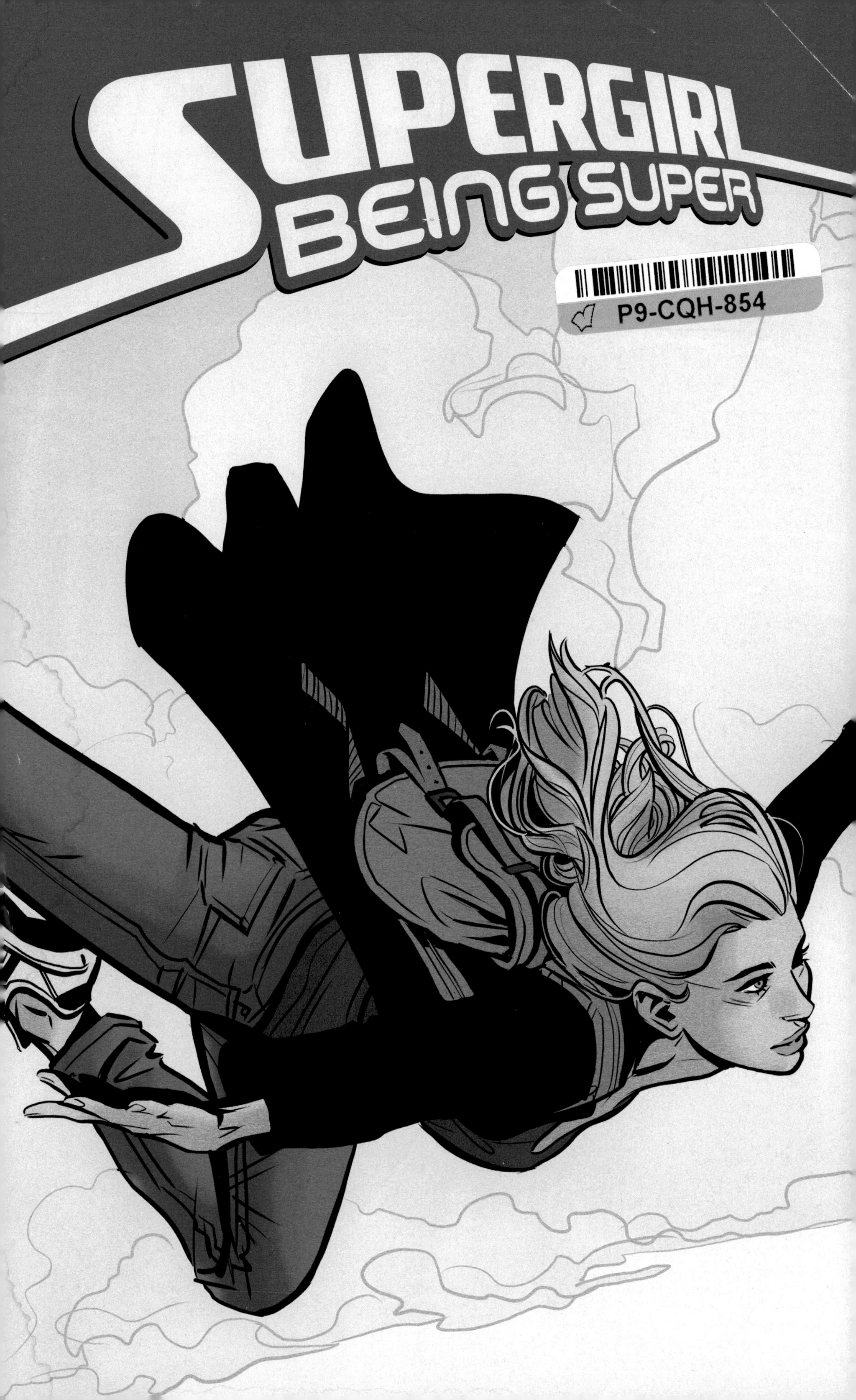
SUPERGIRL
BEING SUPER

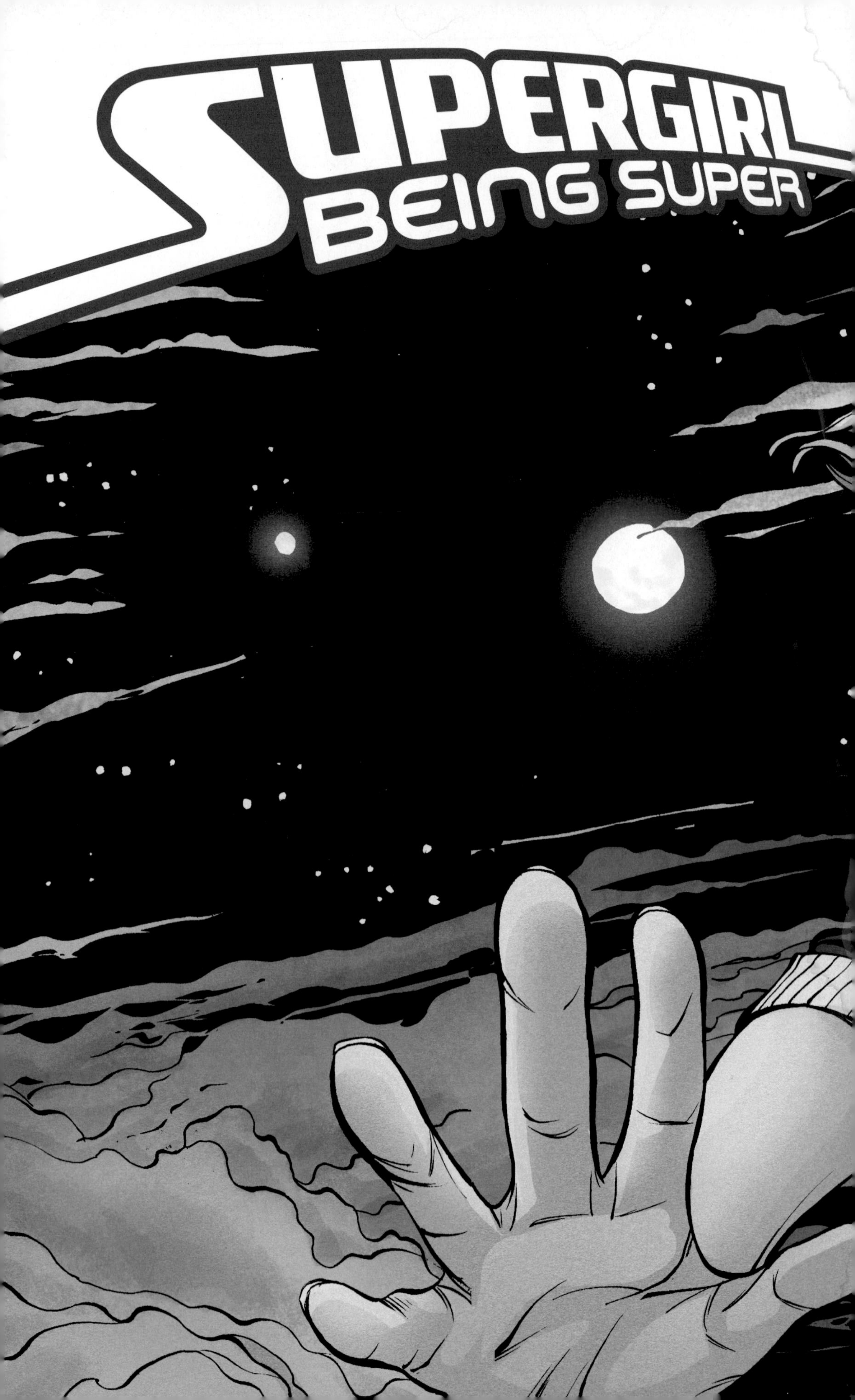
SUPERGIRL
BEING SUPER

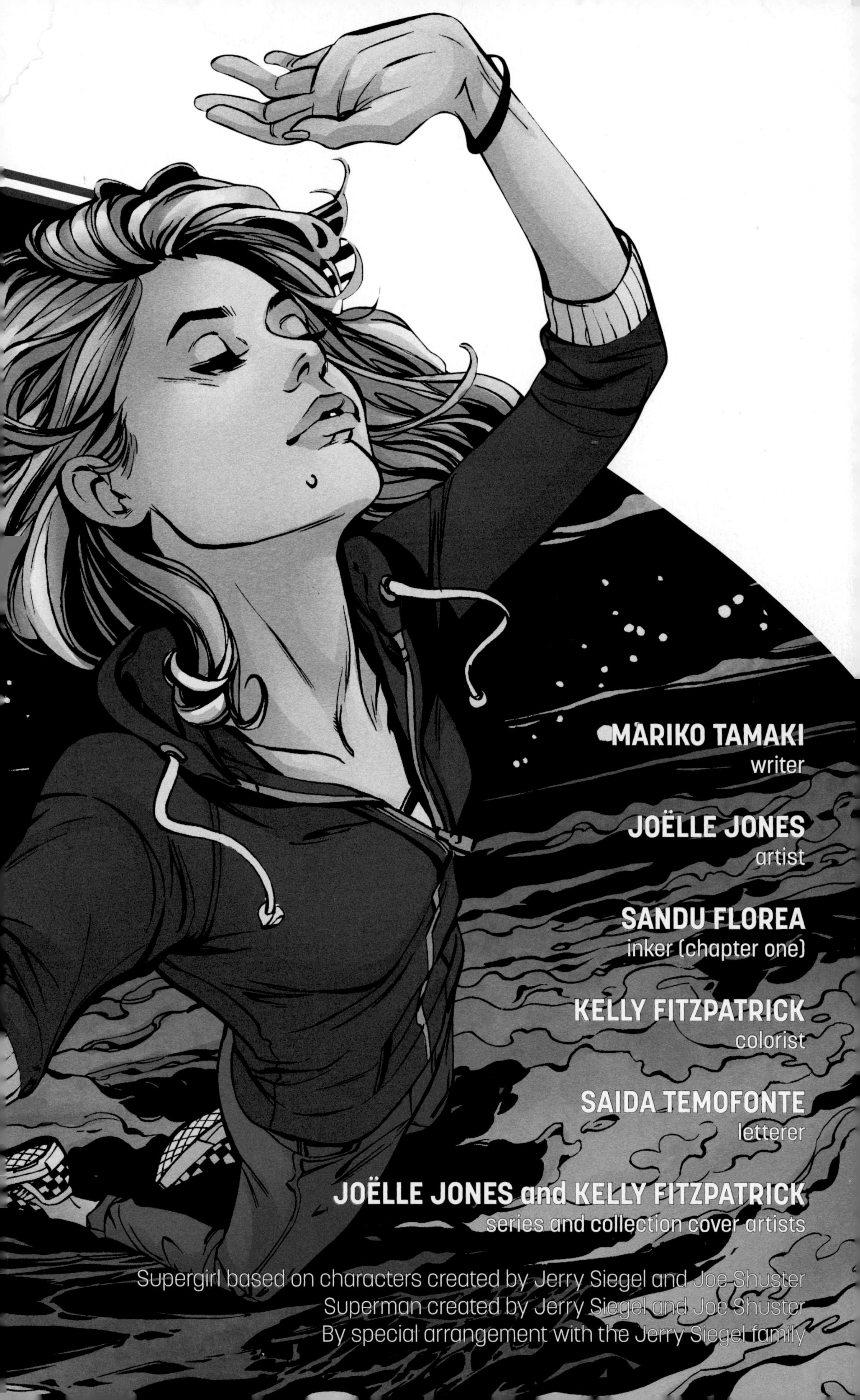

MARIKO TAMAKI
writer

JOËLLE JONES
artist

SANDU FLOREA
inker (chapter one)

KELLY FITZPATRICK
colorist

SAIDA TEMOFONTE
letterer

JOËLLE JONES and KELLY FITZPATRICK
series and collection cover artists

Supergirl based on characters created by Jerry Siegel and Joe Shuster
Superman created by Jerry Siegel and Joe Shuster
By special arrangement with the Jerry Siegel family

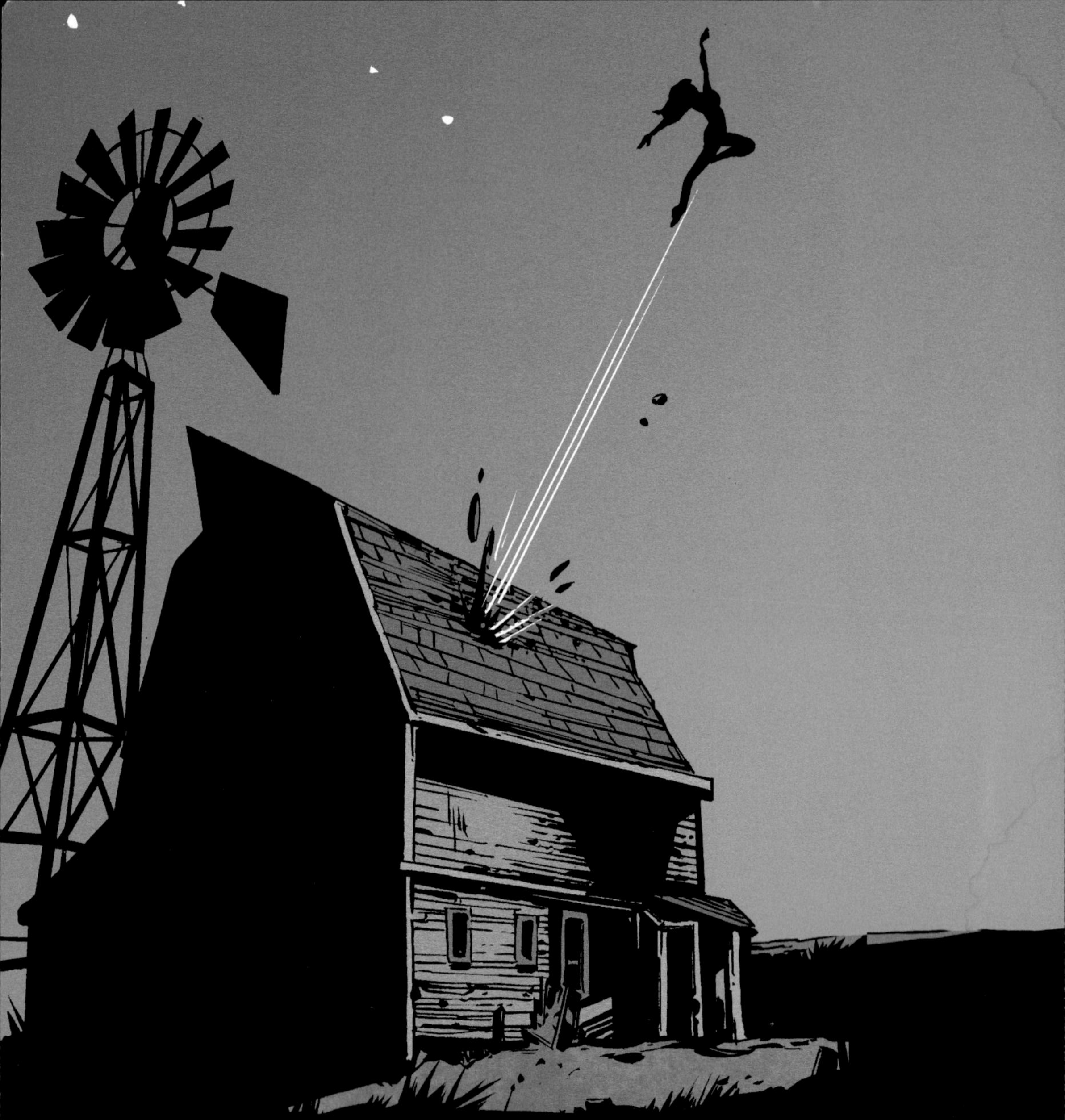

PAUL KAMINSKI and **ANDREW MARINO** Editors – Original Series **JEB WOODARD** Group Editor – Collected Editions
ROBIN WILDMAN Editor – Collected Edition **STEVE COOK** Design Director – Books **SHANNON STEWART** and **MONIQUE NARBONETA** Publication Design
BOB HARRAS Senior VP – Editor-in-Chief, DC Comics **PAT McCALLUM** Executive Editor, DC Comics
DIANE NELSON President **DAN DiDIO** Publisher **JIM LEE** Publisher **GEOFF JOHNS** President & Chief Creative Officer
AMIT DESAI Executive VP – Business & Marketing Strategy, Direct to Consumer & Global Franchise Management **SAM ADES** Senior VP & General Manager, Digital Services
BOBBIE CHASE VP & Executive Editor, Young Reader & Talent Development **MARK CHIARELLO** Senior VP – Art, Design & Collected Editions
JOHN CUNNINGHAM Senior VP – Sales & Trade Marketing **ANNE DePIES** Senior VP – Business Strategy, Finance & Administration **DON FALLETTI** VP – Manufacturing Operations
LAWRENCE GANEM VP – Editorial Administration & Talent Relations **ALISON GILL** Senior VP – Manufacturing & Operations **HANK KANALZ** Senior VP – Editorial Strategy & Administration
JAY KOGAN VP – Legal Affairs **JACK MAHAN** VP – Business Affairs **NICK J. NAPOLITANO** VP – Manufacturing Administration **EDDIE SCANNELL** VP – Consumer Marketing
COURTNEY SIMMONS Senior VP – Publicity & Communications **JIM (SKI) SOKOLOWSKI** VP – Comic Book Specialty Sales & Trade Marketing
NANCY SPEARS VP – Mass, Book, Digital Sales & Trade Marketing **MICHELE R. WELLS** VP – Content Strategy

SUPERGIRL: BEING SUPER

DC Comics, 2900 West Alameda Ave., Burbank, CA 91505
Printed by LSC Communications, Kendallville, IN, USA. 4/27/18. First Printing.
ISBN: 978-1-4012-6894-7

Library of Congress Cataloging-in-Publication Data is available.

PEFC Certified
Printed on paper from sustainably managed forests, controlled sources
PEFC/29-31-337
www.pefc.org

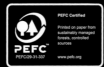

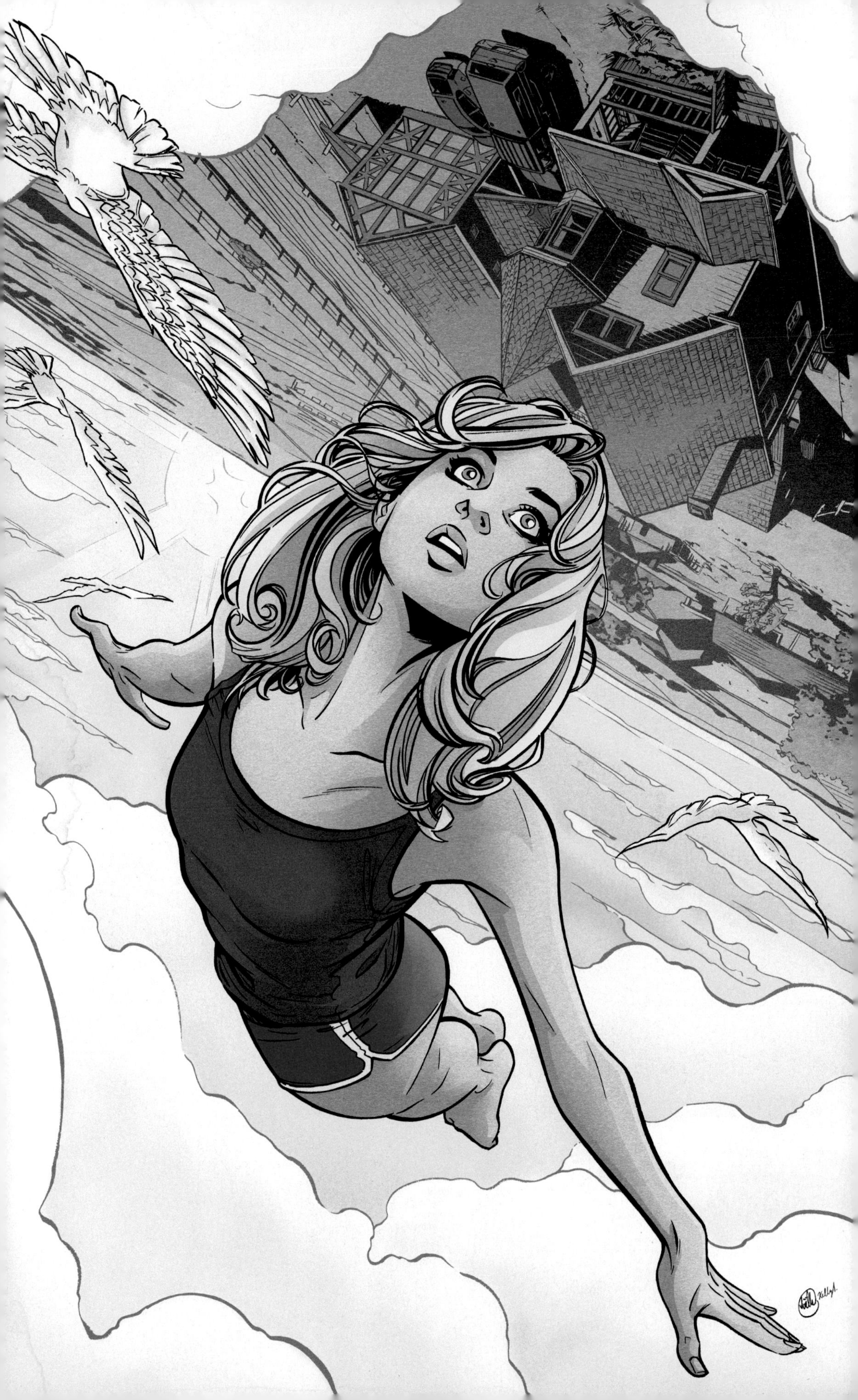

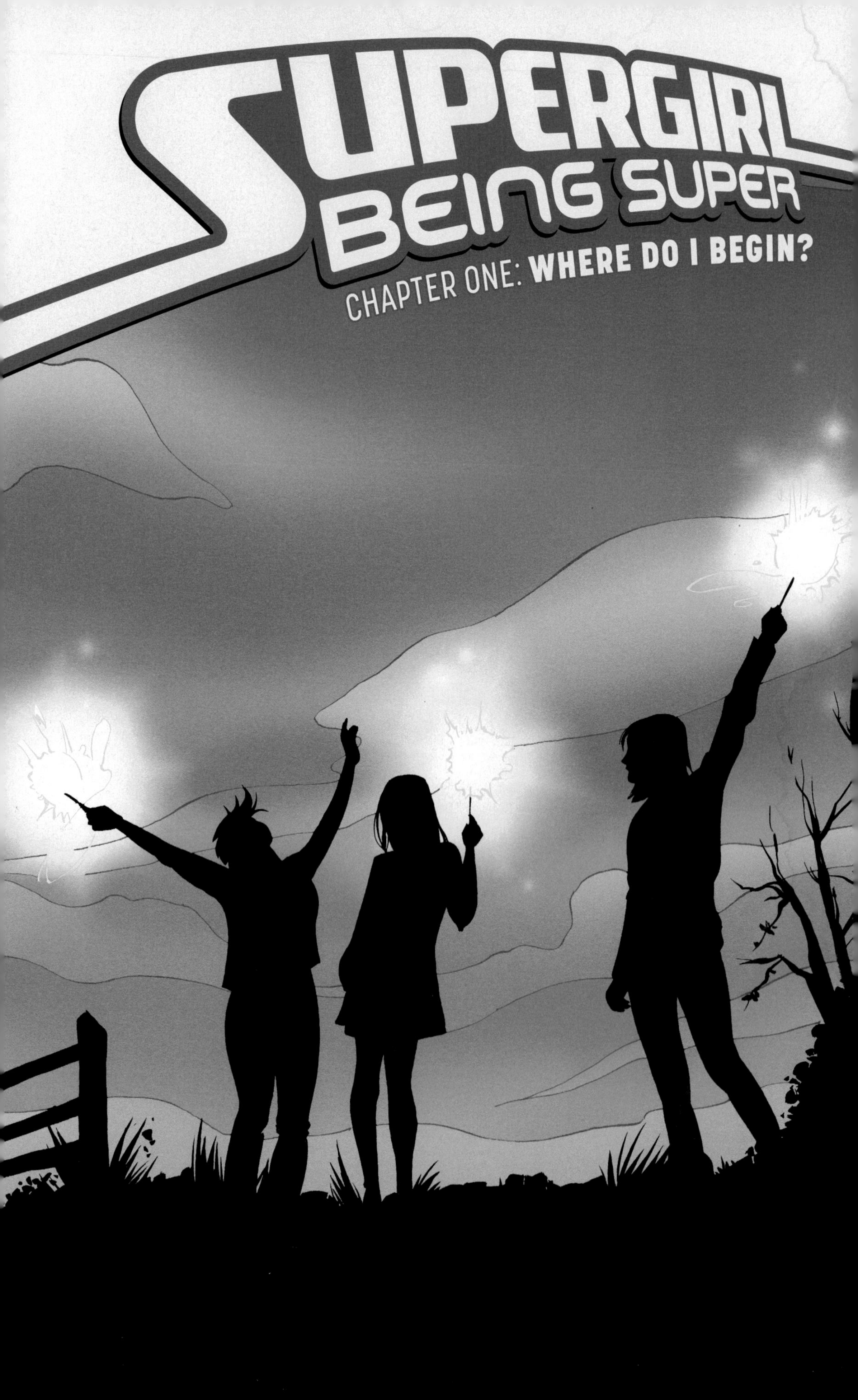
SUPERGIRL
BEING SUPER
CHAPTER ONE: WHERE DO I BEGIN?

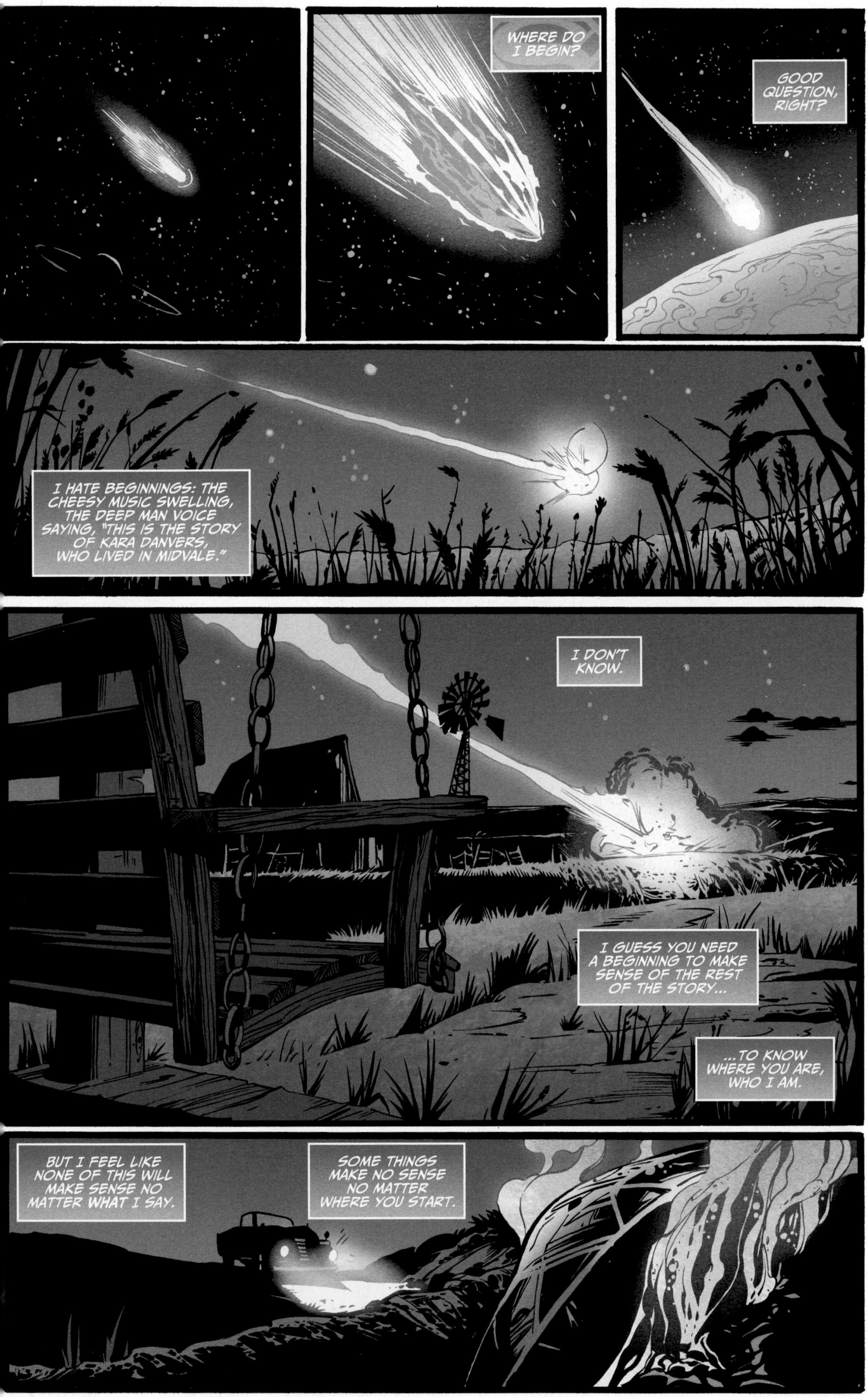
WHERE DO I BEGIN?
GOOD QUESTION, RIGHT?
I HATE BEGINNINGS: THE CHEESY MUSIC SWELLING, THE DEEP MAN VOICE SAYING, "THIS IS THE STORY OF KARA DANVERS, WHO LIVED IN MIDVALE."
I DON'T KNOW.
I GUESS YOU NEED A BEGINNING TO MAKE SENSE OF THE REST OF THE STORY...
...TO KNOW WHERE YOU ARE, WHO I AM.
BUT I FEEL LIKE NONE OF THIS WILL MAKE SENSE NO MATTER WHAT I SAY.
SOME THINGS MAKE NO SENSE NO MATTER WHERE YOU START.

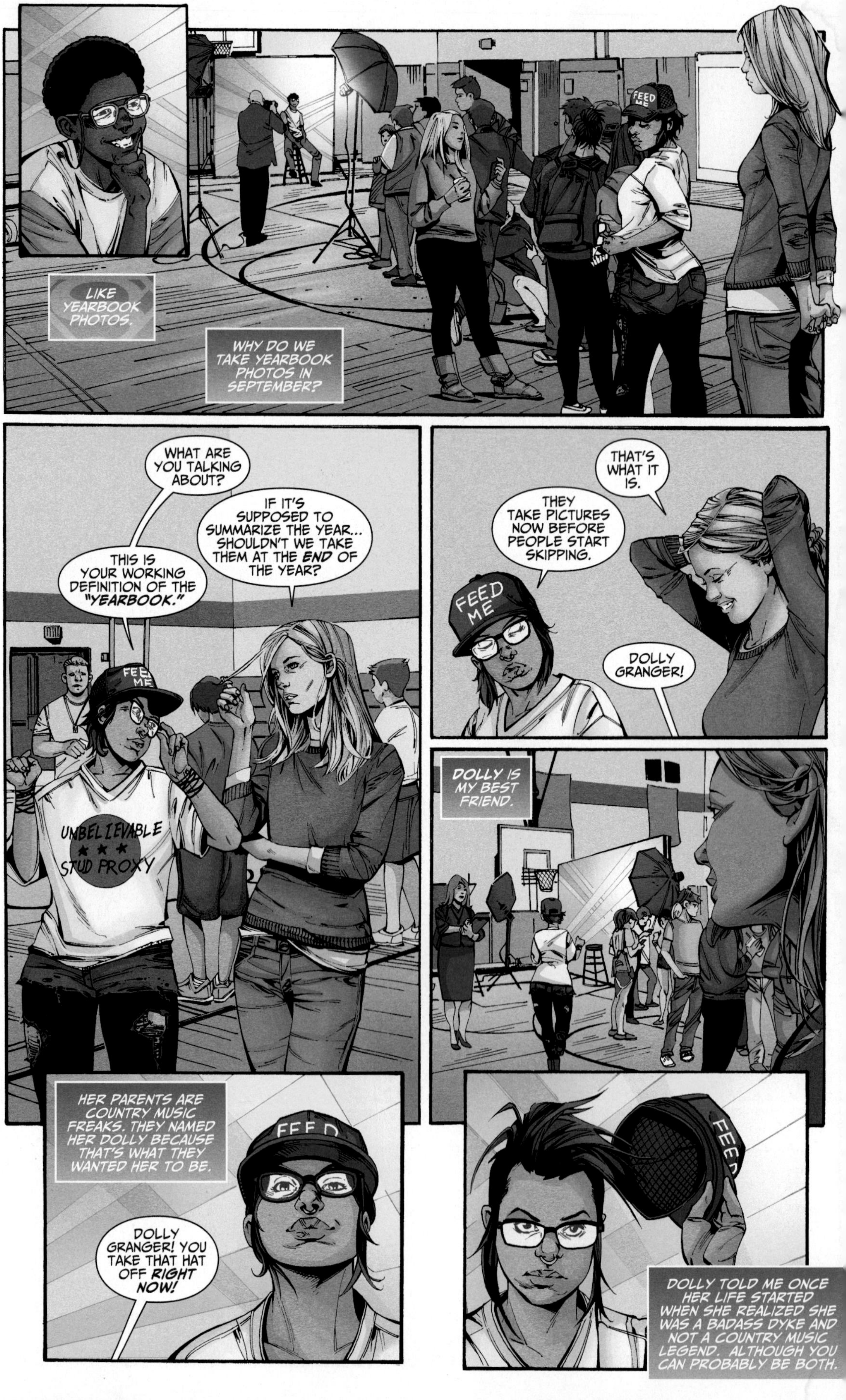

LIKE YEARBOOK PHOTOS.
WHY DO WE TAKE YEARBOOK PHOTOS IN SEPTEMBER?
FEED ME
WHAT ARE YOU TALKING ABOUT?
IF IT'S SUPPOSED TO SUMMARIZE THE YEAR... SHOULDN'T WE TAKE THEM AT THE END OF THE YEAR?
THIS IS YOUR WORKING DEFINITION OF THE "YEARBOOK."
UNBELIEVABLE
STUD PROXY
THAT'S WHAT IT IS.
THEY TAKE PICTURES NOW BEFORE PEOPLE START SKIPPING.
DOLLY GRANGER!
DOLLY IS MY BEST FRIEND.
HER PARENTS ARE COUNTRY MUSIC FREAKS. THEY NAMED HER DOLLY BECAUSE THAT'S WHAT THEY WANTED HER TO BE.
DOLLY GRANGER! YOU TAKE THAT HAT OFF RIGHT NOW!
DOLLY TOLD ME ONCE HER LIFE STARTED WHEN SHE REALIZED SHE WAS A BADASS DYKE AND NOT A COUNTRY MUSIC LEGEND. ALTHOUGH YOU CAN PROBABLY BE BOTH.

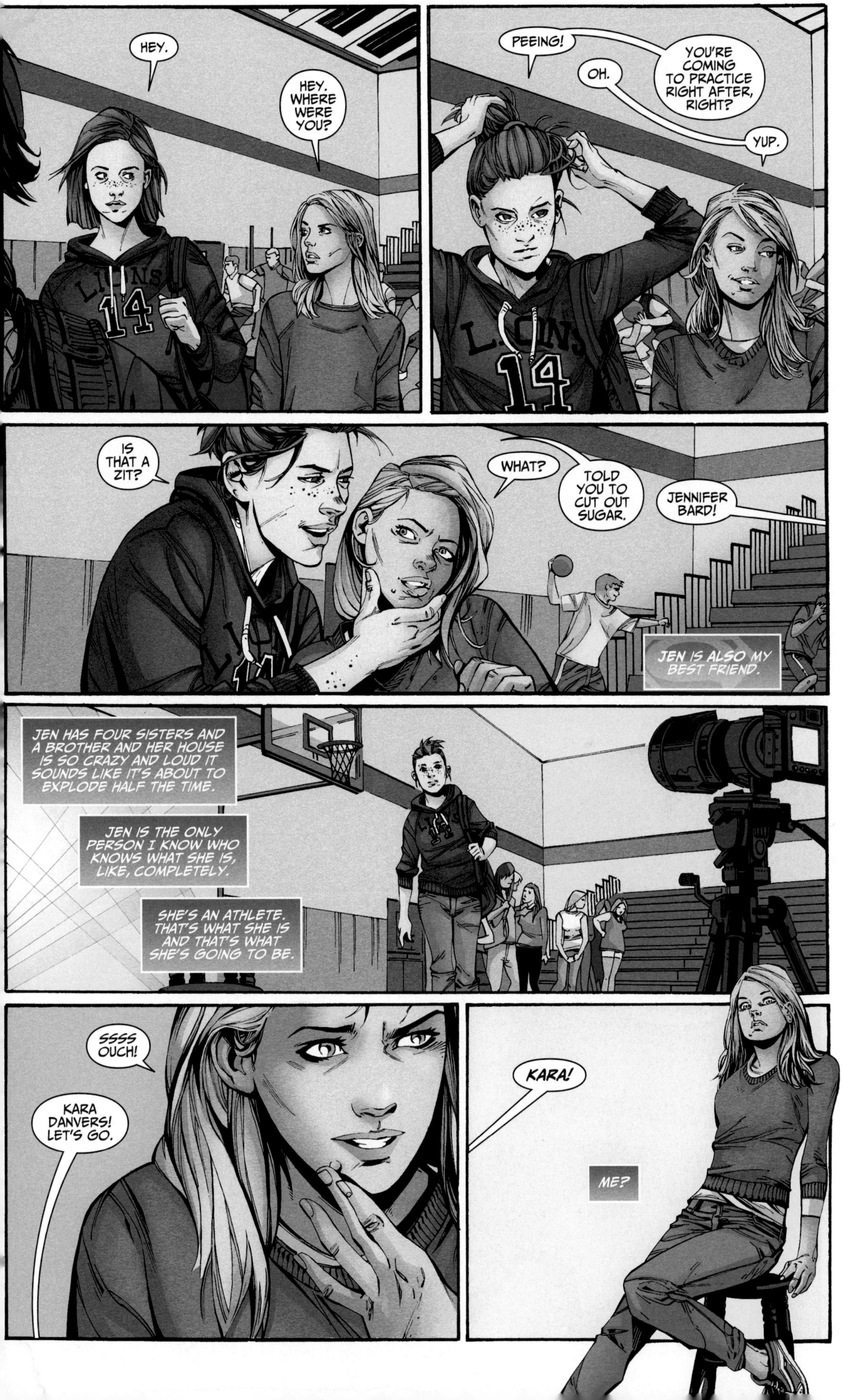
HEY.
HEY. WHERE WERE YOU?
PEEING!
YOU'RE COMING TO PRACTICE RIGHT AFTER, RIGHT?
OH.
YUP.
IS THAT A ZIT?
WHAT?
TOLD YOU TO CUT OUT SUGAR.
JENNIFER BARD!
JEN IS ALSO MY BEST FRIEND.
JEN HAS FOUR SISTERS AND A BROTHER AND HER HOUSE IS SO CRAZY AND LOUD IT SOUNDS LIKE IT'S ABOUT TO EXPLODE HALF THE TIME.
JEN IS THE ONLY PERSON I KNOW WHO KNOWS WHAT SHE IS, LIKE, COMPLETELY.
SHE'S AN ATHLETE. THAT'S WHAT SHE IS AND THAT'S WHAT SHE'S GOING TO BE.
SSSS OUCH!
KARA DANVERS! LET'S GO.
KARA!
ME?

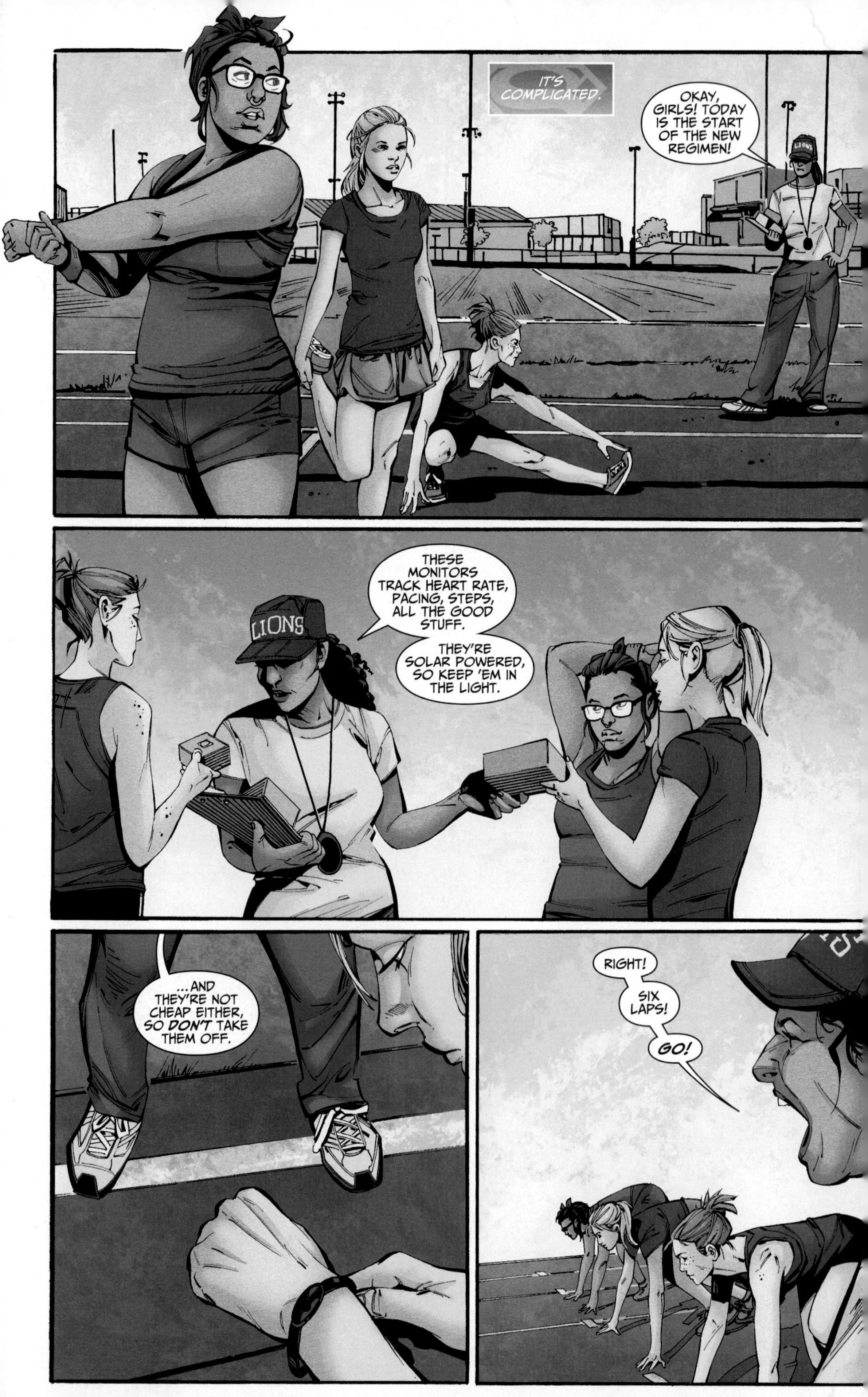
IT'S COMPLICATED.
OKAY, GIRLS! TODAY IS THE START OF THE NEW REGIMEN!
LIONS
THESE MONITORS TRACK HEART RATE, PACING, STEPS, ALL THE GOOD STUFF.
THEY'RE SOLAR POWERED, SO KEEP 'EM IN THE LIGHT.
...AND THEY'RE NOT CHEAP EITHER, SO DON'T TAKE THEM OFF.
RIGHT!
SIX LAPS!
GO!

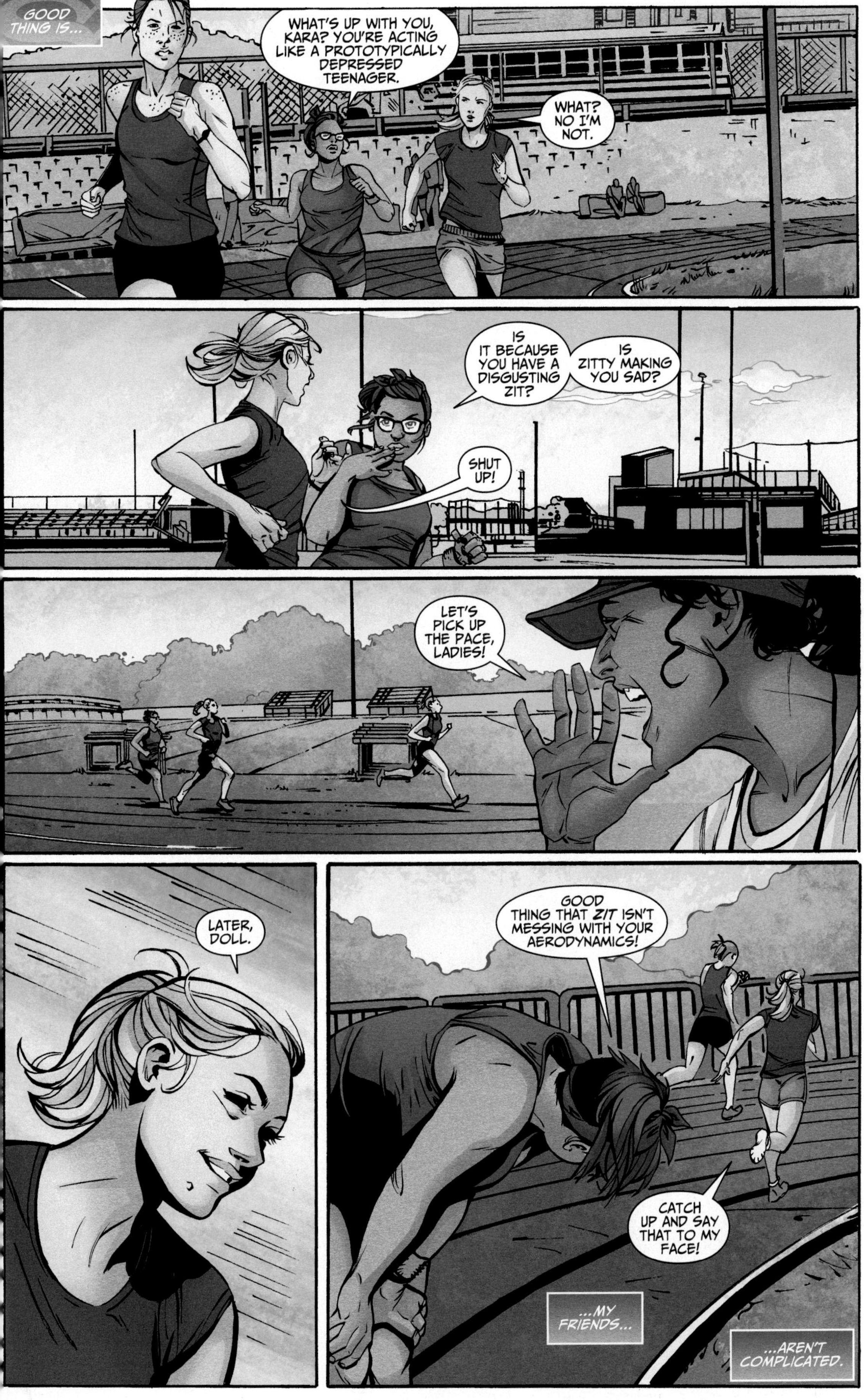
GOOD THING IS...
WHAT'S UP WITH YOU, KARA? YOU'RE ACTING LIKE A PROTOTYPICALLY DEPRESSED TEENAGER.
WHAT? NO I'M NOT.
IS IT BECAUSE YOU HAVE A DISGUSTING ZIT?
IS ZITTY MAKING YOU SAD?
SHUT UP!
LET'S PICK UP THE PACE, LADIES!
LATER, DOLL.
GOOD THING THAT *ZIT* ISN'T MESSING WITH YOUR AERODYNAMICS!
CATCH UP AND SAY THAT TO MY FACE!
...MY FRIENDS...
...AREN'T COMPLICATED.

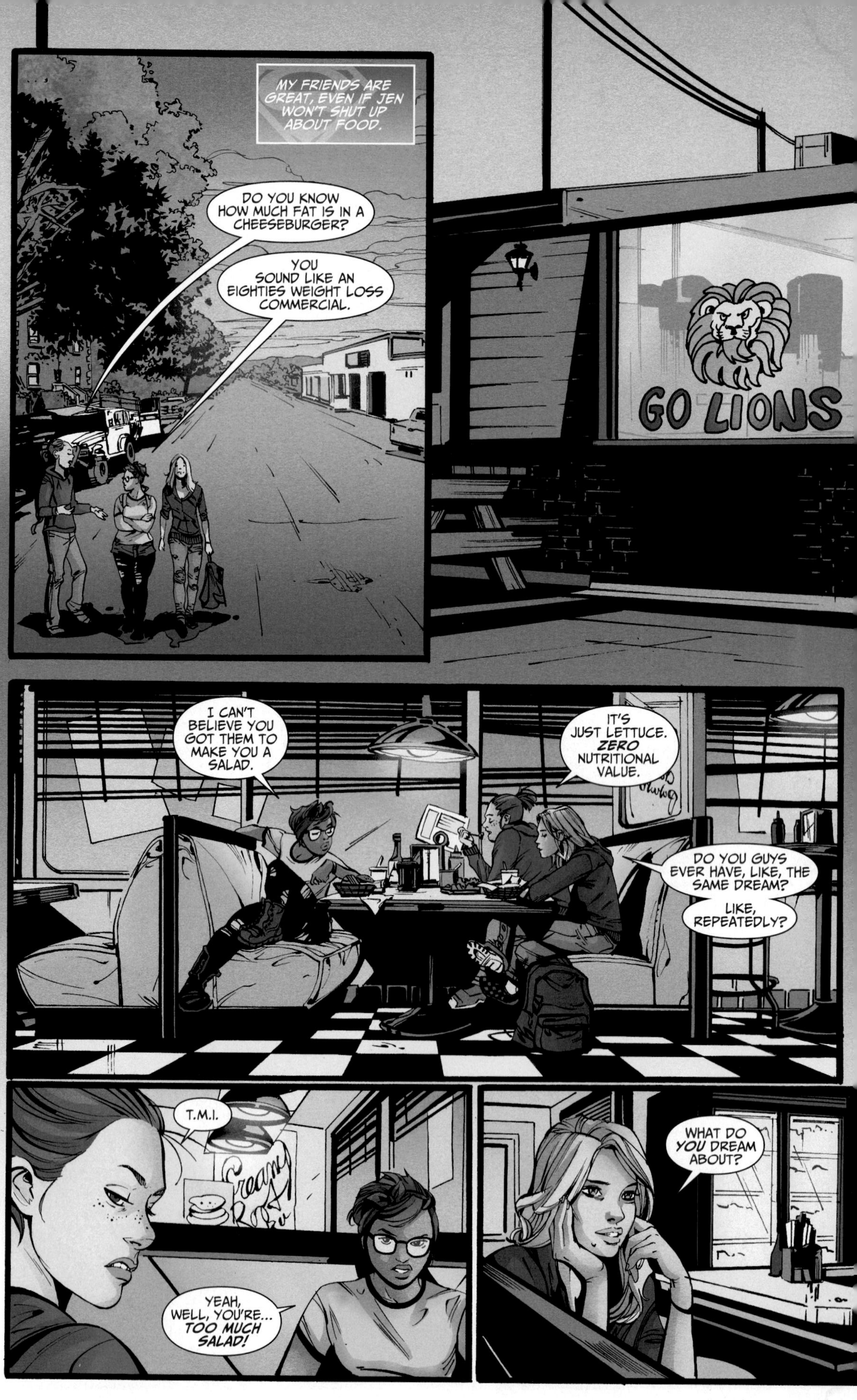

MY FRIENDS ARE GREAT, EVEN IF JEN WON'T SHUT UP ABOUT FOOD.
DO YOU KNOW HOW MUCH FAT IS IN A CHEESEBURGER?
YOU SOUND LIKE AN EIGHTIES WEIGHT LOSS COMMERCIAL.
GO LIONS
I CAN'T BELIEVE YOU GOT THEM TO MAKE YOU A SALAD.
IT'S JUST LETTUCE. ZERO NUTRITIONAL VALUE.
DO YOU GUYS EVER HAVE, LIKE, THE SAME DREAM?
LIKE, REPEATEDLY?
T.M.I.
YEAH, WELL, YOU'RE... TOO MUCH SALAD!
WHAT DO YOU DREAM ABOUT?

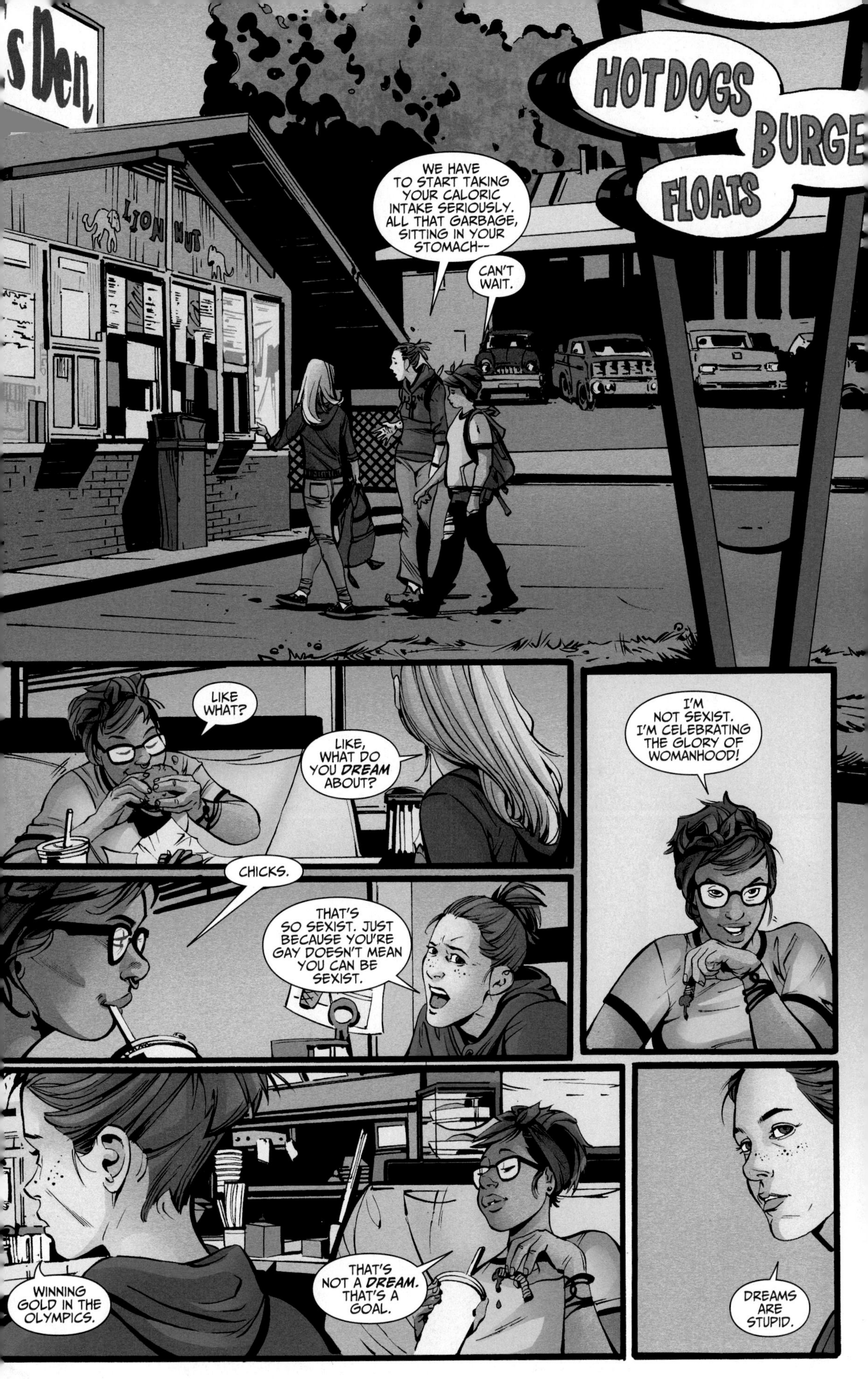
S DEN
LION HUT
HOTDOGS
BURGE
FLOATS
WE HAVE TO START TAKING YOUR CALORIC INTAKE SERIOUSLY. ALL THAT GARBAGE, SITTING IN YOUR STOMACH--
CAN'T WAIT.
LIKE WHAT?
LIKE, WHAT DO YOU DREAM ABOUT?
CHICKS.
THAT'S SO SEXIST. JUST BECAUSE YOU'RE GAY DOESN'T MEAN YOU CAN BE SEXIST.
I'M NOT SEXIST. I'M CELEBRATING THE GLORY OF WOMANHOOD!
WINNING GOLD IN THE OLYMPICS.
THAT'S NOT A DREAM. THAT'S A GOAL.
DREAMS ARE STUPID.

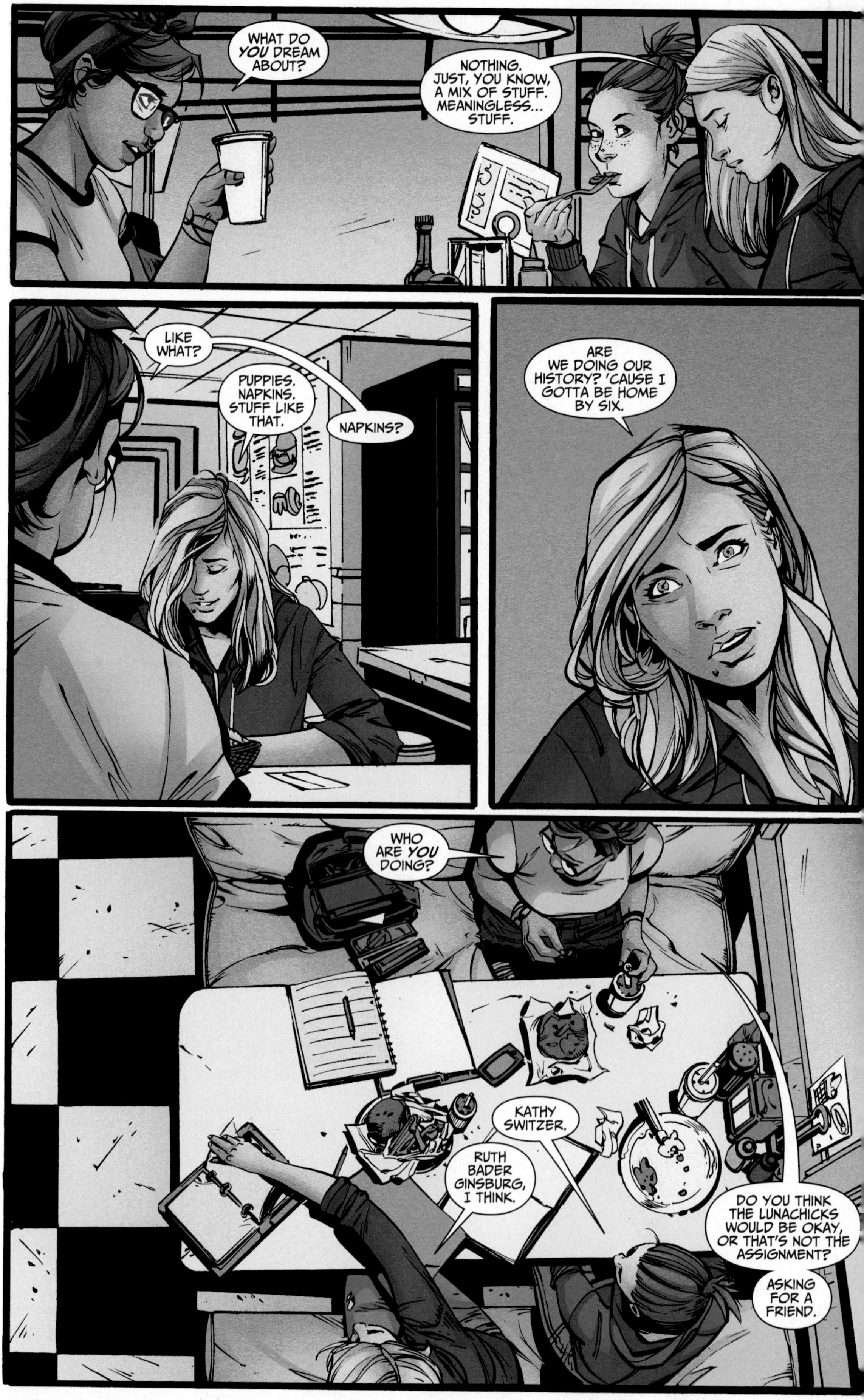
WHAT DO *YOU* DREAM ABOUT?
NOTHING. JUST, YOU KNOW, A MIX OF STUFF. MEANINGLESS... STUFF.
LIKE WHAT?
PUPPIES. NAPKINS. STUFF LIKE THAT.
NAPKINS?
ARE WE DOING OUR HISTORY? 'CAUSE I GOTTA BE HOME BY SIX.
WHO ARE *YOU* DOING?
KATHY SWITZER.
RUTH BADER GINSBURG, I THINK.
DO YOU THINK THE LUNACHICKS WOULD BE OKAY, OR THAT'S NOT THE ASSIGNMENT?
ASKING FOR A FRIEND.

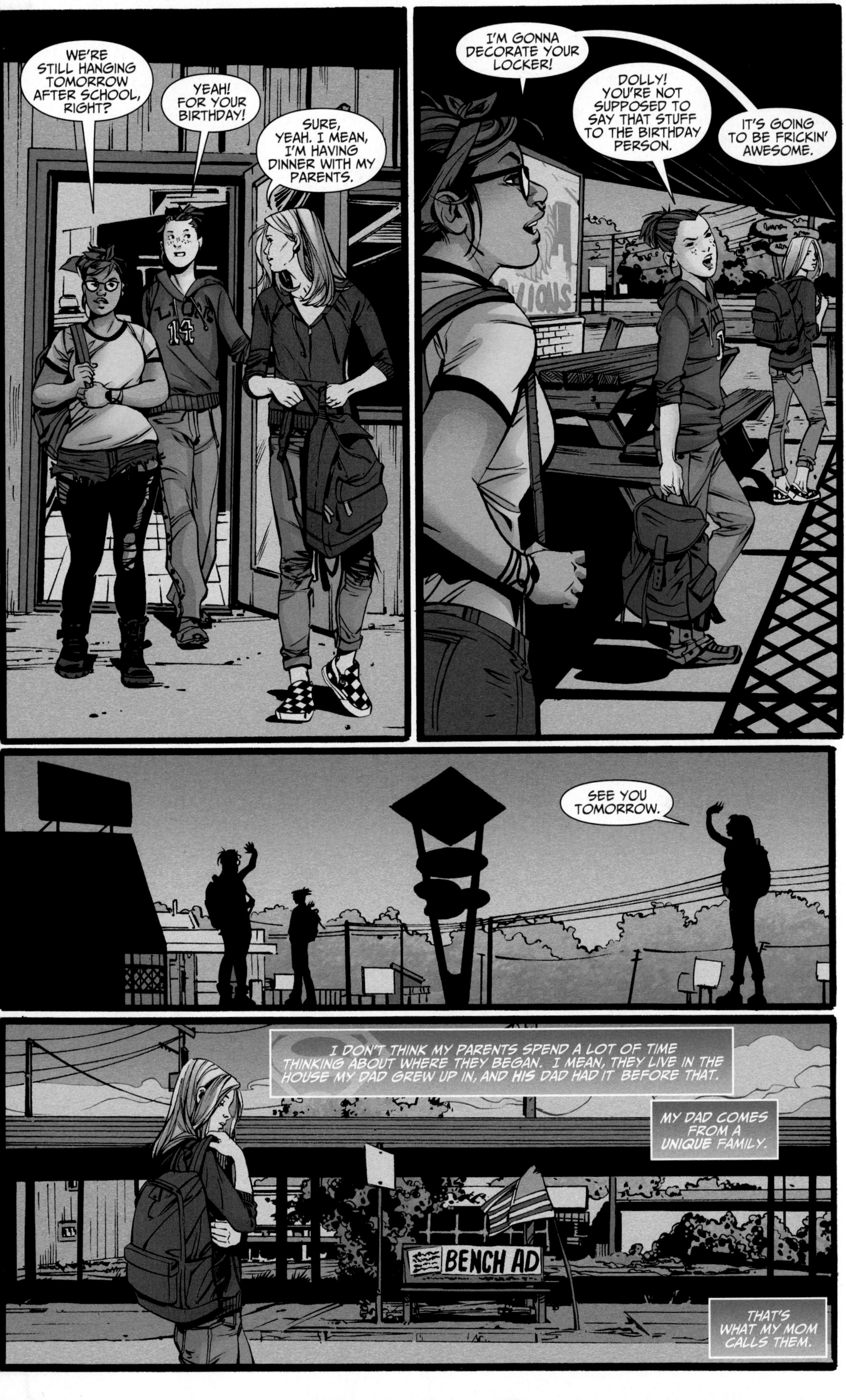
WE'RE STILL HANGING TOMORROW AFTER SCHOOL, RIGHT?
YEAH! FOR YOUR BIRTHDAY!
SURE, YEAH. I MEAN, I'M HAVING DINNER WITH MY PARENTS.
I'M GONNA DECORATE YOUR LOCKER!
DOLLY! YOU'RE NOT SUPPOSED TO SAY THAT STUFF TO THE BIRTHDAY PERSON.
IT'S GOING TO BE FRICKIN' AWESOME.
SEE YOU TOMORROW.
I DON'T THINK MY PARENTS SPEND A LOT OF TIME THINKING ABOUT WHERE THEY BEGAN. I MEAN, THEY LIVE IN THE HOUSE MY DAD GREW UP IN, AND HIS DAD HAD IT BEFORE THAT.
MY DAD COMES FROM A UNIQUE FAMILY.
BENCH AD
THAT'S WHAT MY MOM CALLS THEM.

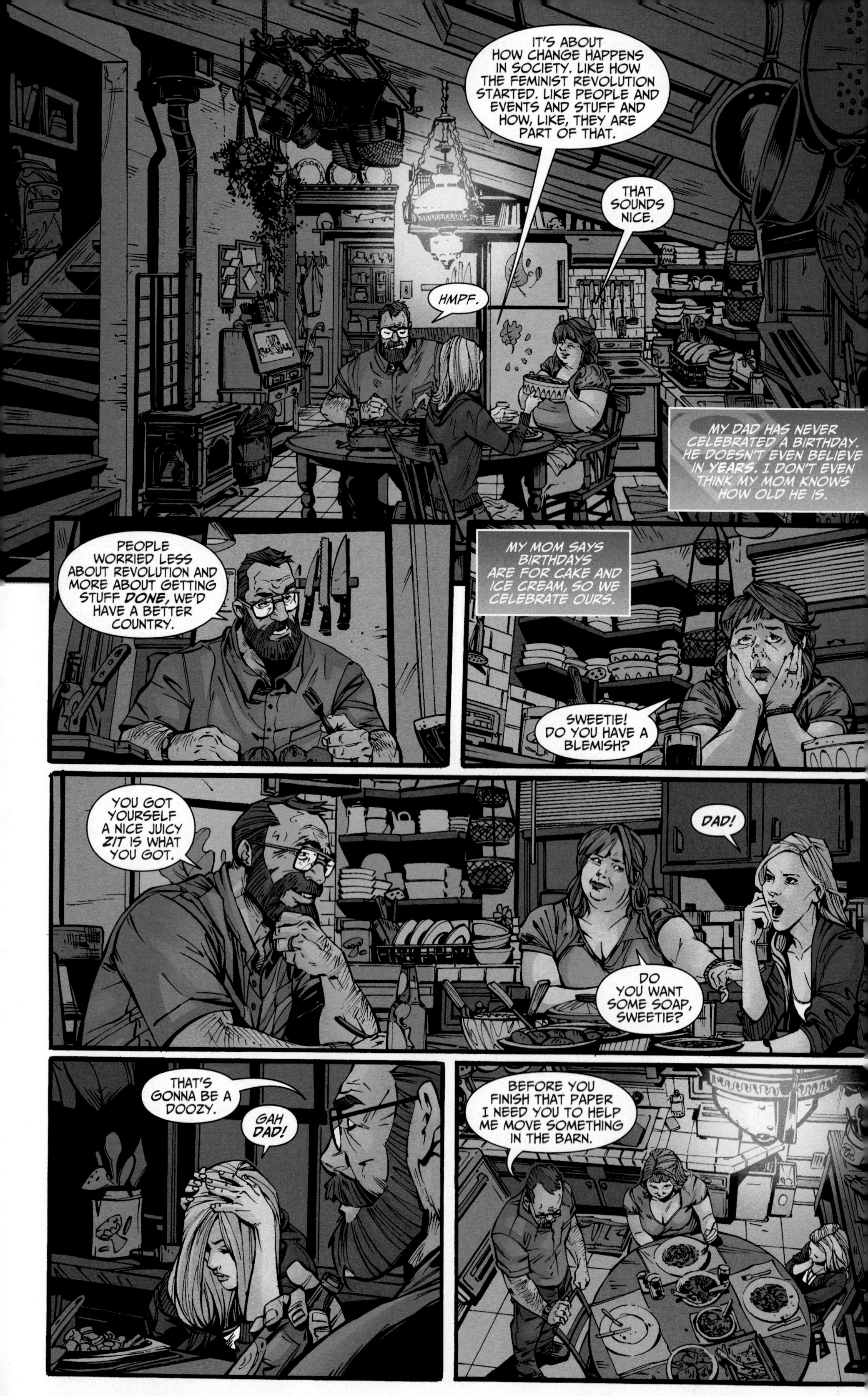
IT'S ABOUT HOW CHANGE HAPPENS IN SOCIETY. LIKE HOW THE FEMINIST REVOLUTION STARTED. LIKE PEOPLE AND EVENTS AND STUFF AND HOW, LIKE, THEY ARE PART OF THAT.
THAT SOUNDS NICE.
HMPF.
MY DAD HAS NEVER CELEBRATED A BIRTHDAY. HE DOESN'T EVEN BELIEVE IN YEARS. I DON'T EVEN THINK MY MOM KNOWS HOW OLD HE IS.
PEOPLE WORRIED LESS ABOUT REVOLUTION AND MORE ABOUT GETTING STUFF DONE, WE'D HAVE A BETTER COUNTRY.
MY MOM SAYS BIRTHDAYS ARE FOR CAKE AND ICE CREAM, SO WE CELEBRATE OURS.
SWEETIE! DO YOU HAVE A BLEMISH?
YOU GOT YOURSELF A NICE JUICY ZIT IS WHAT YOU GOT.
DAD!
DO YOU WANT SOME SOAP, SWEETIE?
THAT'S GONNA BE A DOOZY.
GAH DAD!
BEFORE YOU FINISH THAT PAPER I NEED YOU TO HELP ME MOVE SOMETHING IN THE BARN.

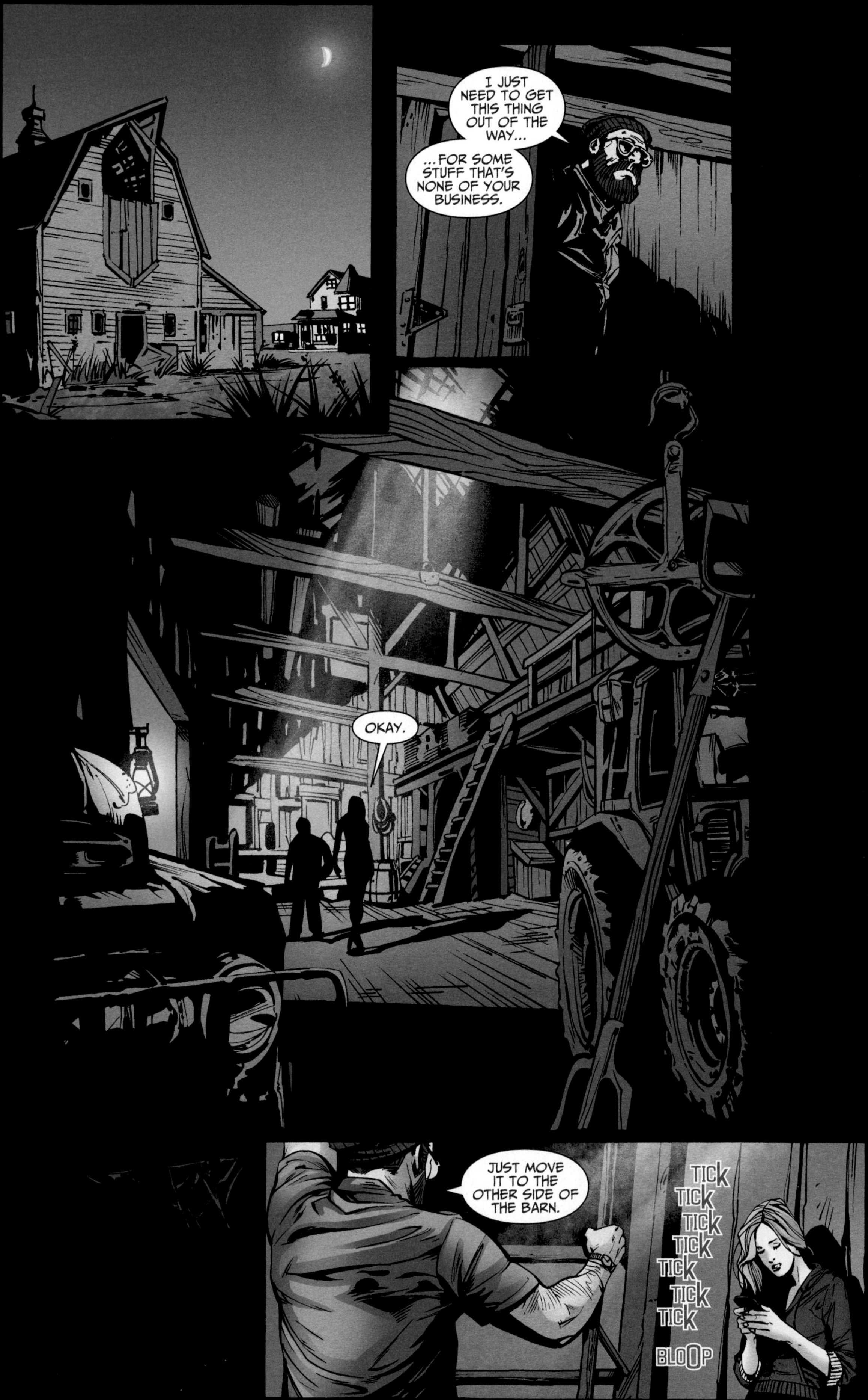
I JUST NEED TO GET THIS THING OUT OF THE WAY...
...FOR SOME STUFF THAT'S NONE OF YOUR BUSINESS.
OKAY.
JUST MOVE IT TO THE OTHER SIDE OF THE BARN.
TICK TICK TICK TICK TICK TICK TICK
BLOOP

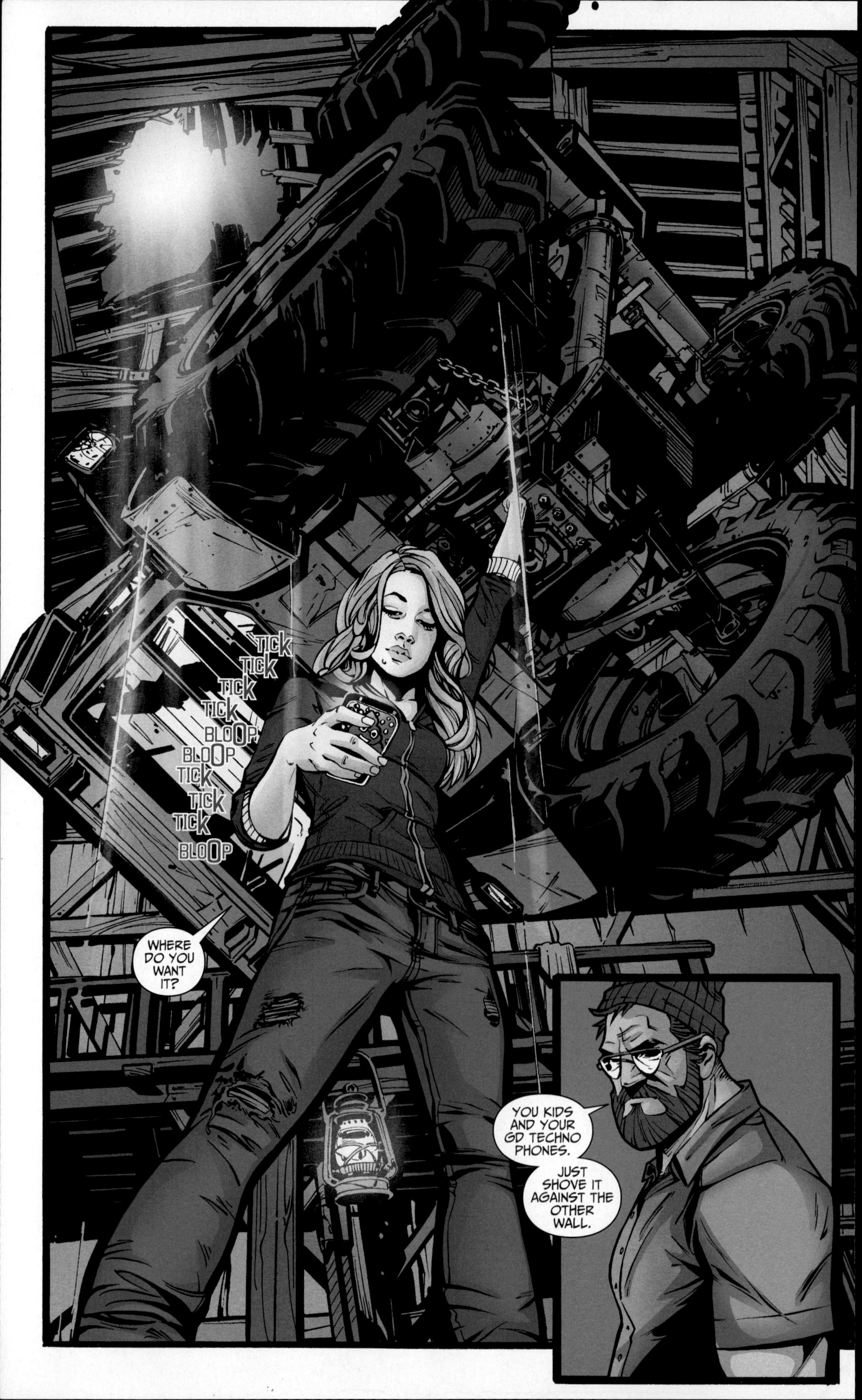
TICK
TICK
TICK
TICK
BLOOP
BLOOP
TICK
TICK
TICK
BLOOP
WHERE DO YOU WANT IT?
YOU KIDS AND YOUR GD TECHNO PHONES.
JUST SHOVE IT AGAINST THE OTHER WALL.

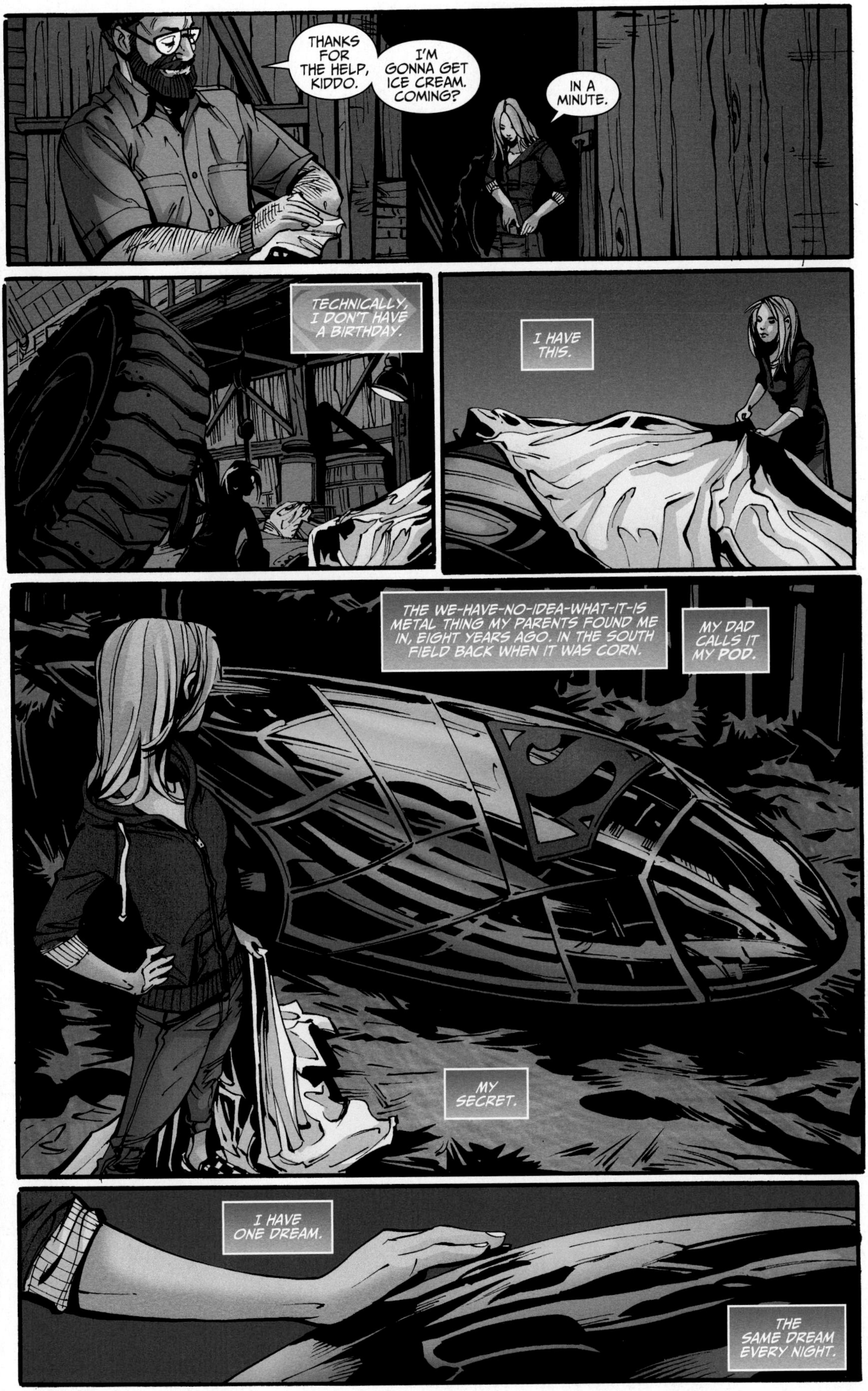
THANKS FOR THE HELP, KIDDO.
I'M GONNA GET ICE CREAM. COMING?
IN A MINUTE.
TECHNICALLY, I DON'T HAVE A BIRTHDAY.
I HAVE THIS.
THE WE-HAVE-NO-IDEA-WHAT-IT-IS METAL THING MY PARENTS FOUND ME IN, EIGHT YEARS AGO. IN THE SOUTH FIELD BACK WHEN IT WAS CORN.
MY DAD CALLS IT MY POD.
MY SECRET.
I HAVE ONE DREAM.
THE SAME DREAM EVERY NIGHT.

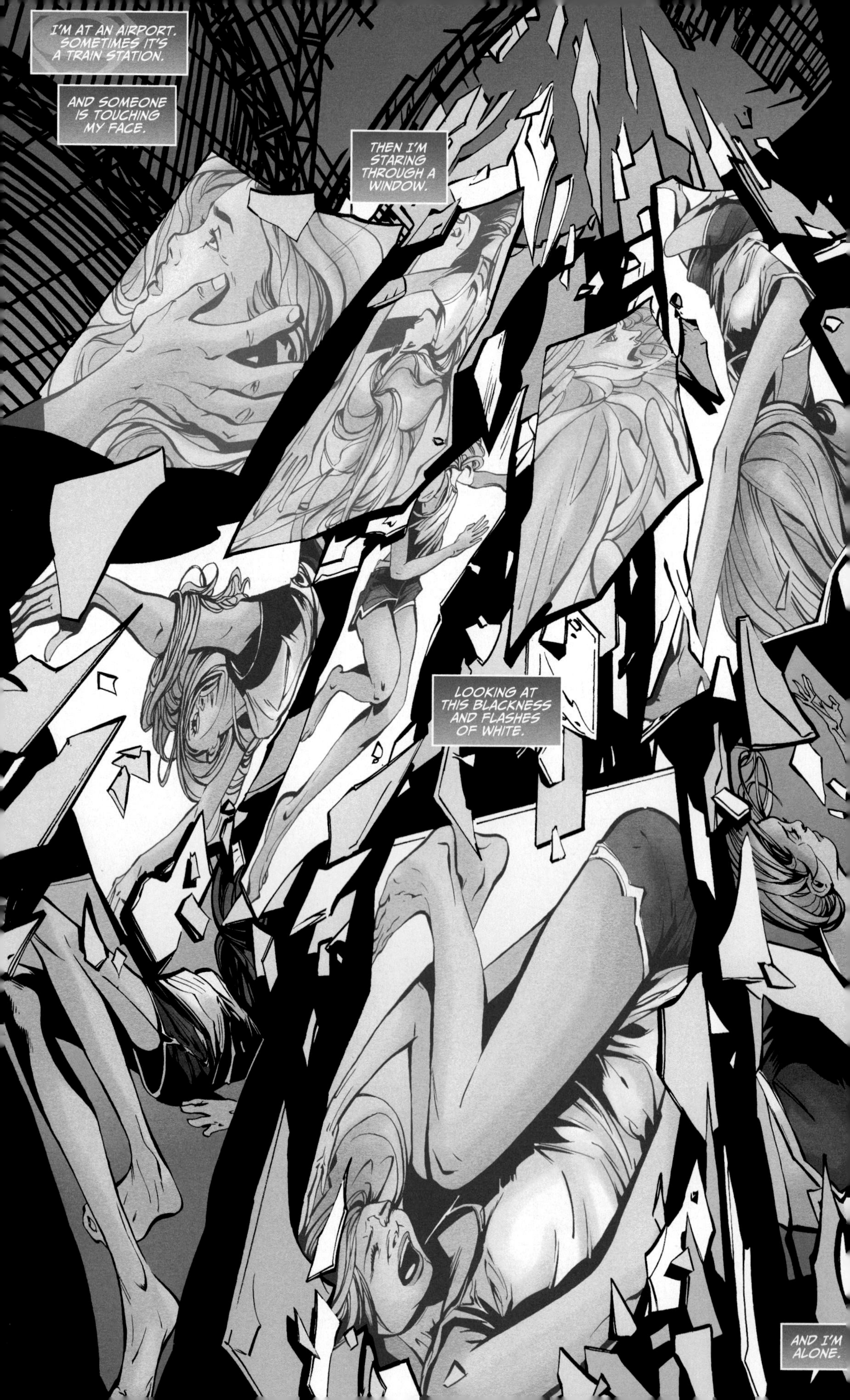
I'M AT AN AIRPORT. SOMETIMES IT'S A TRAIN STATION.
AND SOMEONE IS TOUCHING MY FACE.
THEN I'M STARING THROUGH A WINDOW.
LOOKING AT THIS BLACKNESS AND FLASHES OF WHITE.
AND I'M ALONE.

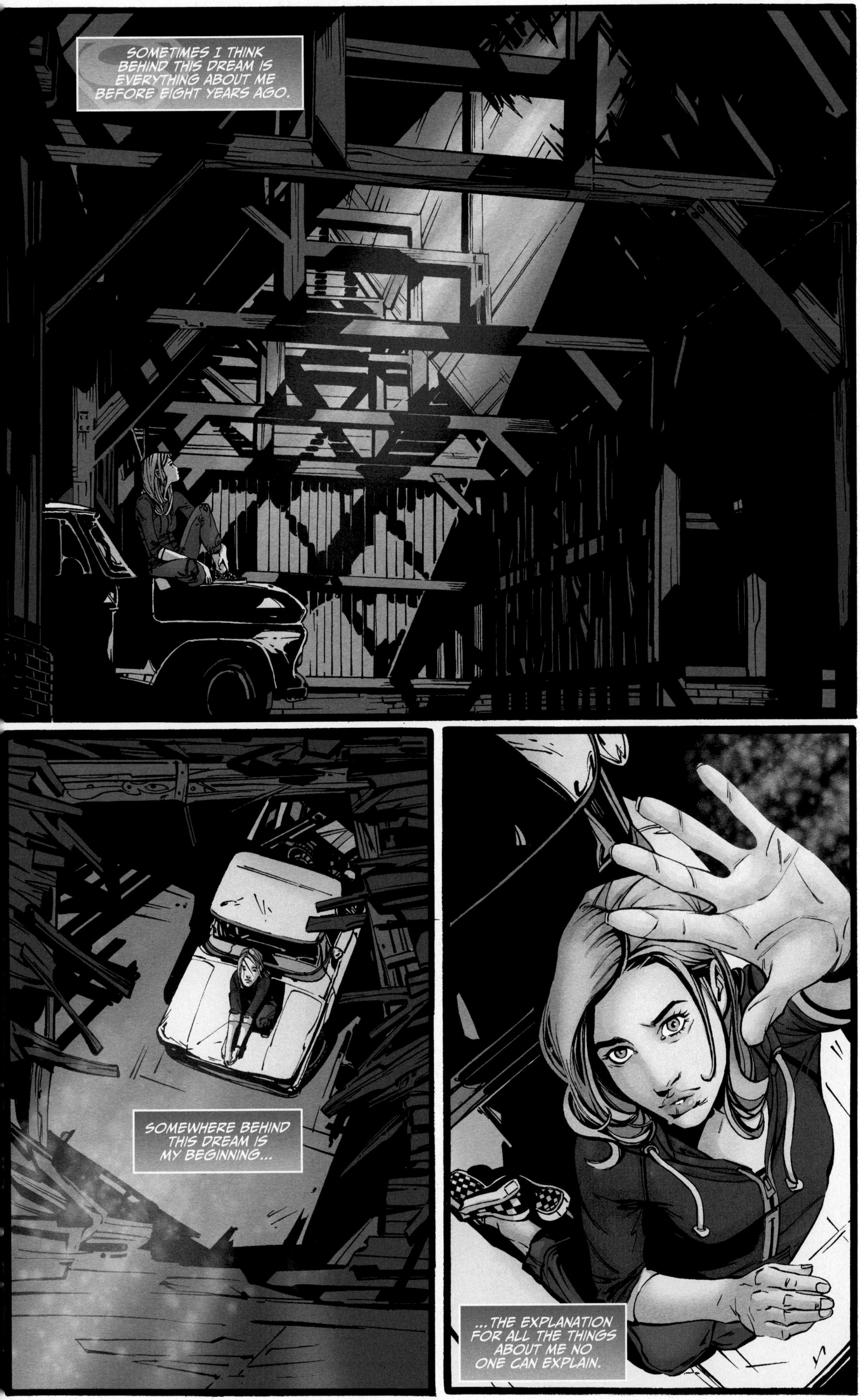
SOMETIMES I THINK BEHIND THIS DREAM IS EVERYTHING ABOUT ME BEFORE EIGHT YEARS AGO.
SOMEWHERE BEHIND THIS DREAM IS MY BEGINNING...
...THE EXPLANATION FOR ALL THE THINGS ABOUT ME NO ONE CAN EXPLAIN.

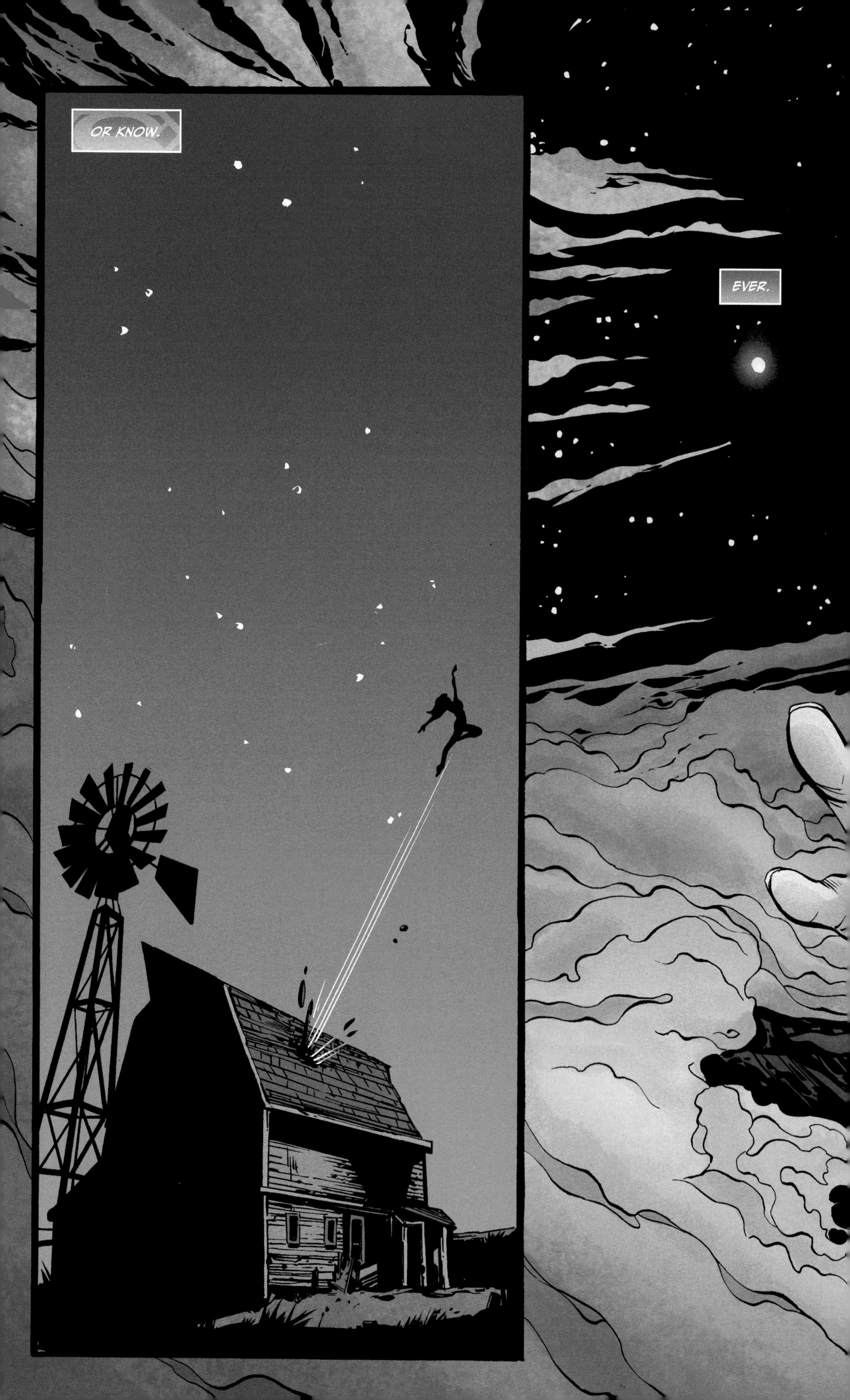
OR KNOW.
EVER.

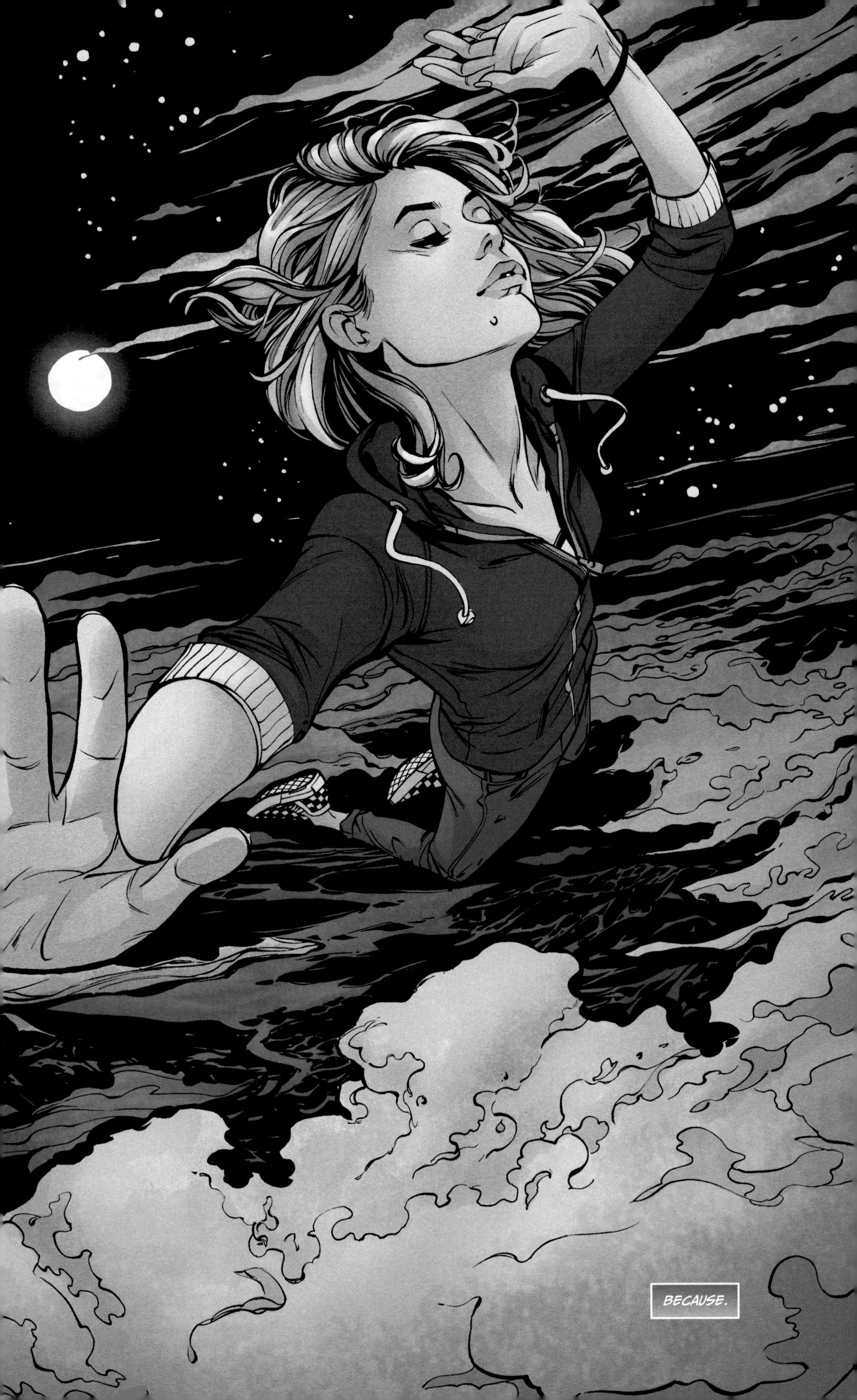
BECAUSE.

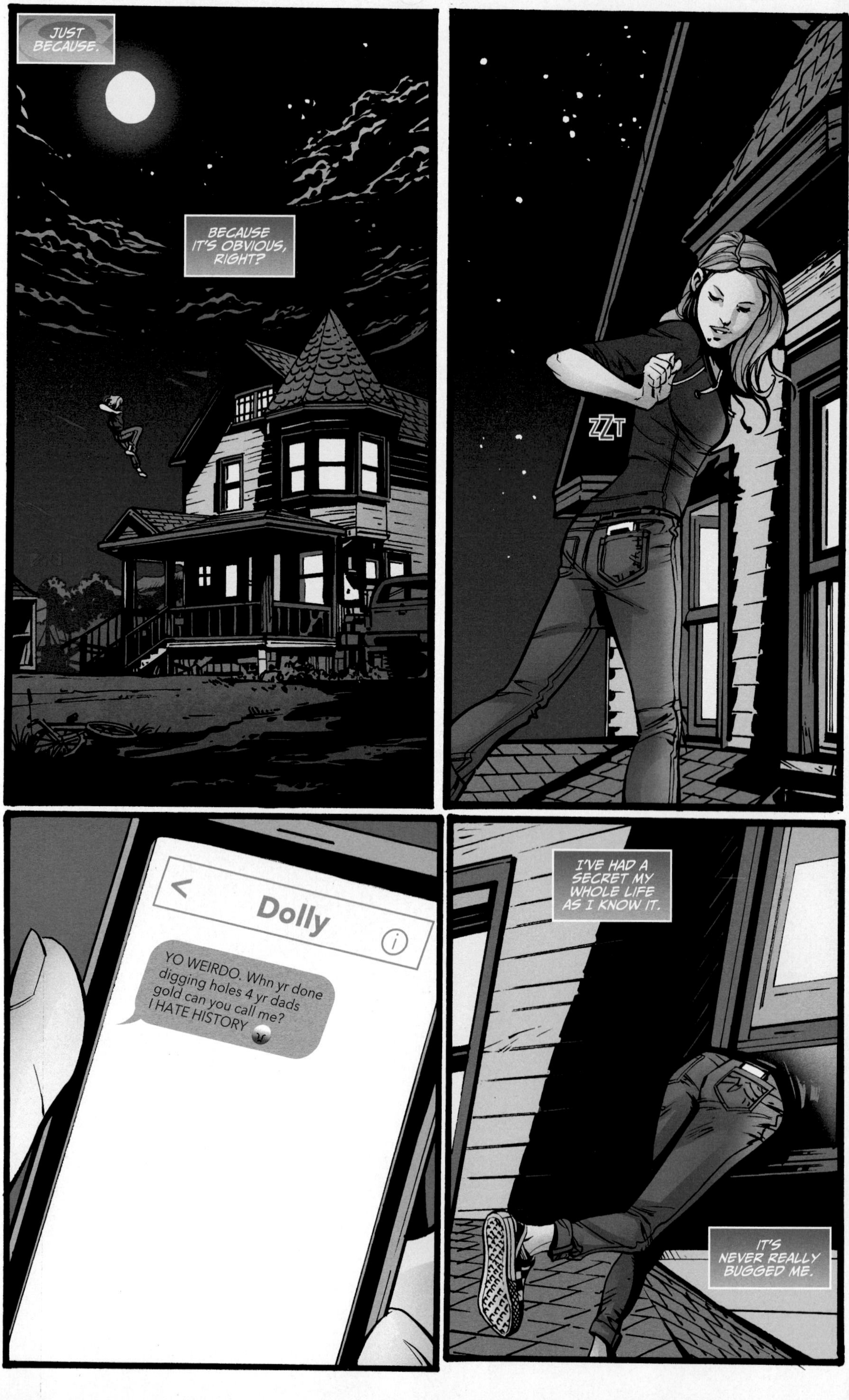
JUST BECAUSE.
BECAUSE IT'S OBVIOUS, RIGHT?
ZZZT
<
Dolly
YO WEIRDO. Whn yr done digging holes 4 yr dads gold can you call me? I HATE HISTORY
I'VE HAD A SECRET MY WHOLE LIFE AS I KNOW IT.
IT'S NEVER REALLY BUGGED ME.

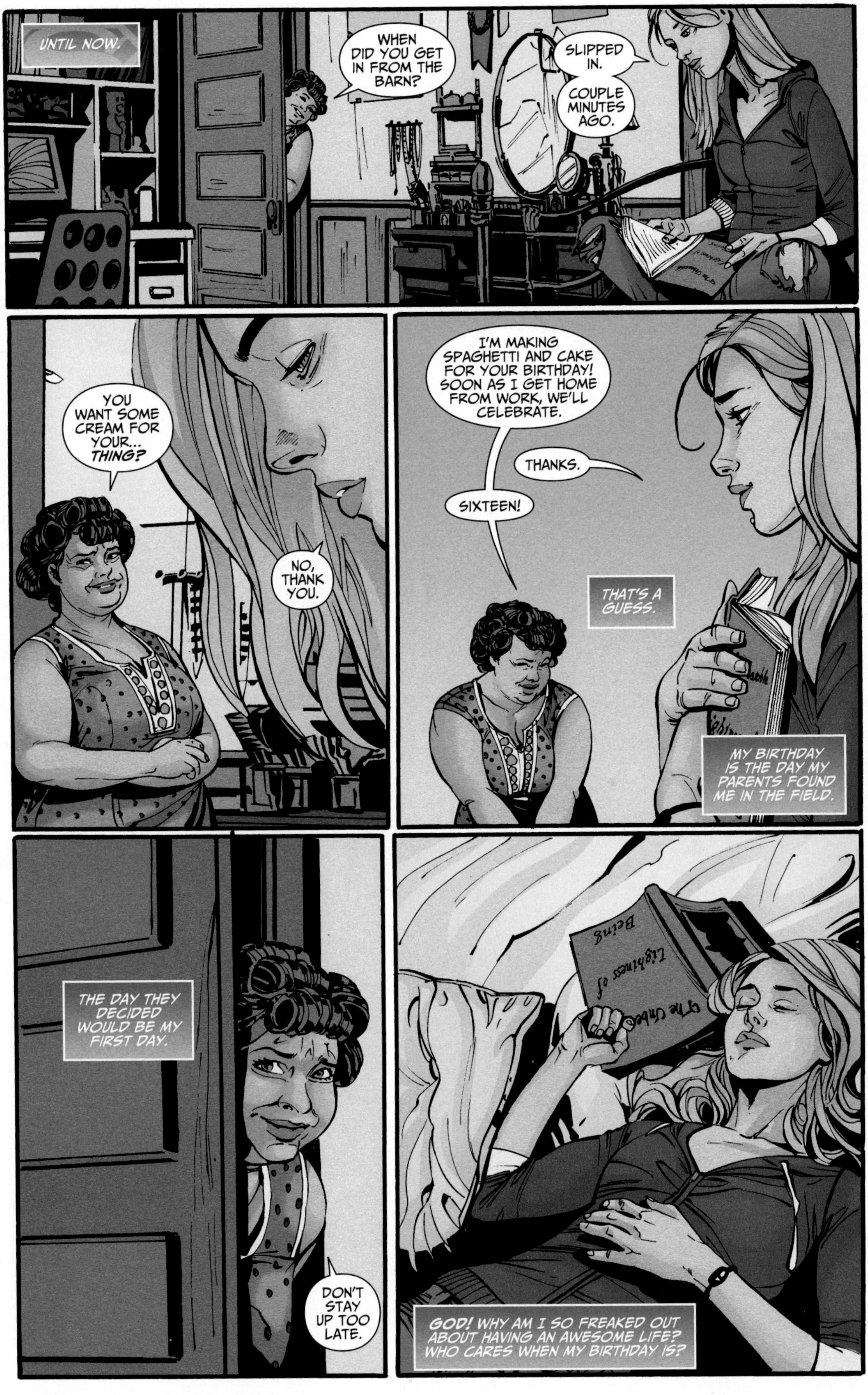
UNTIL NOW.
WHEN DID YOU GET IN FROM THE BARN?
SLIPPED IN.
COUPLE MINUTES AGO.
YOU WANT SOME CREAM FOR YOUR... THING?
NO, THANK YOU.
I'M MAKING SPAGHETTI AND CAKE FOR YOUR BIRTHDAY! SOON AS I GET HOME FROM WORK, WE'LL CELEBRATE.
THANKS.
SIXTEEN!
THAT'S A GUESS.
MY BIRTHDAY IS THE DAY MY PARENTS FOUND ME IN THE FIELD.
THE DAY THEY DECIDED WOULD BE MY FIRST DAY.
DON'T STAY UP TOO LATE.
The Unbearable Lightness of Being
GOD! WHY AM I SO FREAKED OUT ABOUT HAVING AN AWESOME LIFE? WHO CARES WHEN MY BIRTHDAY IS?

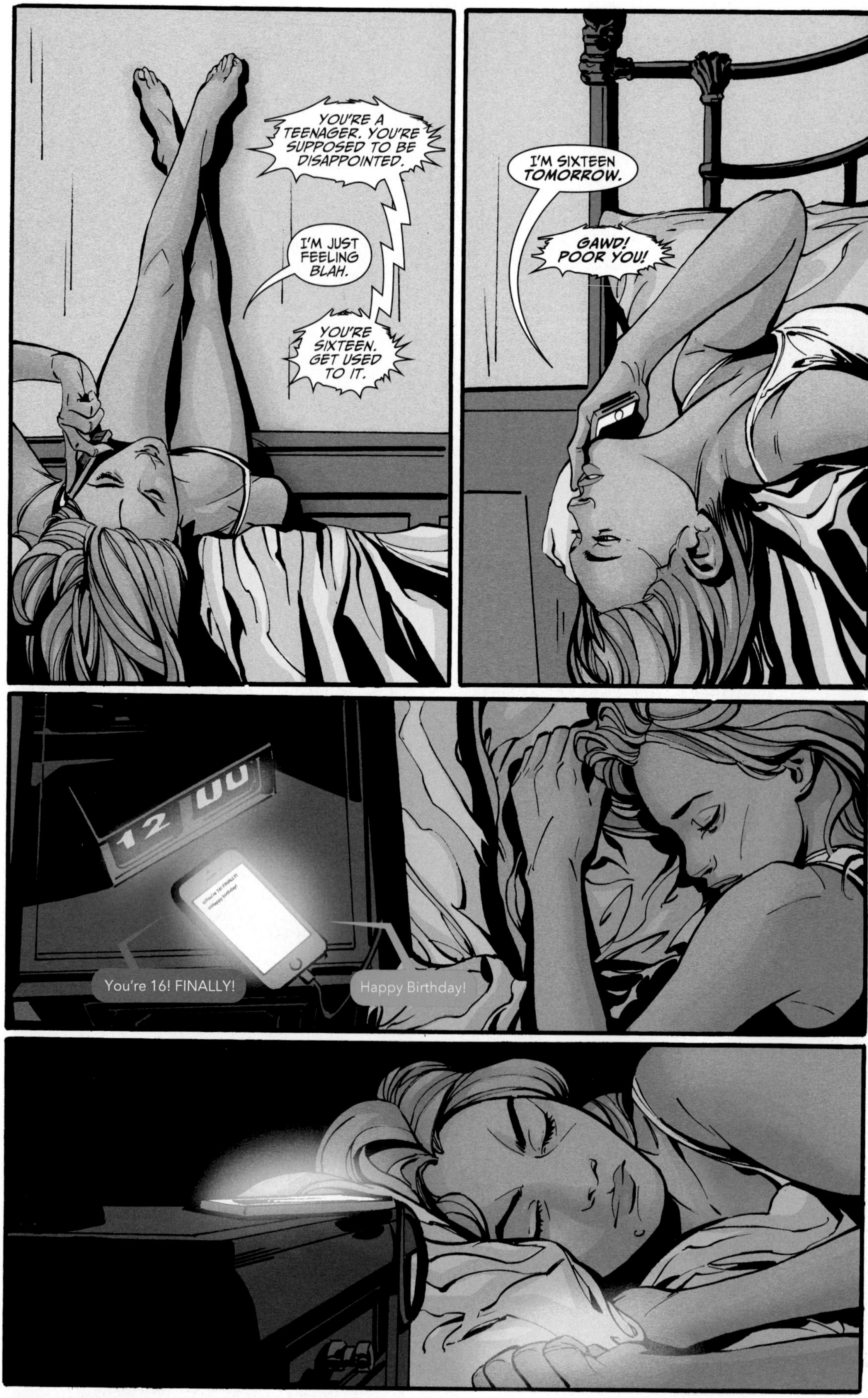
YOU'RE A TEENAGER. YOU'RE SUPPOSED TO BE DISAPPOINTED.
I'M JUST FEELING BLAH.
YOU'RE SIXTEEN. GET USED TO IT.
I'M SIXTEEN TOMORROW.
GAWD! POOR YOU!
12 00
You're 16! FINALLY!
Happy Birthday!

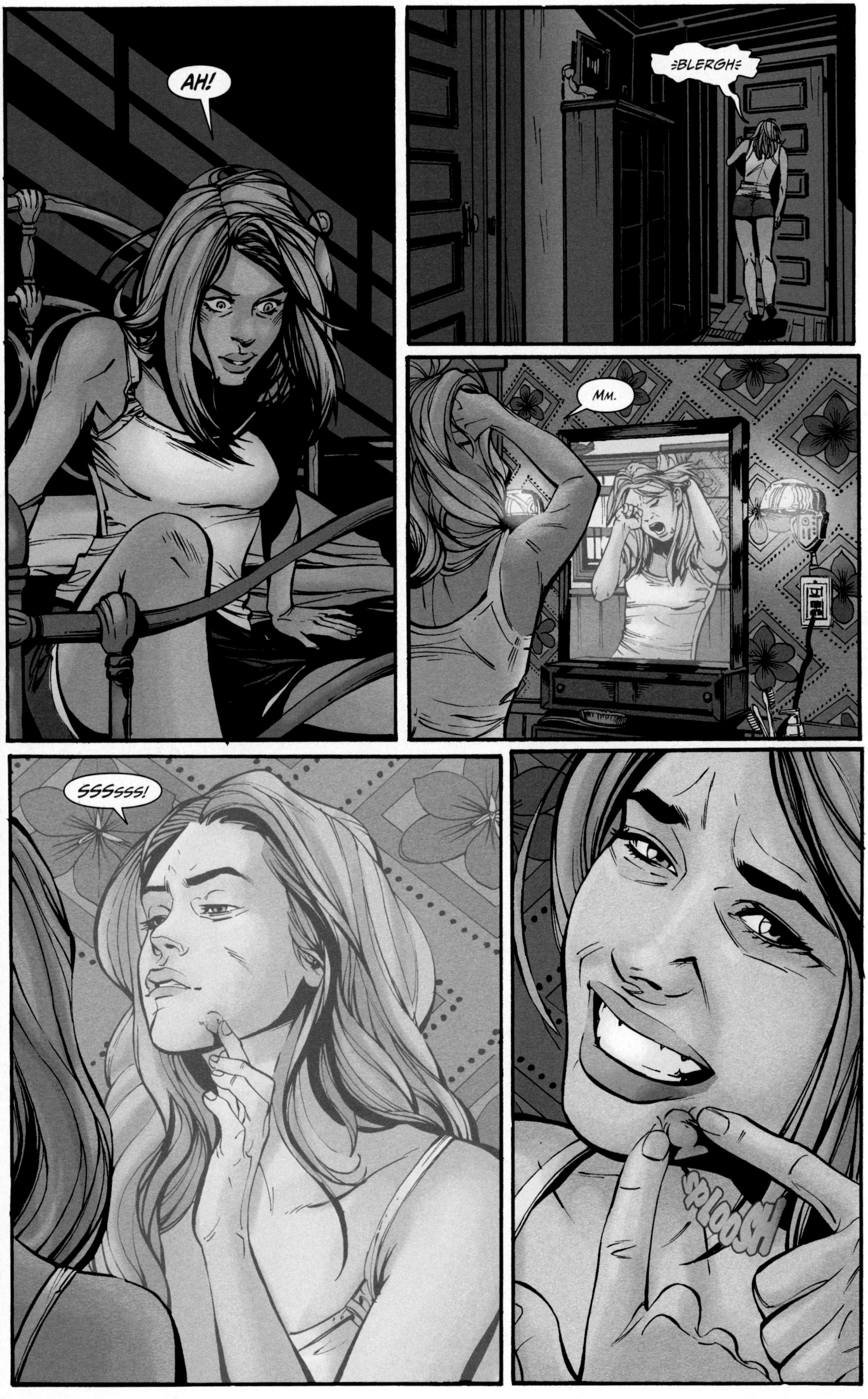
AH!
BLERGH
MM.
SSSSSS!
SPLOOSH

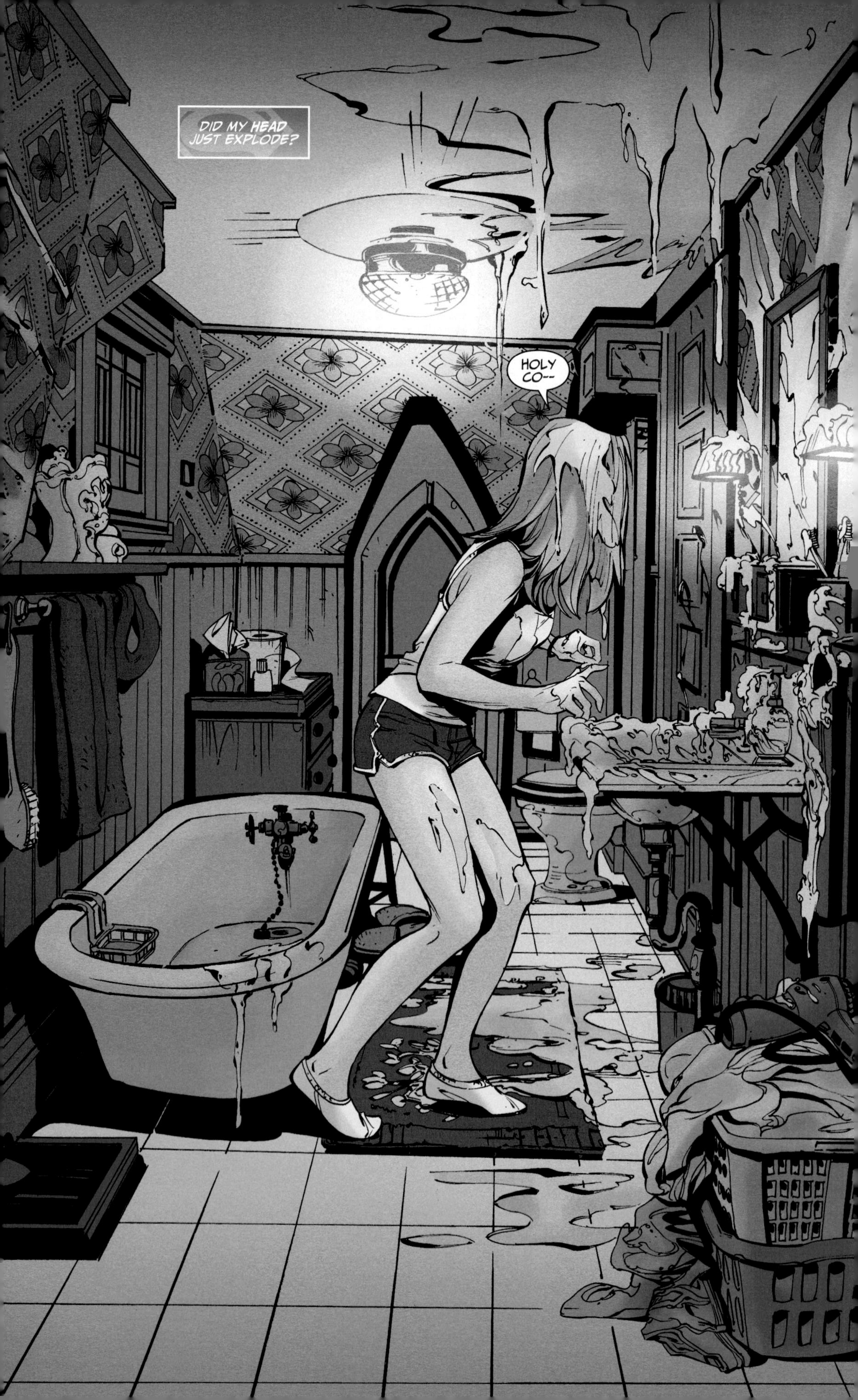
DID MY HEAD JUST EXPLODE?
HOLY CO--

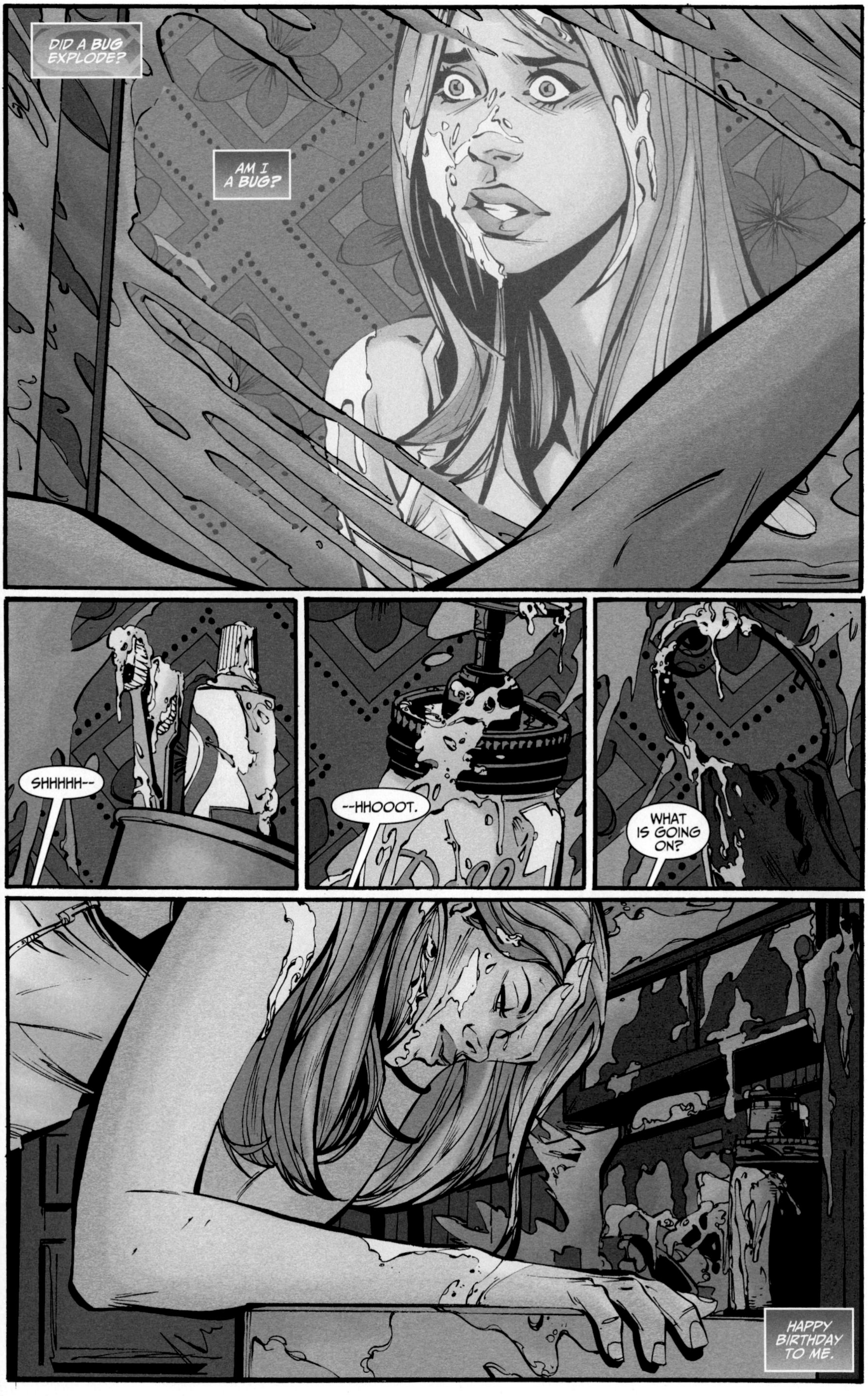
DID A BUG EXPLODE?
AM I A BUG?
SHHHHH--
--HHOOOT.
WHAT IS GOING ON?
HAPPY BIRTHDAY TO ME.

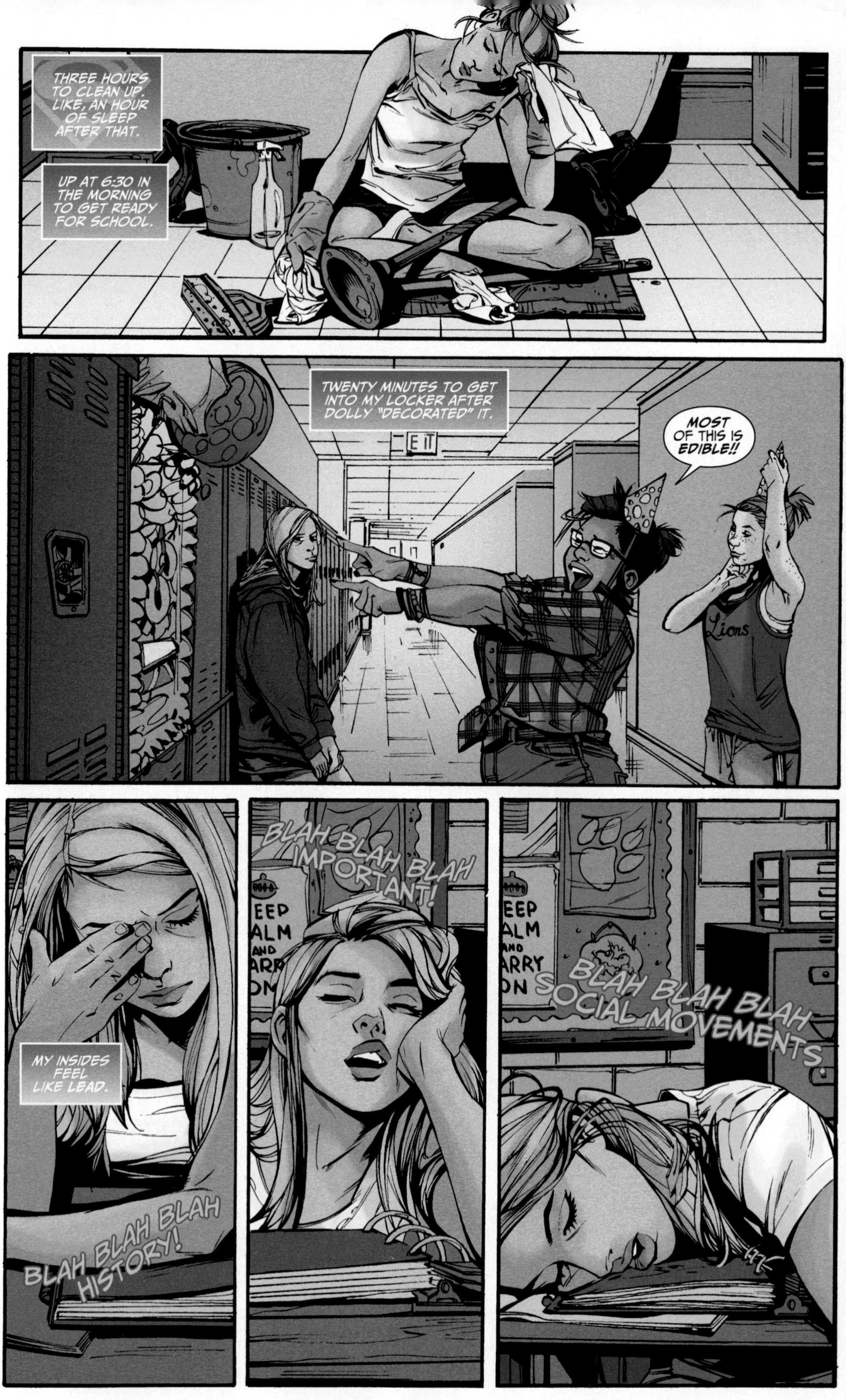
THREE HOURS TO CLEAN UP. LIKE, AN HOUR OF SLEEP AFTER THAT.
UP AT 6:30 IN THE MORNING TO GET READY FOR SCHOOL.
TWENTY MINUTES TO GET INTO MY LOCKER AFTER DOLLY "DECORATED" IT.
MOST OF THIS IS EDIBLE!!
MY INSIDES FEEL LIKE LEAD.
BLAH BLAH BLAH HISTORY!
BLAH BLAH BLAH IMPORTANT!
BLAH BLAH BLAH SOCIAL MOVEMENTS.

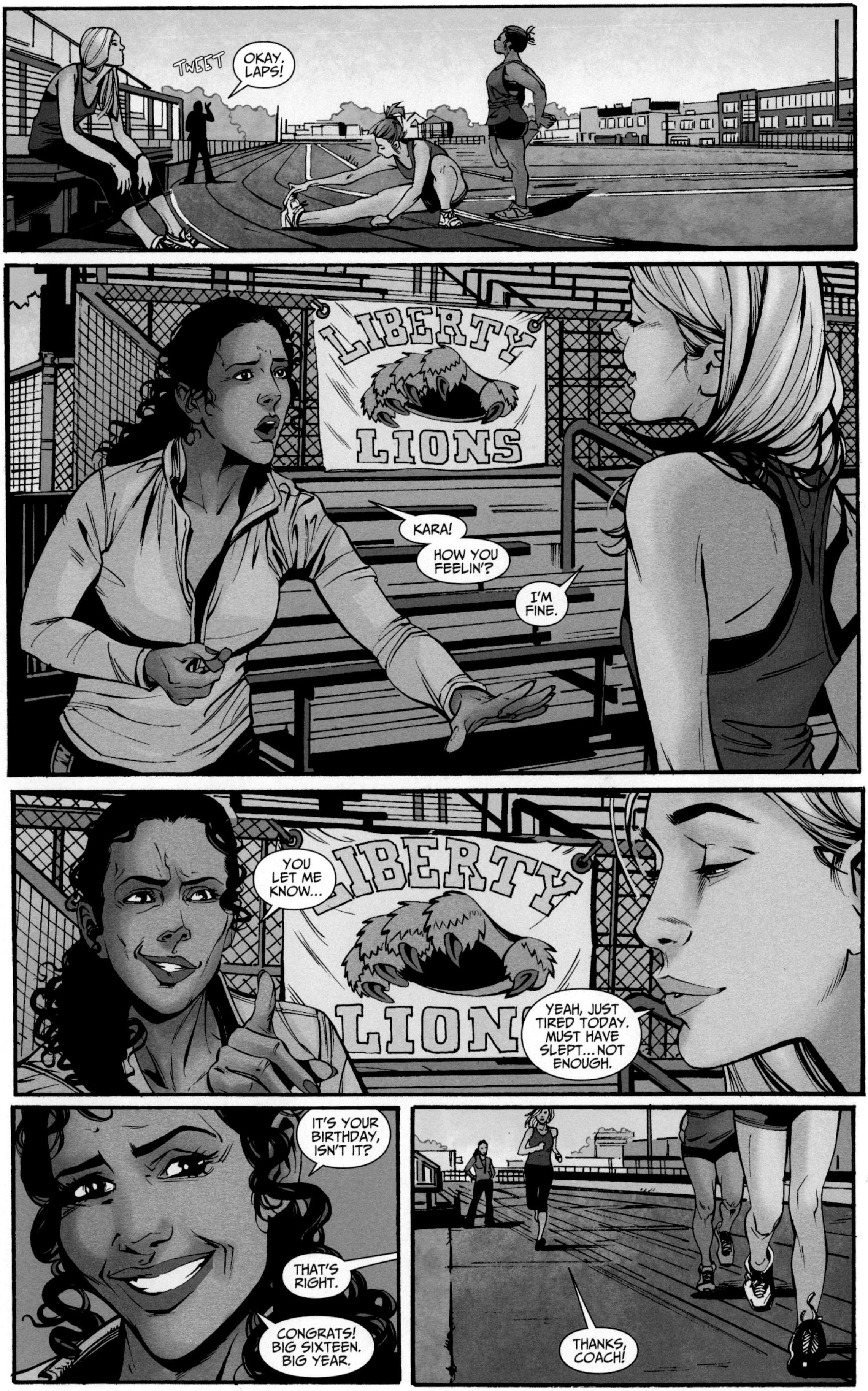
TWEET
OKAY. LAPS!
LIBERTY
LIONS
KARA!
HOW YOU FEELIN'?
I'M FINE.
LIBERTY
YOU LET ME KNOW...
YEAH, JUST TIRED TODAY. MUST HAVE SLEPT...NOT ENOUGH.
IT'S YOUR BIRTHDAY, ISN'T IT?
THAT'S RIGHT.
CONGRATS! BIG SIXTEEN. BIG YEAR.
THANKS, COACH!

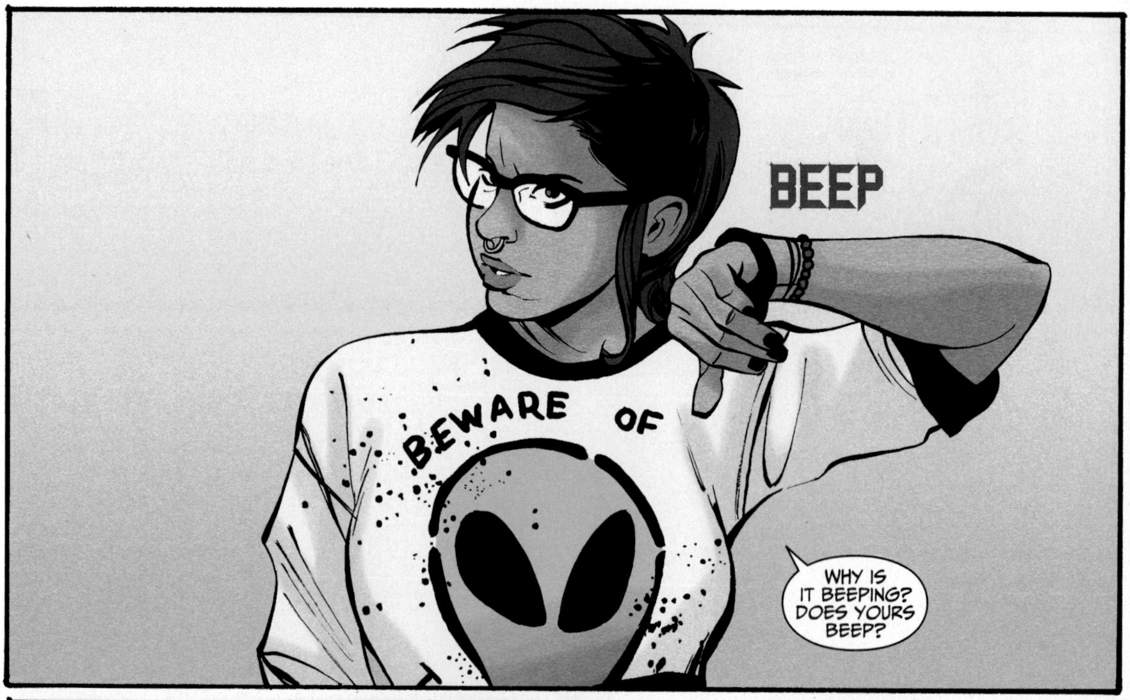
BEEP
BEWARE OF
WHY IS IT BEEPING? DOES YOURS BEEP?

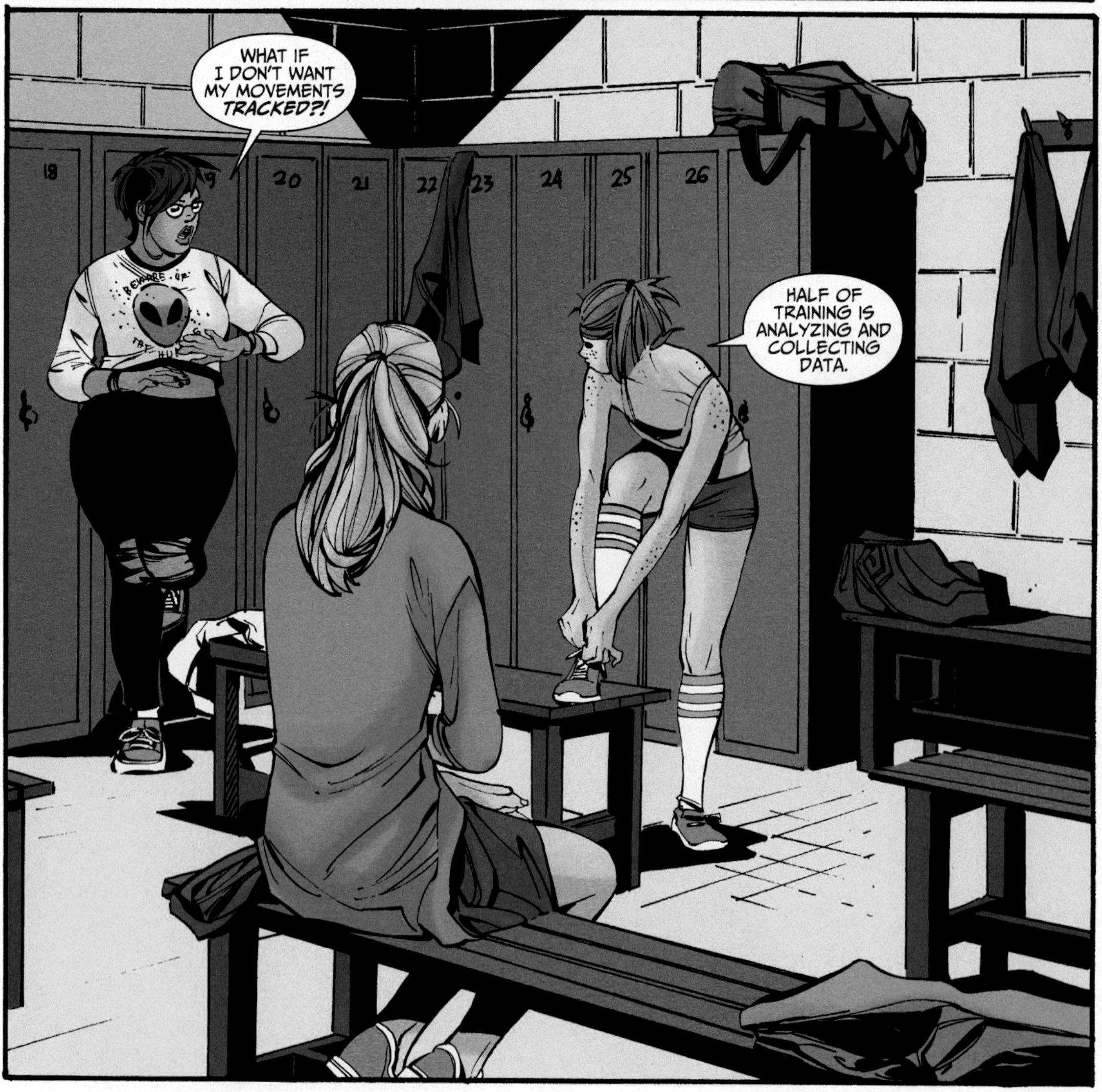
WHAT IF I DON'T WANT MY MOVEMENTS *TRACKED?!*
HALF OF TRAINING IS ANALYZING AND COLLECTING DATA.

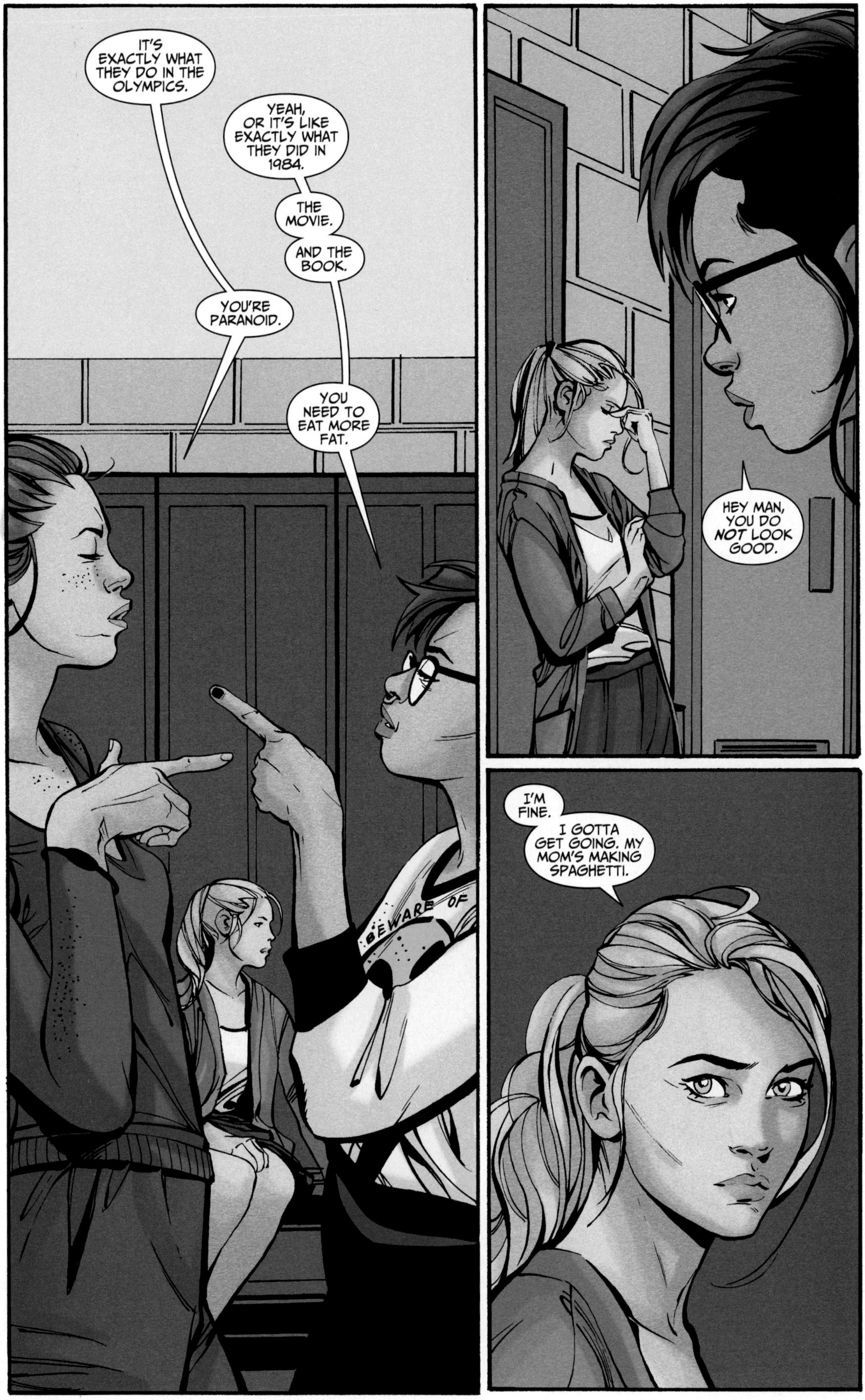

IT'S EXACTLY WHAT THEY DO IN THE OLYMPICS.
YEAH, OR IT'S LIKE EXACTLY WHAT THEY DID IN 1984.
THE MOVIE.
AND THE BOOK.
YOU'RE PARANOID.
YOU NEED TO EAT MORE FAT.
BEWARE OF
HEY MAN, YOU DO *NOT* LOOK GOOD.
I'M FINE.
I GOTTA GET GOING. MY MOM'S MAKING SPAGHETTI.

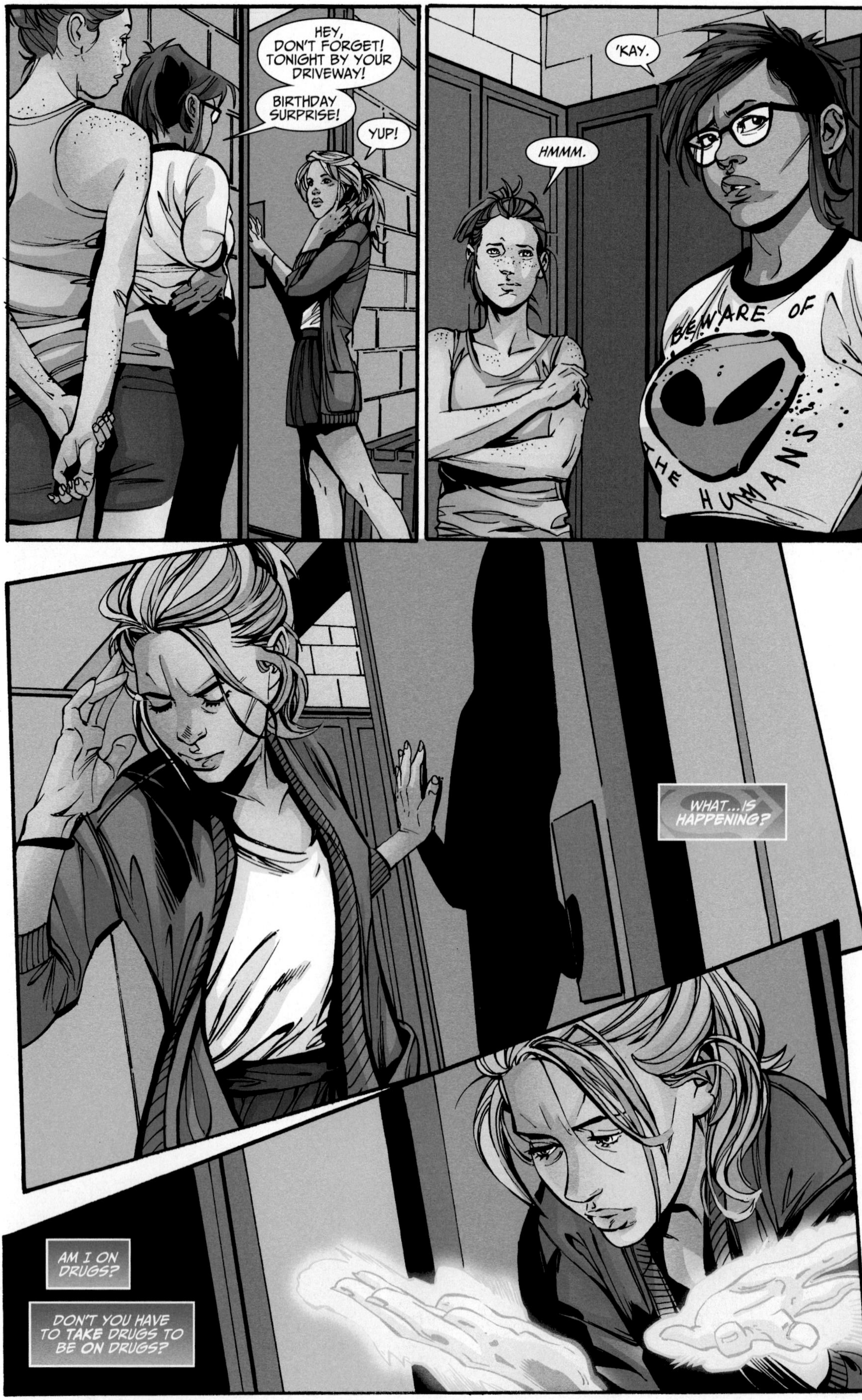
HEY, DON'T FORGET! TONIGHT BY YOUR DRIVEWAY!
BIRTHDAY SURPRISE!
YUP!
'KAY.
HMMM.
BEWARE OF THE HUMANS
WHAT...IS HAPPENING?
AM I ON DRUGS?
DON'T YOU HAVE TO TAKE DRUGS TO BE ON DRUGS?

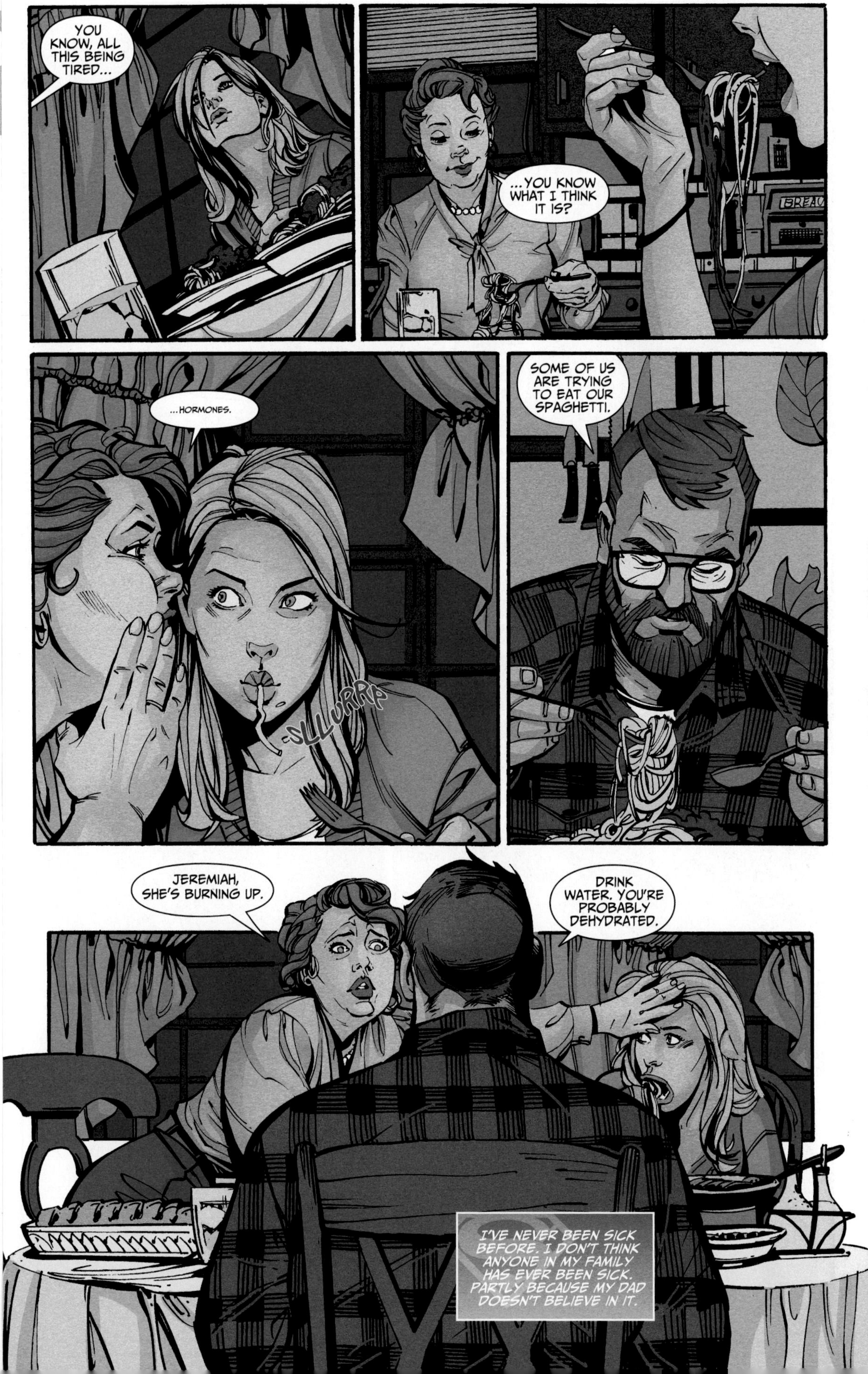
YOU KNOW, ALL THIS BEING TIRED...
...YOU KNOW WHAT I THINK IT IS?
...HORMONES.
-SLLURRP
SOME OF US ARE TRYING TO EAT OUR SPAGHETTI.
JEREMIAH, SHE'S BURNING UP.
DRINK WATER. YOU'RE PROBABLY DEHYDRATED.
I'VE NEVER BEEN SICK BEFORE. I DON'T THINK ANYONE IN MY FAMILY HAS EVER BEEN SICK. PARTLY BECAUSE MY DAD DOESN'T BELIEVE IN IT.

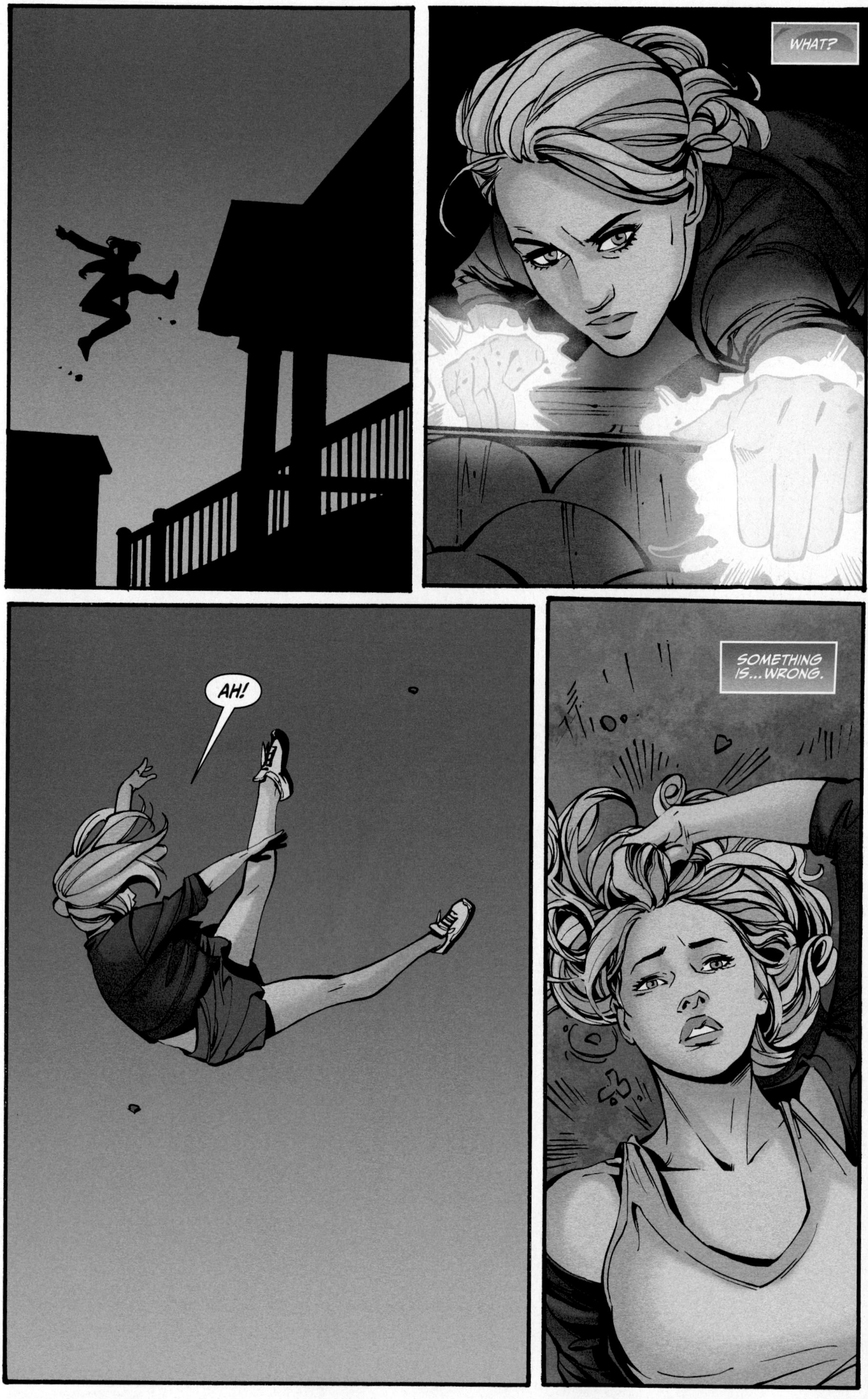
WHAT?
AH!
SOMETHING IS...WRONG.

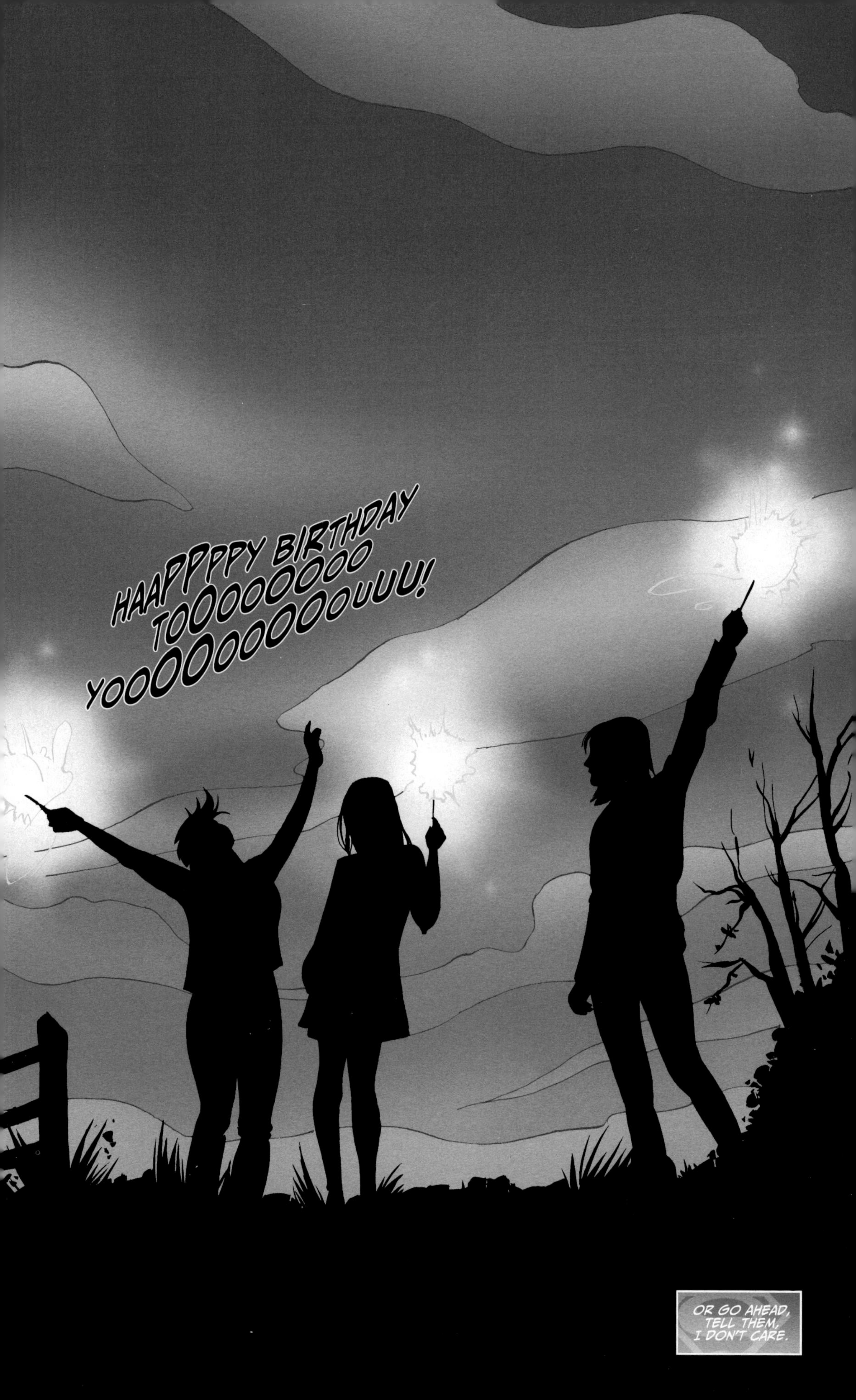
HAAPPPPY BIRTHDAY TOOOOOOOOO YOOOOOOOOOOOUUUU!
OR GO AHEAD, TELL THEM, I DON'T CARE.

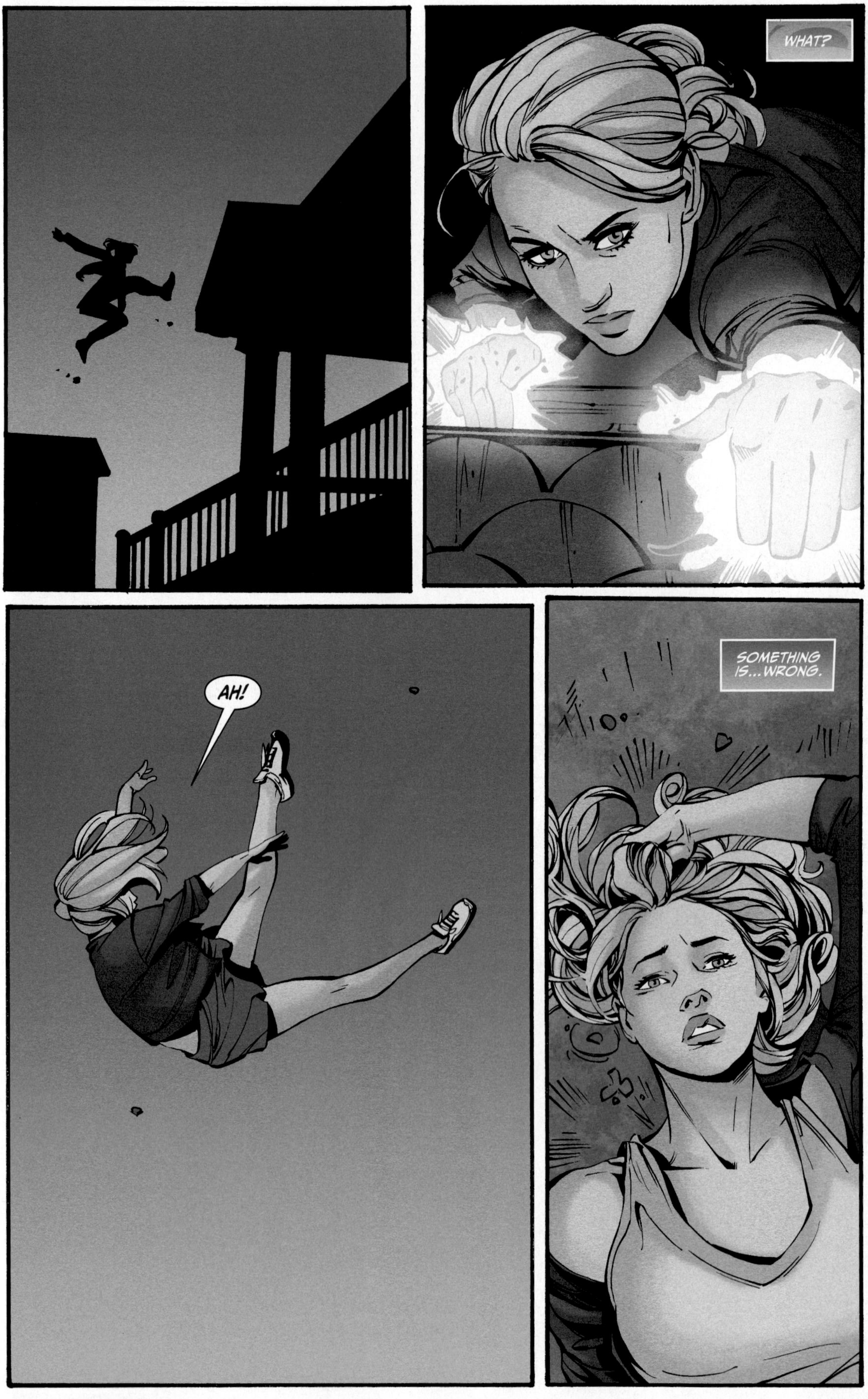
WHAT?
AH!
SOMETHING IS...WRONG.

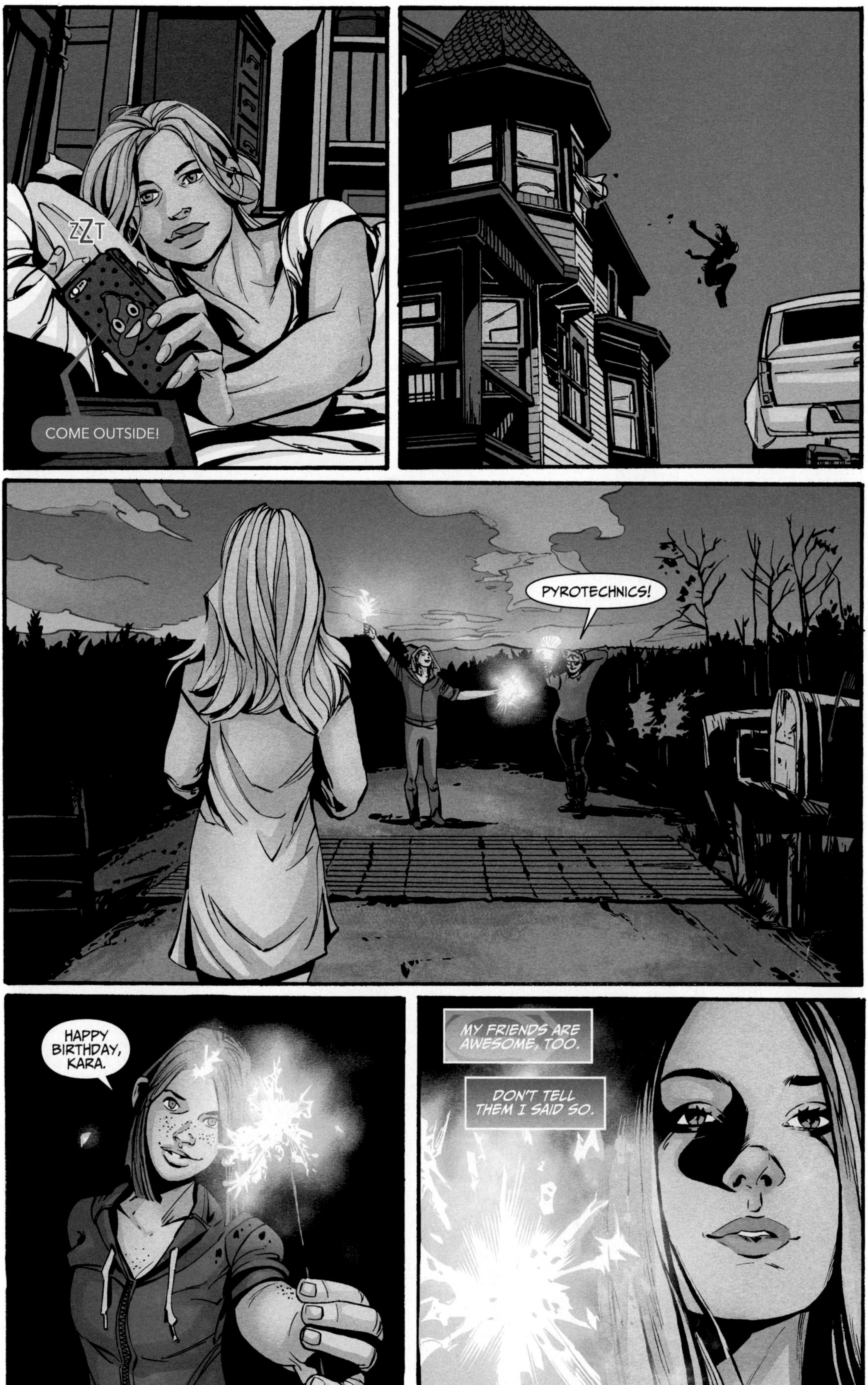
ZZT
COME OUTSIDE!
PYROTECHNICS!
HAPPY BIRTHDAY, KARA.
MY FRIENDS ARE AWESOME, TOO.
DON'T TELL THEM I SAID SO.

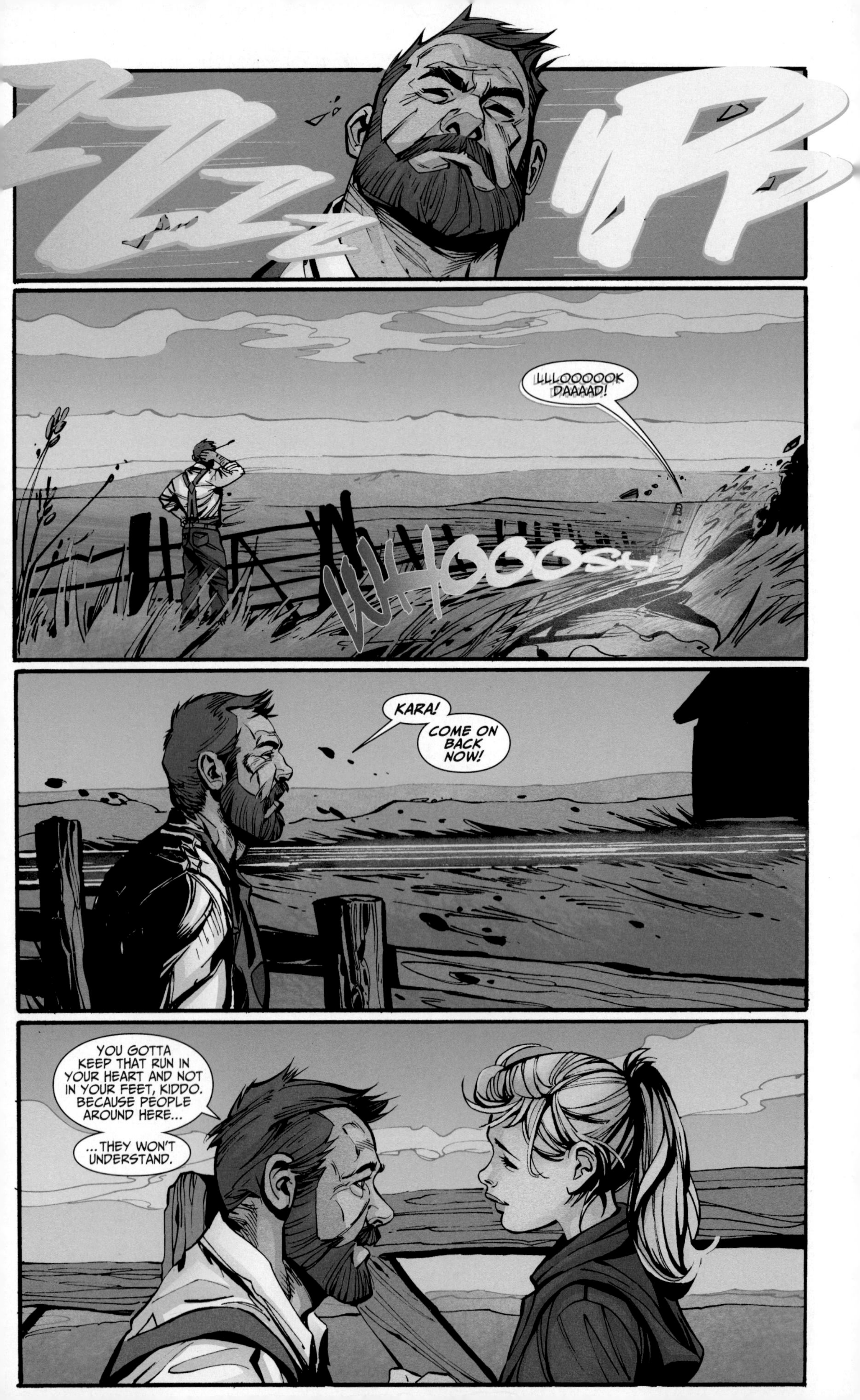
ZZZZZWPP
LLLOOOOOK DAAAAD!
WHOOOOSH
KARA!
COME ON BACK NOW!
YOU GOTTA KEEP THAT RUN IN YOUR HEART AND NOT IN YOUR FEET, KIDDO. BECAUSE PEOPLE AROUND HERE...
...THEY WON'T UNDERSTAND.

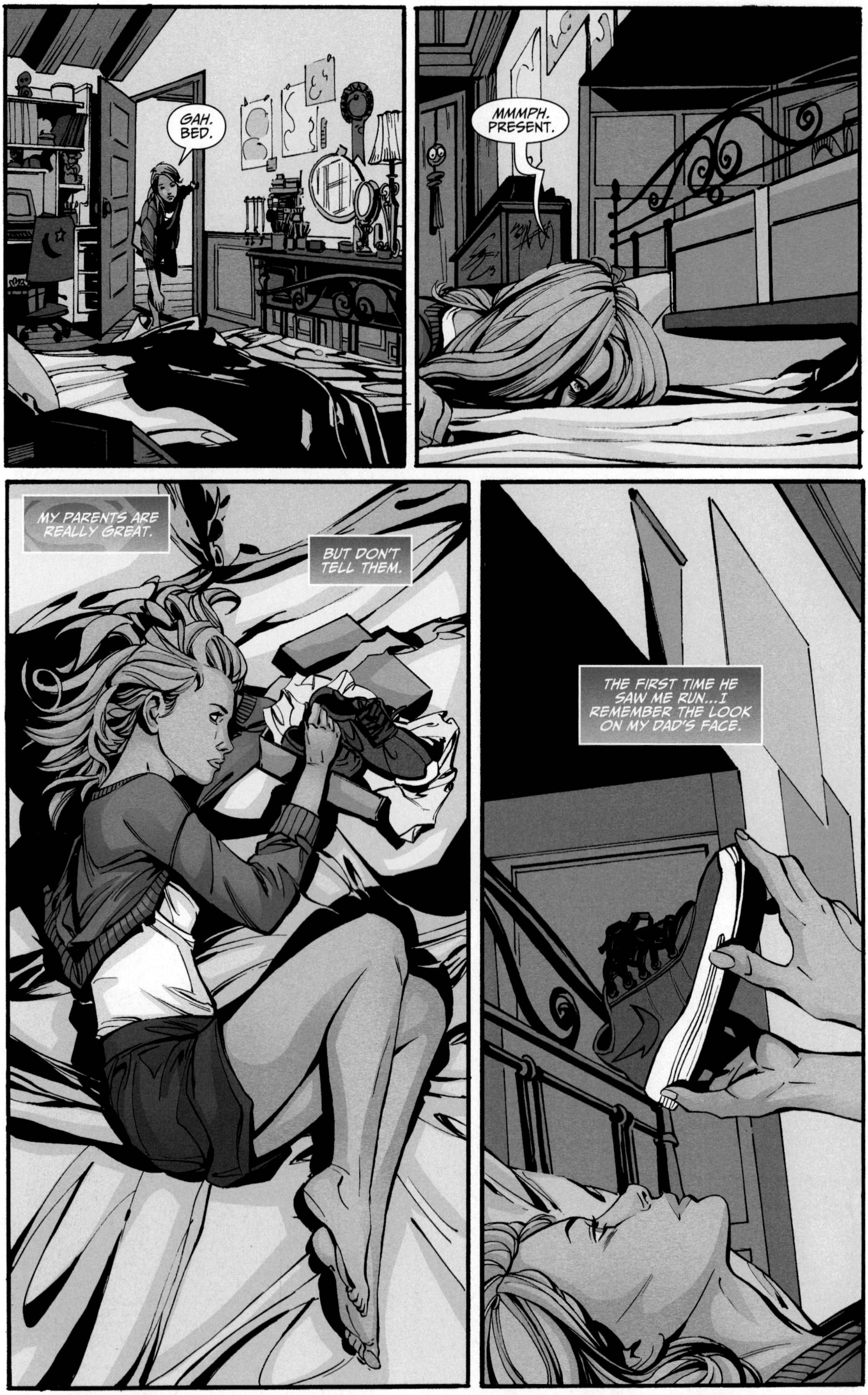
GAH. BED.
MMMPH. PRESENT.
MY PARENTS ARE REALLY GREAT.
BUT DON'T TELL THEM.
THE FIRST TIME HE SAW ME RUN...I REMEMBER THE LOOK ON MY DAD'S FACE.

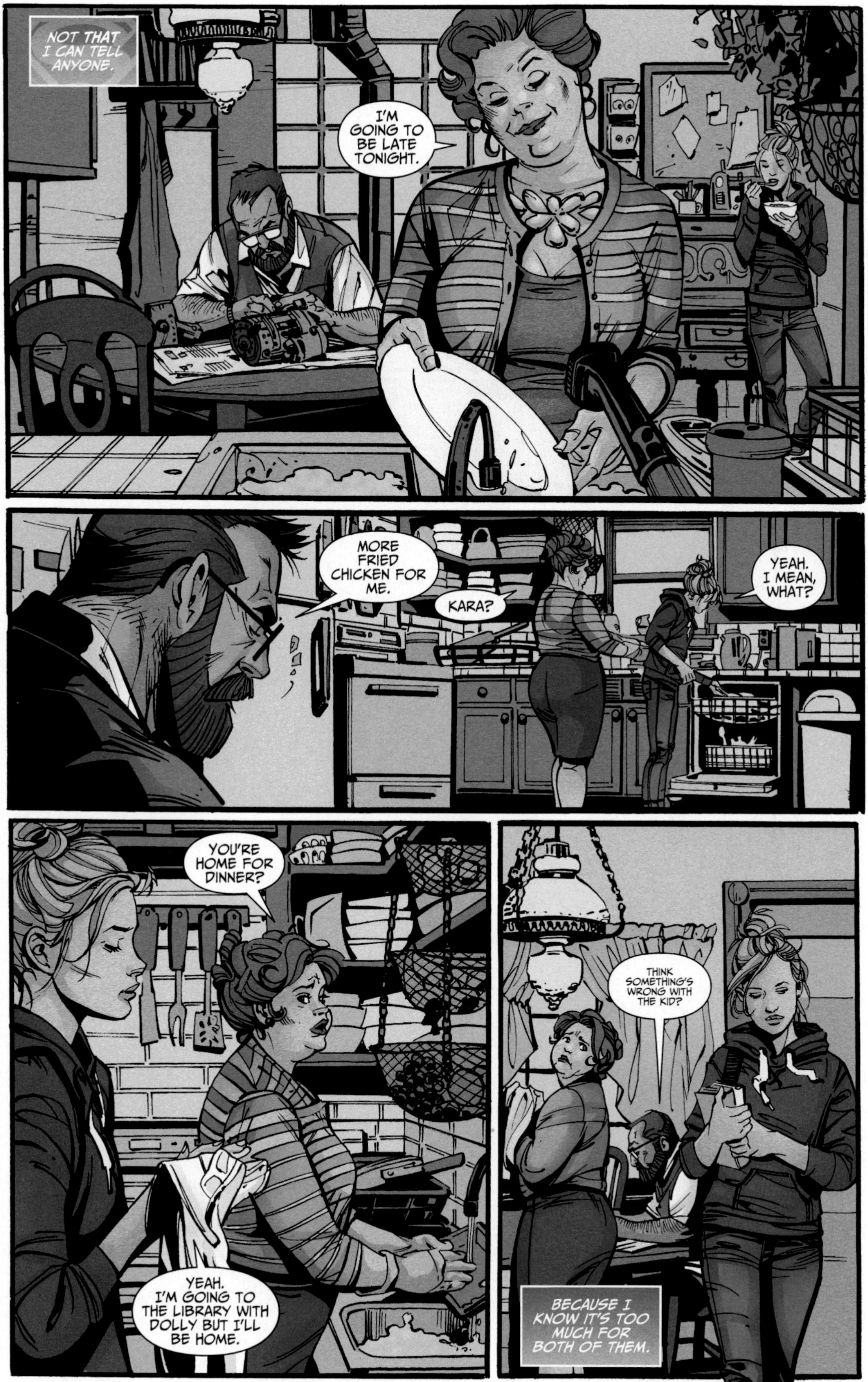
NOT THAT I CAN TELL ANYONE.
I'M GOING TO BE LATE TONIGHT.
MORE FRIED CHICKEN FOR ME.
KARA?
YEAH. I MEAN, WHAT?
YOU'RE HOME FOR DINNER?
YEAH. I'M GOING TO THE LIBRARY WITH DOLLY BUT I'LL BE HOME.
THINK SOMETHING'S WRONG WITH THE KID?
BECAUSE I KNOW IT'S TOO MUCH FOR BOTH OF THEM.

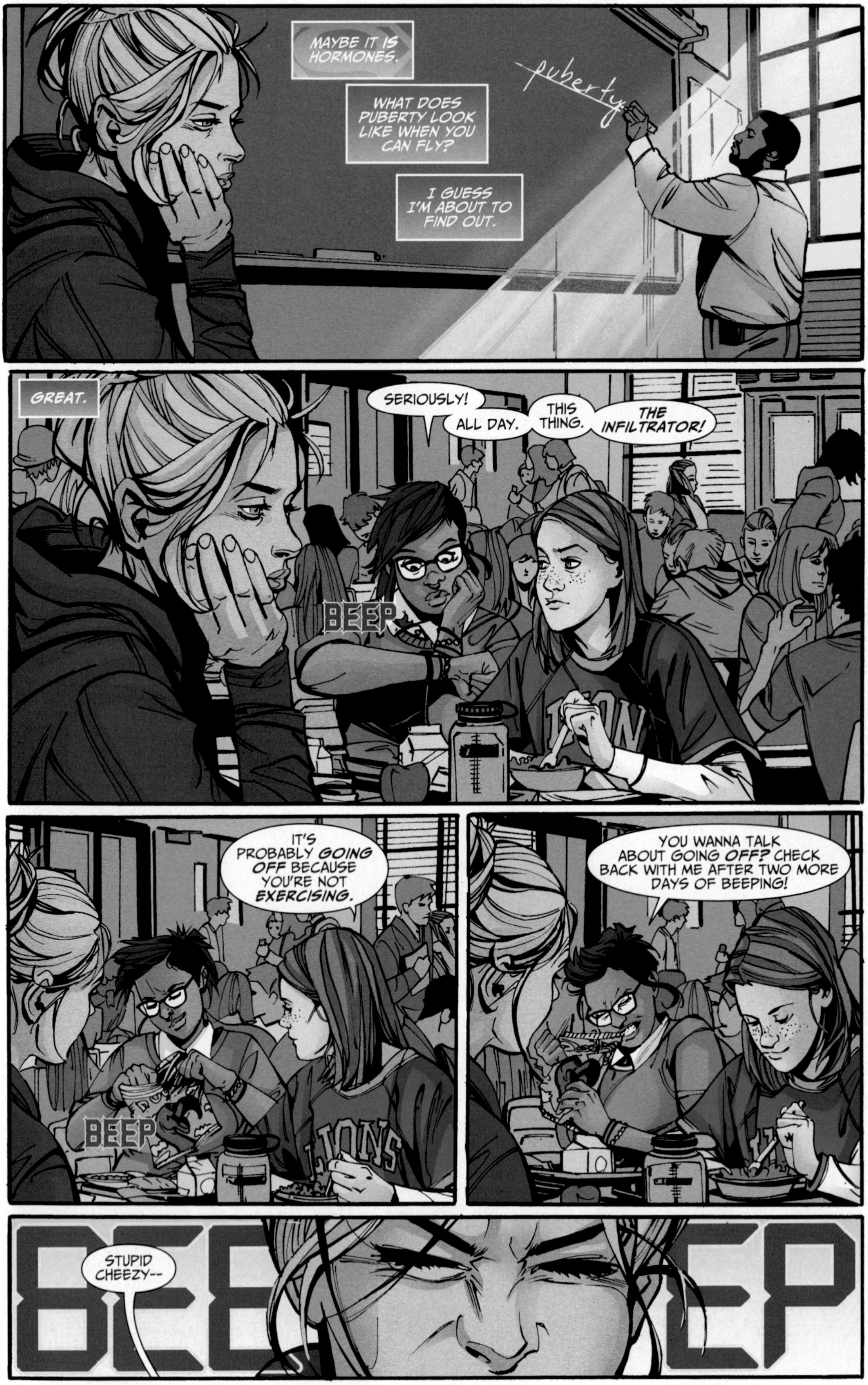
MAYBE IT IS HORMONES.
WHAT DOES PUBERTY LOOK LIKE WHEN YOU CAN FLY?
I GUESS I'M ABOUT TO FIND OUT.
puberty
GREAT.
SERIOUSLY!
ALL DAY.
THIS THING.
THE INFILTRATOR!
BEEP
IT'S PROBABLY GOING OFF BECAUSE YOU'RE NOT EXERCISING.
BEEP
YOU WANNA TALK ABOUT GOING OFF? CHECK BACK WITH ME AFTER TWO MORE DAYS OF BEEPING!
STUPID CHEEZY--
BEEEP

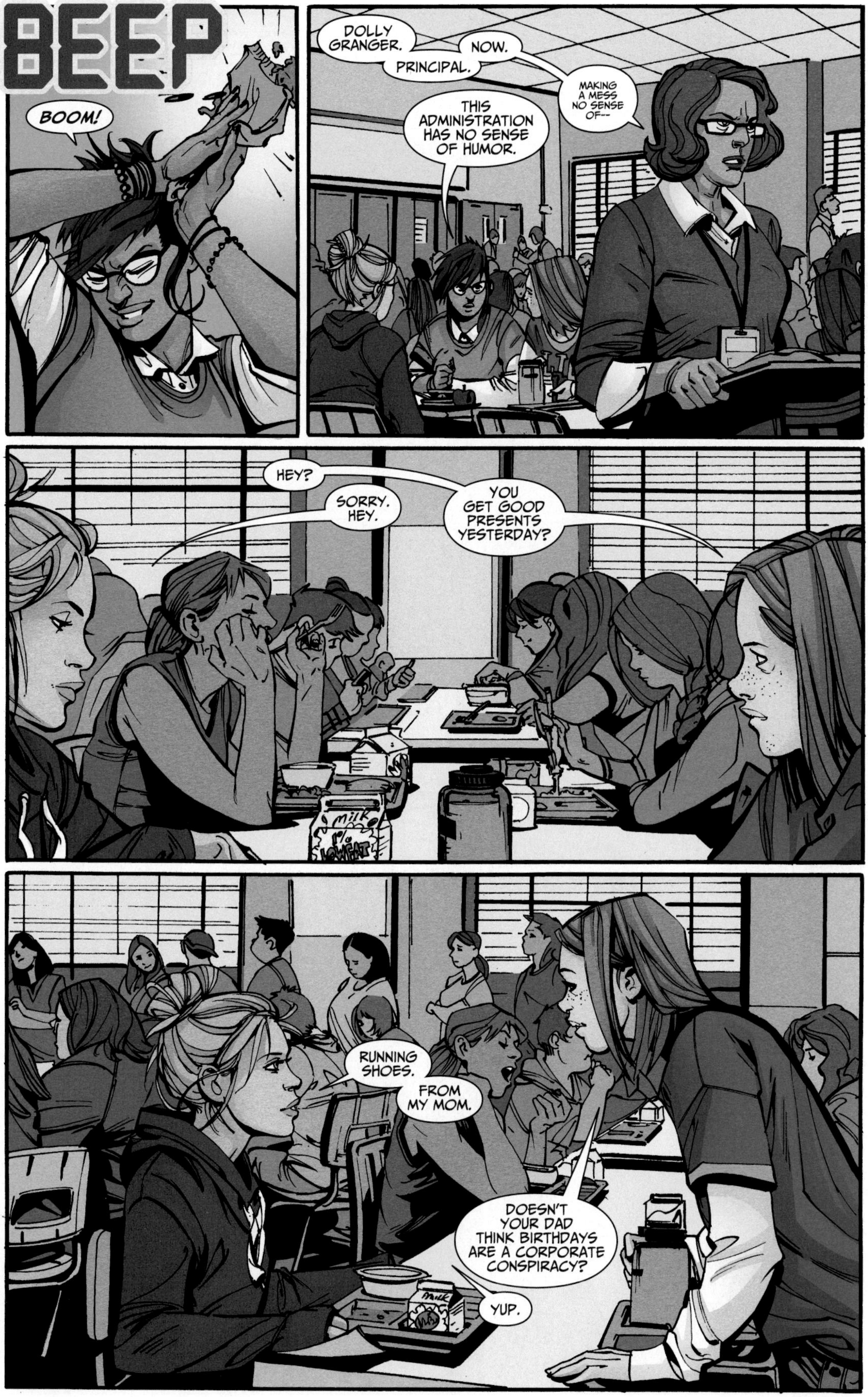
BEEP
BOOM!
DOLLY GRANGER.
PRINCIPAL.
NOW.
MAKING A MESS NO SENSE OF--
THIS ADMINISTRATION HAS NO SENSE OF HUMOR.
HEY?
SORRY. HEY.
YOU GET GOOD PRESENTS YESTERDAY?
RUNNING SHOES.
FROM MY MOM.
DOESN'T YOUR DAD THINK BIRTHDAYS ARE A CORPORATE CONSPIRACY?
YUP.

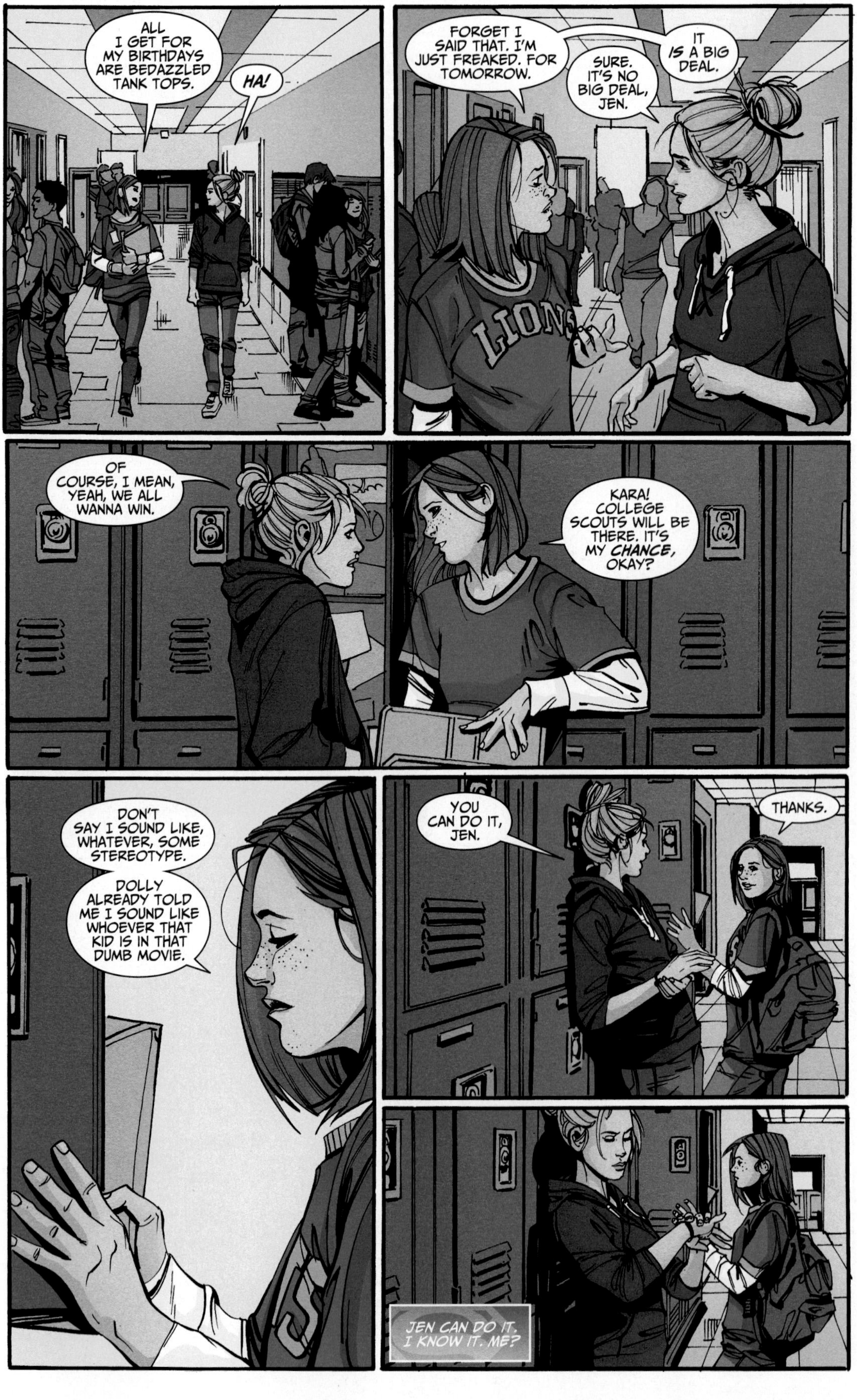
ALL I GET FOR MY BIRTHDAYS ARE BEDAZZLED TANK TOPS.
HA!
FORGET I SAID THAT. I'M JUST FREAKED. FOR TOMORROW.
SURE. IT'S NO BIG DEAL, JEN.
IT IS A BIG DEAL.
LIONS
OF COURSE, I MEAN, YEAH, WE ALL WANNA WIN.
KARA! COLLEGE SCOUTS WILL BE THERE. IT'S MY CHANCE, OKAY?
DON'T SAY I SOUND LIKE, WHATEVER, SOME STEREOTYPE.
DOLLY ALREADY TOLD ME I SOUND LIKE WHOEVER THAT KID IS IN THAT DUMB MOVIE.
YOU CAN DO IT, JEN.
THANKS.
JEN CAN DO IT. I KNOW IT. ME?

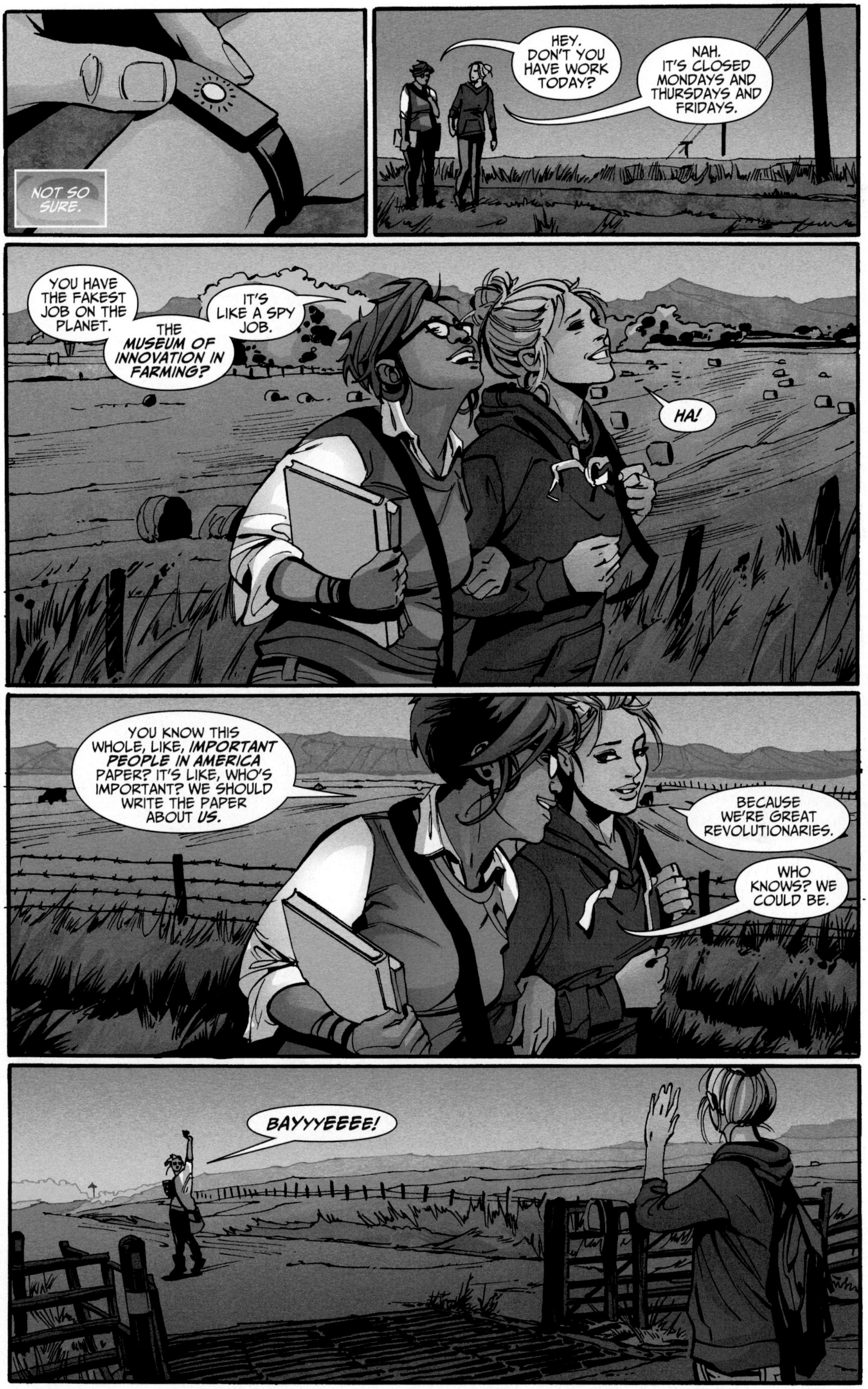
NOT SO SURE.
HEY. DON'T YOU HAVE WORK TODAY?
NAH. IT'S CLOSED MONDAYS AND THURSDAYS AND FRIDAYS.
YOU HAVE THE FAKEST JOB ON THE PLANET.
THE *MUSEUM OF INNOVATION IN FARMING?*
IT'S LIKE A SPY JOB.
HA!
YOU KNOW THIS WHOLE, LIKE, *IMPORTANT PEOPLE IN AMERICA* PAPER? IT'S LIKE, WHO'S IMPORTANT? WE SHOULD WRITE THE PAPER ABOUT *US.*
BECAUSE WE'RE GREAT REVOLUTIONARIES.
WHO KNOWS? WE COULD BE.
BAYYYEEEE!

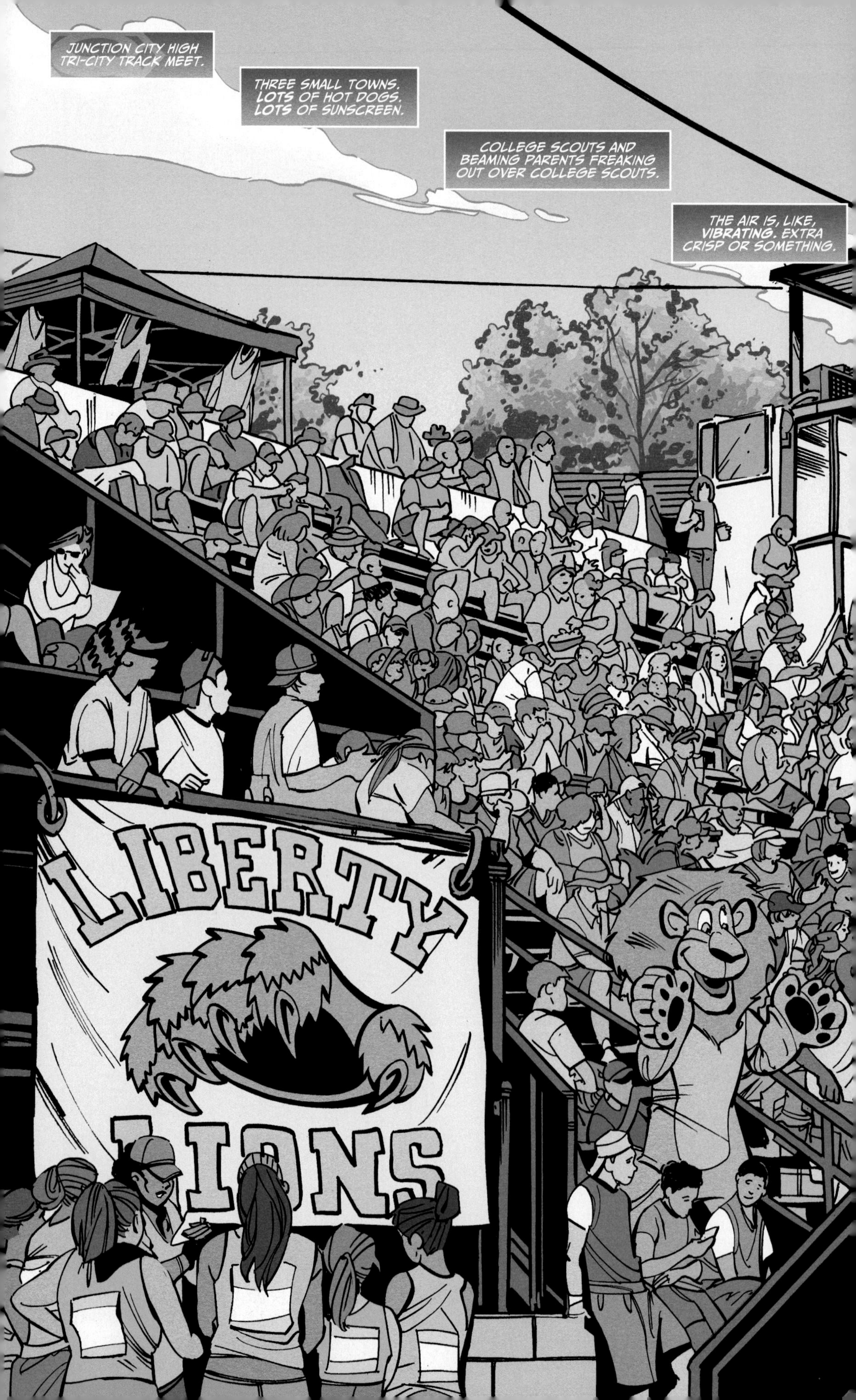
JUNCTION CITY HIGH TRI-CITY TRACK MEET.
THREE SMALL TOWNS. LOTS OF HOT DOGS. LOTS OF SUNSCREEN.
COLLEGE SCOUTS AND BEAMING PARENTS FREAKING OUT OVER COLLEGE SCOUTS.
THE AIR IS, LIKE, VIBRATING. EXTRA CRISP OR SOMETHING.
LIBERTY
LIONS

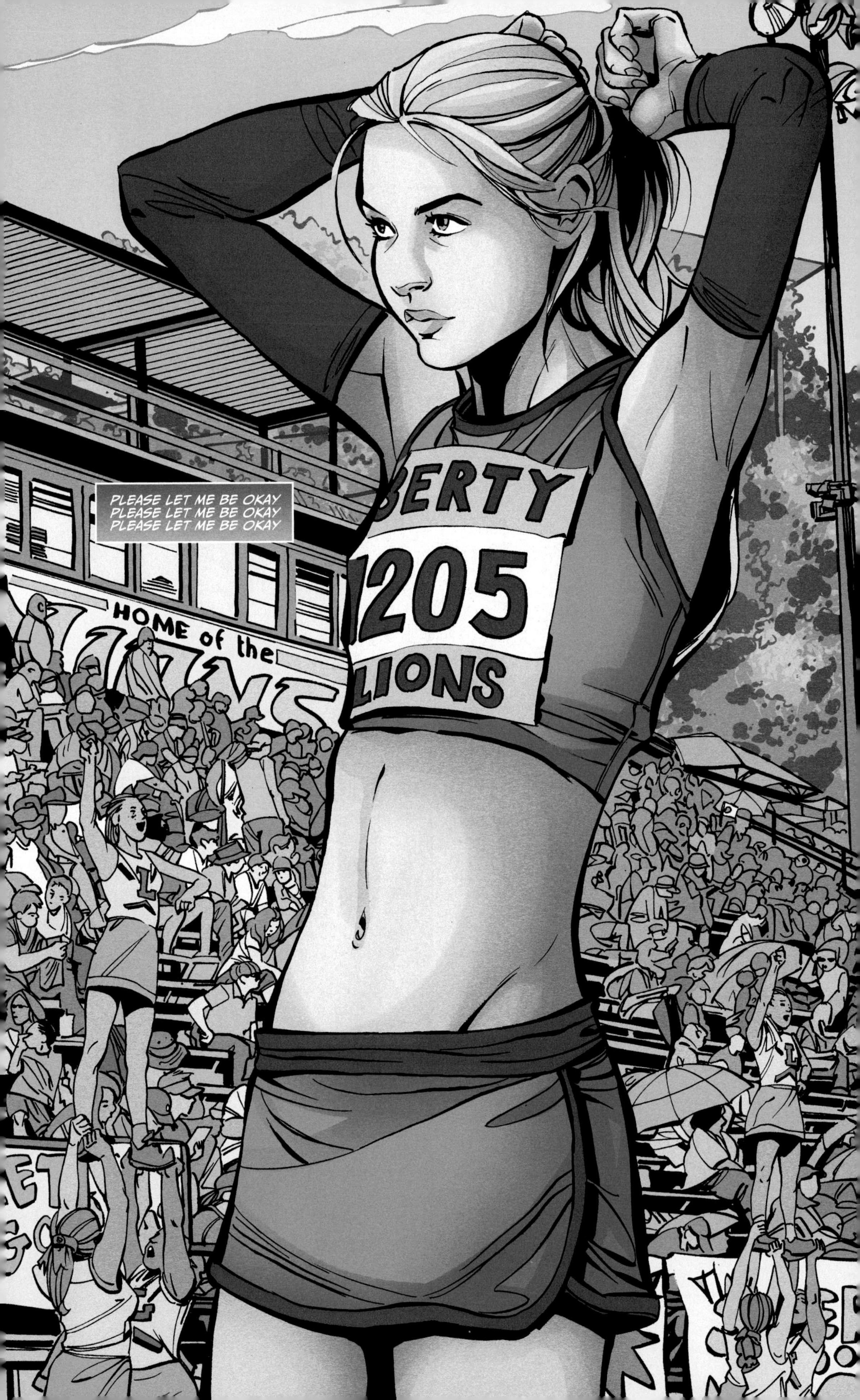
PLEASE LET ME BE OKAY
PLEASE LET ME BE OKAY
PLEASE LET ME BE OKAY
HOME of the
BERTY
1205
LIONS

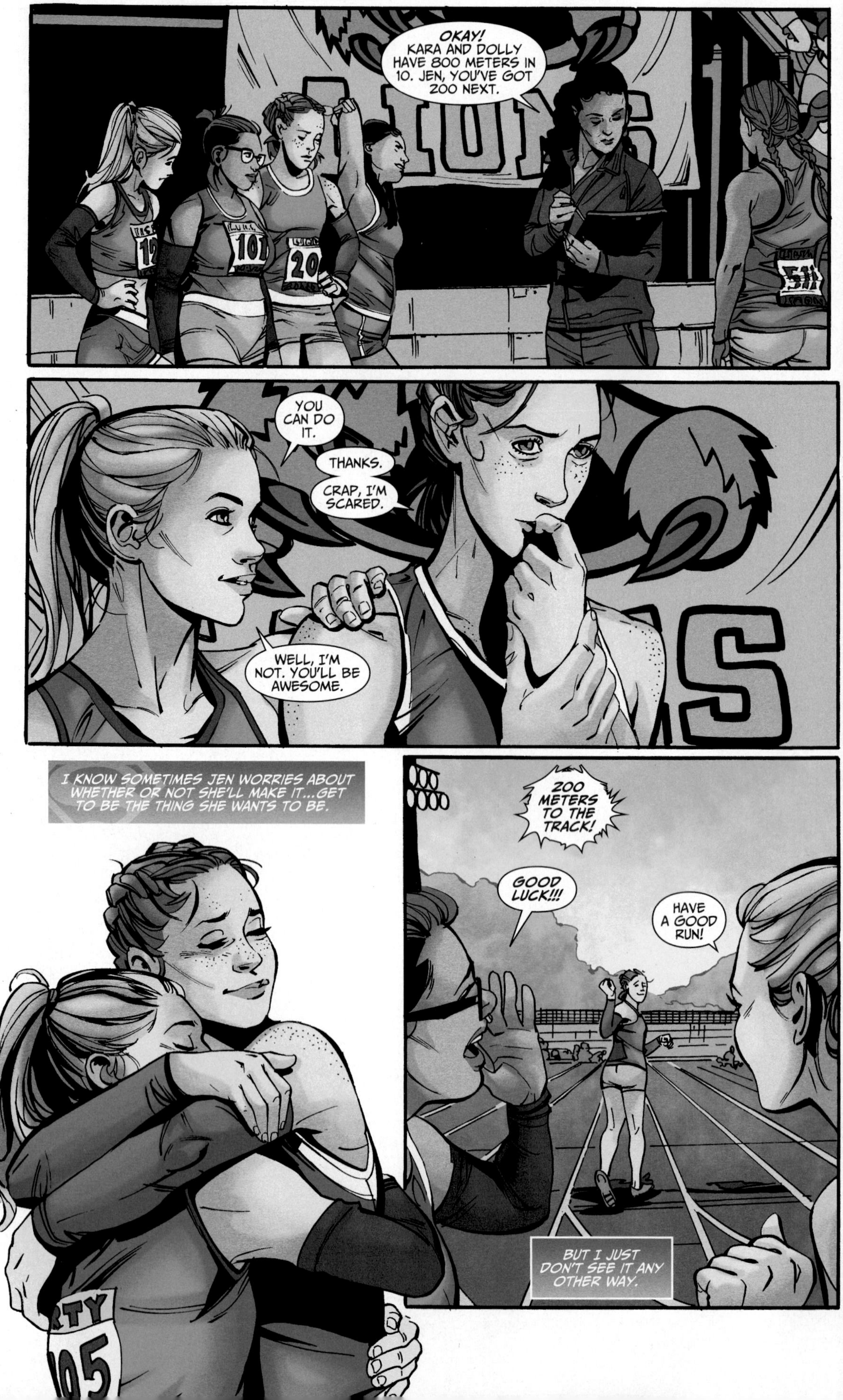
OKAY! KARA AND DOLLY HAVE 800 METERS IN 10. JEN, YOU'VE GOT 200 NEXT.
YOU CAN DO IT.
THANKS.
CRAP, I'M SCARED.
WELL, I'M NOT. YOU'LL BE AWESOME.
I KNOW SOMETIMES JEN WORRIES ABOUT WHETHER OR NOT SHE'LL MAKE IT...GET TO BE THE THING SHE WANTS TO BE.
200 METERS TO THE TRACK!
GOOD LUCK!!!
HAVE A GOOD RUN!
BUT I JUST DON'T SEE IT ANY OTHER WAY.

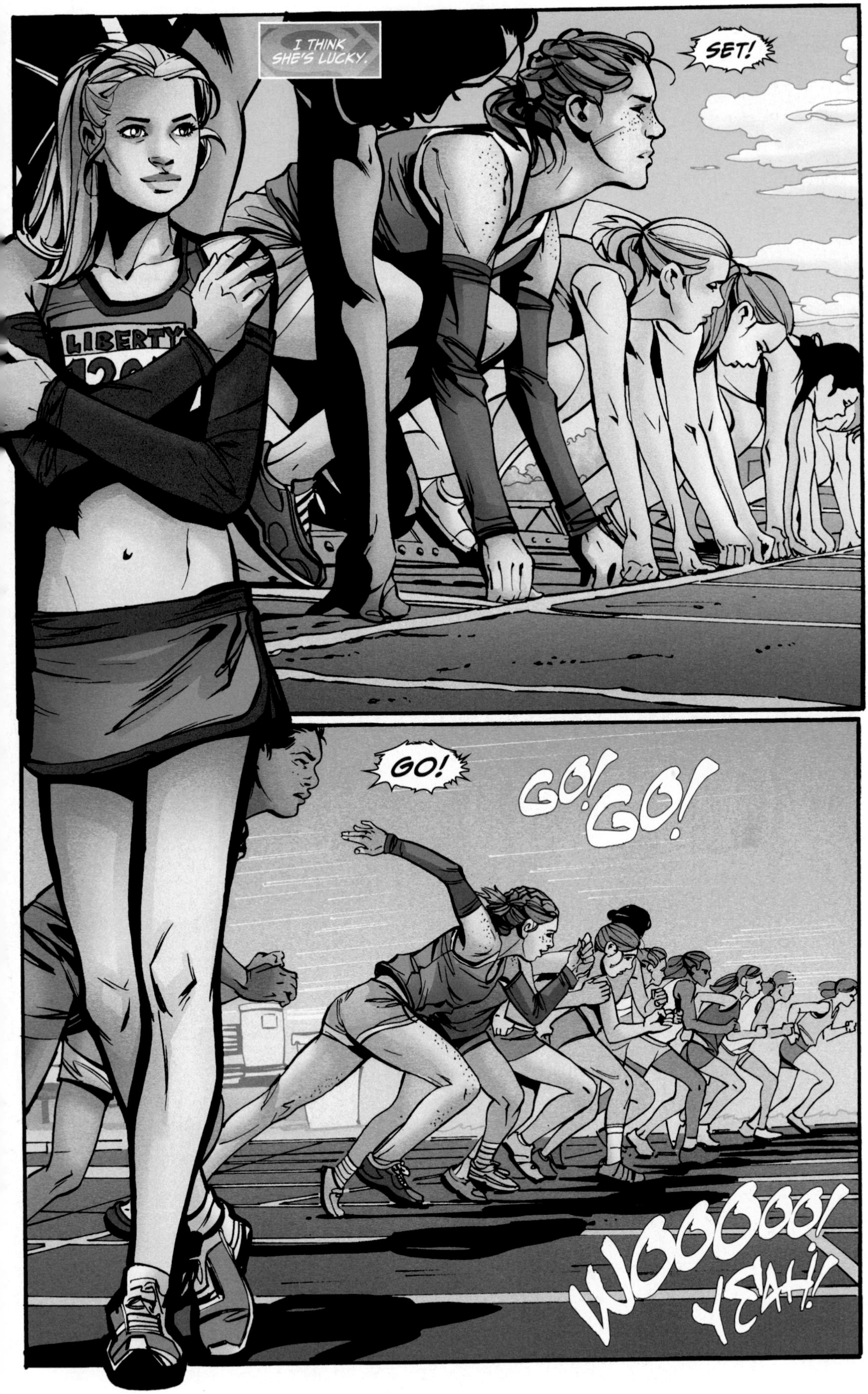

I THINK SHE'S LUCKY.
SET!
LIBERTY
GO!
GO! GO!
WOOOOO! YEAH!

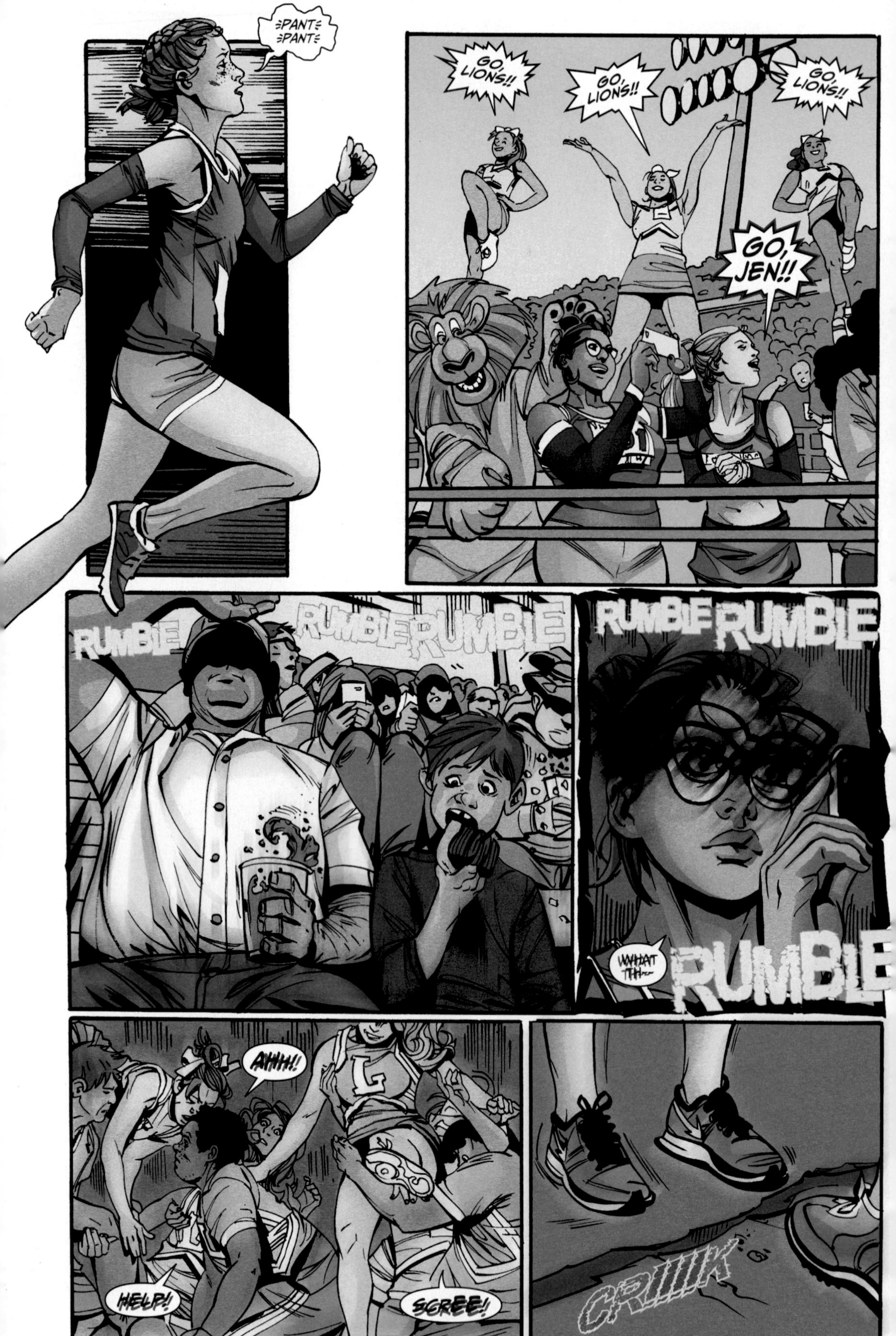

PANT
PANT
GO, LIONS!!
GO, LIONS!!
GO, LIONS!!
GO, JEN!!
RUMBLE
RUMBLE RUMBLE
RUMBLE RUMBLE
WHAT TH--
RUMBLE
AHHH!
HELP!
SCREE!
CRIIIIK

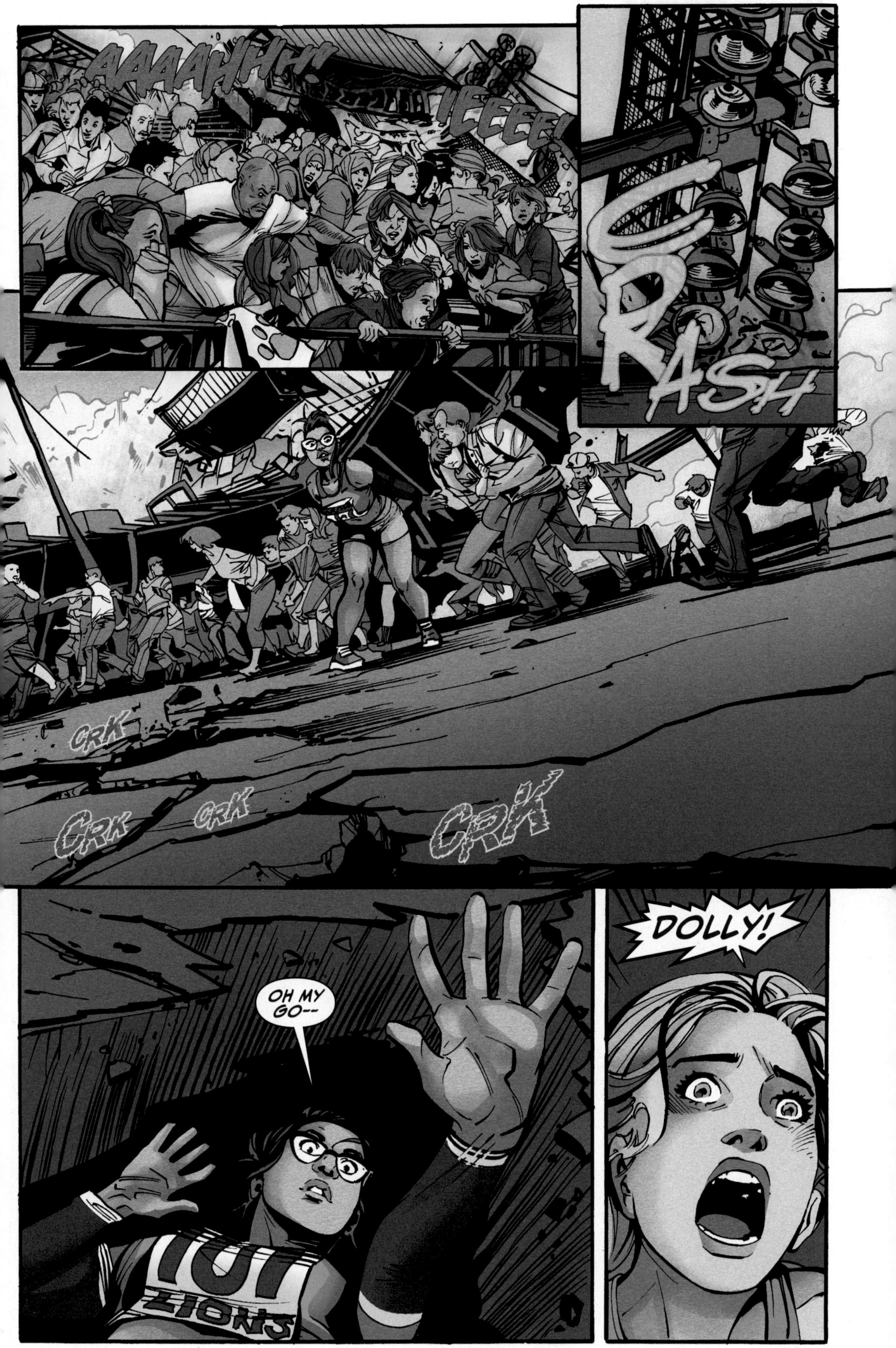
AAAAHHH!!
IEEEE!
CRASH
CRK
CRK
CRK
CRK
OH MY GO--
DOLLY!

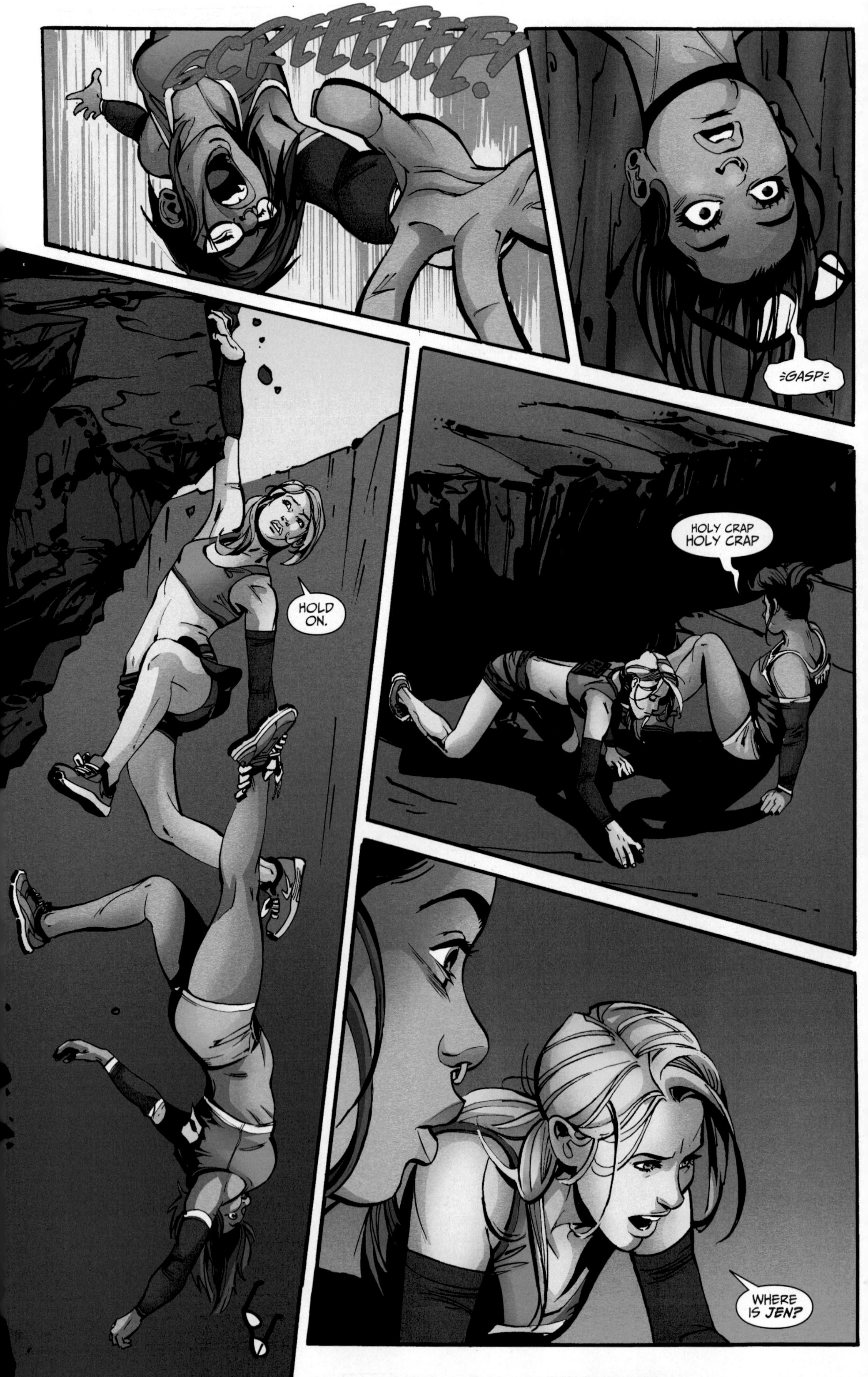
SCREEEEEEE!
GASP
HOLD ON.
HOLY CRAP HOLY CRAP
WHERE IS JEN?

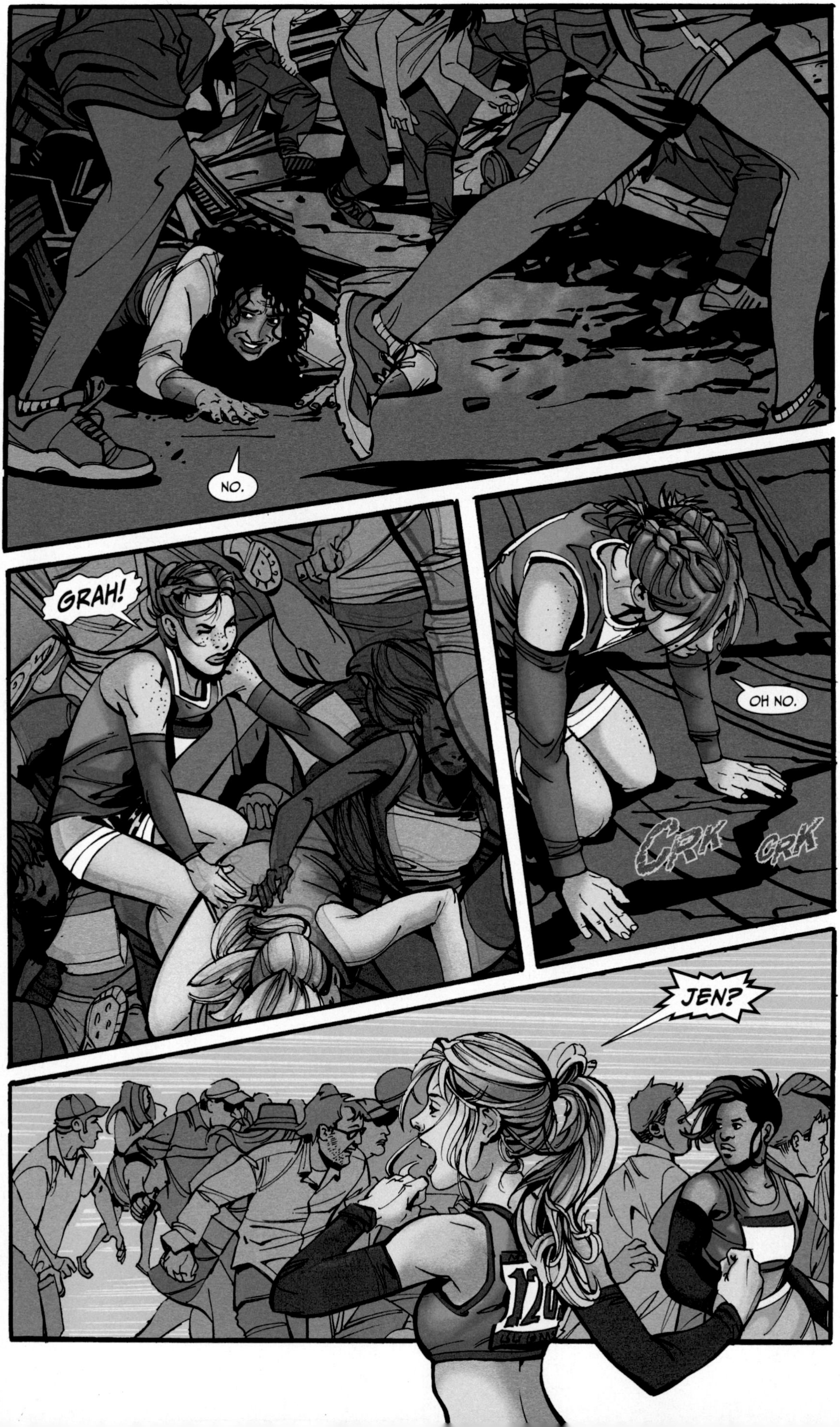
NO.
GRAH!
OH NO.
CRK CRK
JEN?

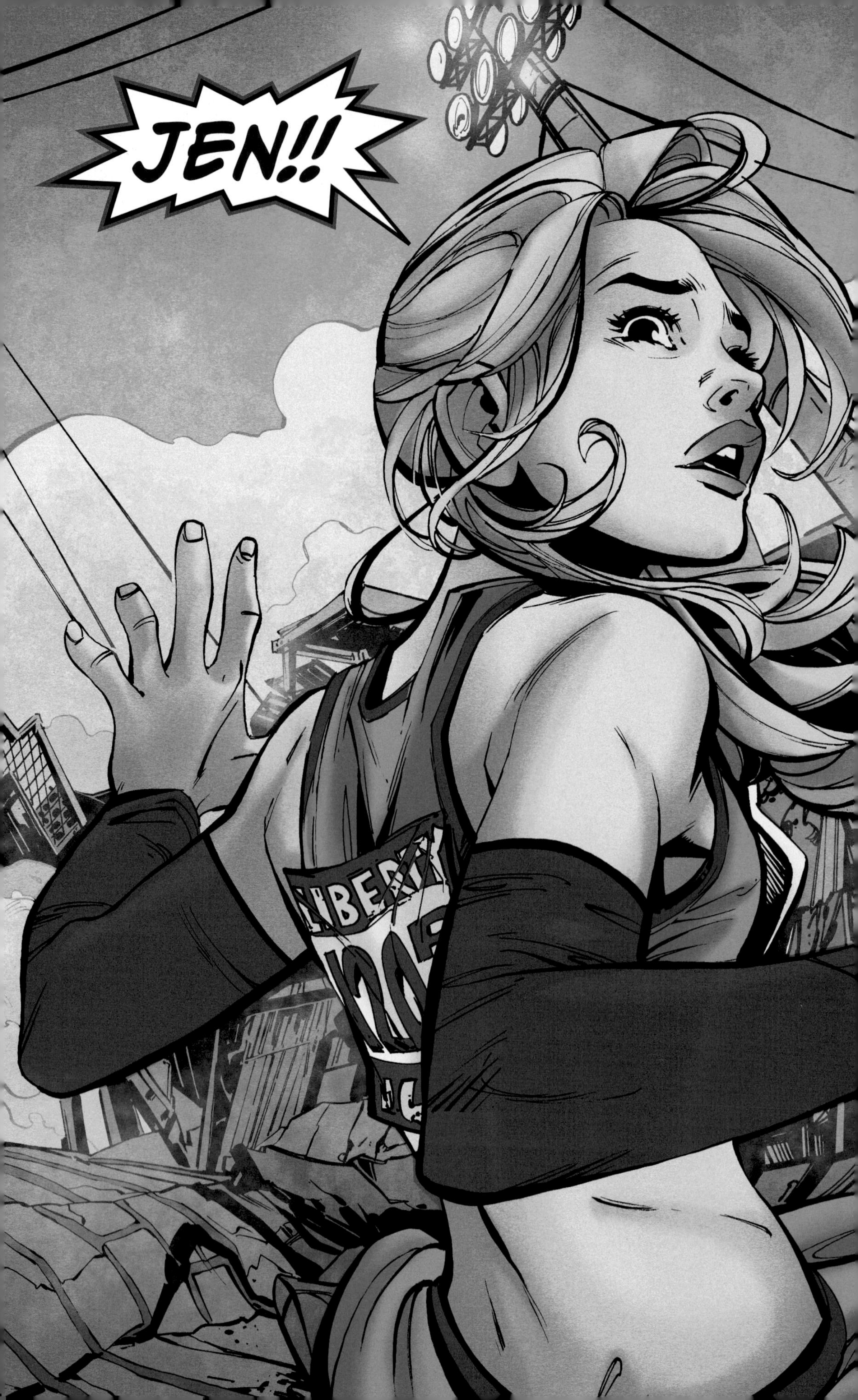
JEN!!

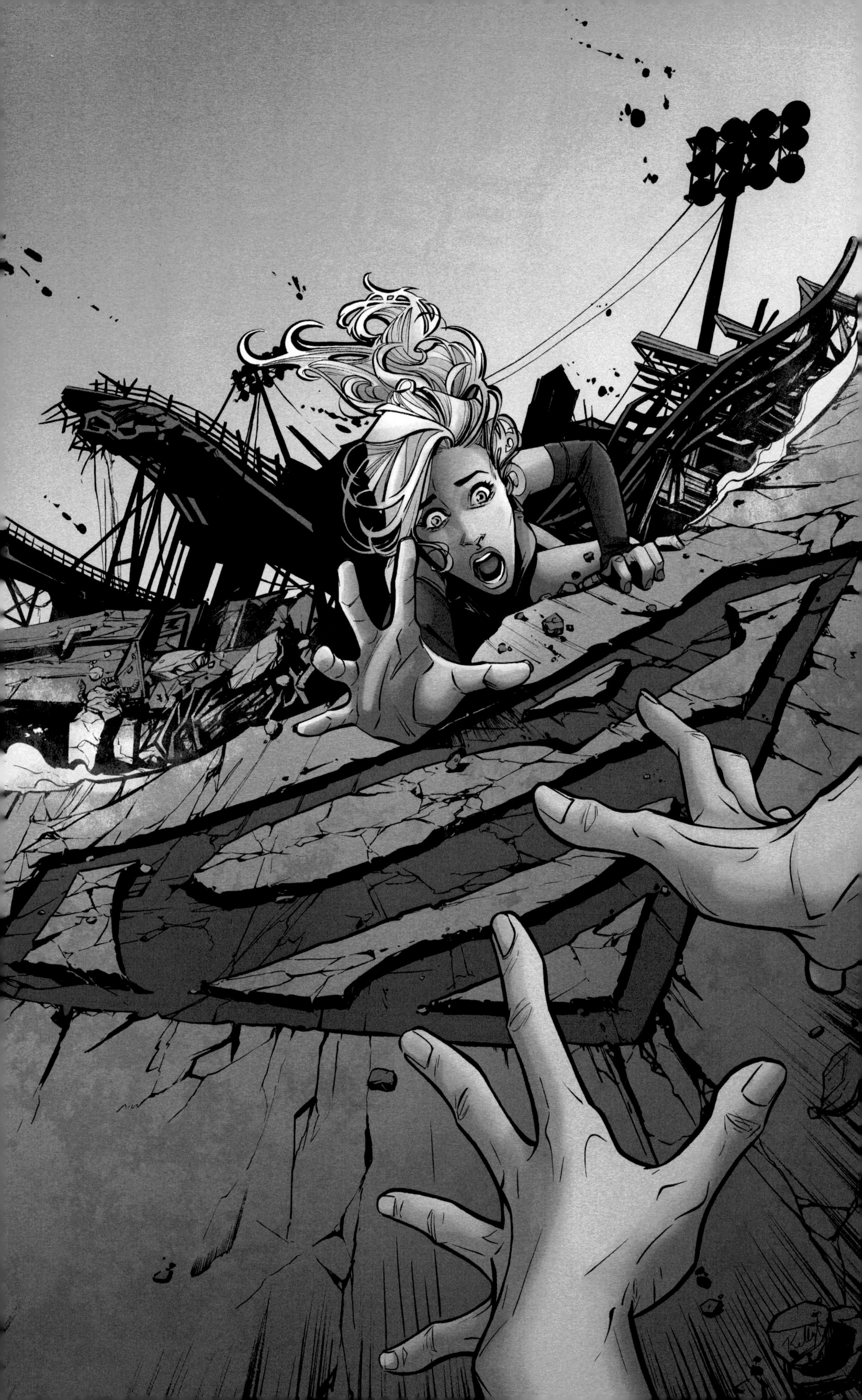

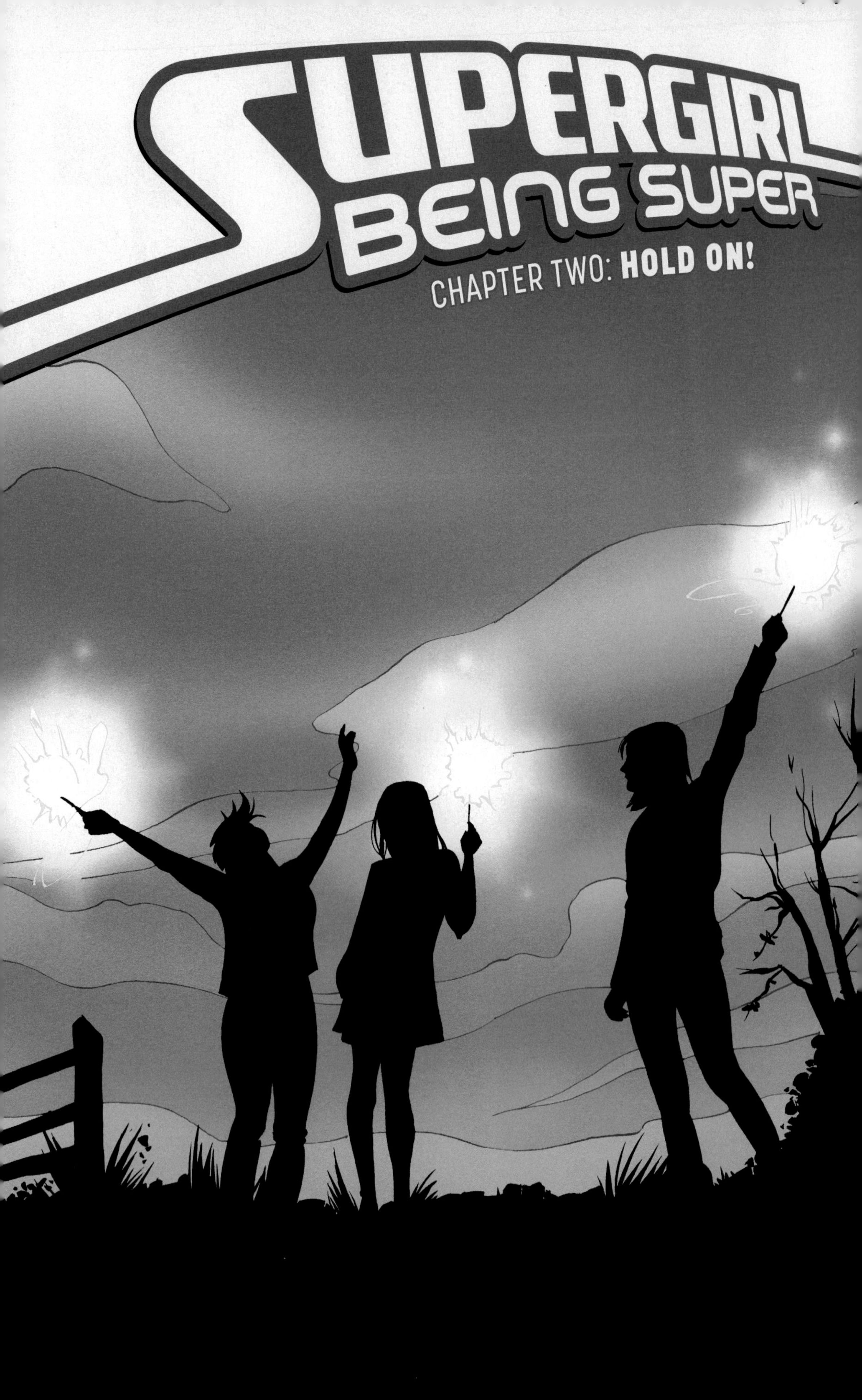
SUPERGIRL
BEING SUPER
CHAPTER TWO: HOLD ON!

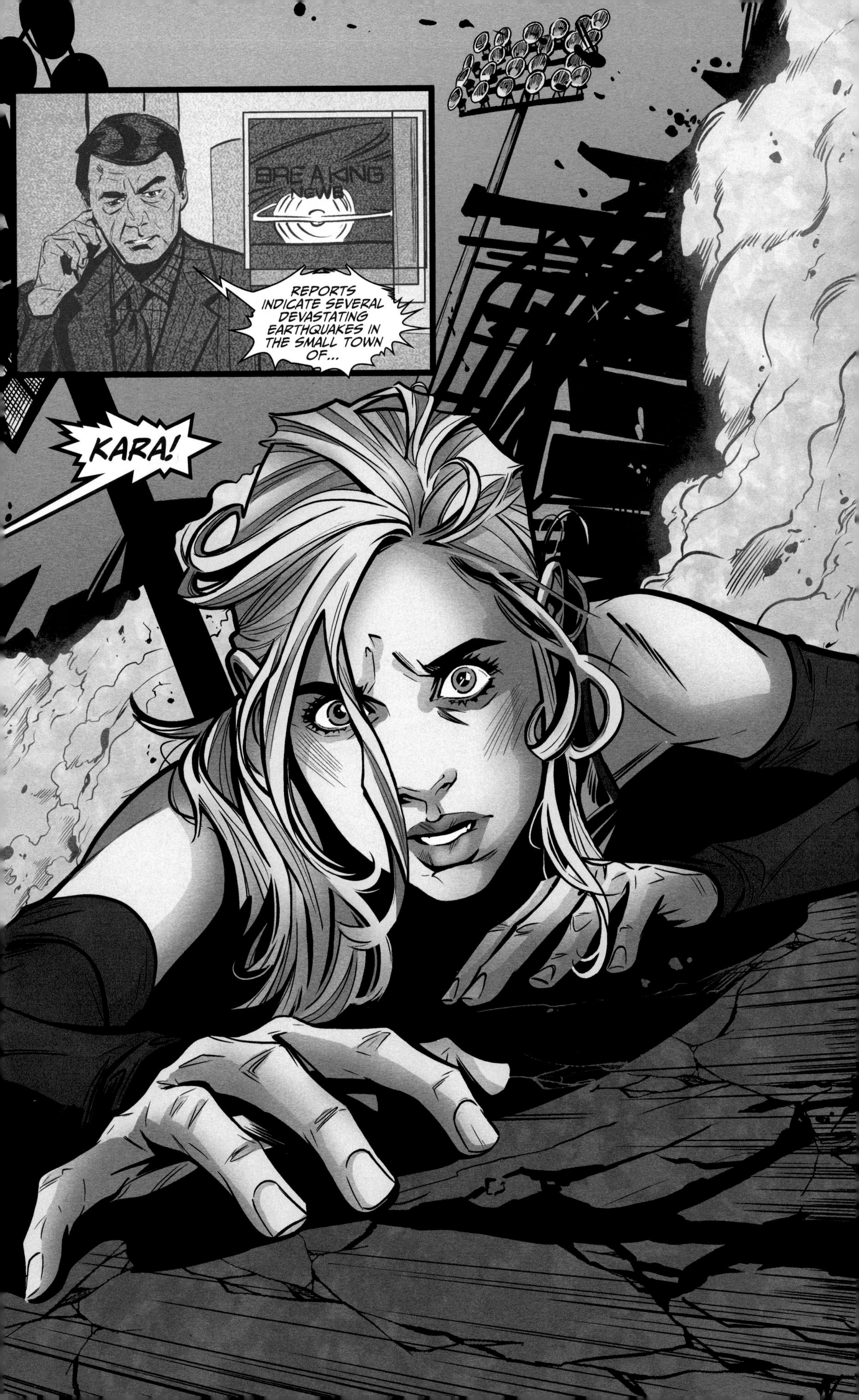
BREAKING NEWS
REPORTS INDICATE SEVERAL DEVASTATING EARTHQUAKES IN THE SMALL TOWN OF...
KARA!

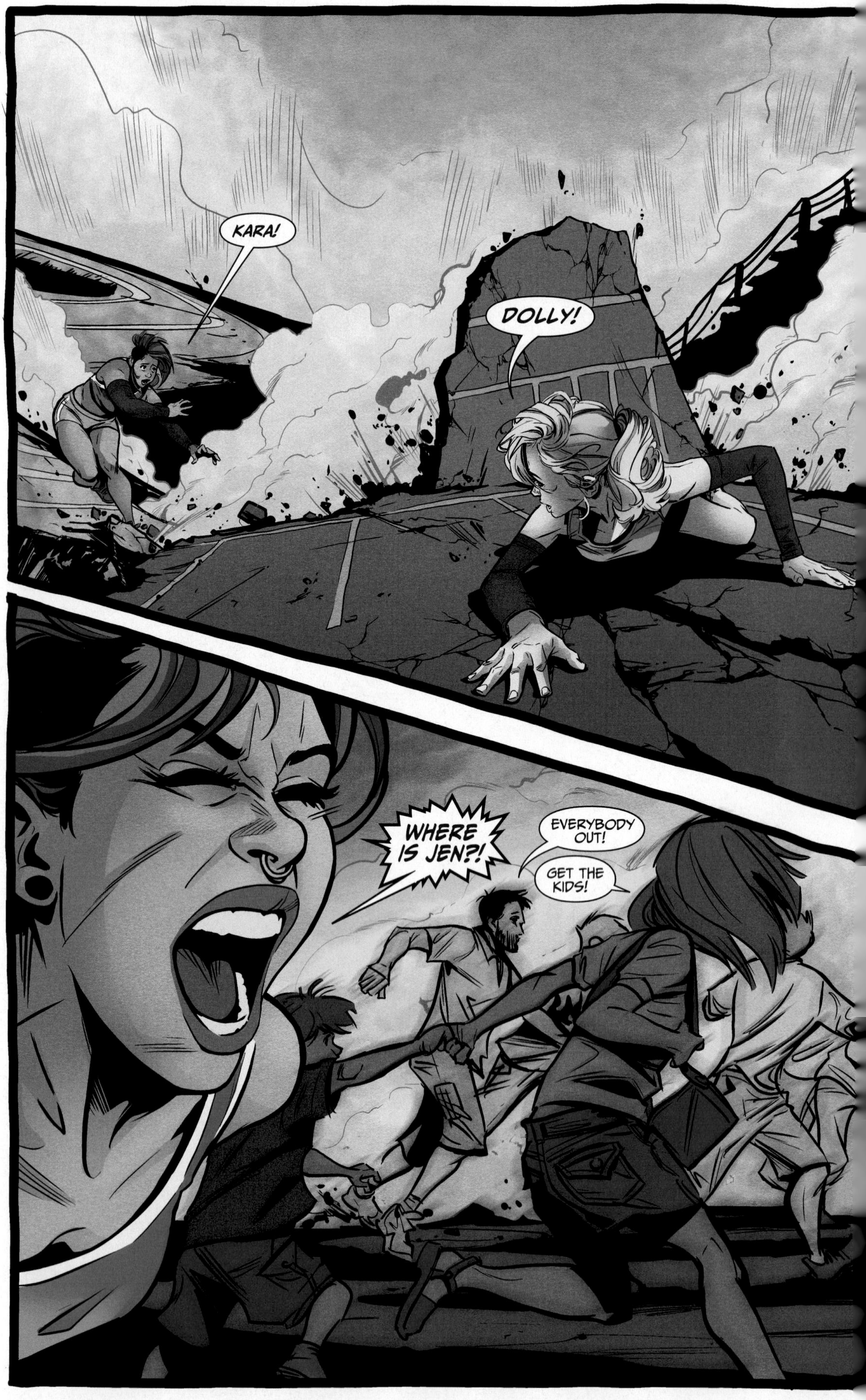
KARA!
DOLLY!
WHERE IS JEN?!
EVERYBODY OUT!
GET THE KIDS!

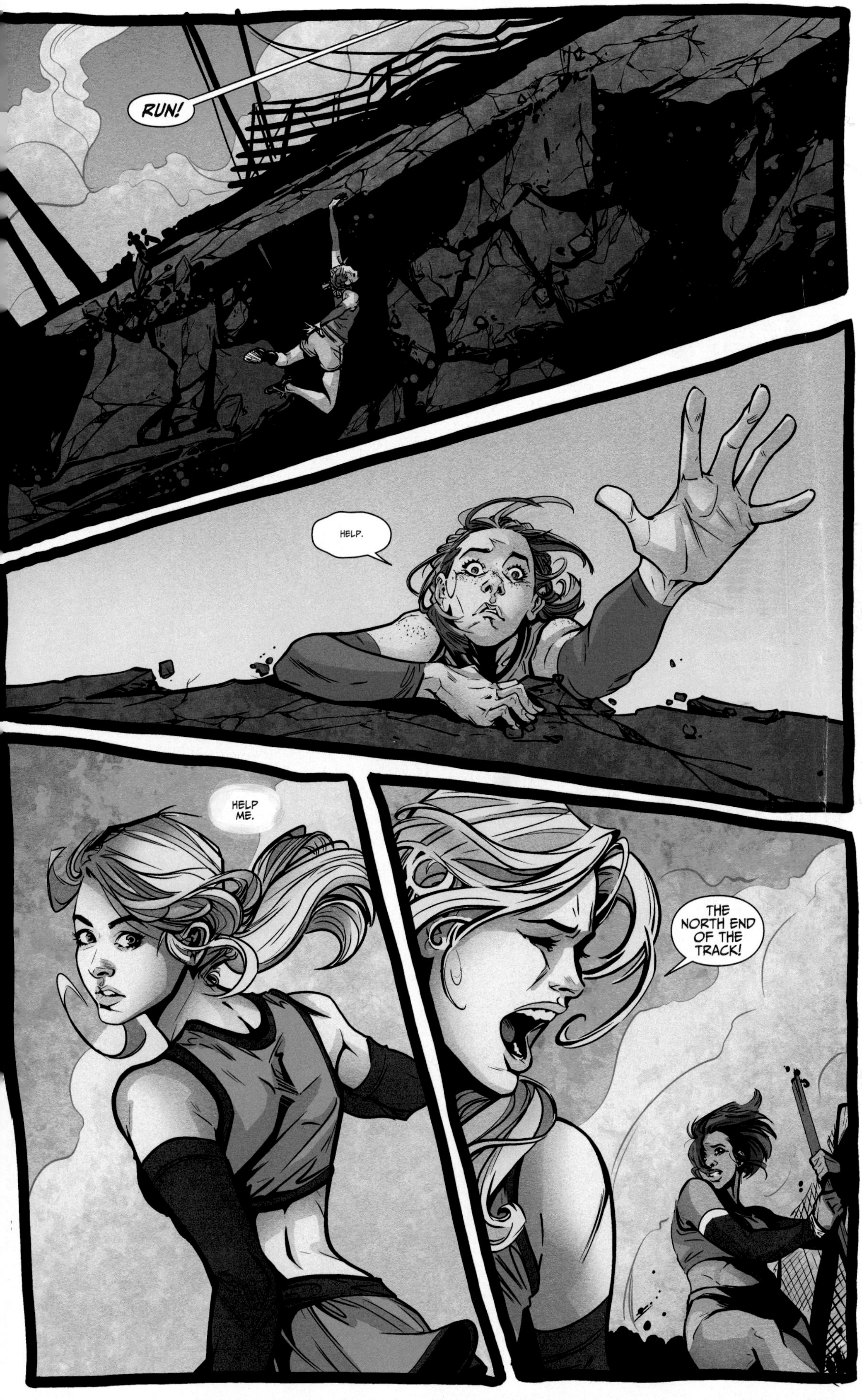
RUN!
HELP.
HELP ME.
THE NORTH END OF THE TRACK!

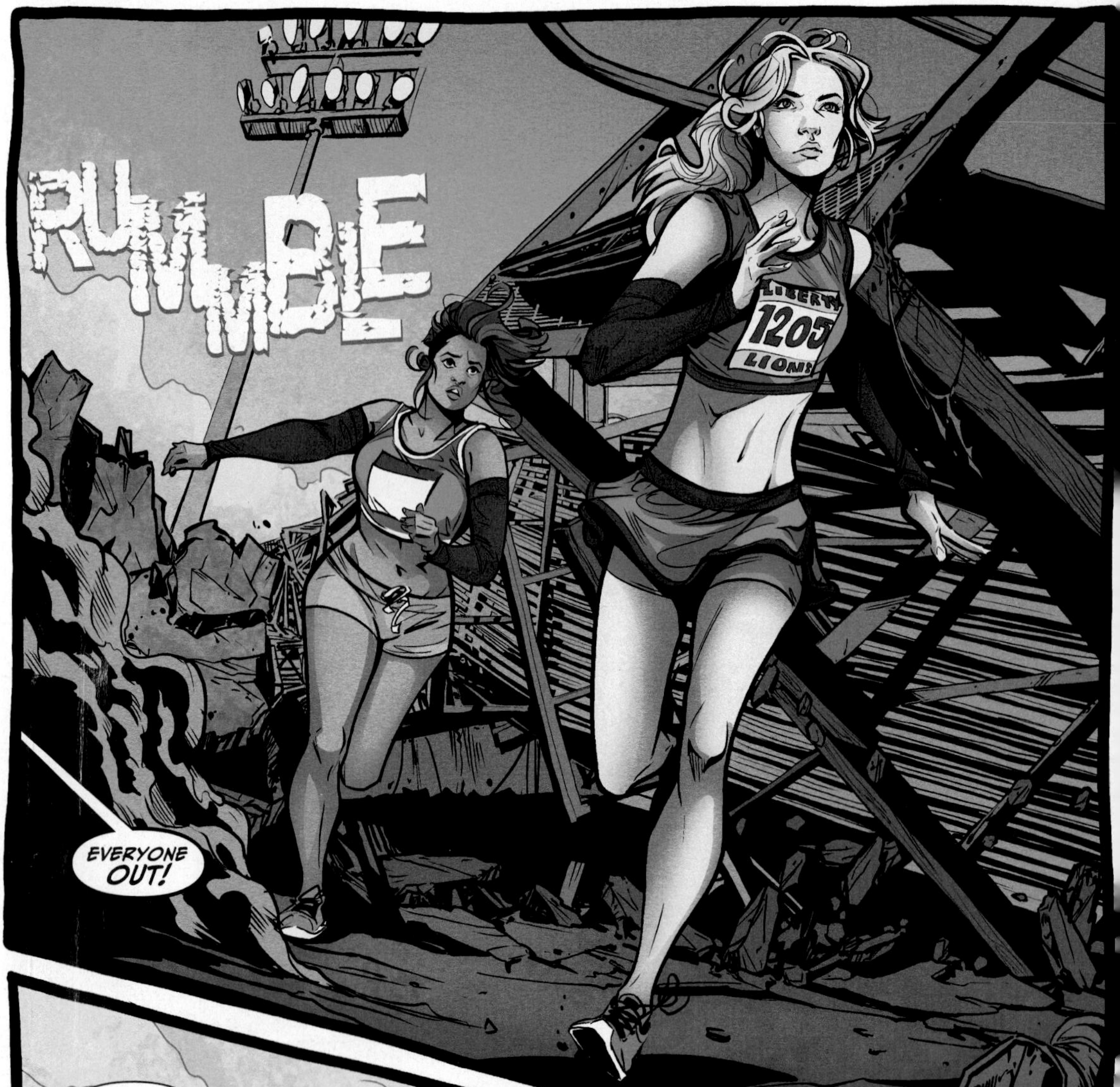
RUMMBLE
EVERYONE OUT!

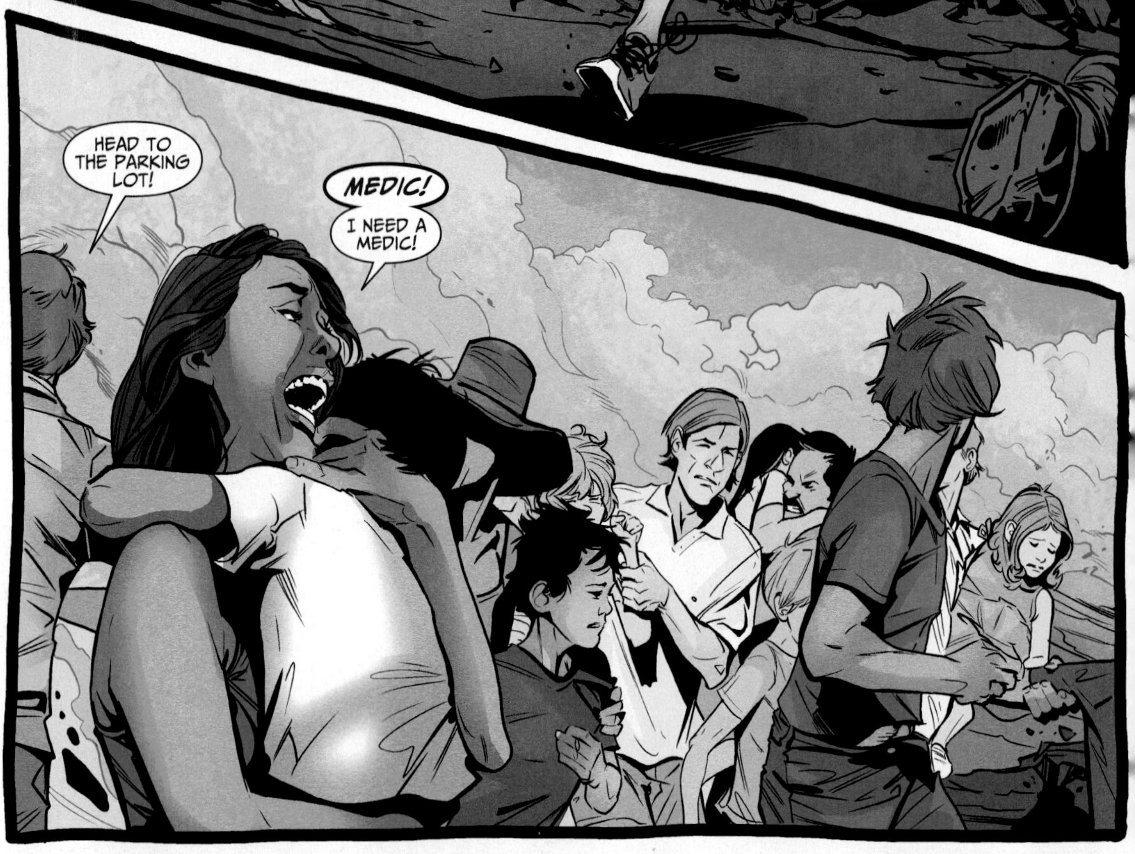
HEAD TO THE PARKING LOT!
MEDIC!
I NEED A MEDIC!

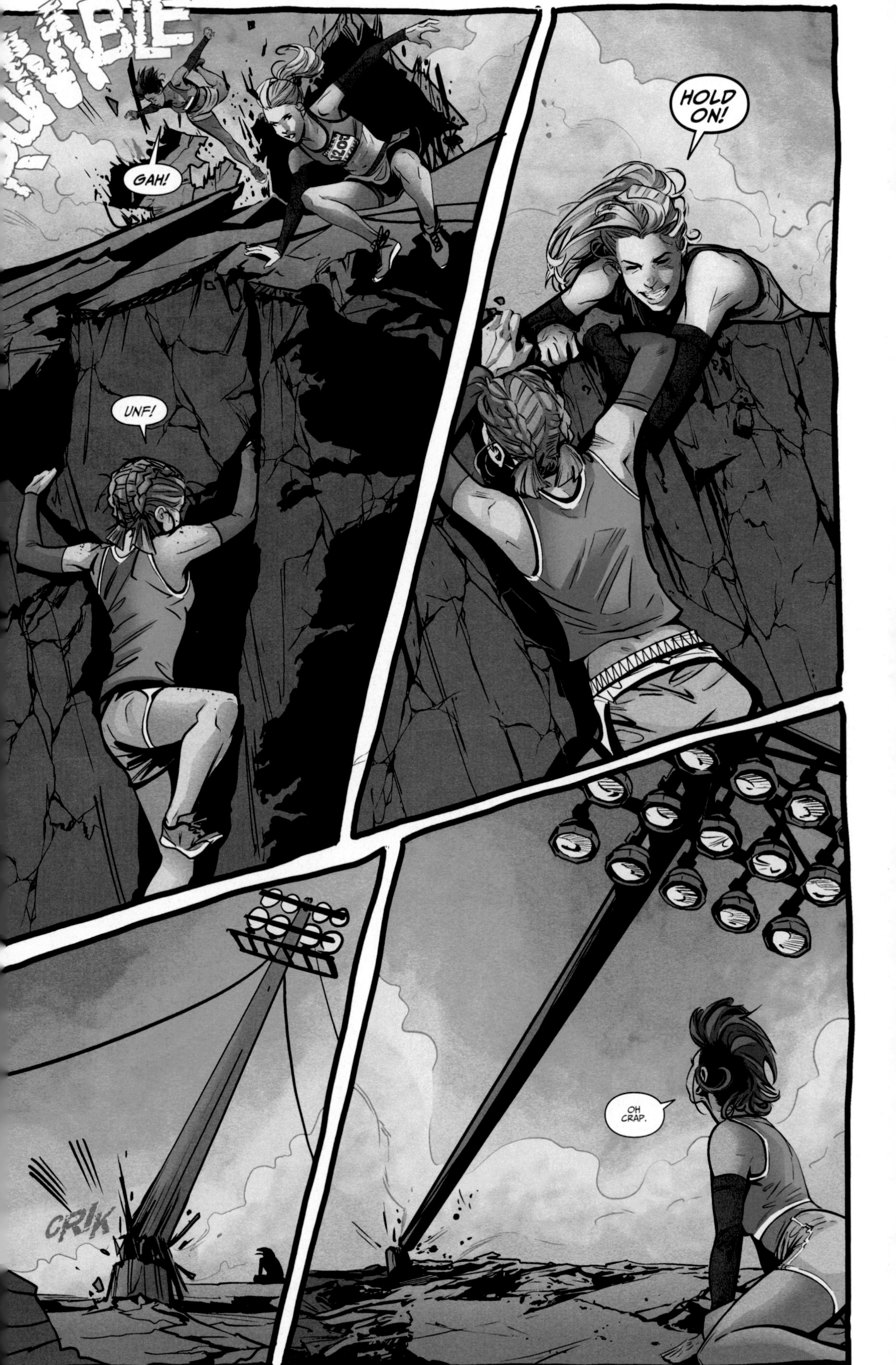
RUMBLE
GAH!
UNF!
HOLD ON!
CRIK
OH CRAP.

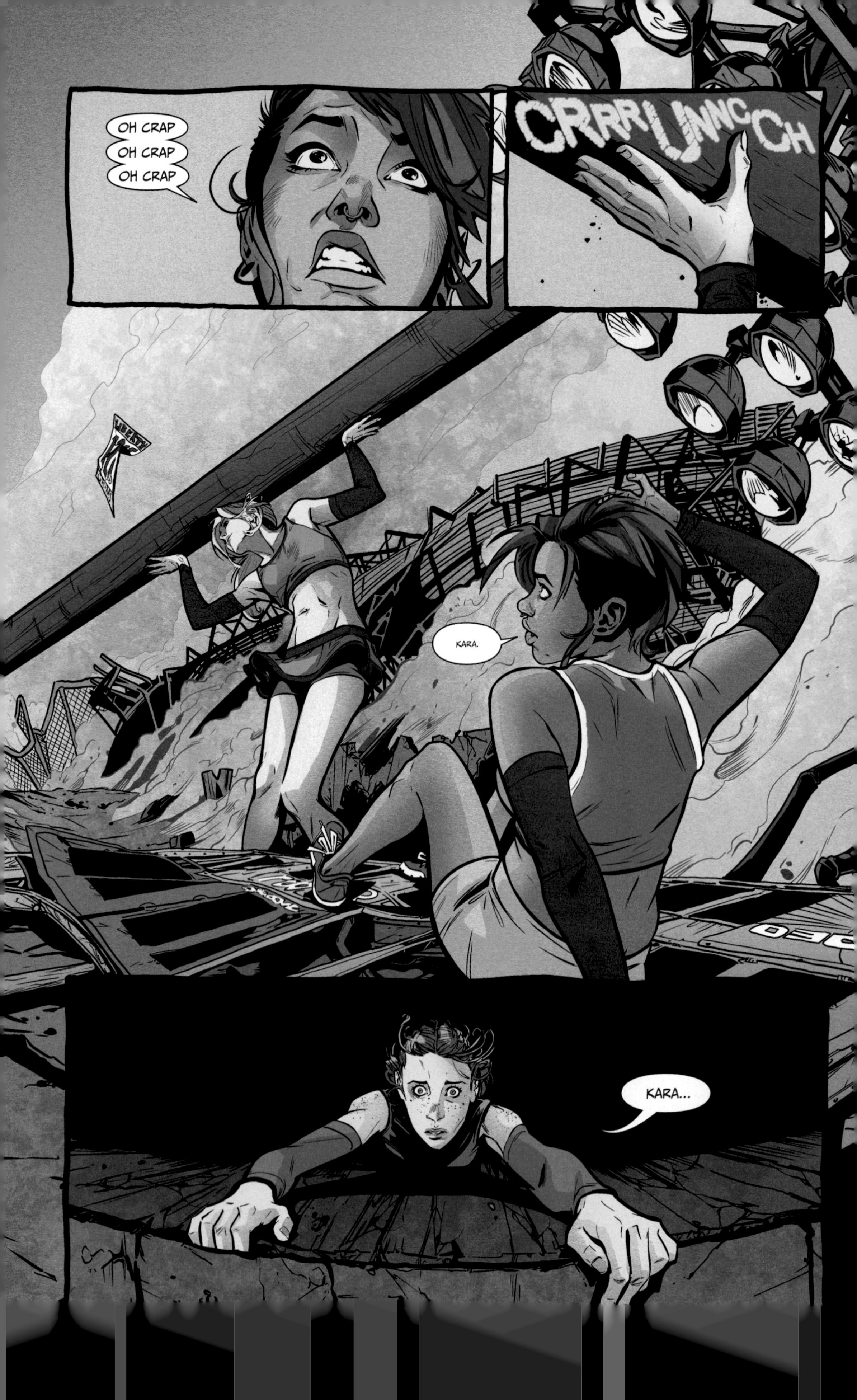
OH CRAP
OH CRAP
OH CRAP
CRRRUNNCCH
KARA.
KARA...

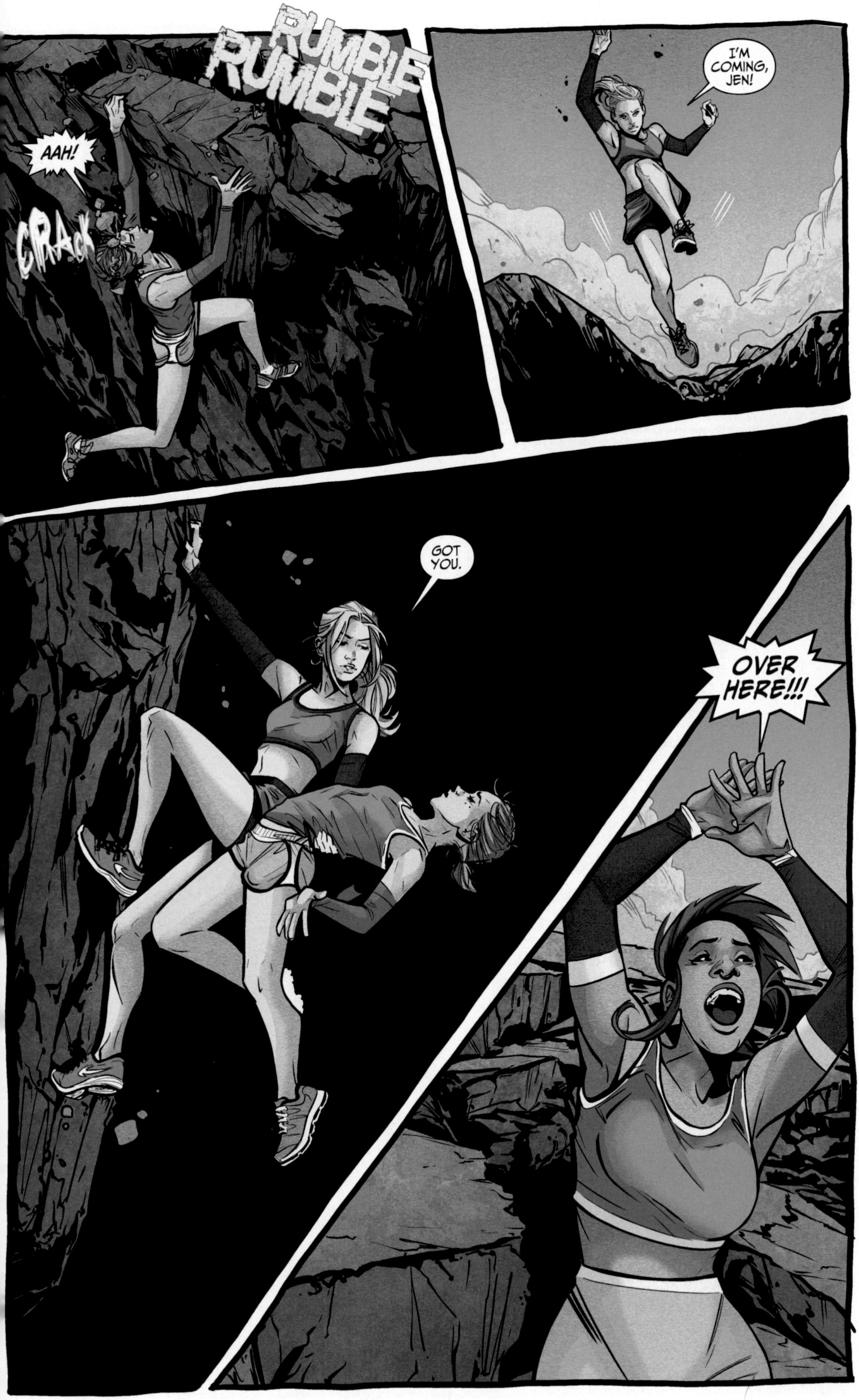
RUMBLE RUMBLE
AAH!
CRACK
I'M COMING, JEN!
GOT YOU.
OVER HERE!!!

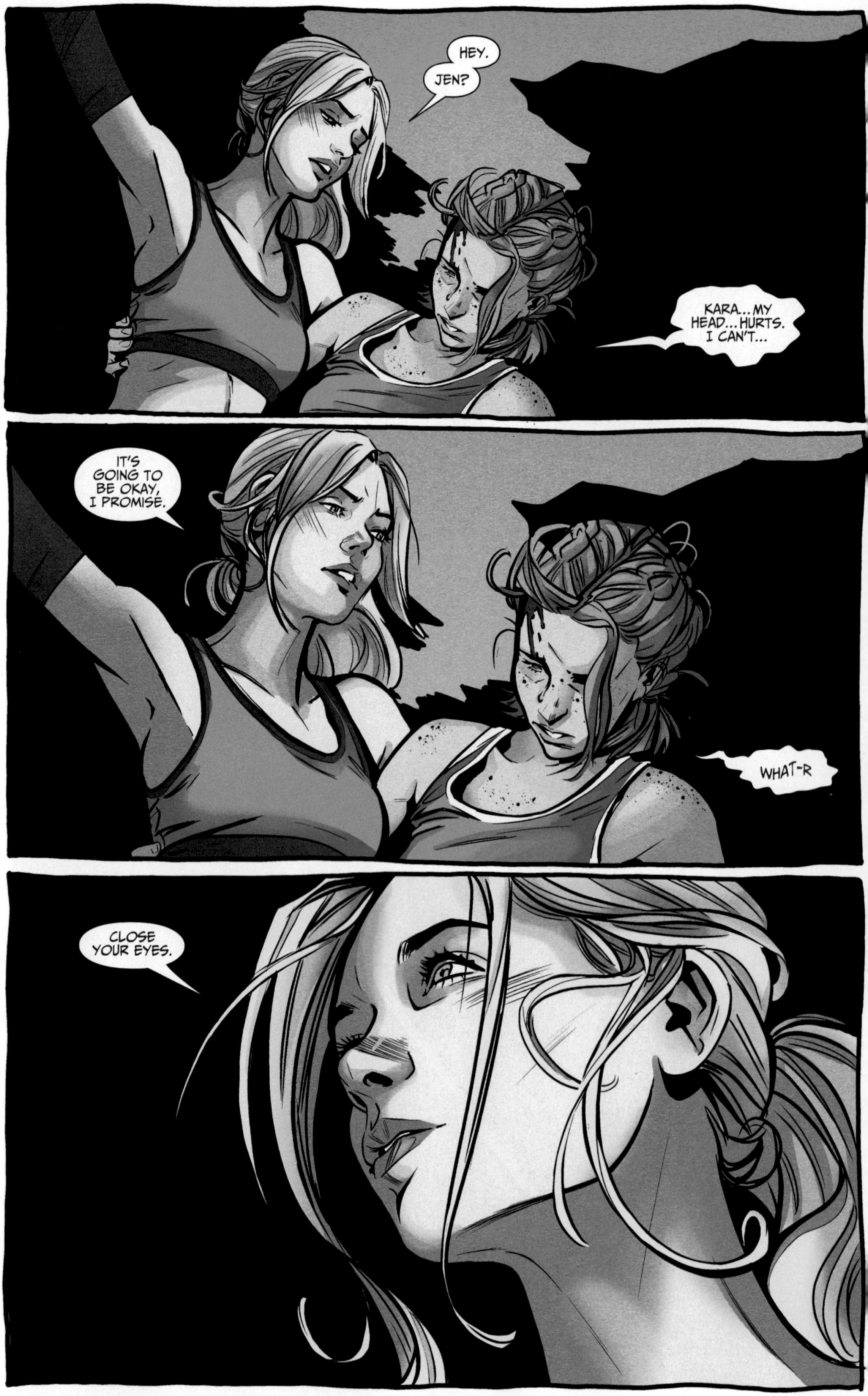
HEY.
JEN?
KARA... MY HEAD... HURTS. I CAN'T...
IT'S GOING TO BE OKAY, I PROMISE.
WHAT-R
CLOSE YOUR EYES.

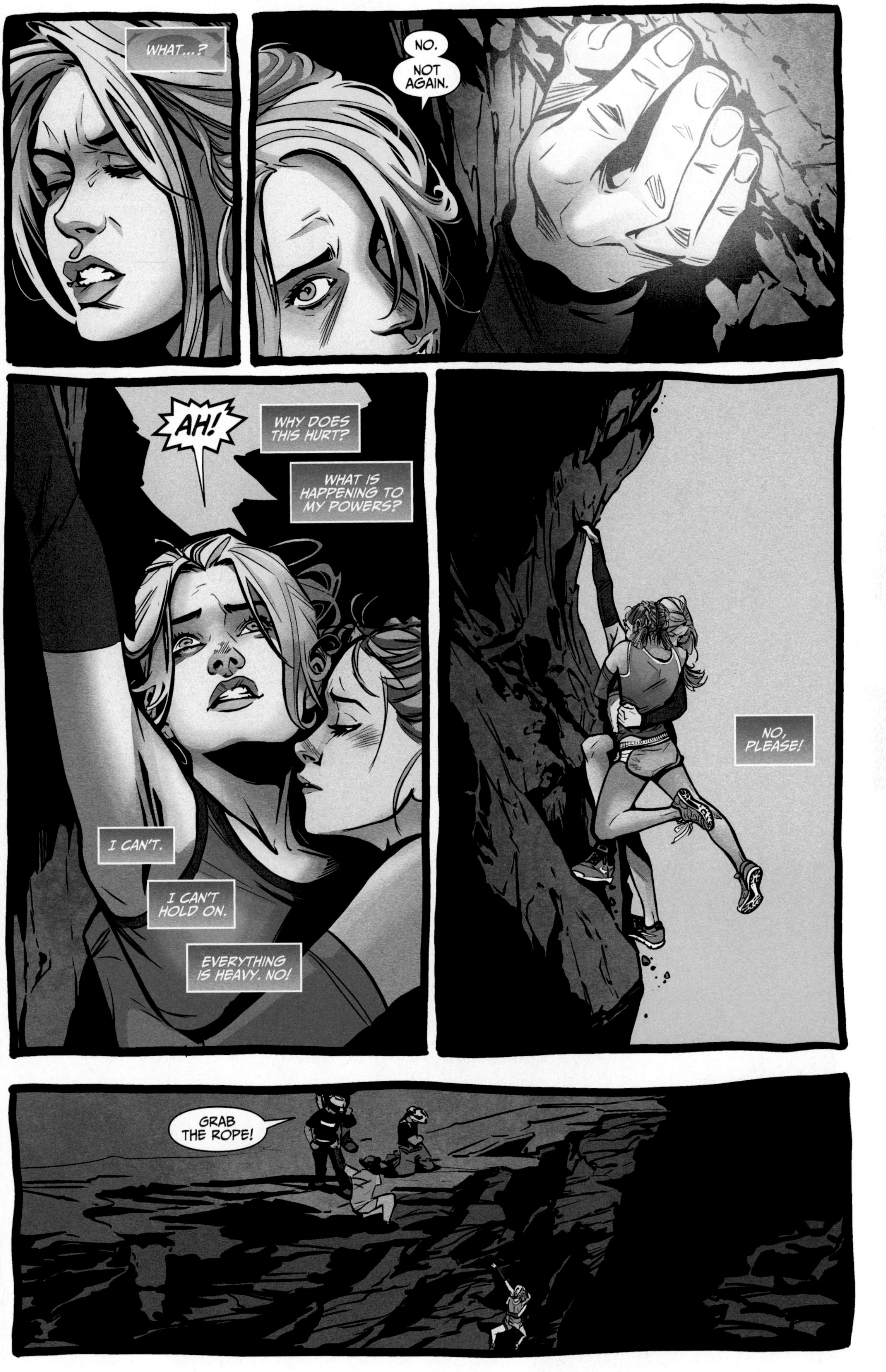
WHAT...?
NO.
NOT AGAIN.
AH!
WHY DOES THIS HURT?
WHAT IS HAPPENING TO MY POWERS?
I CAN'T.
I CAN'T HOLD ON.
EVERYTHING IS HEAVY. NO!
NO, PLEASE!
GRAB THE ROPE!

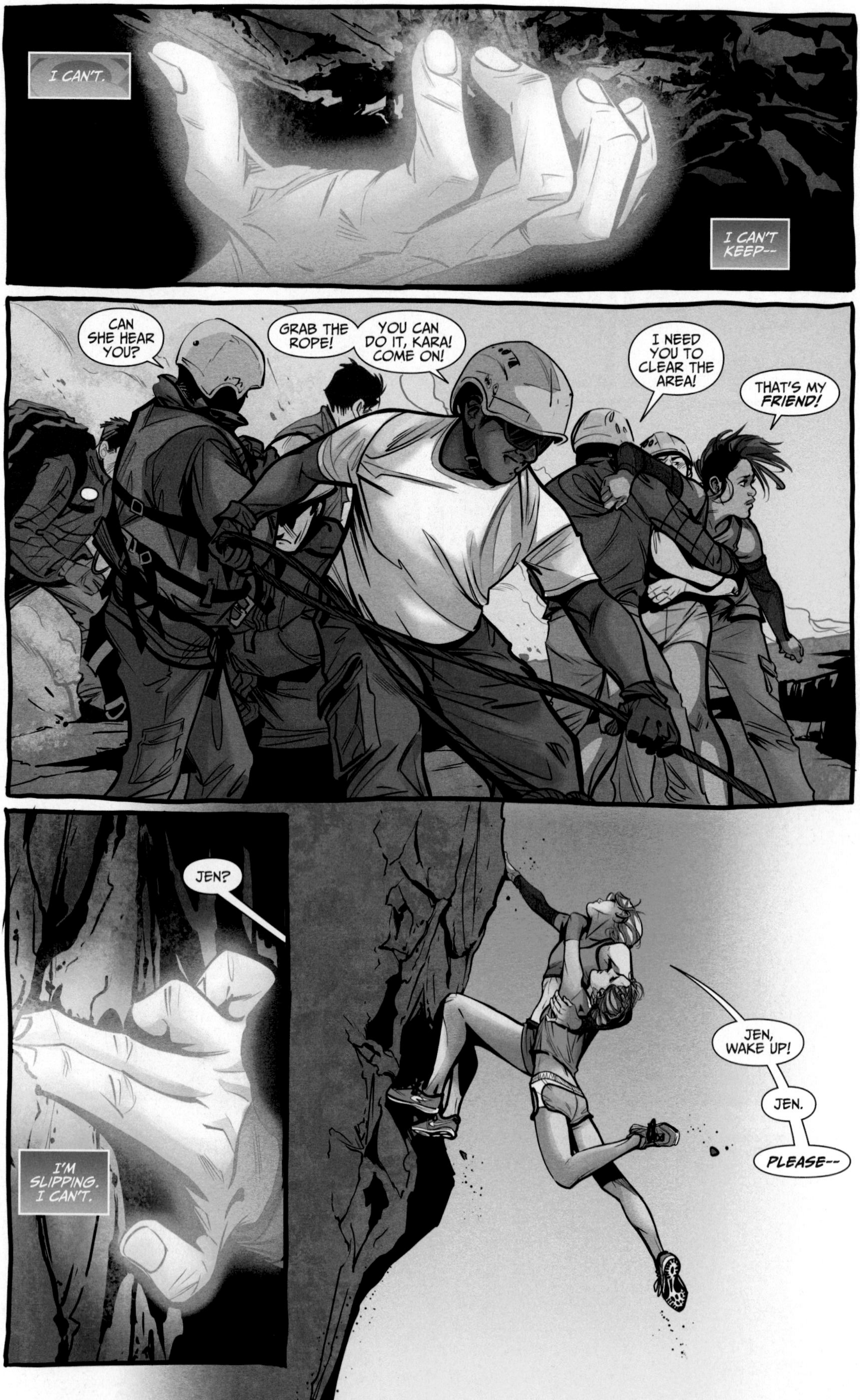
I CAN'T.
I CAN'T KEEP--
CAN SHE HEAR YOU?
GRAB THE ROPE!
YOU CAN DO IT, KARA! COME ON!
I NEED YOU TO CLEAR THE AREA!
THAT'S MY FRIEND!
JEN?
I'M SLIPPING. I CAN'T.
JEN, WAKE UP!
JEN.
PLEASE--

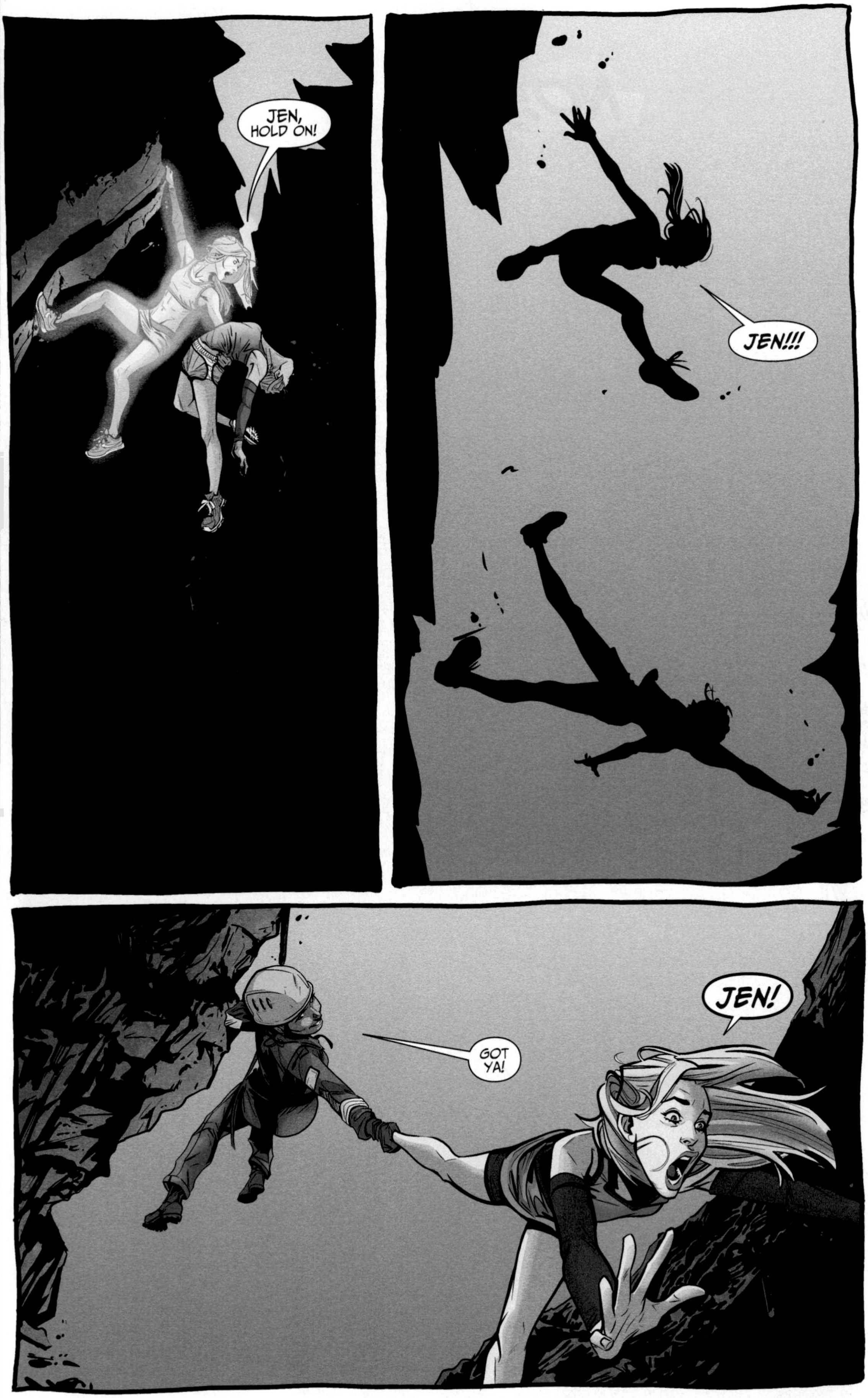
JEN, HOLD ON!
JEN!!!
JEN!
GOT YA!

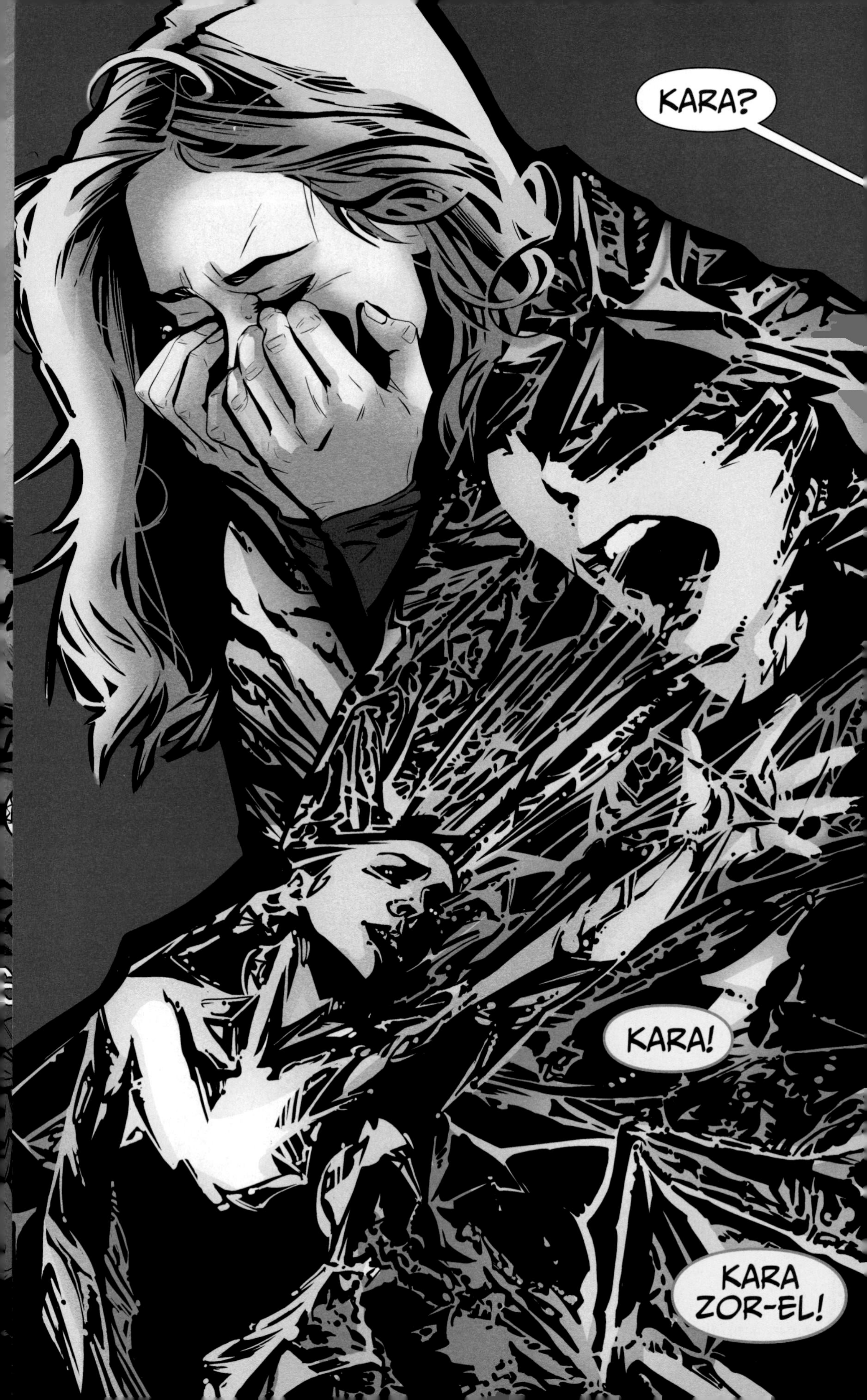
KARA?
KARA!
KARA ZOR-EL!

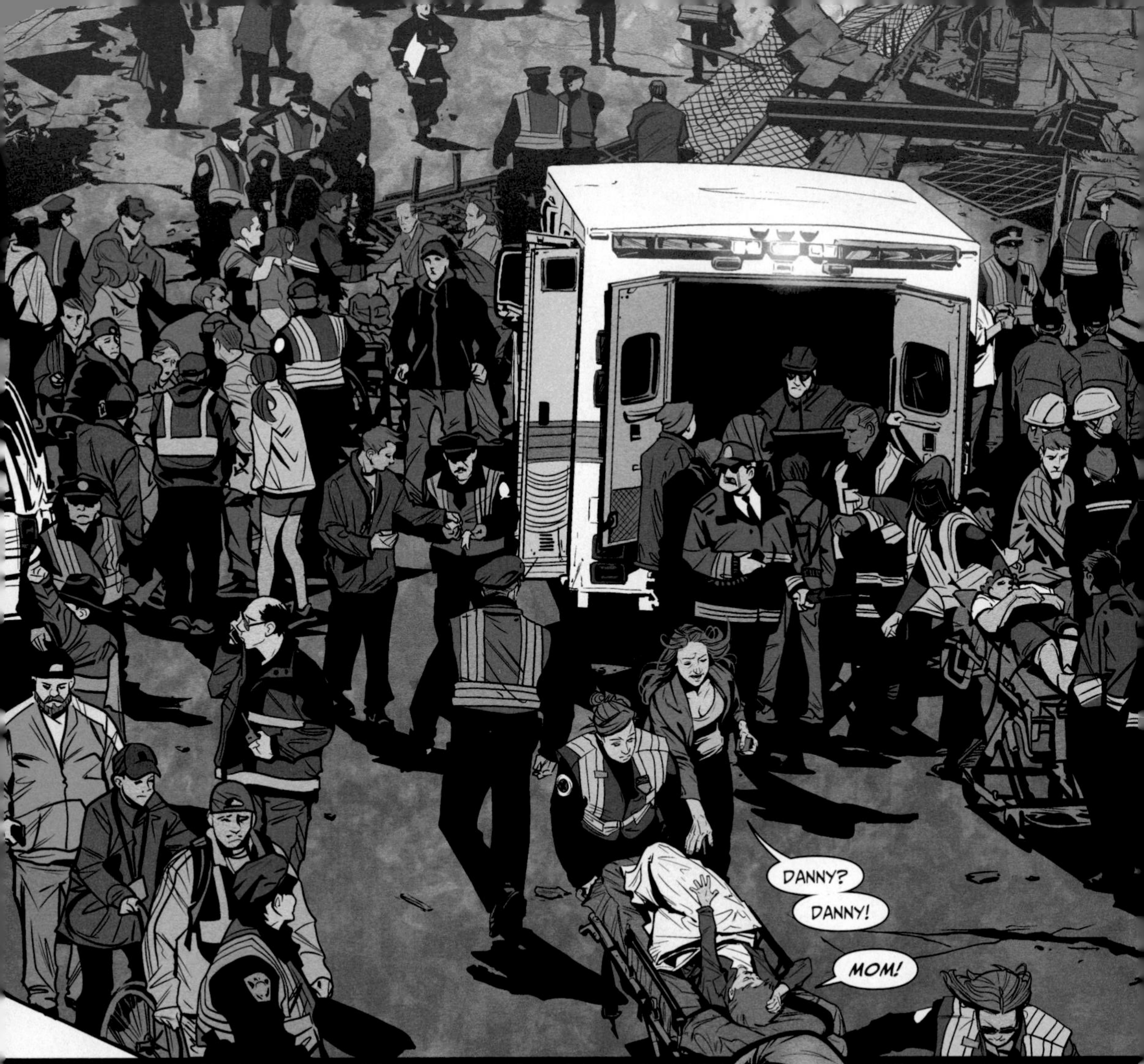
DANNY?
DANNY!
MOM!

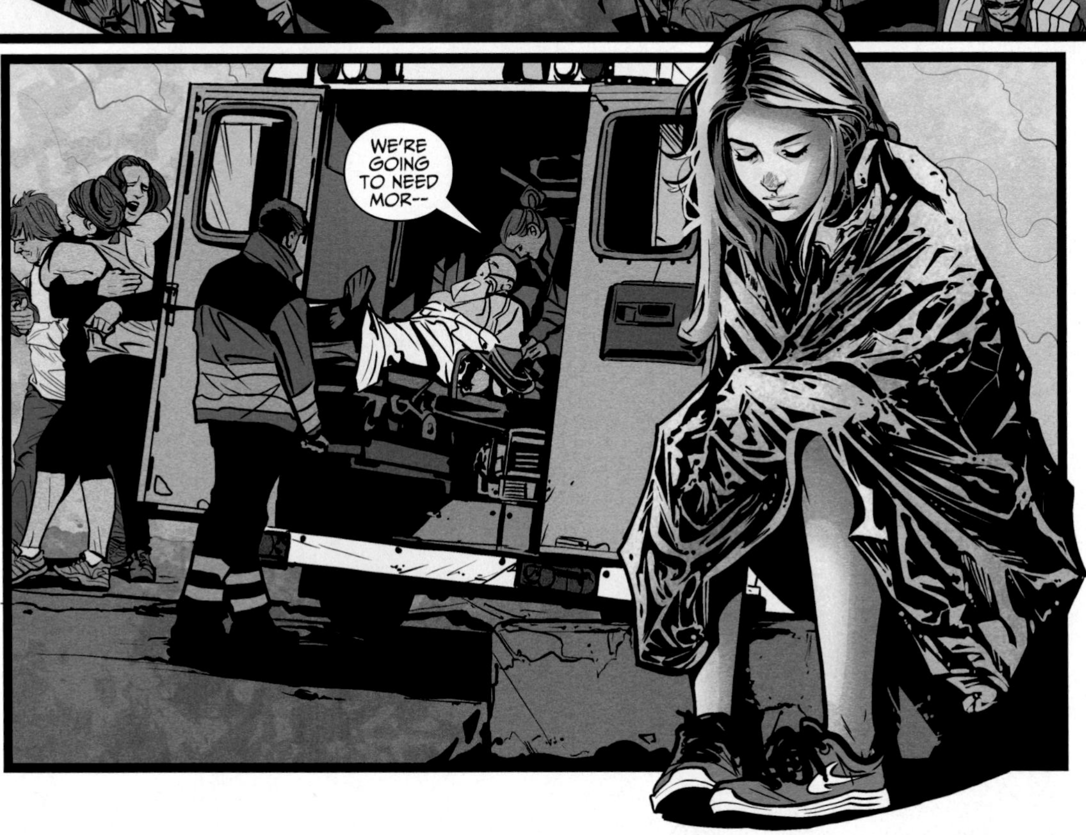
WE'RE GOING TO NEED MOR--

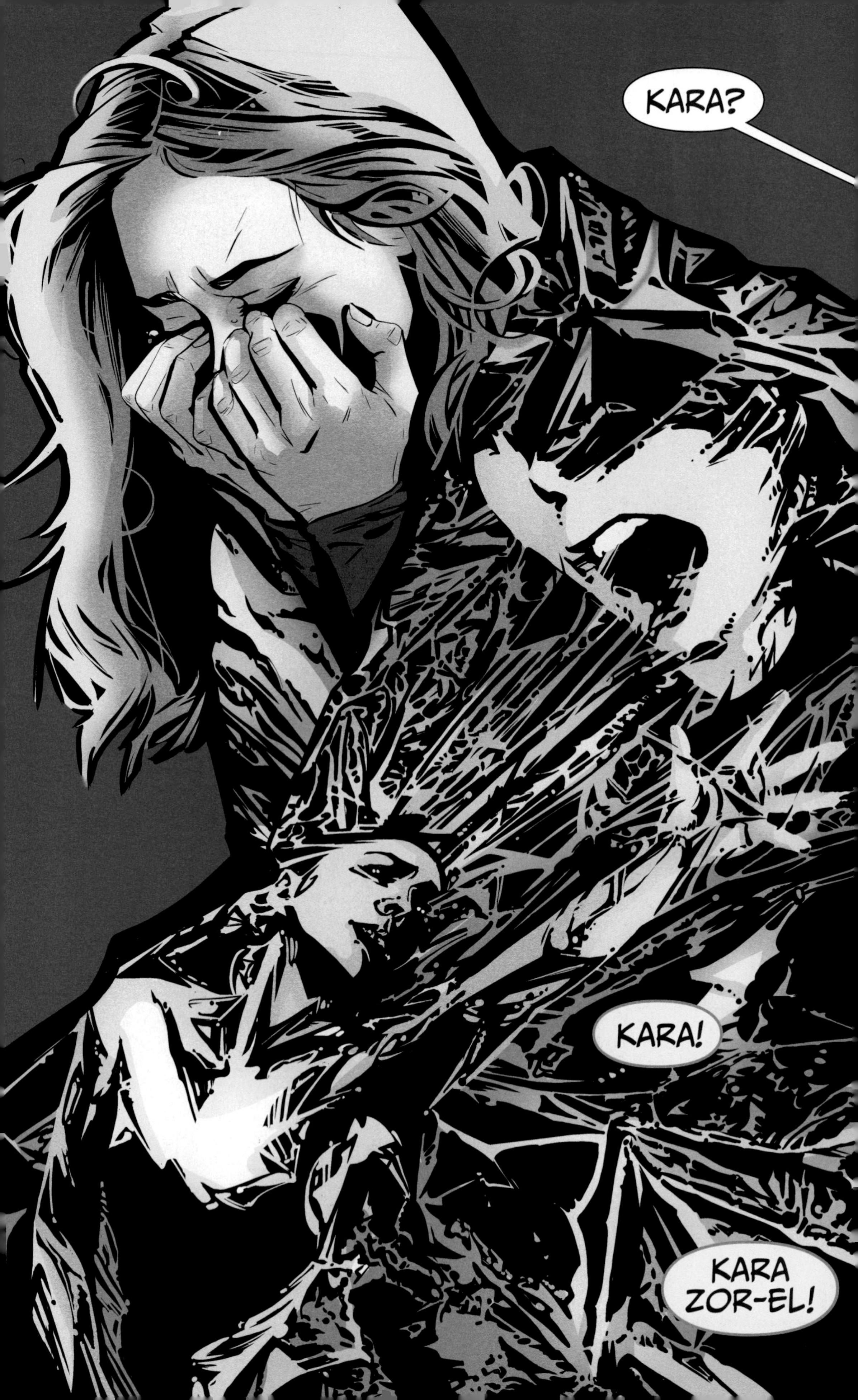
KARA?
KARA!
KARA ZOR-EL!

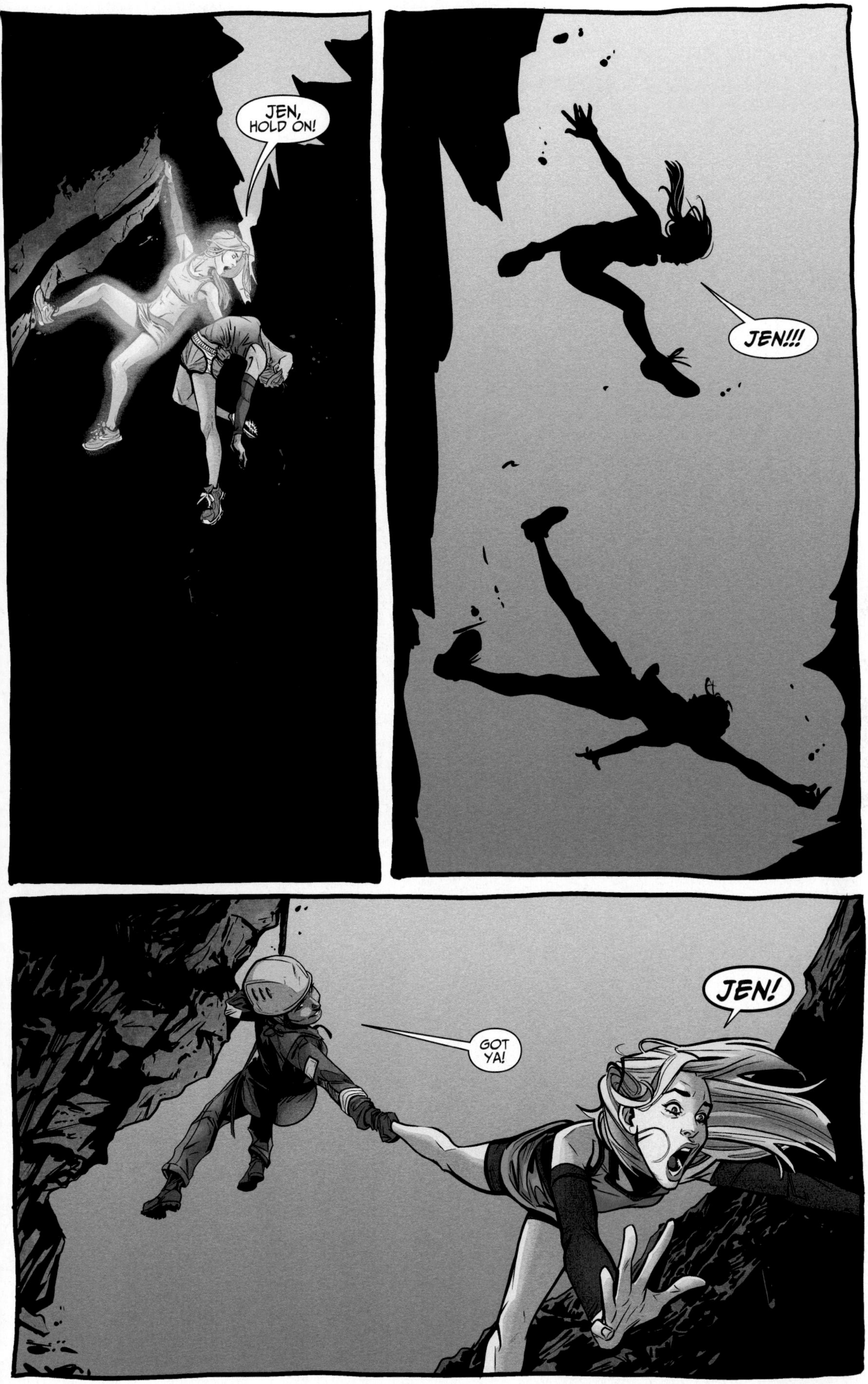
JEN, HOLD ON!
JEN!!!
JEN!
GOT YA!

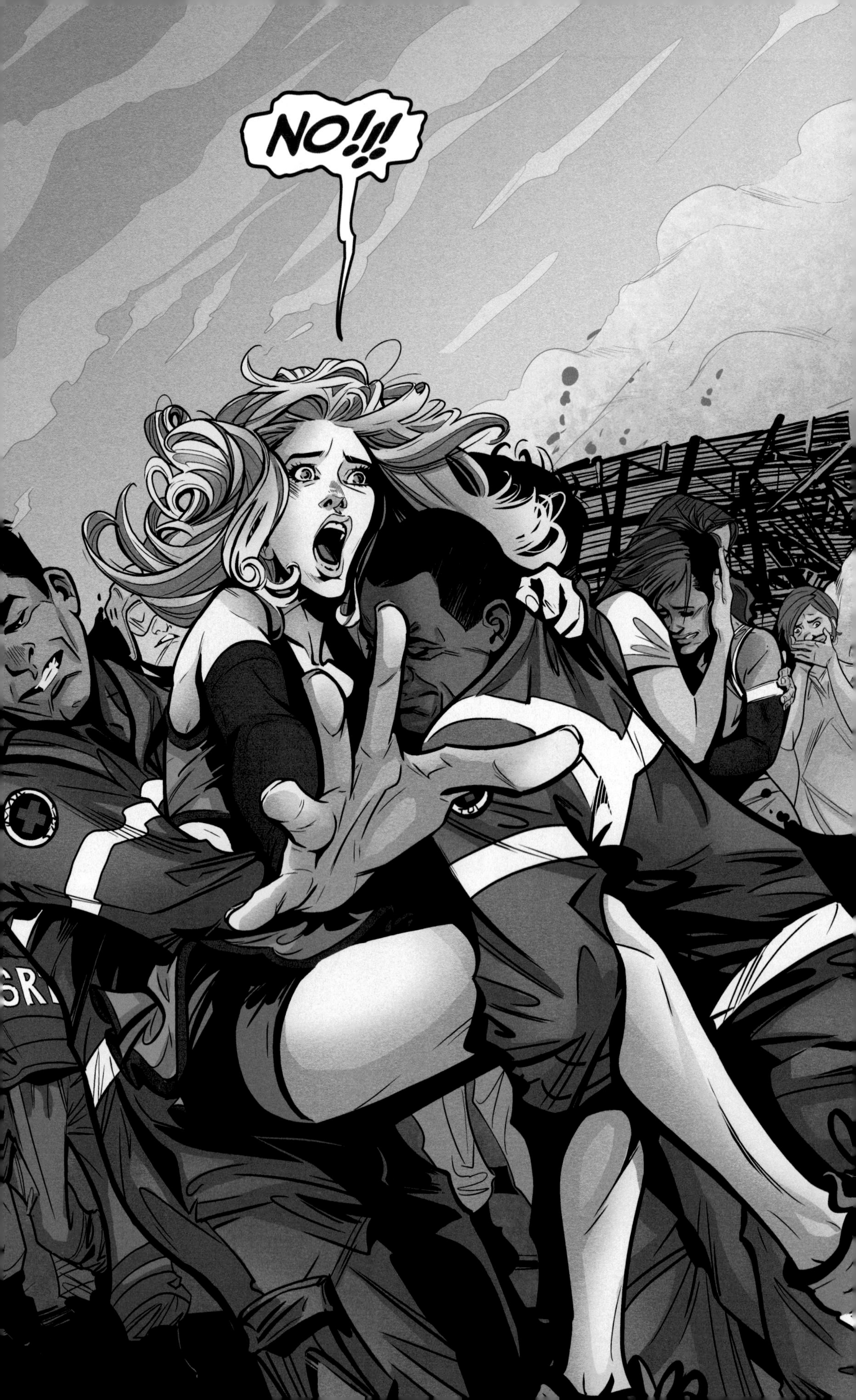
NO!!!

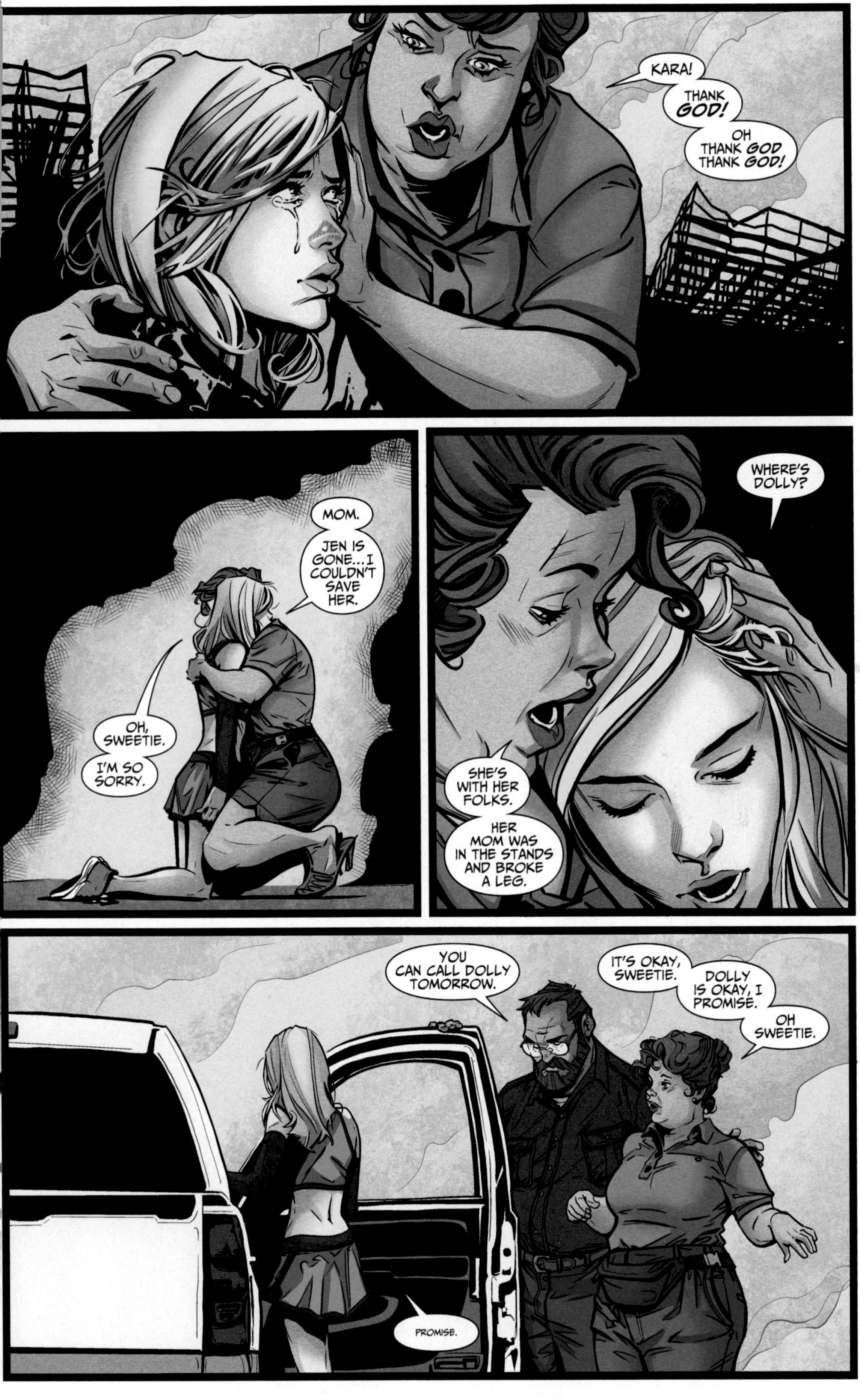
KARA!
THANK GOD!
OH THANK GOD THANK GOD!
MOM.
JEN IS GONE...I COULDN'T SAVE HER.
OH, SWEETIE.
I'M SO SORRY.
WHERE'S DOLLY?
SHE'S WITH HER FOLKS.
HER MOM WAS IN THE STANDS AND BROKE A LEG.
YOU CAN CALL DOLLY TOMORROW.
IT'S OKAY, SWEETIE.
DOLLY IS OKAY, I PROMISE.
OH SWEETIE.
PROMISE.

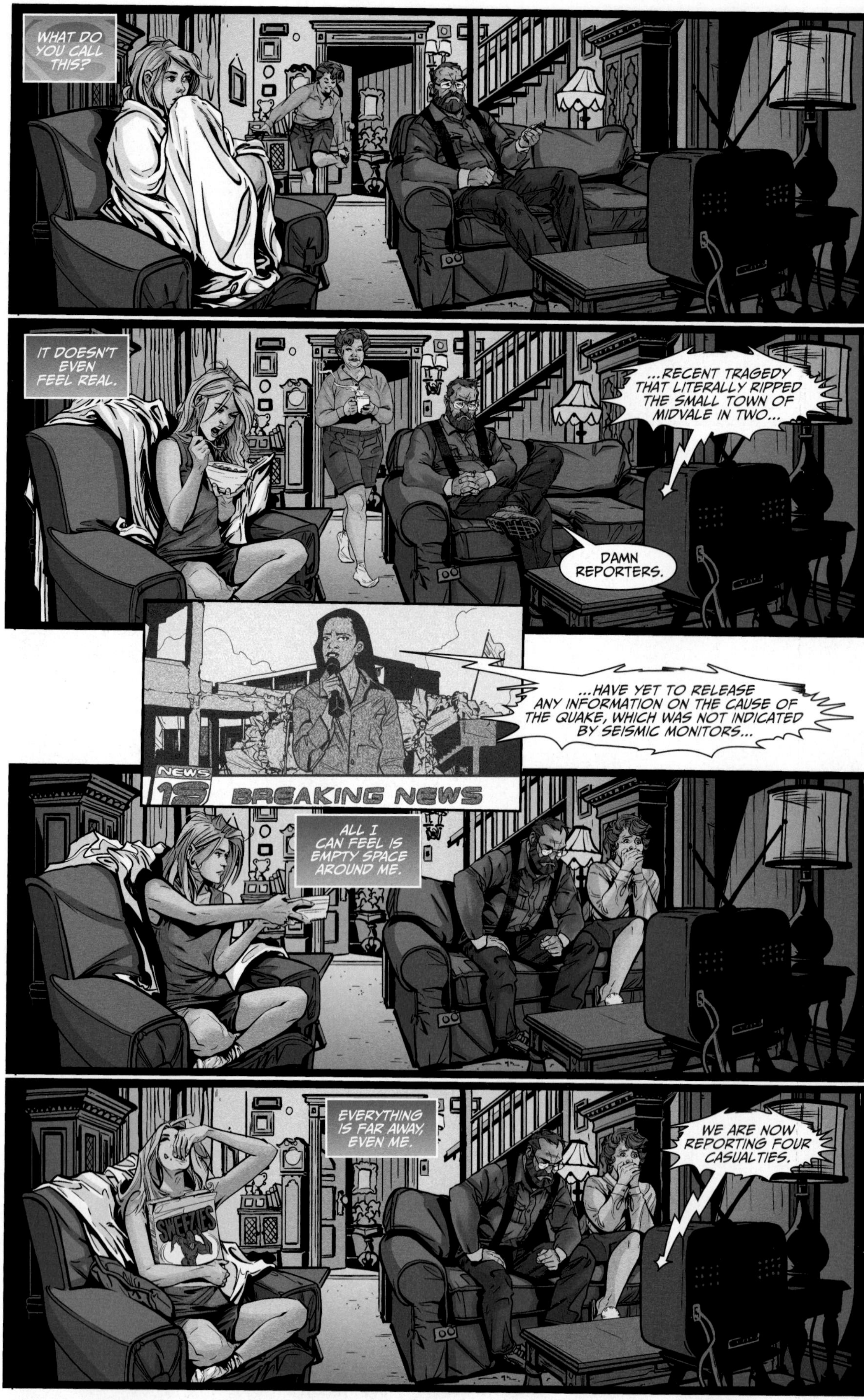
WHAT DO YOU CALL THIS?
IT DOESN'T EVEN FEEL REAL.
...RECENT TRAGEDY THAT LITERALLY RIPPED THE SMALL TOWN OF MIDVALE IN TWO...
DAMN REPORTERS.
...HAVE YET TO RELEASE ANY INFORMATION ON THE CAUSE OF THE QUAKE, WHICH WAS NOT INDICATED BY SEISMIC MONITORS...
NEWS 19
BREAKING NEWS
ALL I CAN FEEL IS EMPTY SPACE AROUND ME.
EVERYTHING IS FAR AWAY, EVEN ME.
WE ARE NOW REPORTING FOUR CASUALTIES.
SNEEZIES

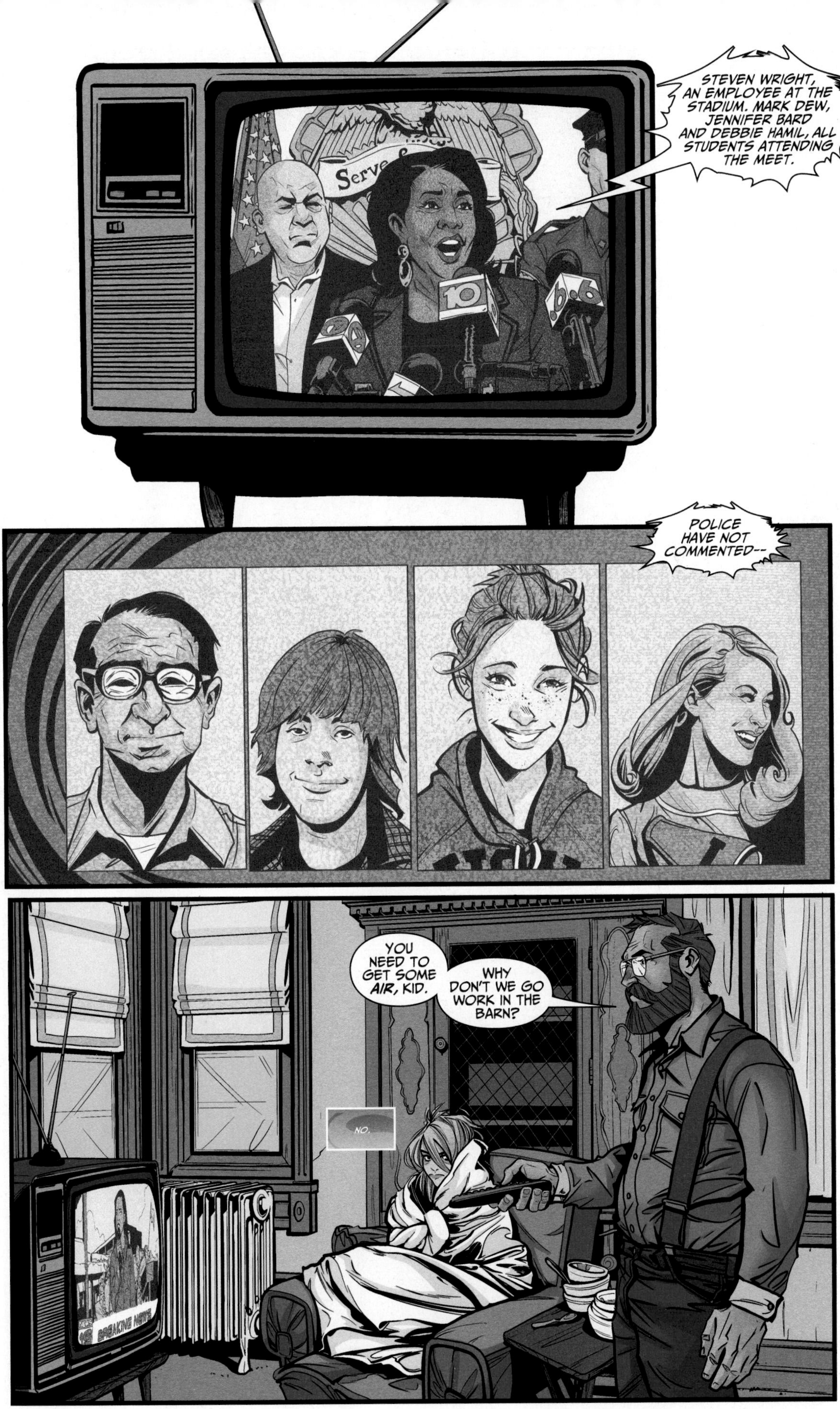
STEVEN WRIGHT, AN EMPLOYEE AT THE STADIUM. MARK DEW, JENNIFER BARD AND DEBBIE HAMIL, ALL STUDENTS ATTENDING THE MEET.
POLICE HAVE NOT COMMENTED--
YOU NEED TO GET SOME AIR, KID.
WHY DON'T WE GO WORK IN THE BARN?
NO.
BREAKING NEWS

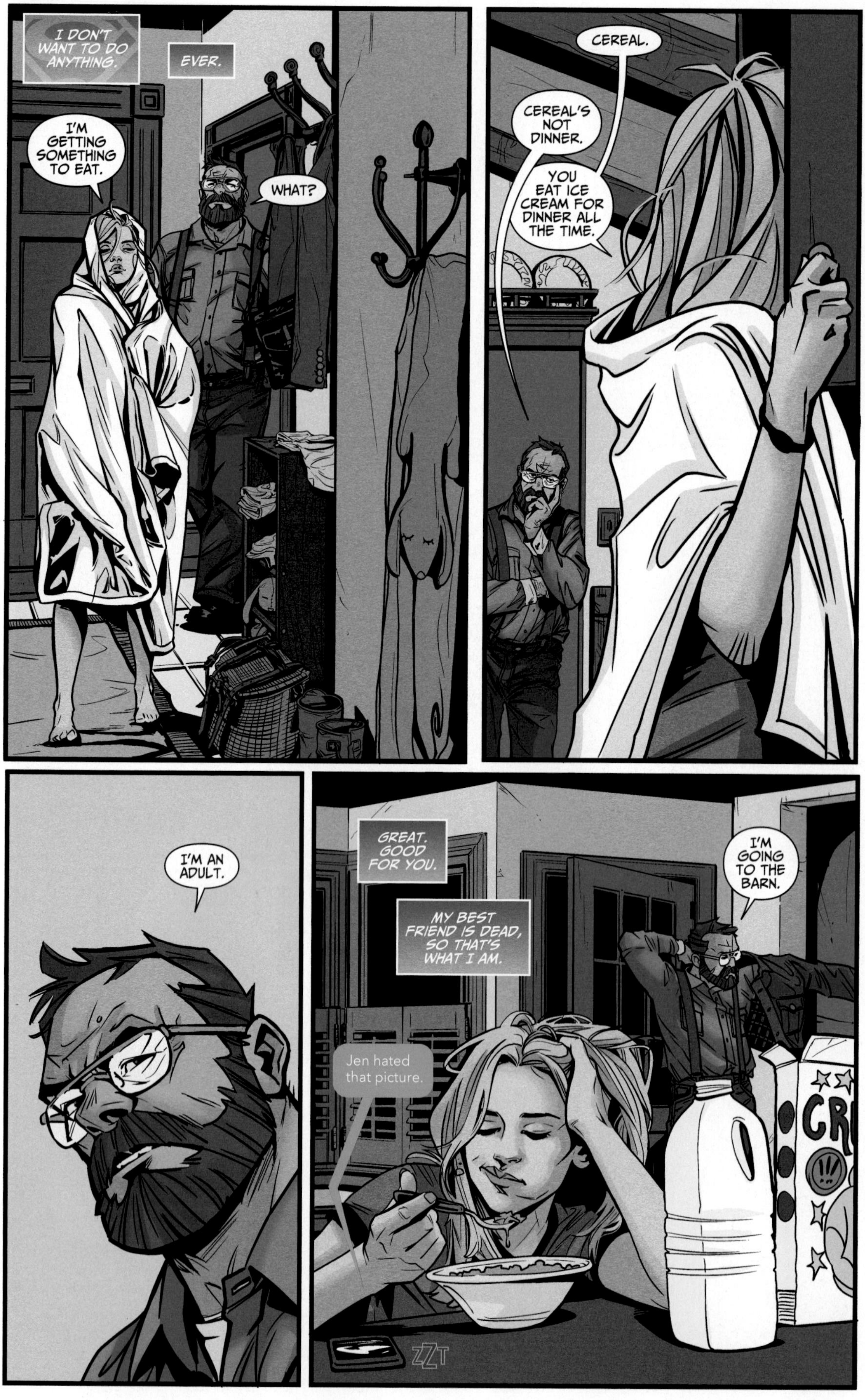

I DON'T WANT TO DO ANYTHING.
EVER.
I'M GETTING SOMETHING TO EAT.
WHAT?
CEREAL.
CEREAL'S NOT DINNER.
YOU EAT ICE CREAM FOR DINNER ALL THE TIME.
I'M AN ADULT.
GREAT. GOOD FOR YOU.
MY BEST FRIEND IS DEAD, SO THAT'S WHAT I AM.
I'M GOING TO THE BARN.
Jen hated that picture.
ZZT

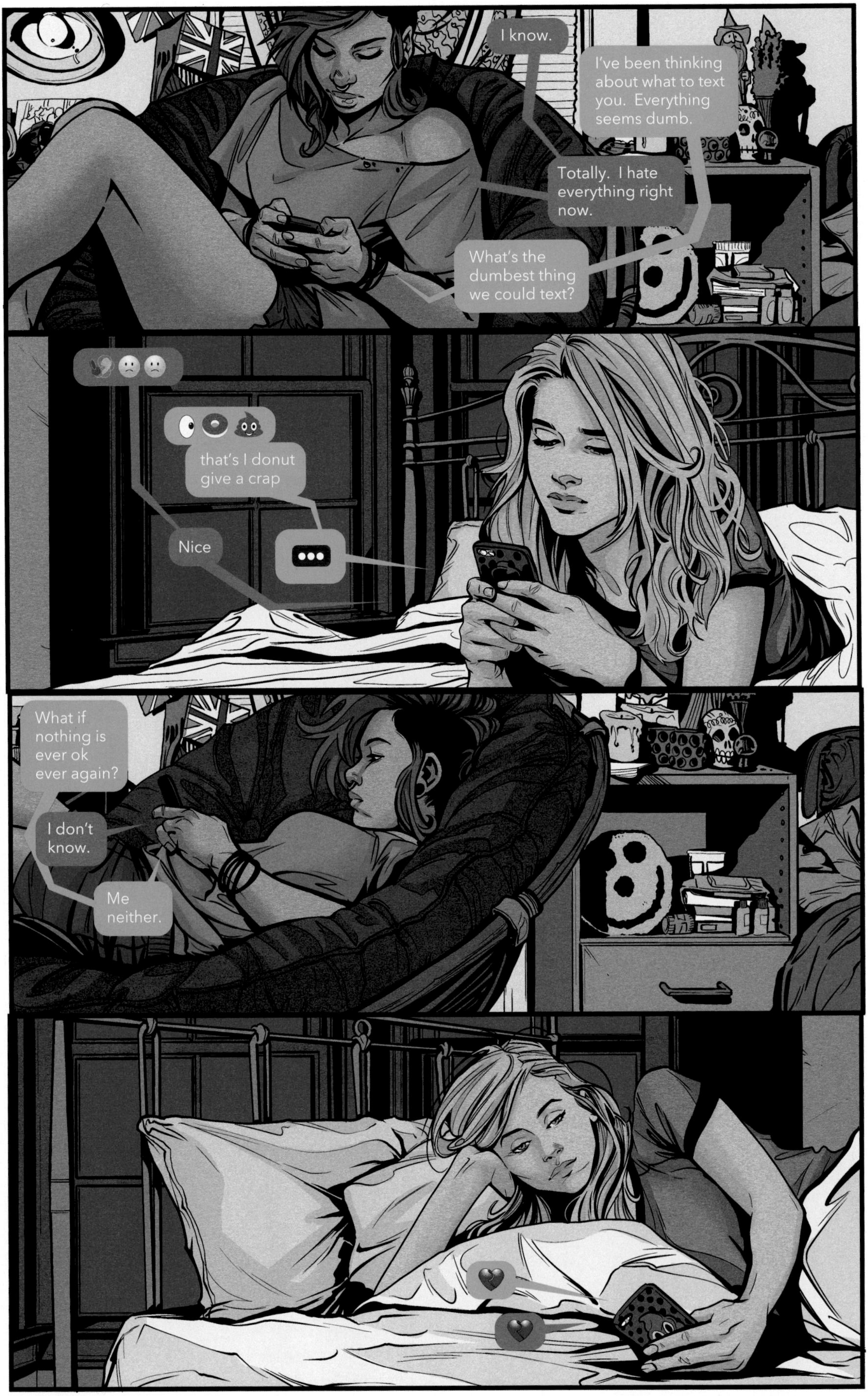
I know.
I've been thinking about what to text you. Everything seems dumb.
Totally. I hate everything right now.
What's the dumbest thing we could text?
that's I donut give a crap
Nice
What if nothing is ever ok ever again?
I don't know.
Me neither.

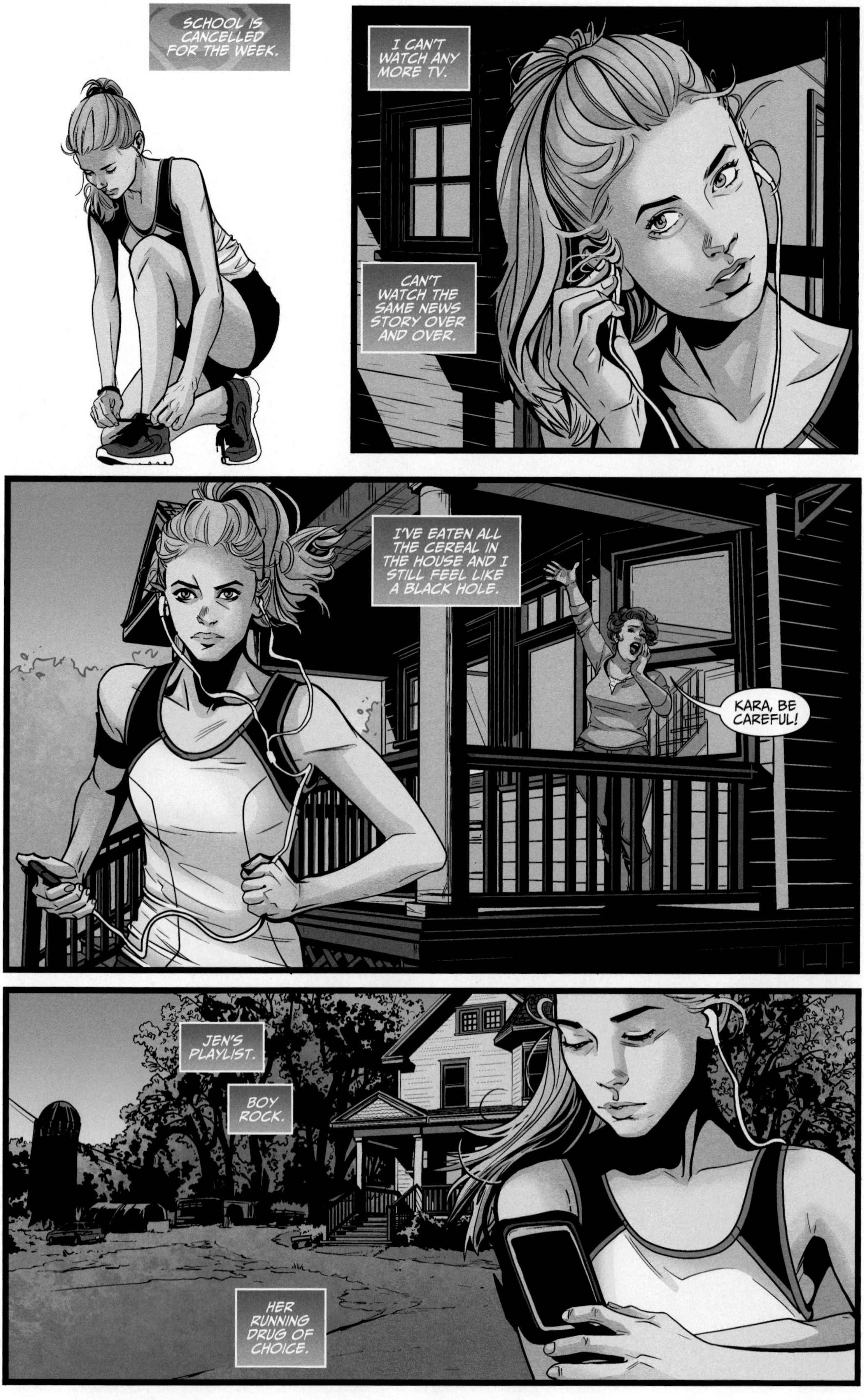

SCHOOL IS CANCELLED FOR THE WEEK.
I CAN'T WATCH ANY MORE TV.
CAN'T WATCH THE SAME NEWS STORY OVER AND OVER.
I'VE EATEN ALL THE CEREAL IN THE HOUSE AND I STILL FEEL LIKE A BLACK HOLE.
KARA, BE CAREFUL!
JEN'S PLAYLIST.
BOY ROCK.
HER RUNNING DRUG OF CHOICE.

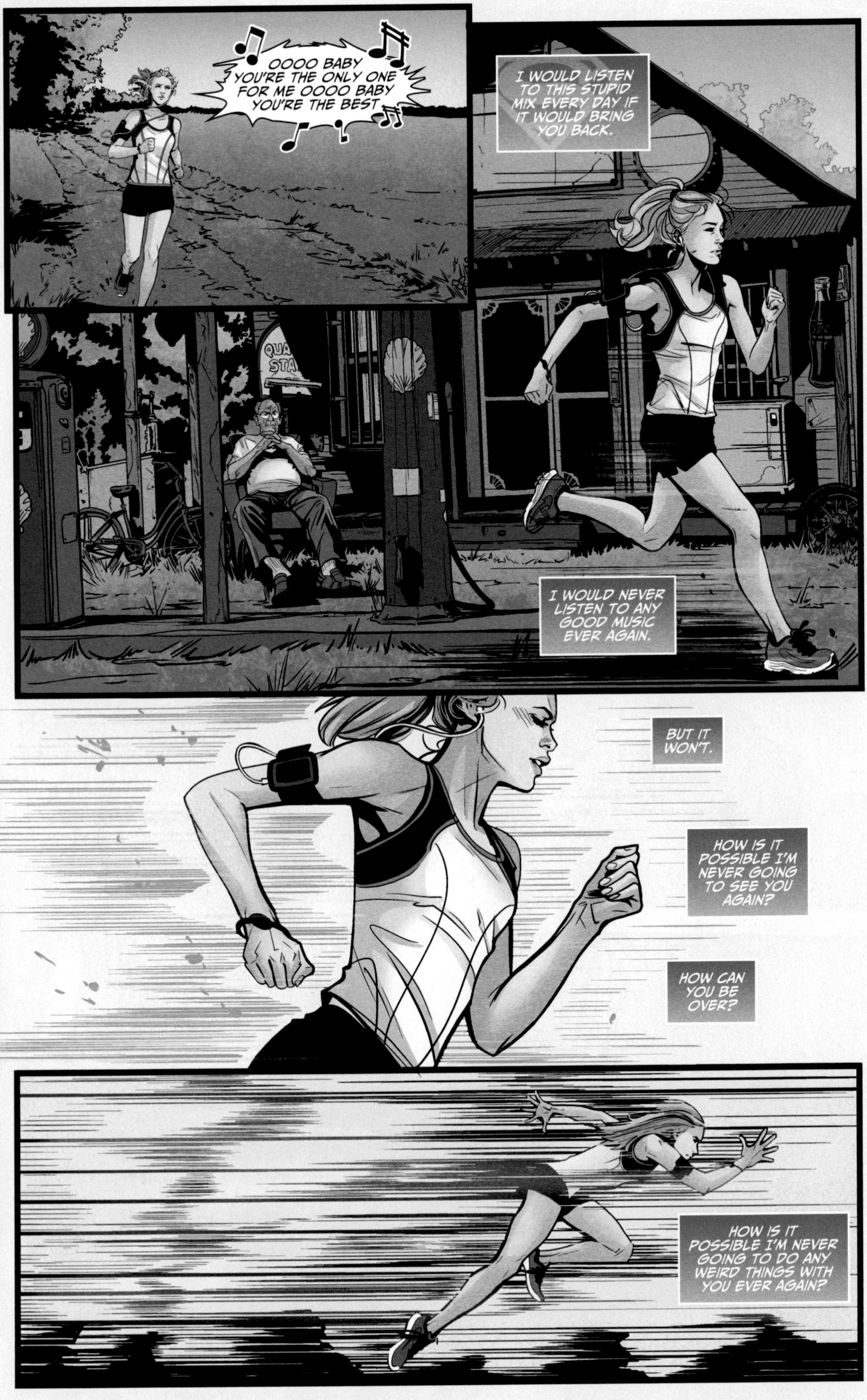
OOOO BABY YOU'RE THE ONLY ONE FOR ME OOOO BABY YOU'RE THE BEST
I WOULD LISTEN TO THIS STUPID MIX EVERY DAY IF IT WOULD BRING YOU BACK.
I WOULD NEVER LISTEN TO ANY GOOD MUSIC EVER AGAIN.
BUT IT WON'T.
HOW IS IT POSSIBLE I'M NEVER GOING TO SEE YOU AGAIN?
HOW CAN YOU BE OVER?
HOW IS IT POSSIBLE I'M NEVER GOING TO DO ANY WEIRD THINGS WITH YOU EVER AGAIN?

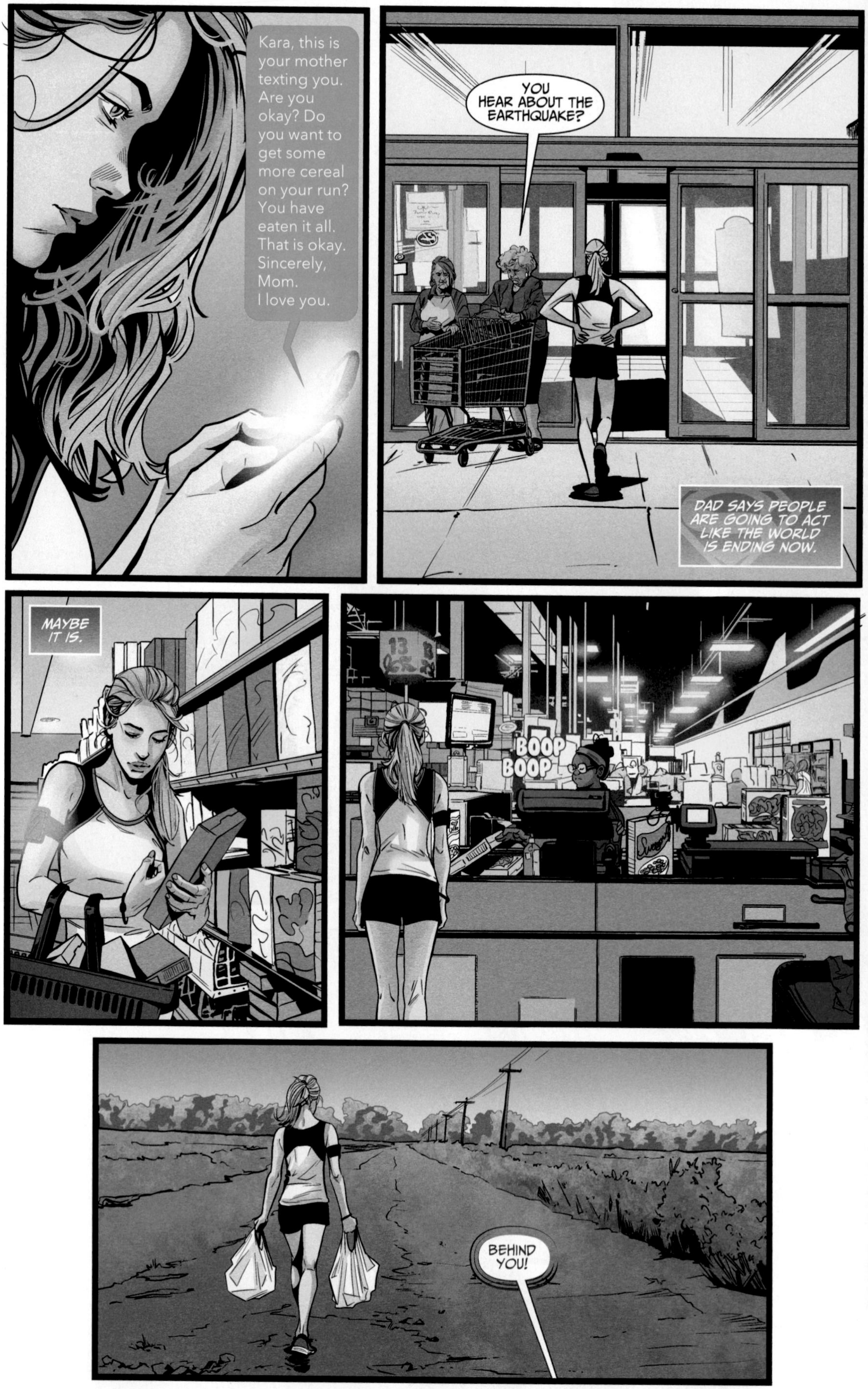
Kara, this is your mother texting you. Are you okay? Do you want to get some more cereal on your run? You have eaten it all. That is okay. Sincerely, Mom. I love you.
YOU HEAR ABOUT THE EARTHQUAKE?
DAD SAYS PEOPLE ARE GOING TO ACT LIKE THE WORLD IS ENDING NOW.
MAYBE IT IS.
BOOP BOOP
BEHIND YOU!

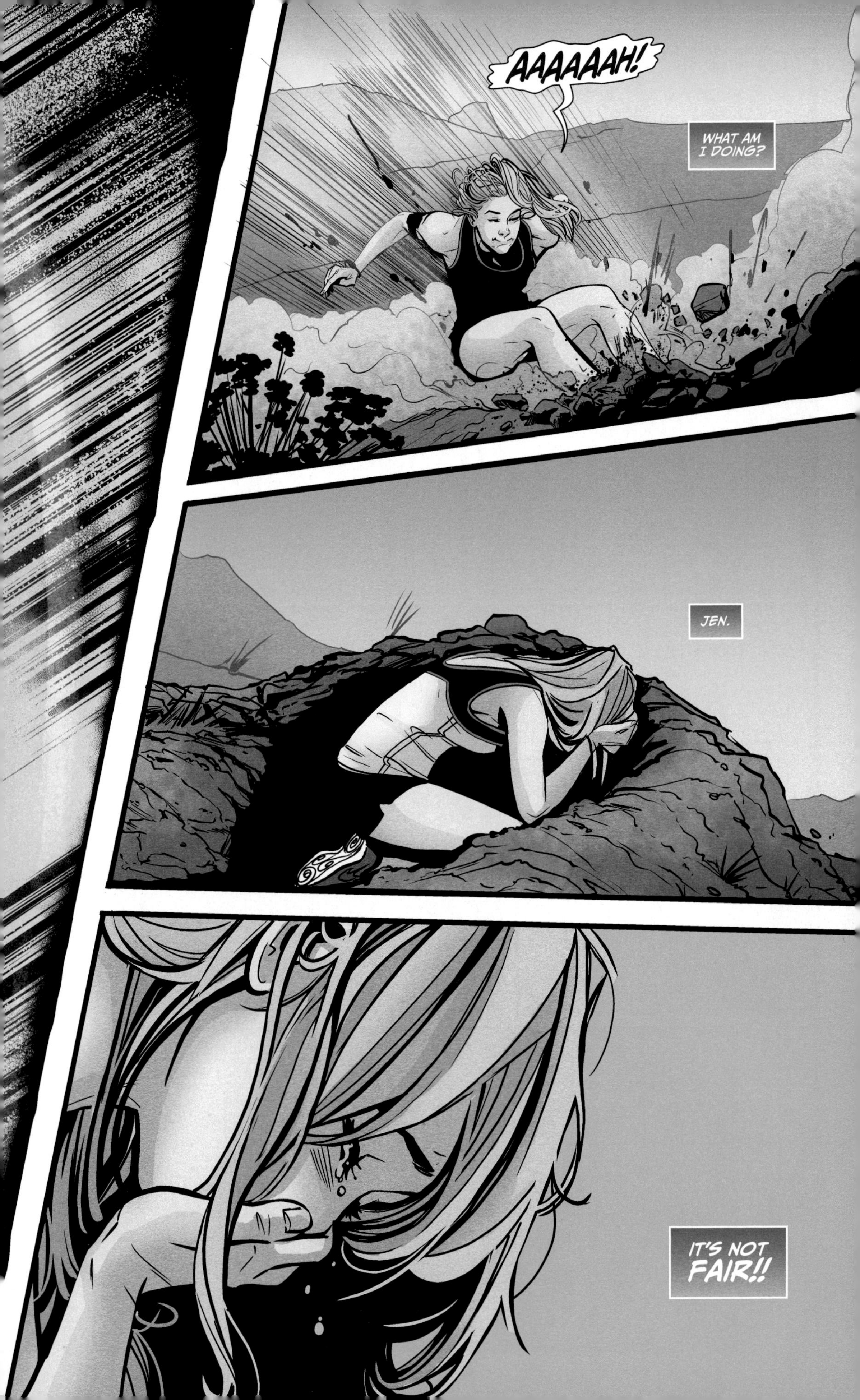
AAAAAAH!
WHAT AM I DOING?
JEN.
IT'S NOT FAIR!!

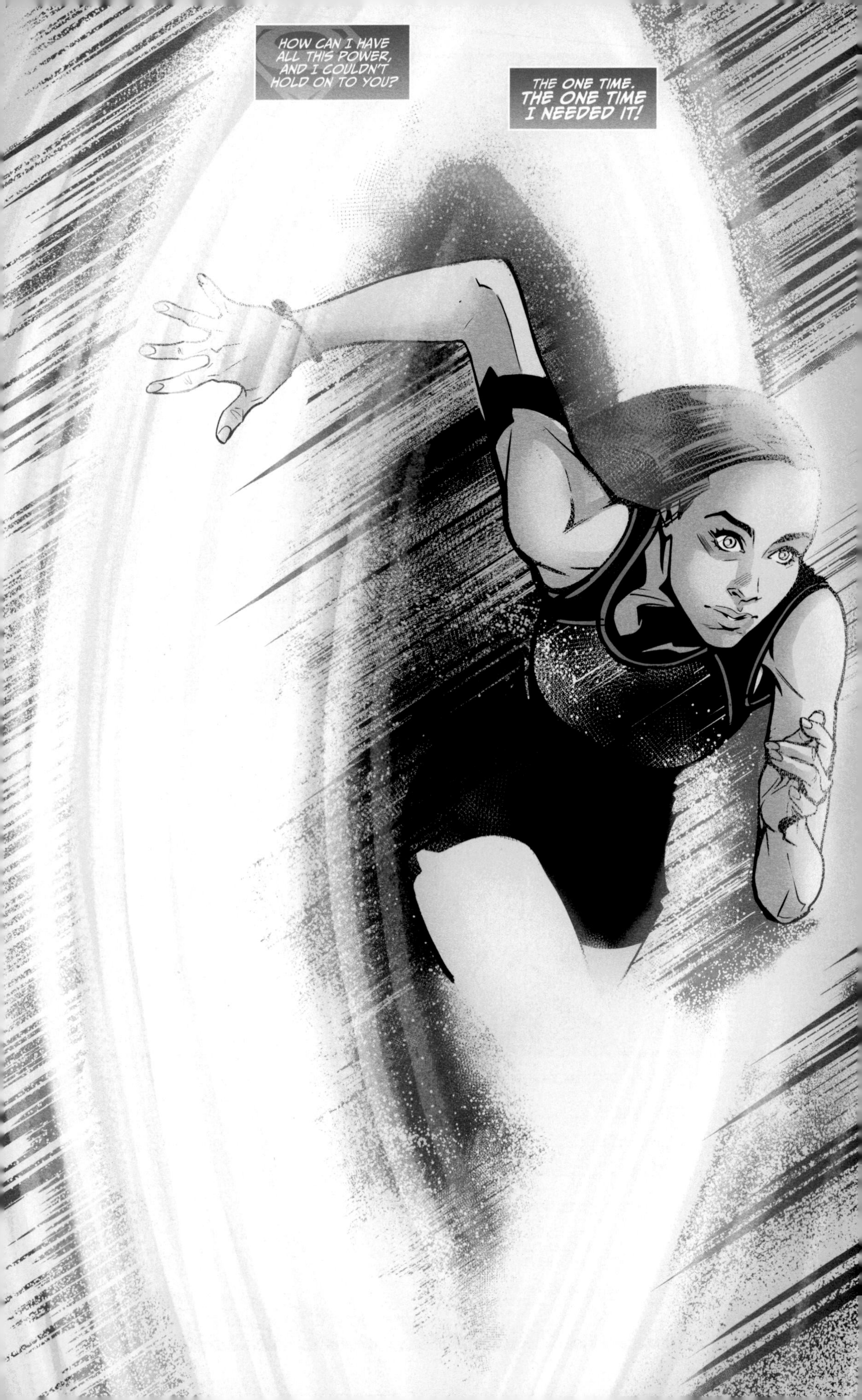
HOW CAN I HAVE ALL THIS POWER, AND I COULDN'T HOLD ON TO YOU?
THE ONE TIME. THE ONE TIME I NEEDED IT!

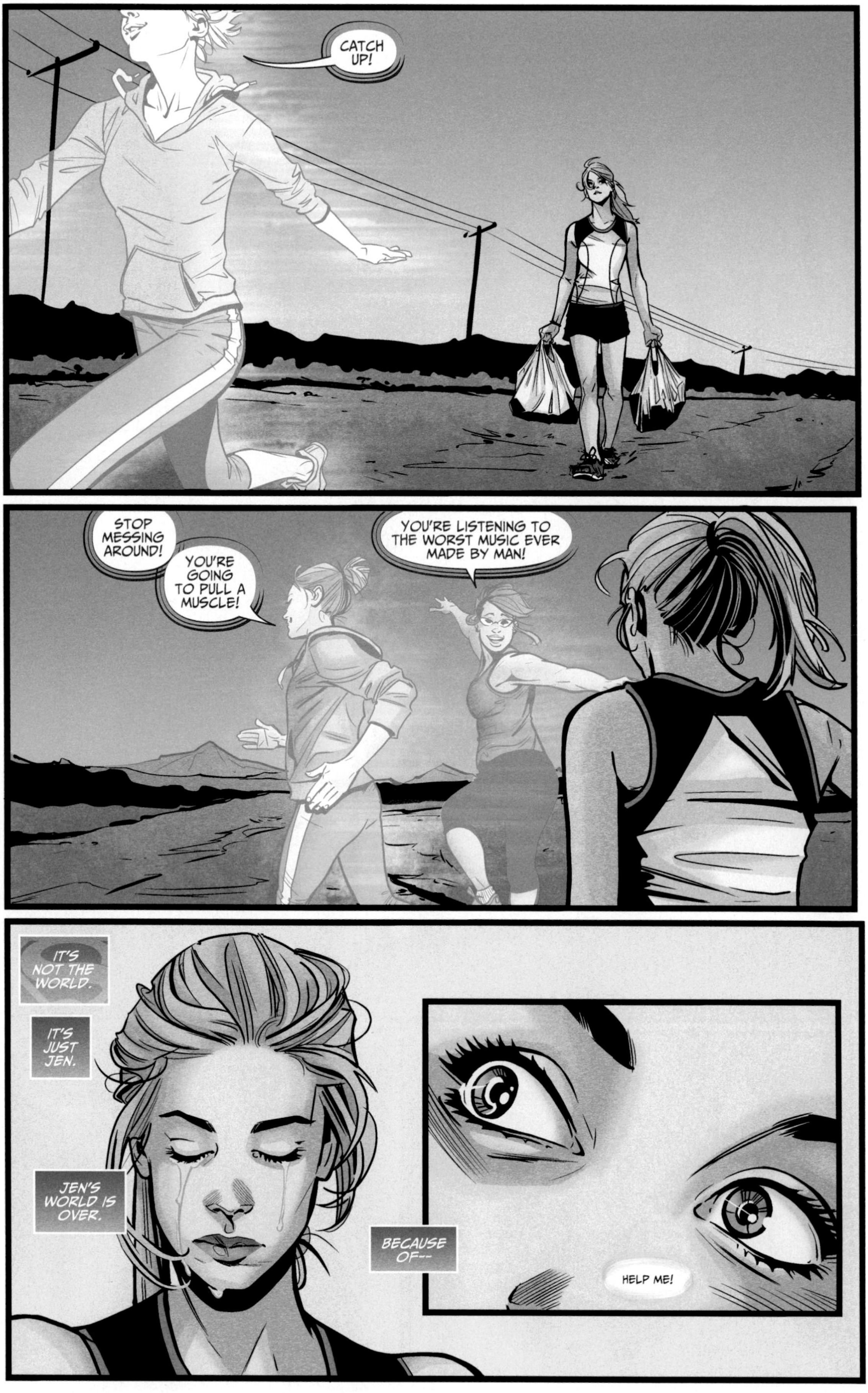
CATCH UP!
STOP MESSING AROUND!
YOU'RE GOING TO PULL A MUSCLE!
YOU'RE LISTENING TO THE WORST MUSIC EVER MADE BY MAN!
IT'S NOT THE WORLD.
IT'S JUST JEN.
JEN'S WORLD IS OVER.
BECAUSE OF--
HELP ME!

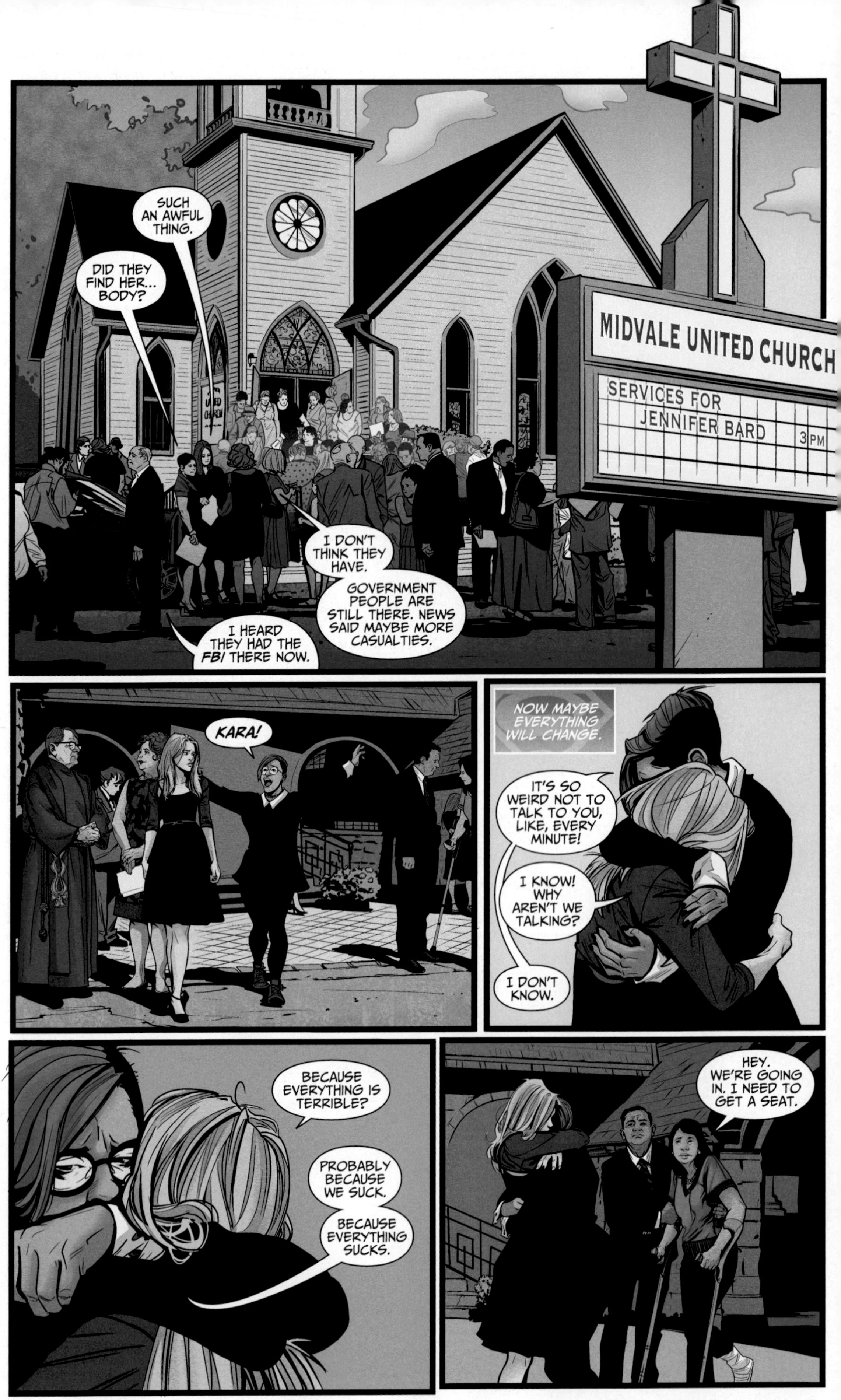
SUCH AN AWFUL THING.
DID THEY FIND HER... BODY?
MIDVALE UNITED CHURCH
SERVICES FOR JENNIFER BARD 3PM
I DON'T THINK THEY HAVE.
GOVERNMENT PEOPLE ARE STILL THERE. NEWS SAID MAYBE MORE CASUALTIES.
I HEARD THEY HAD THE *FBI* THERE NOW.
KARA!
NOW MAYBE EVERYTHING WILL CHANGE.
IT'S SO WEIRD NOT TO TALK TO YOU, LIKE, EVERY MINUTE!
I KNOW! WHY AREN'T WE TALKING?
I DON'T KNOW.
BECAUSE EVERYTHING IS TERRIBLE?
PROBABLY BECAUSE WE SUCK.
BECAUSE EVERYTHING SUCKS.
HEY. WE'RE GOING IN. I NEED TO GET A SEAT.

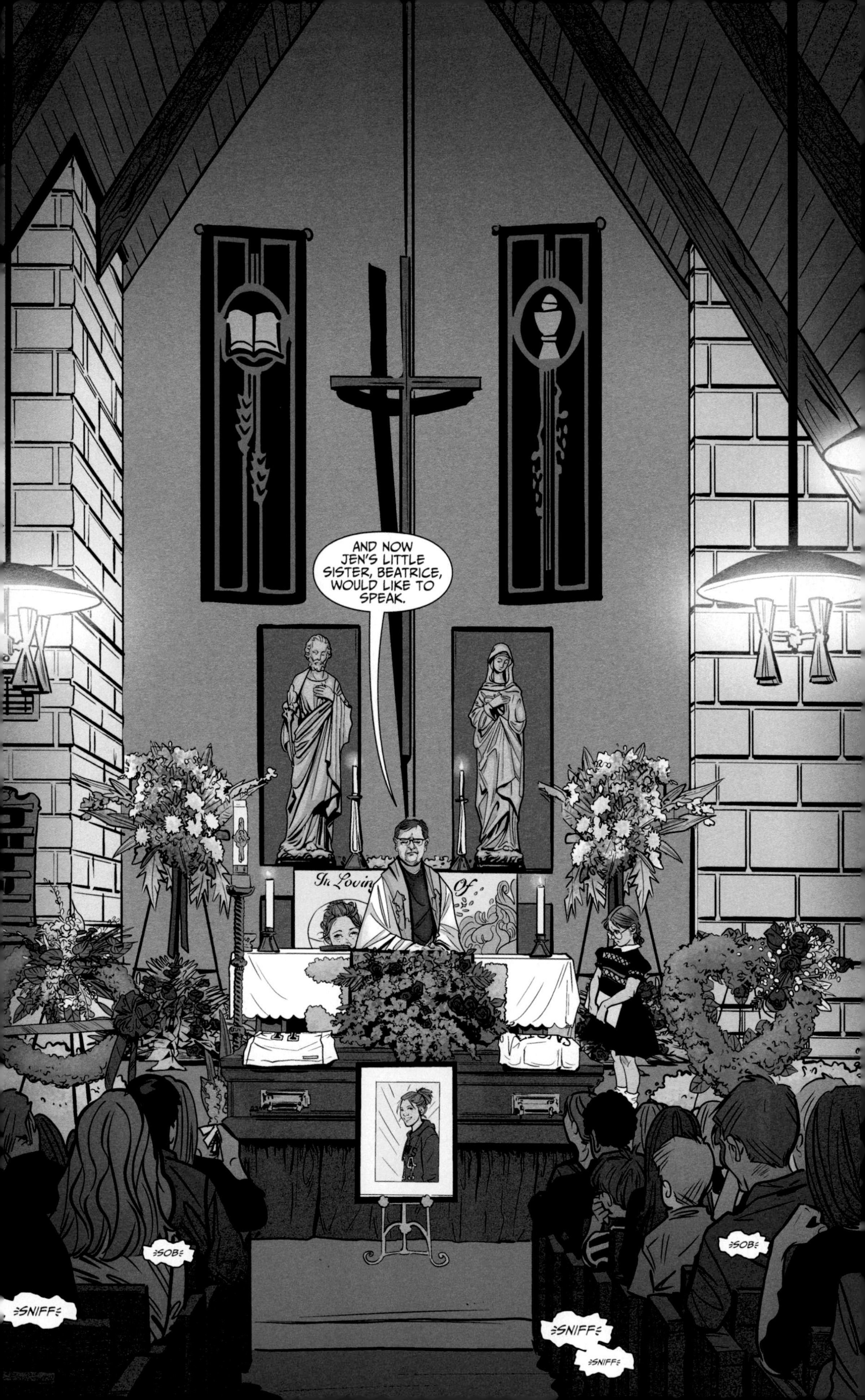
AND NOW JEN'S LITTLE SISTER, BEATRICE, WOULD LIKE TO SPEAK.
SOB
SOB
SNIFF
SNIFF
SNIFF

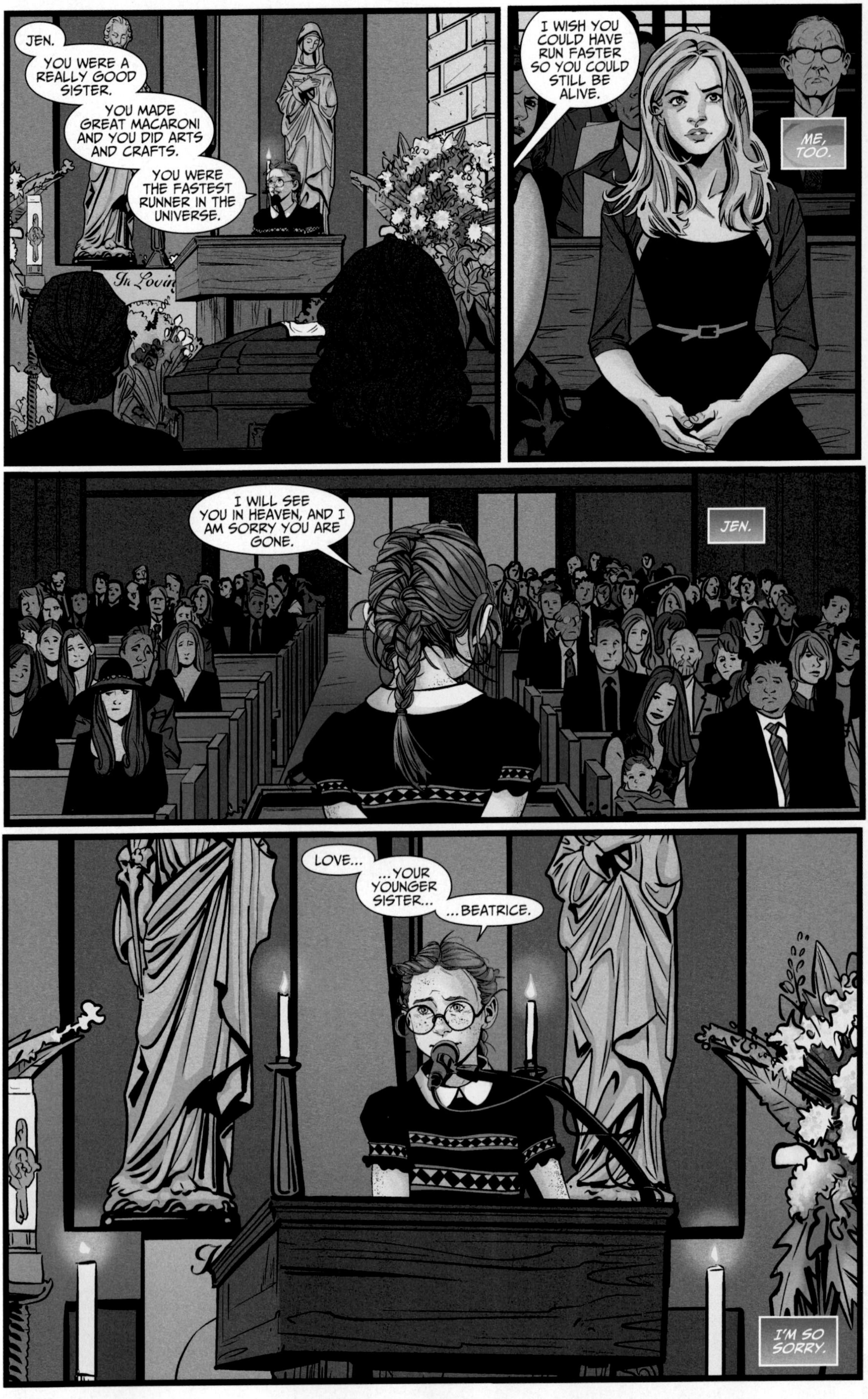

JEN.
YOU WERE A REALLY GOOD SISTER.
YOU MADE GREAT MACARONI AND YOU DID ARTS AND CRAFTS.
YOU WERE THE FASTEST RUNNER IN THE UNIVERSE.
I WISH YOU COULD HAVE RUN FASTER SO YOU COULD STILL BE ALIVE.
ME, TOO.
I WILL SEE YOU IN HEAVEN, AND I AM SORRY YOU ARE GONE.
JEN.
LOVE...
...YOUR YOUNGER SISTER...
...BEATRICE.
I'M SO SORRY.

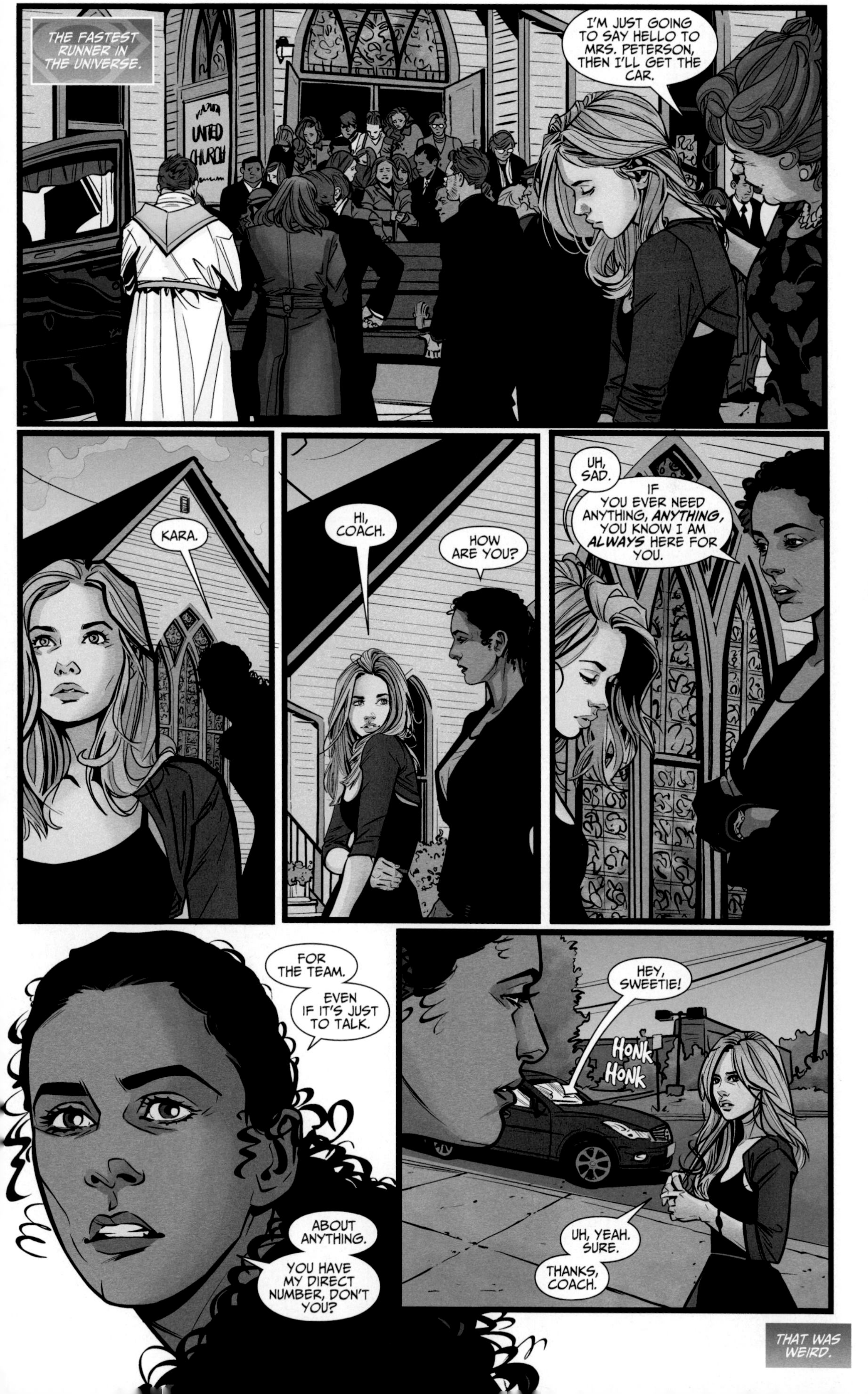
THE FASTEST RUNNER IN THE UNIVERSE.
I'M JUST GOING TO SAY HELLO TO MRS. PETERSON, THEN I'LL GET THE CAR.
UNITED CHURCH
KARA.
HI, COACH.
HOW ARE YOU?
UH, SAD.
IF YOU EVER NEED ANYTHING, ANYTHING, YOU KNOW I AM ALWAYS HERE FOR YOU.
FOR THE TEAM.
EVEN IF IT'S JUST TO TALK.
ABOUT ANYTHING.
YOU HAVE MY DIRECT NUMBER, DON'T YOU?
HEY, SWEETIE!
HONK HONK
UH, YEAH. SURE.
THANKS, COACH.
THAT WAS WEIRD.

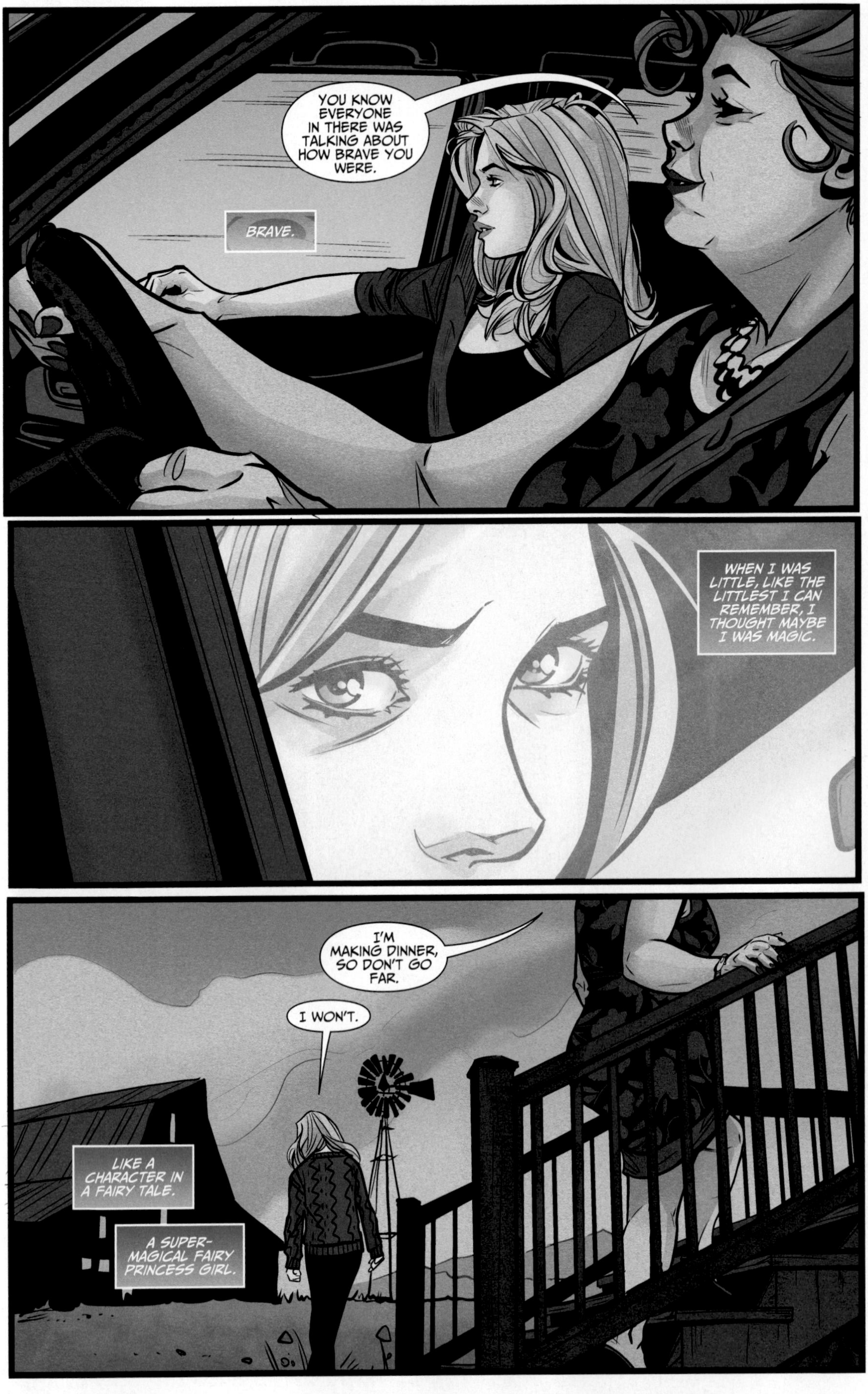
YOU KNOW EVERYONE IN THERE WAS TALKING ABOUT HOW BRAVE YOU WERE.
BRAVE.
WHEN I WAS LITTLE, LIKE THE LITTLEST I CAN REMEMBER, I THOUGHT MAYBE I WAS MAGIC.
I'M MAKING DINNER, SO DON'T GO FAR.
I WON'T.
LIKE A CHARACTER IN A FAIRY TALE.
A SUPER-MAGICAL FAIRY PRINCESS GIRL.

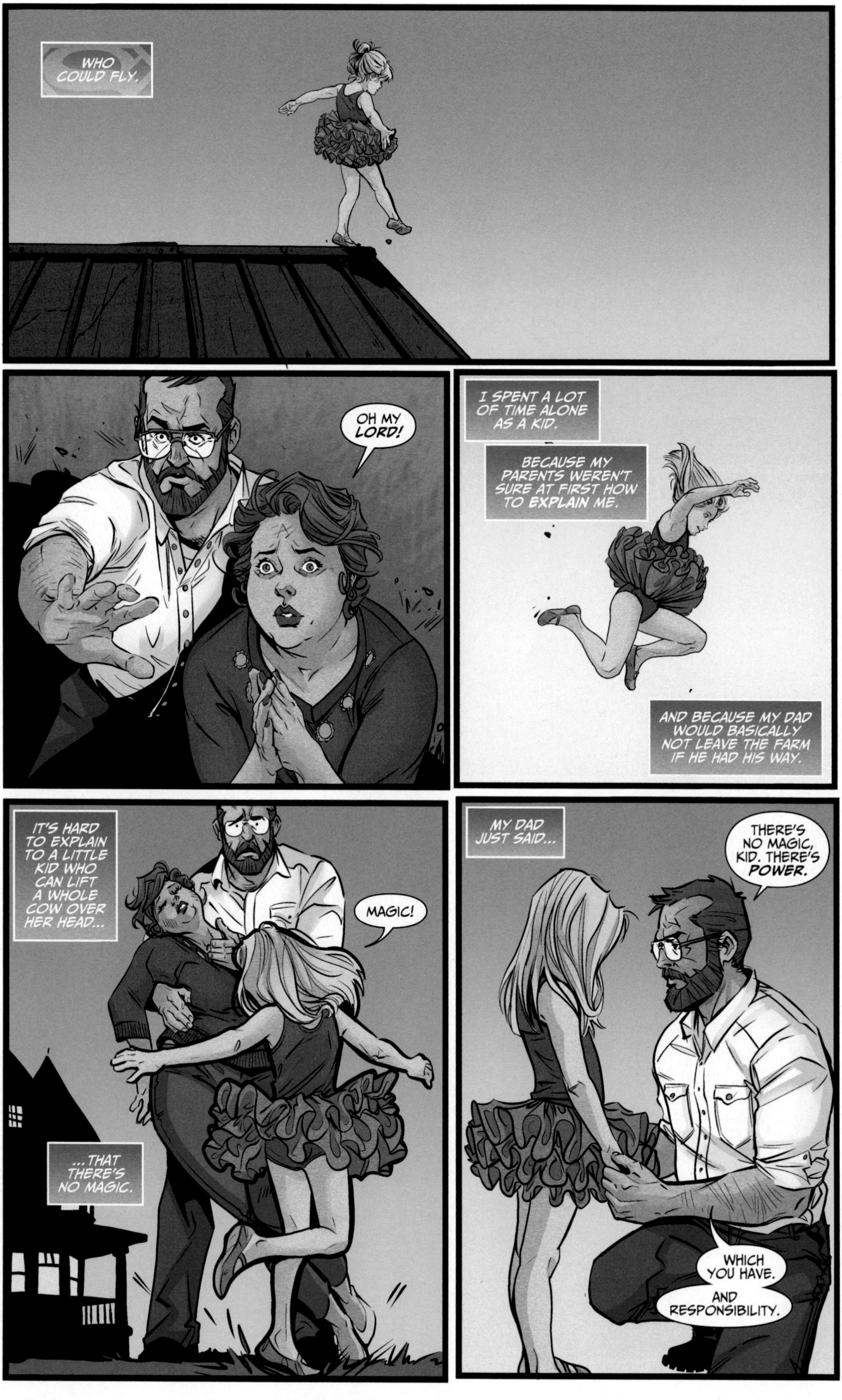
WHO COULD FLY.
OH MY LORD!
I SPENT A LOT OF TIME ALONE AS A KID.
BECAUSE MY PARENTS WEREN'T SURE AT FIRST HOW TO EXPLAIN ME.
AND BECAUSE MY DAD WOULD BASICALLY NOT LEAVE THE FARM IF HE HAD HIS WAY.
IT'S HARD TO EXPLAIN TO A LITTLE KID WHO CAN LIFT A WHOLE COW OVER HER HEAD...
MAGIC!
...THAT THERE'S NO MAGIC.
MY DAD JUST SAID...
THERE'S NO MAGIC, KID. THERE'S POWER.
WHICH YOU HAVE.
AND RESPONSIBILITY.

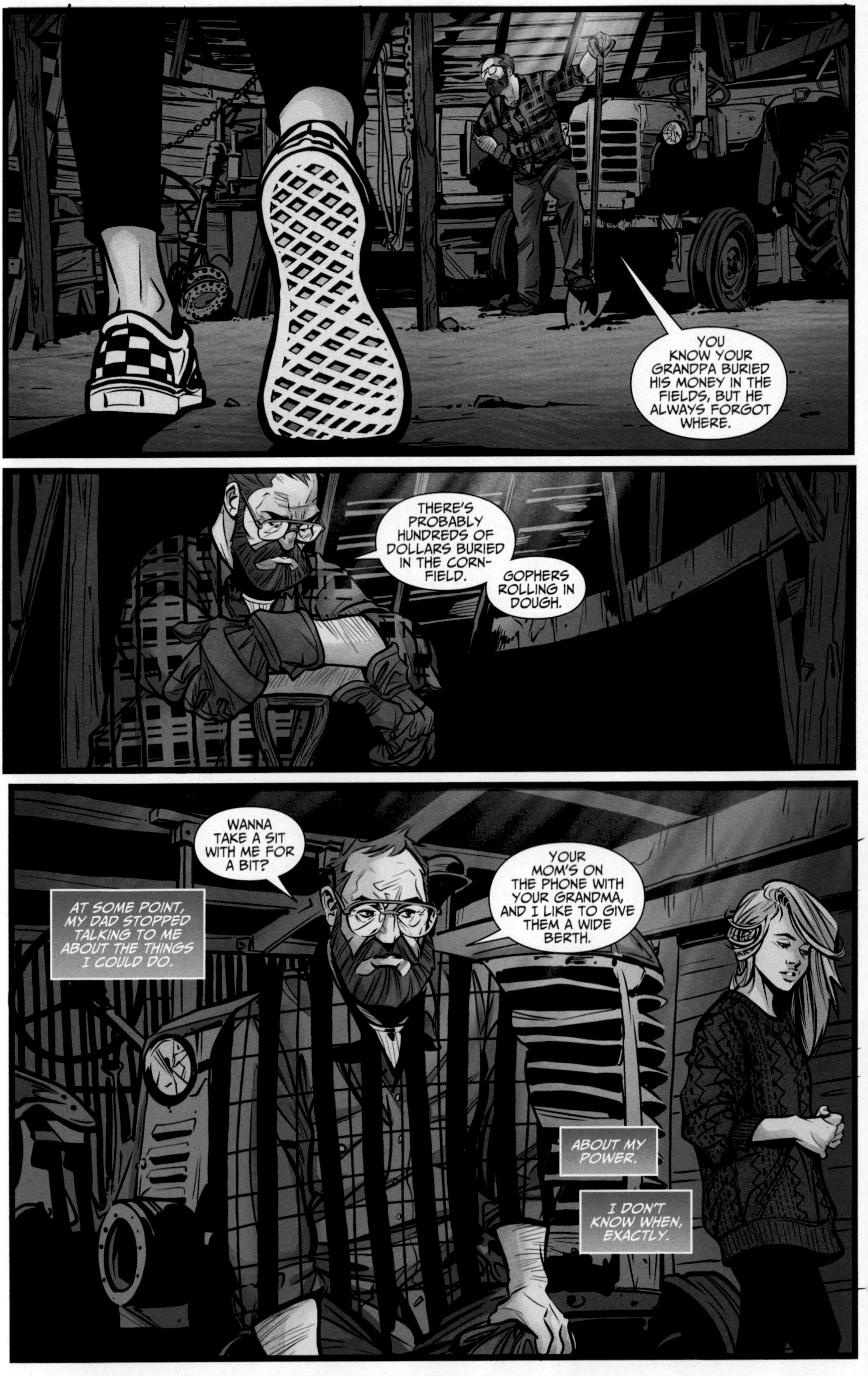

YOU KNOW YOUR GRANDPA BURIED HIS MONEY IN THE FIELDS, BUT HE ALWAYS FORGOT WHERE.
THERE'S PROBABLY HUNDREDS OF DOLLARS BURIED IN THE CORN-FIELD.
GOPHERS ROLLING IN DOUGH.
AT SOME POINT, MY DAD STOPPED TALKING TO ME ABOUT THE THINGS I COULD DO.
WANNA TAKE A SIT WITH ME FOR A BIT?
YOUR MOM'S ON THE PHONE WITH YOUR GRANDMA, AND I LIKE TO GIVE THEM A WIDE BERTH.
ABOUT MY POWER.
I DON'T KNOW WHEN, EXACTLY.

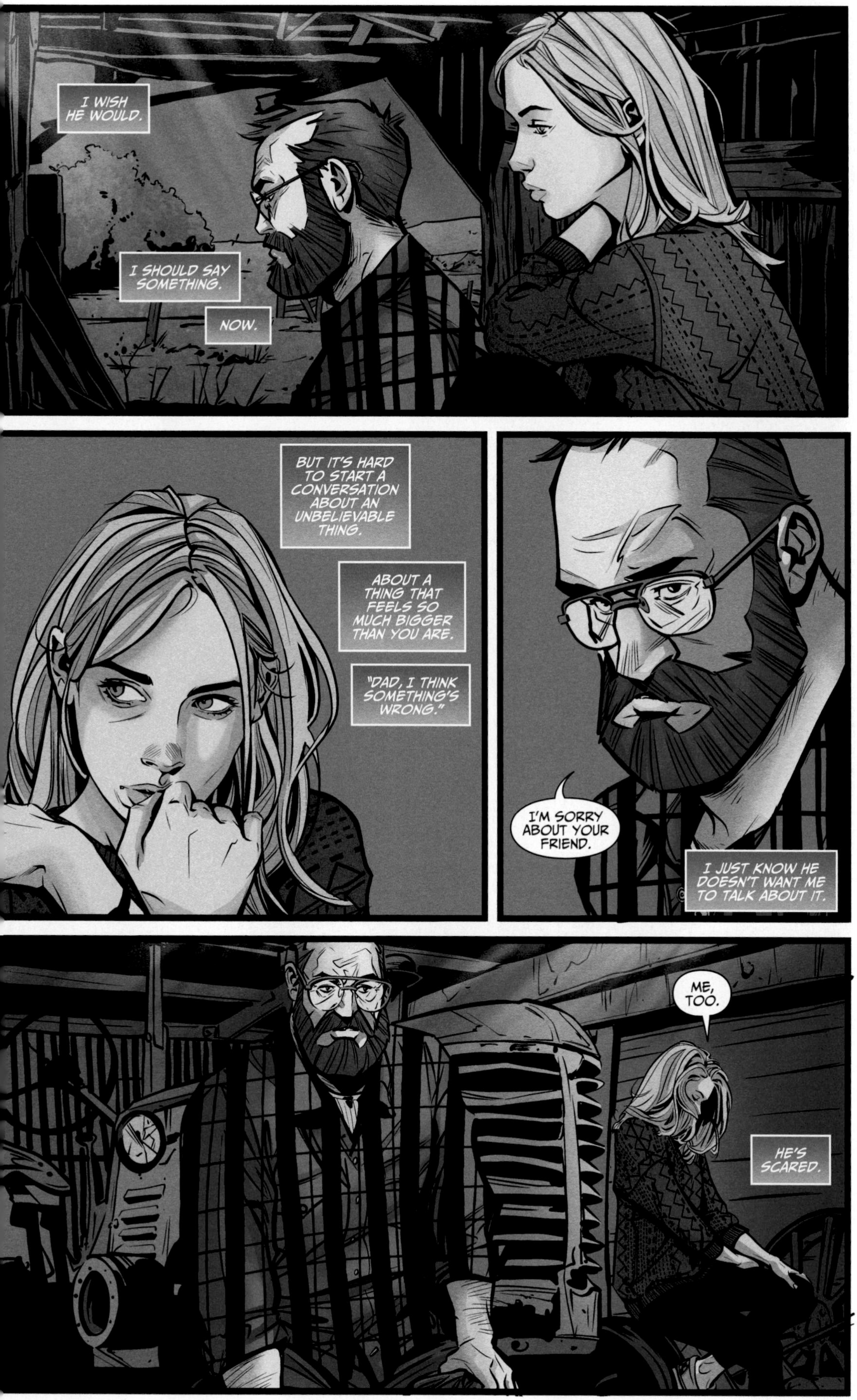
I WISH HE WOULD.
I SHOULD SAY SOMETHING.
NOW.
BUT IT'S HARD TO START A CONVERSATION ABOUT AN UNBELIEVABLE THING.
ABOUT A THING THAT FEELS SO MUCH BIGGER THAN YOU ARE.
"DAD, I THINK SOMETHING'S WRONG."
I'M SORRY ABOUT YOUR FRIEND.
I JUST KNOW HE DOESN'T WANT ME TO TALK ABOUT IT.
ME, TOO.
HE'S SCARED.

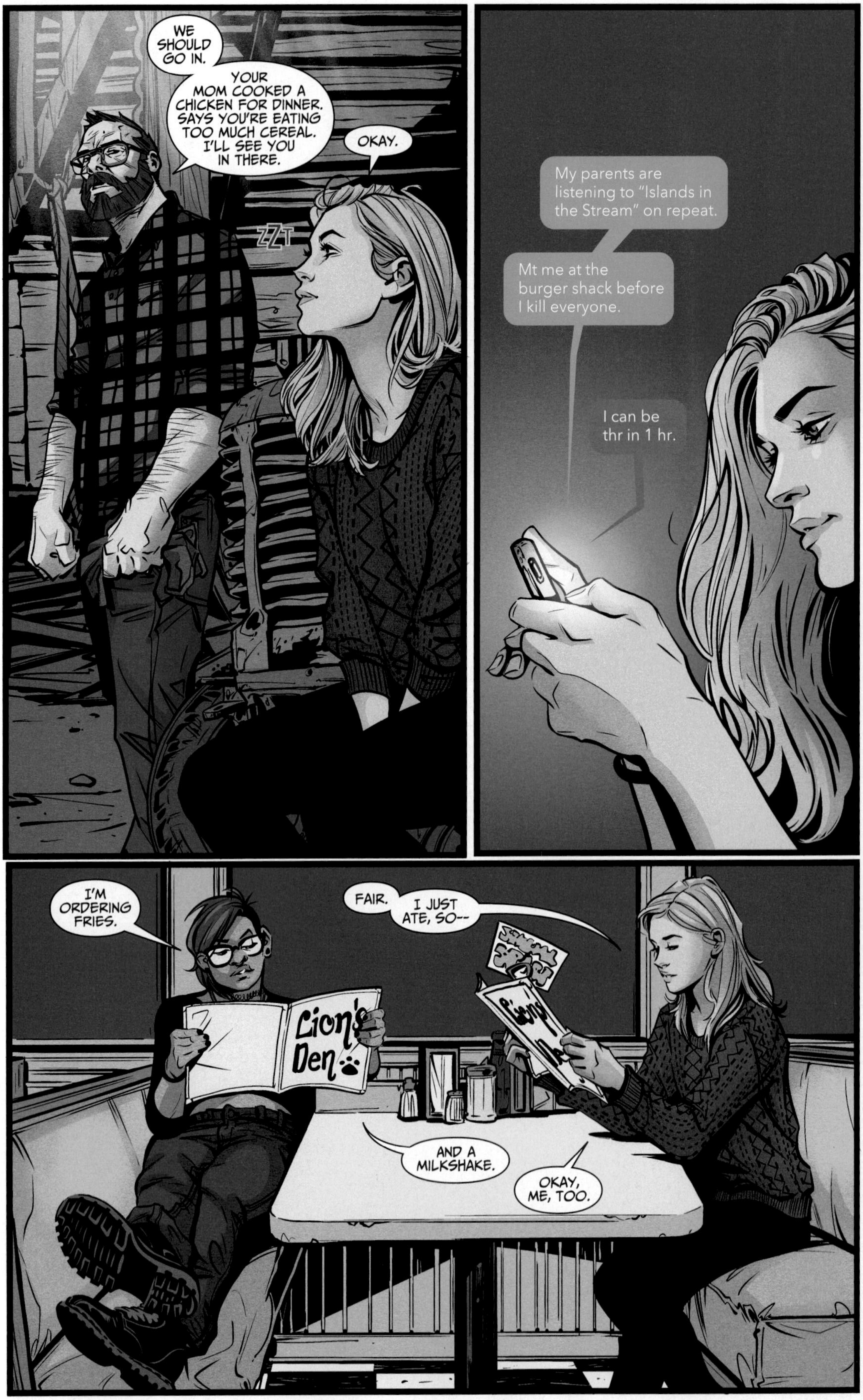
WE SHOULD GO IN.
YOUR MOM COOKED A CHICKEN FOR DINNER. SAYS YOU'RE EATING TOO MUCH CEREAL. I'LL SEE YOU IN THERE.
OKAY.
ZZT
My parents are listening to "Islands in the Stream" on repeat.
Mt me at the burger shack before I kill everyone.
I can be thr in 1 hr.
I'M ORDERING FRIES.
FAIR.
I JUST ATE, SO--
Lion's Den
AND A MILKSHAKE.
OKAY, ME, TOO.

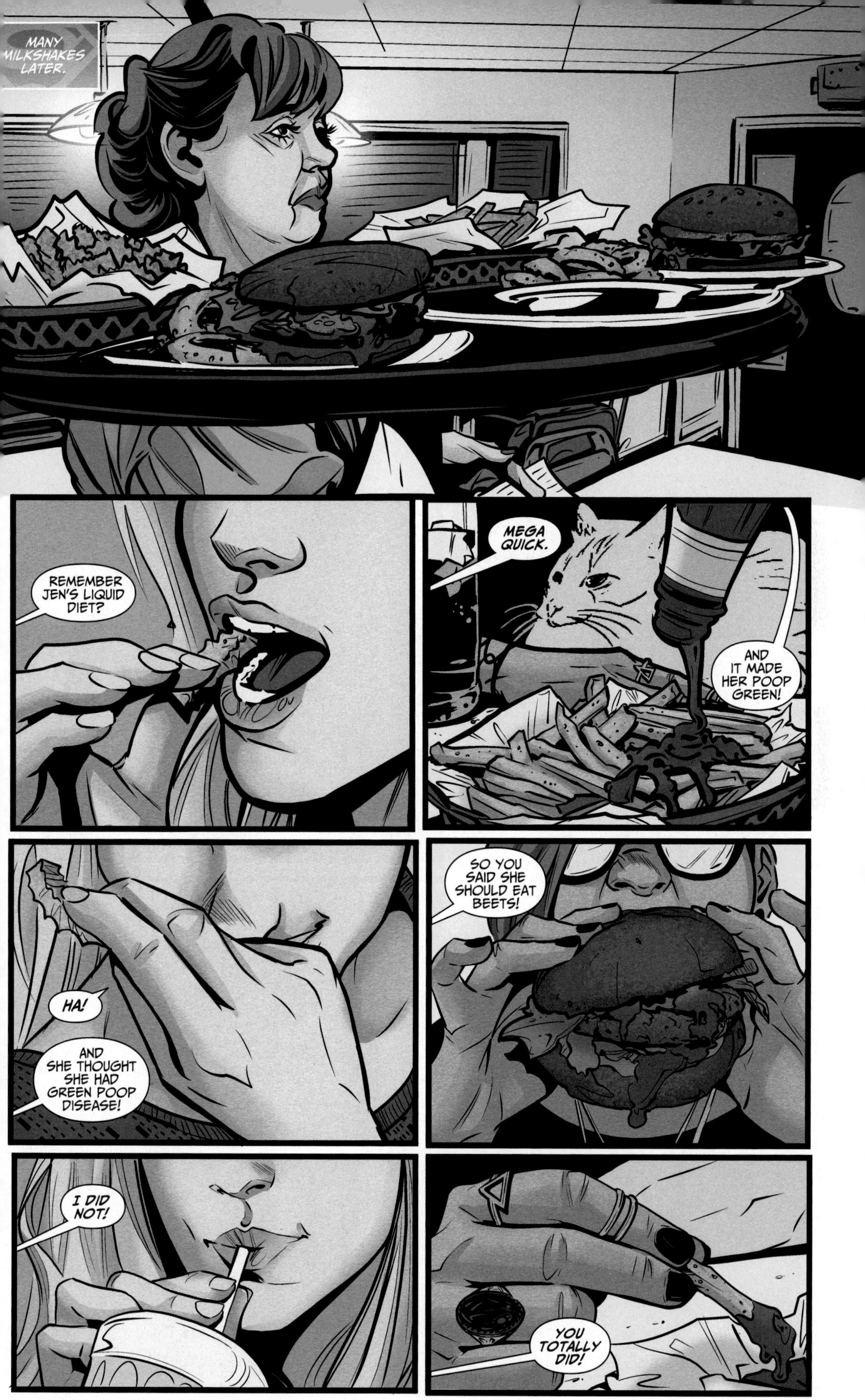
MANY MILKSHAKES LATER.
REMEMBER JEN'S LIQUID DIET?
MEGA QUICK.
AND IT MADE HER POOP GREEN!
HA!
AND SHE THOUGHT SHE HAD GREEN POOP DISEASE!
SO YOU SAID SHE SHOULD EAT BEETS!
I DID NOT!
YOU TOTALLY DID!

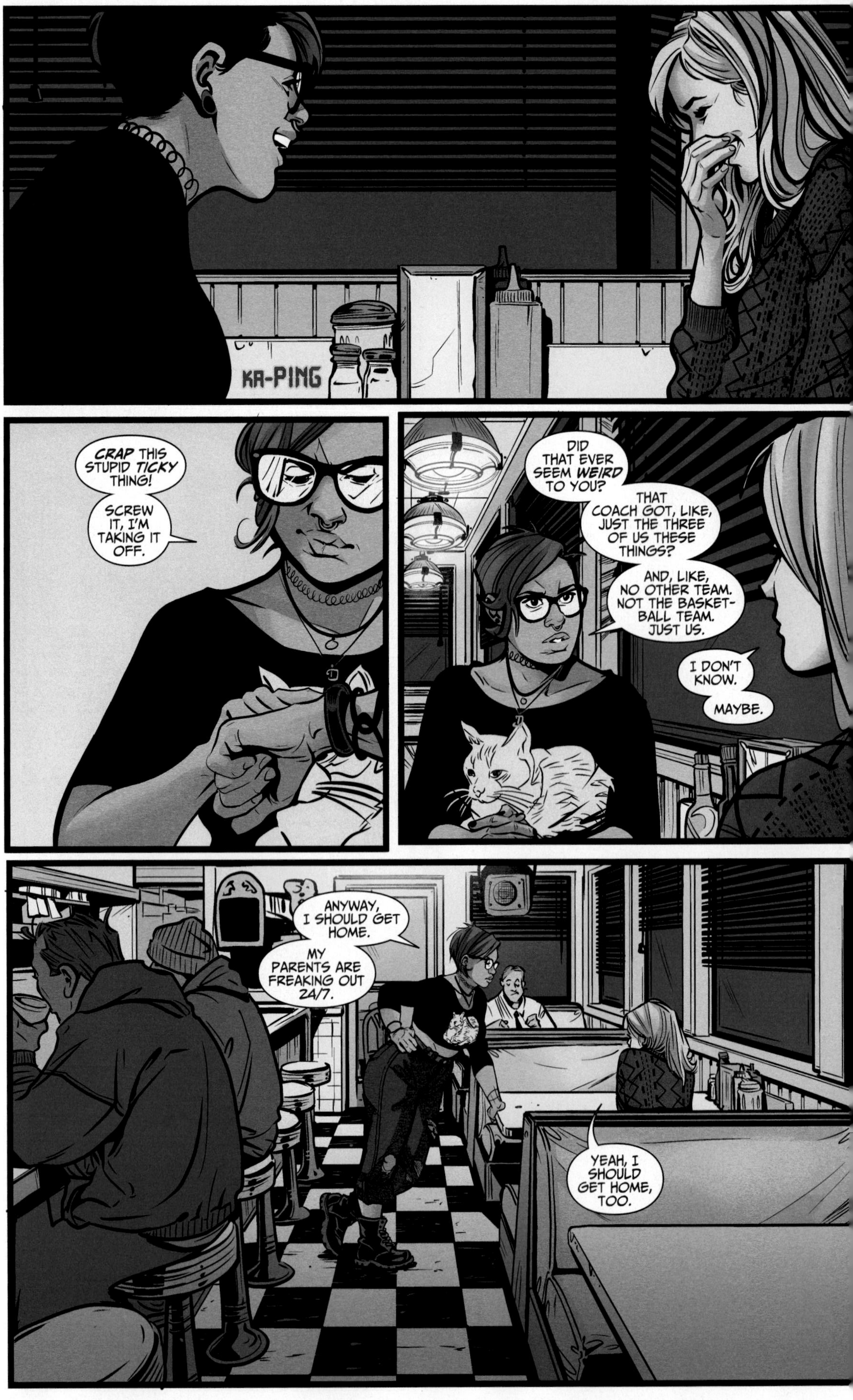
KA-PING
CRAP THIS STUPID TICKY THING!
SCREW IT, I'M TAKING IT OFF.
DID THAT EVER SEEM WEIRD TO YOU?
THAT COACH GOT, LIKE, JUST THE THREE OF US THESE THINGS?
AND, LIKE, NO OTHER TEAM. NOT THE BASKET-BALL TEAM. JUST US.
I DON'T KNOW.
MAYBE.
ANYWAY, I SHOULD GET HOME.
MY PARENTS ARE FREAKING OUT 24/7.
YEAH, I SHOULD GET HOME, TOO.

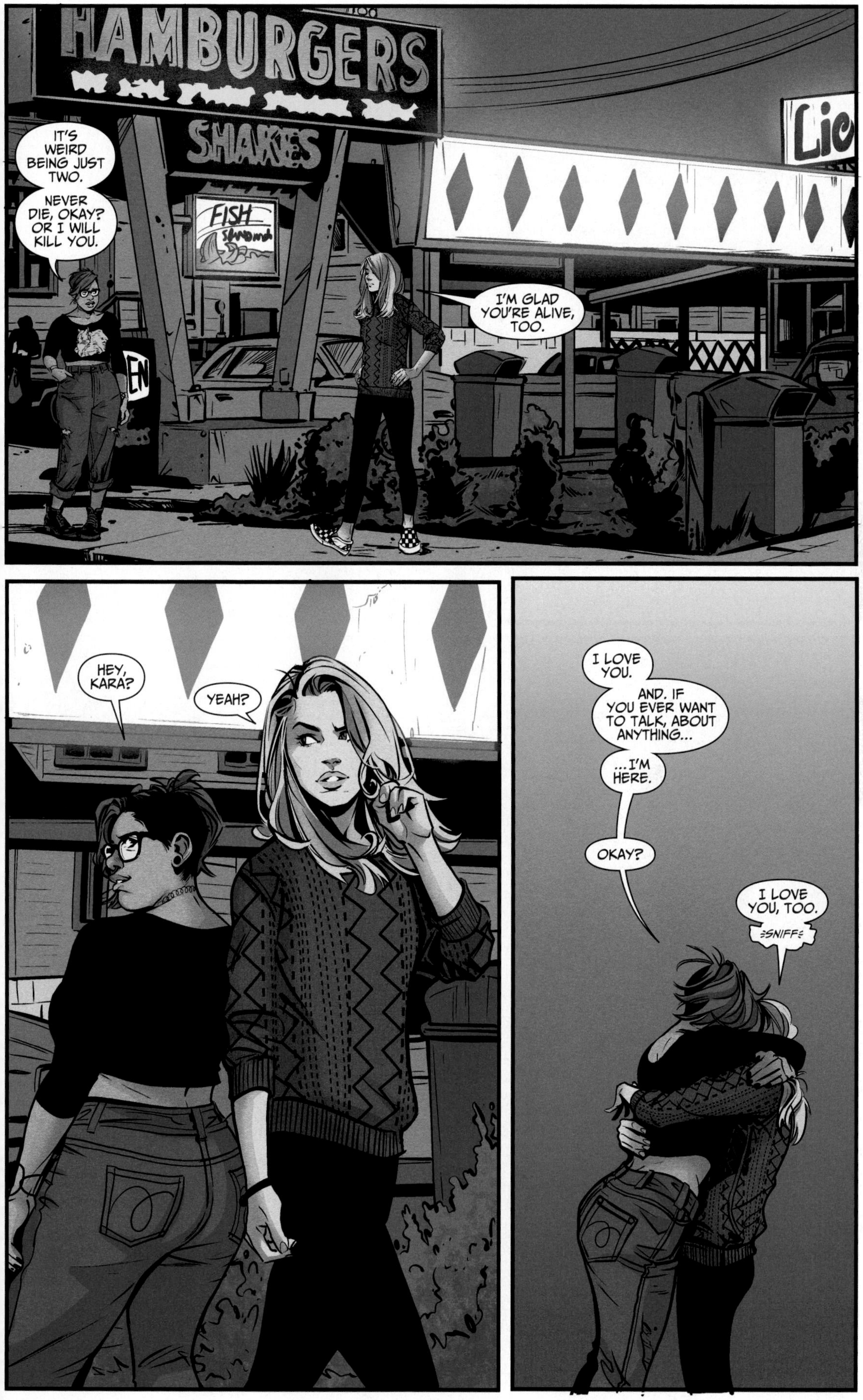
HAMBURGERS
SHAKES
FISH
IT'S WEIRD BEING JUST TWO.
NEVER DIE, OKAY? OR I WILL KILL YOU.
I'M GLAD YOU'RE ALIVE, TOO.
HEY, KARA?
YEAH?
I LOVE YOU.
AND. IF YOU EVER WANT TO TALK, ABOUT ANYTHING...
...I'M HERE.
OKAY?
I LOVE YOU, TOO.
SNIFF

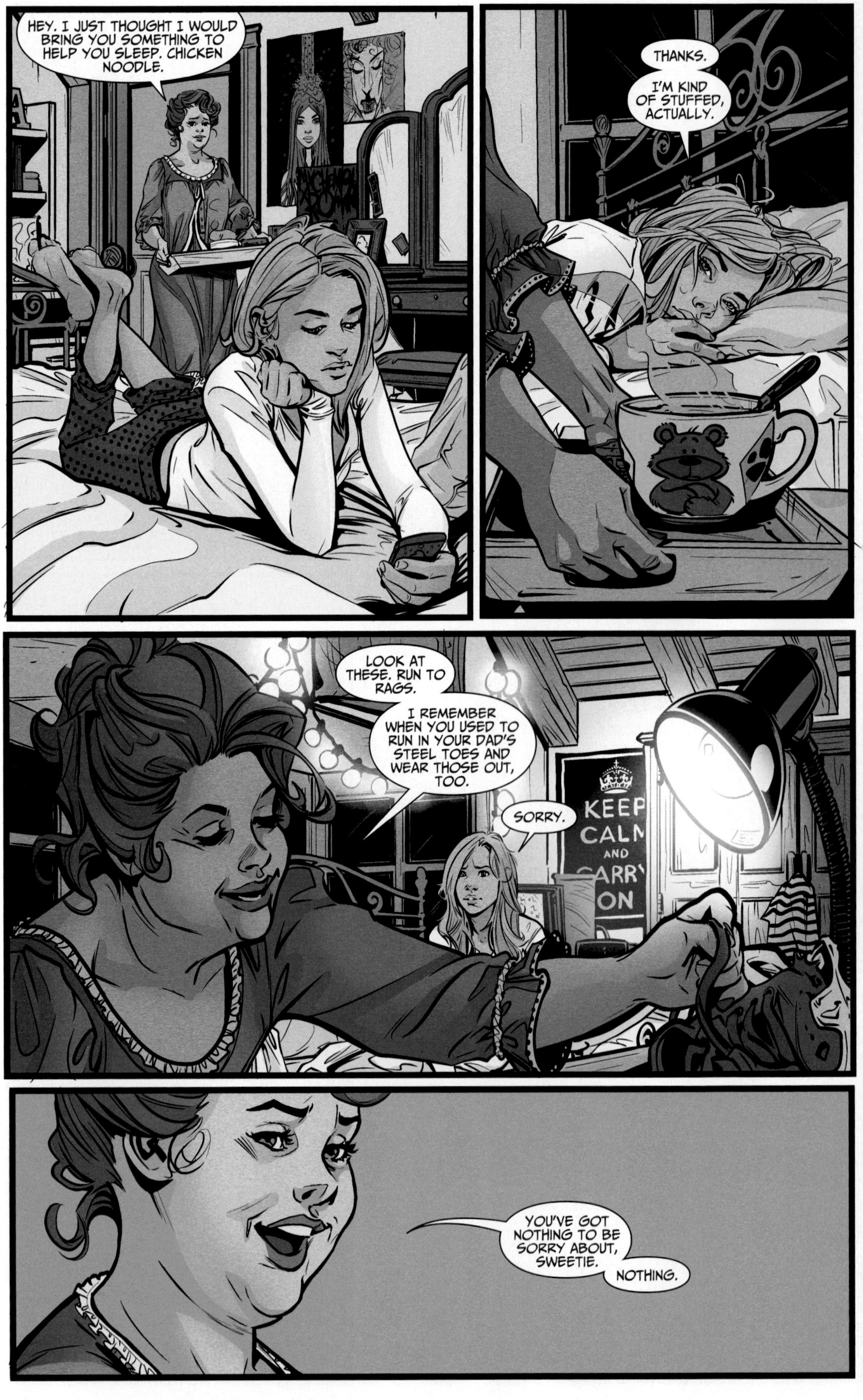
HEY. I JUST THOUGHT I WOULD BRING YOU SOMETHING TO HELP YOU SLEEP. CHICKEN NOODLE.
THANKS.
I'M KIND OF STUFFED, ACTUALLY.
LOOK AT THESE. RUN TO RAGS.
I REMEMBER WHEN YOU USED TO RUN IN YOUR DAD'S STEEL TOES AND WEAR THOSE OUT, TOO.
SORRY.
YOU'VE GOT NOTHING TO BE SORRY ABOUT, SWEETIE.
NOTHING.

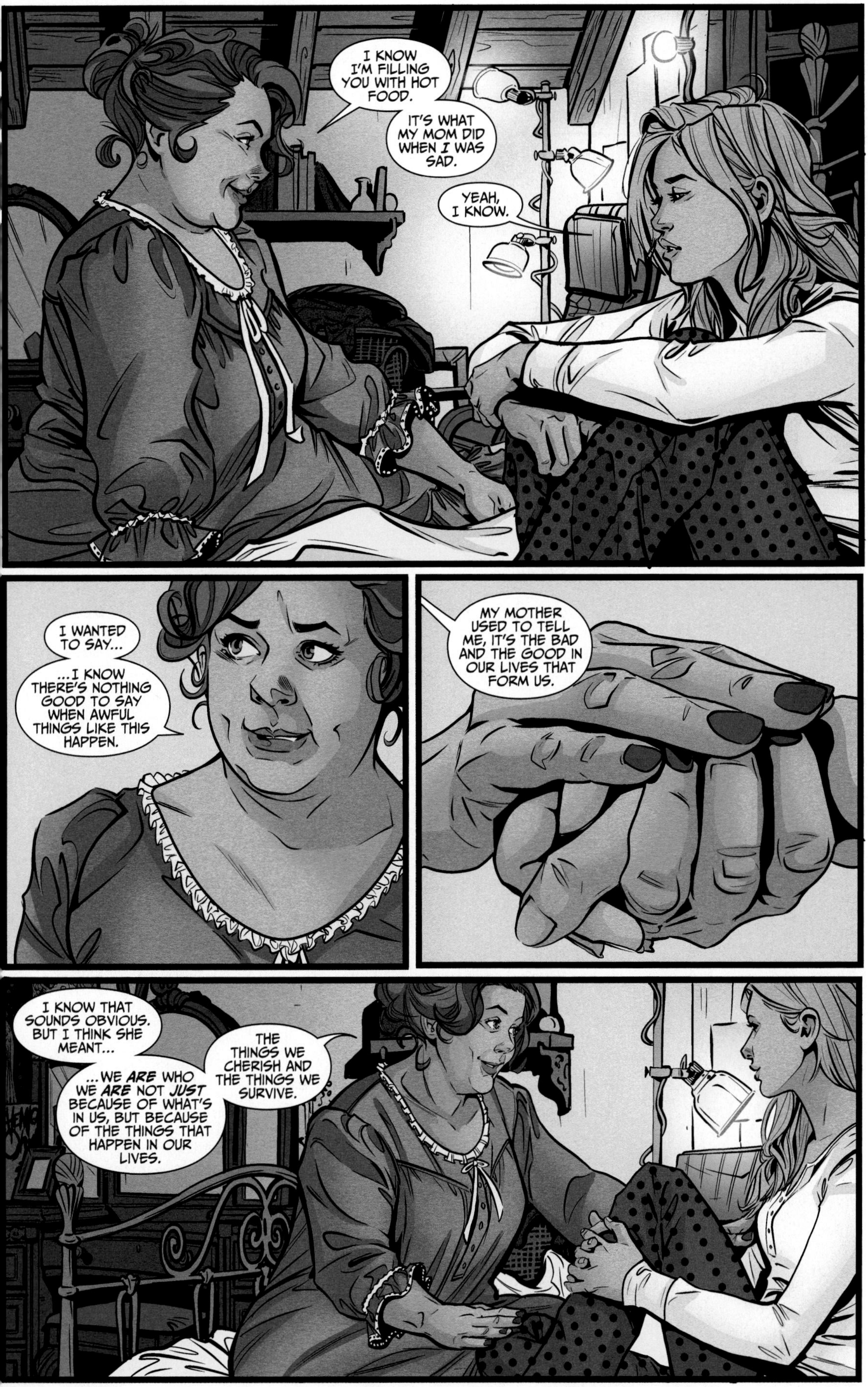
I KNOW I'M FILLING YOU WITH HOT FOOD.
IT'S WHAT MY MOM DID WHEN *I* WAS SAD.
YEAH, I KNOW.
I WANTED TO SAY...
...I KNOW THERE'S NOTHING GOOD TO SAY WHEN AWFUL THINGS LIKE THIS HAPPEN.
MY MOTHER USED TO TELL ME, IT'S THE BAD AND THE GOOD IN OUR LIVES THAT FORM US.
I KNOW THAT SOUNDS OBVIOUS. BUT I THINK SHE MEANT...
...WE ***ARE*** WHO WE ***ARE*** NOT ***JUST*** BECAUSE OF WHAT'S IN US, BUT BECAUSE OF THE THINGS THAT HAPPEN IN OUR LIVES.
THE THINGS WE CHERISH AND THE THINGS WE SURVIVE.

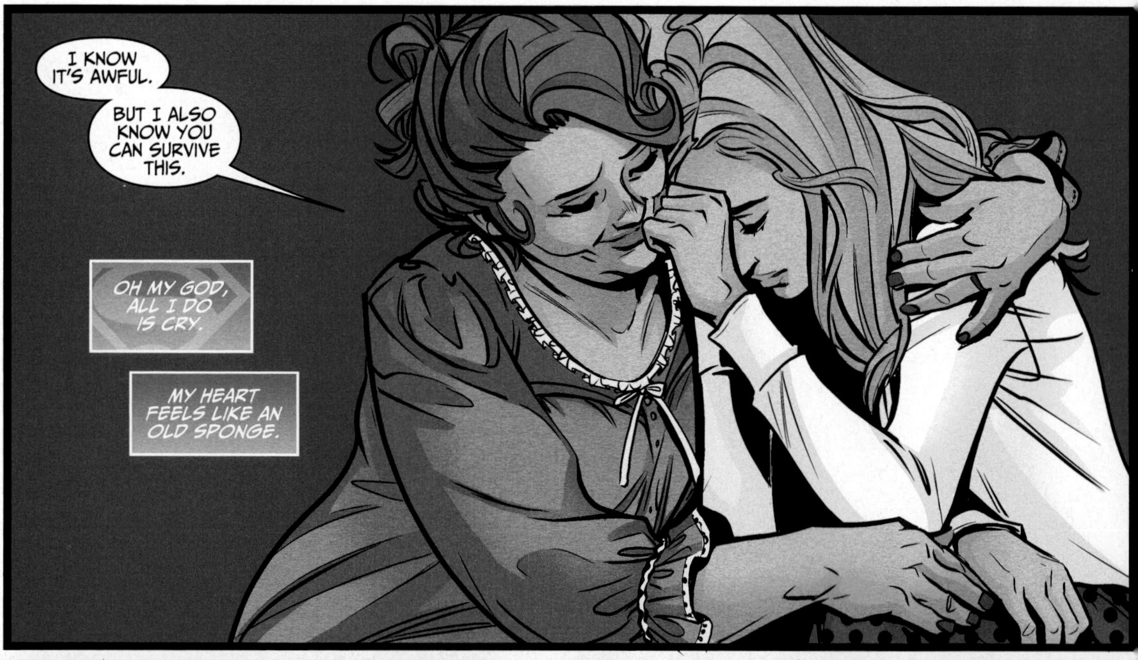
I KNOW IT'S AWFUL.
BUT I ALSO KNOW YOU CAN SURVIVE THIS.
OH MY GOD, ALL I DO IS CRY.
MY HEART FEELS LIKE AN OLD SPONGE.

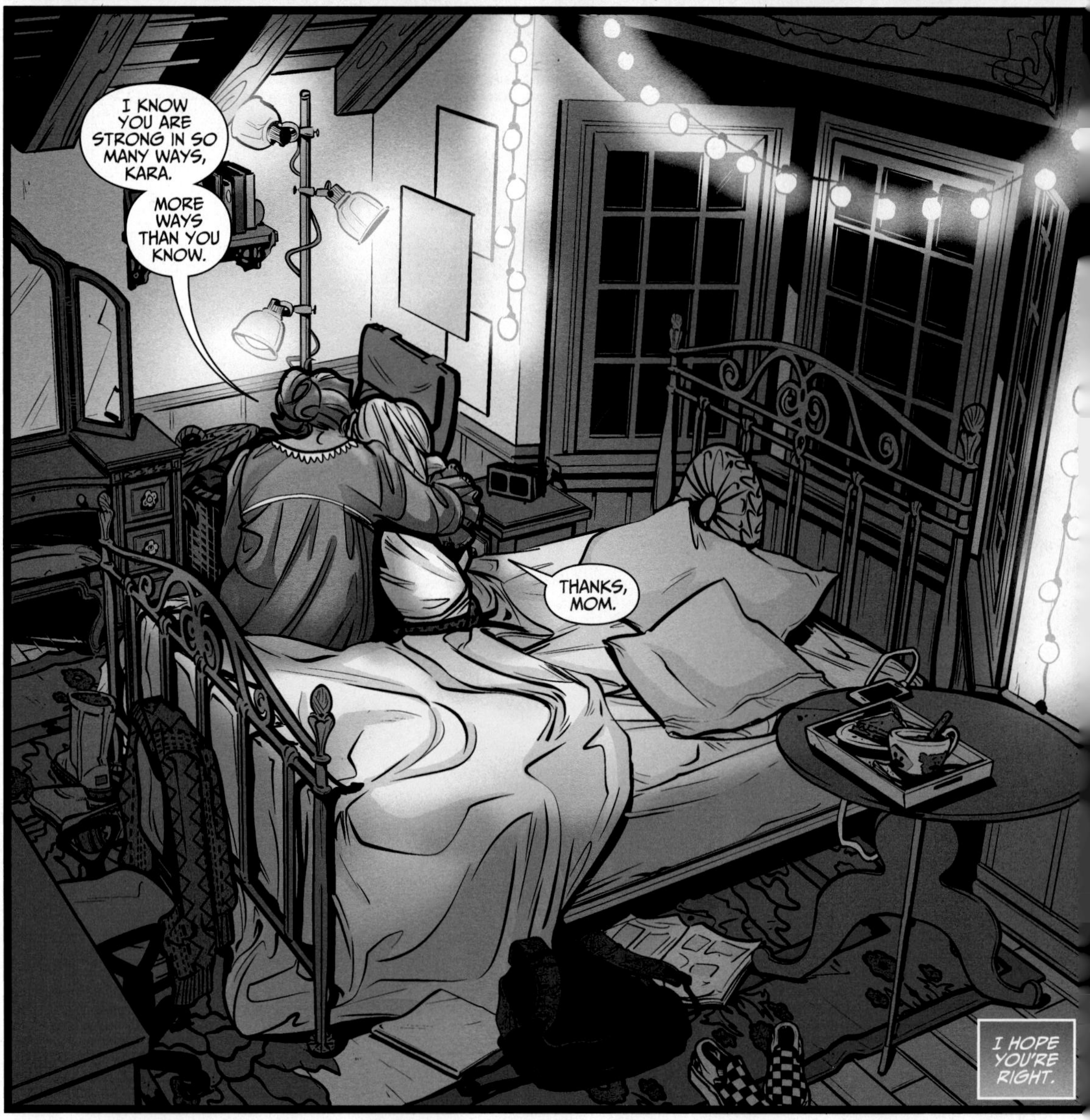
I KNOW YOU ARE STRONG IN SO MANY WAYS, KARA.
MORE WAYS THAN YOU KNOW.
THANKS, MOM.
I HOPE YOU'RE RIGHT.

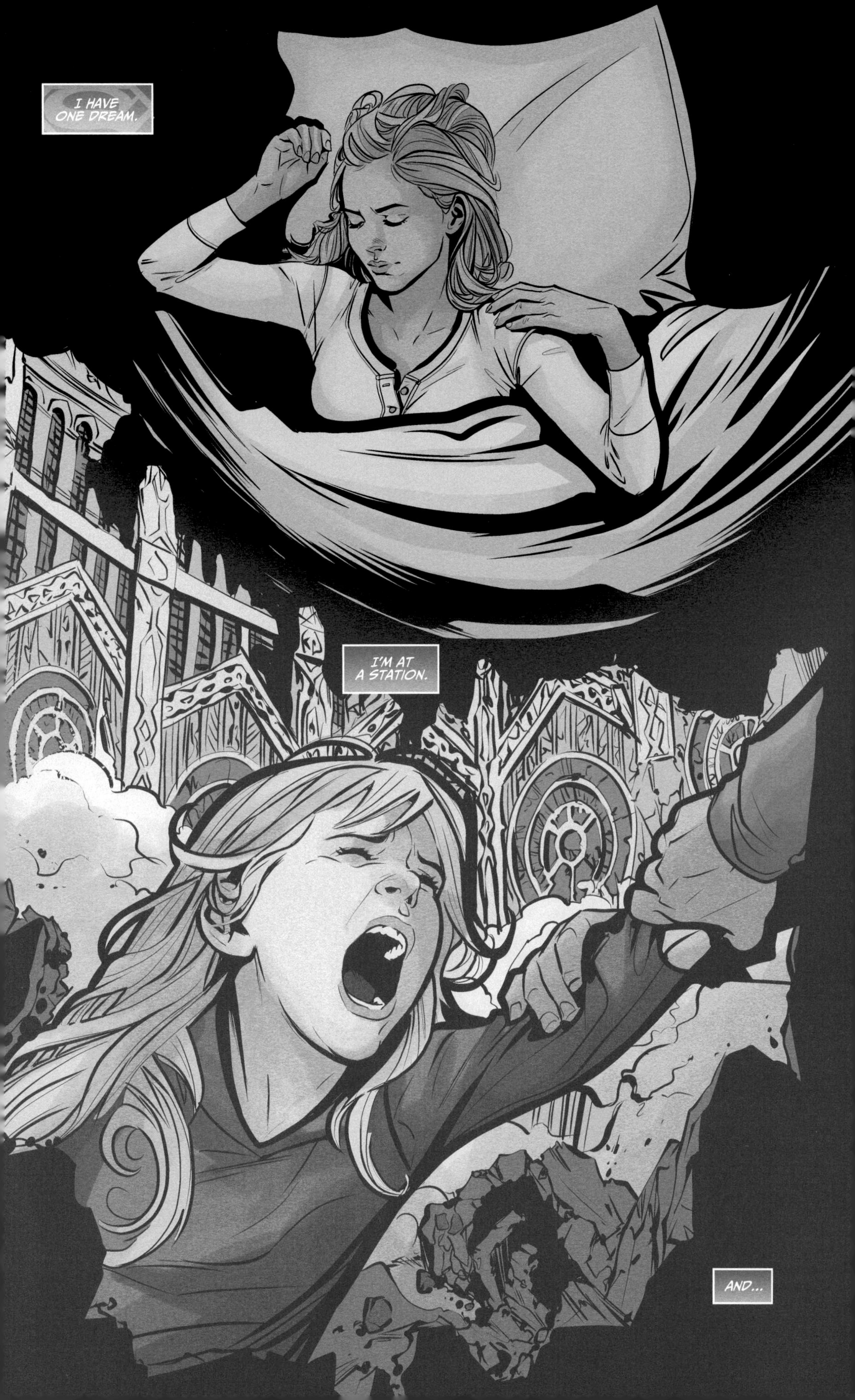
I HAVE ONE DREAM.
I'M AT A STATION.
AND...

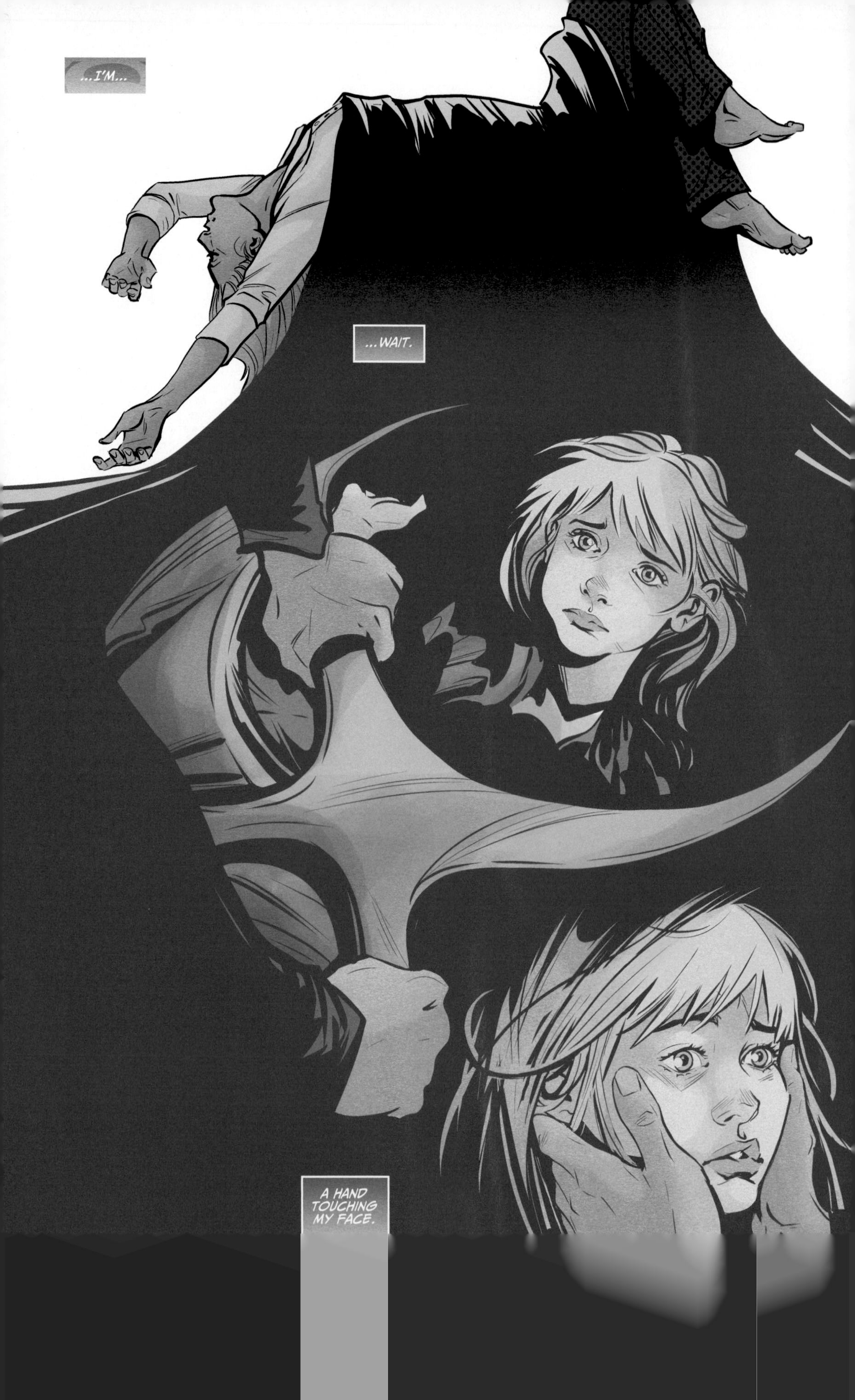
...I'M...
...WAIT.
A HAND TOUCHING MY FACE.

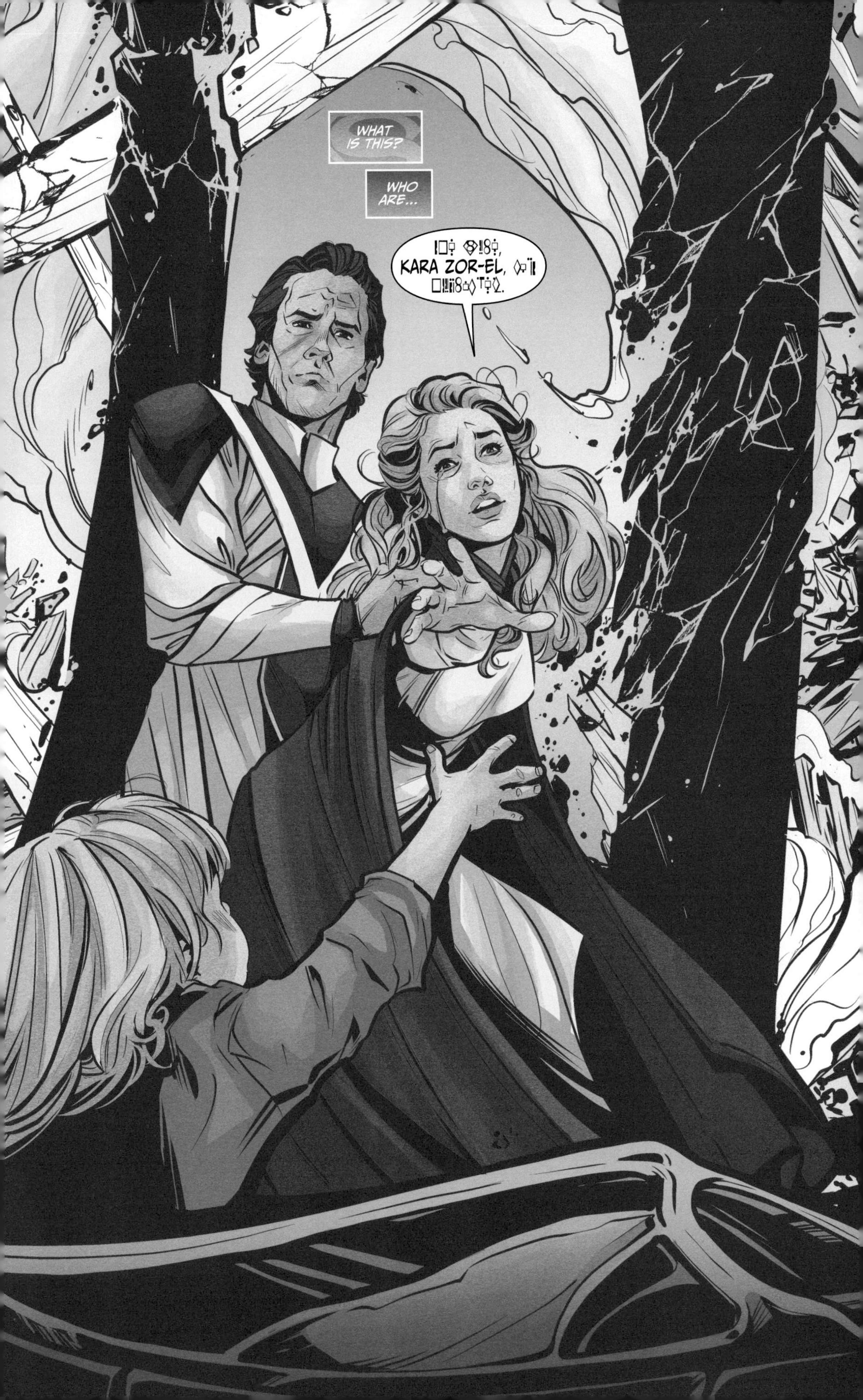
WHAT IS THIS?
WHO ARE...
KARA ZOR-EL,

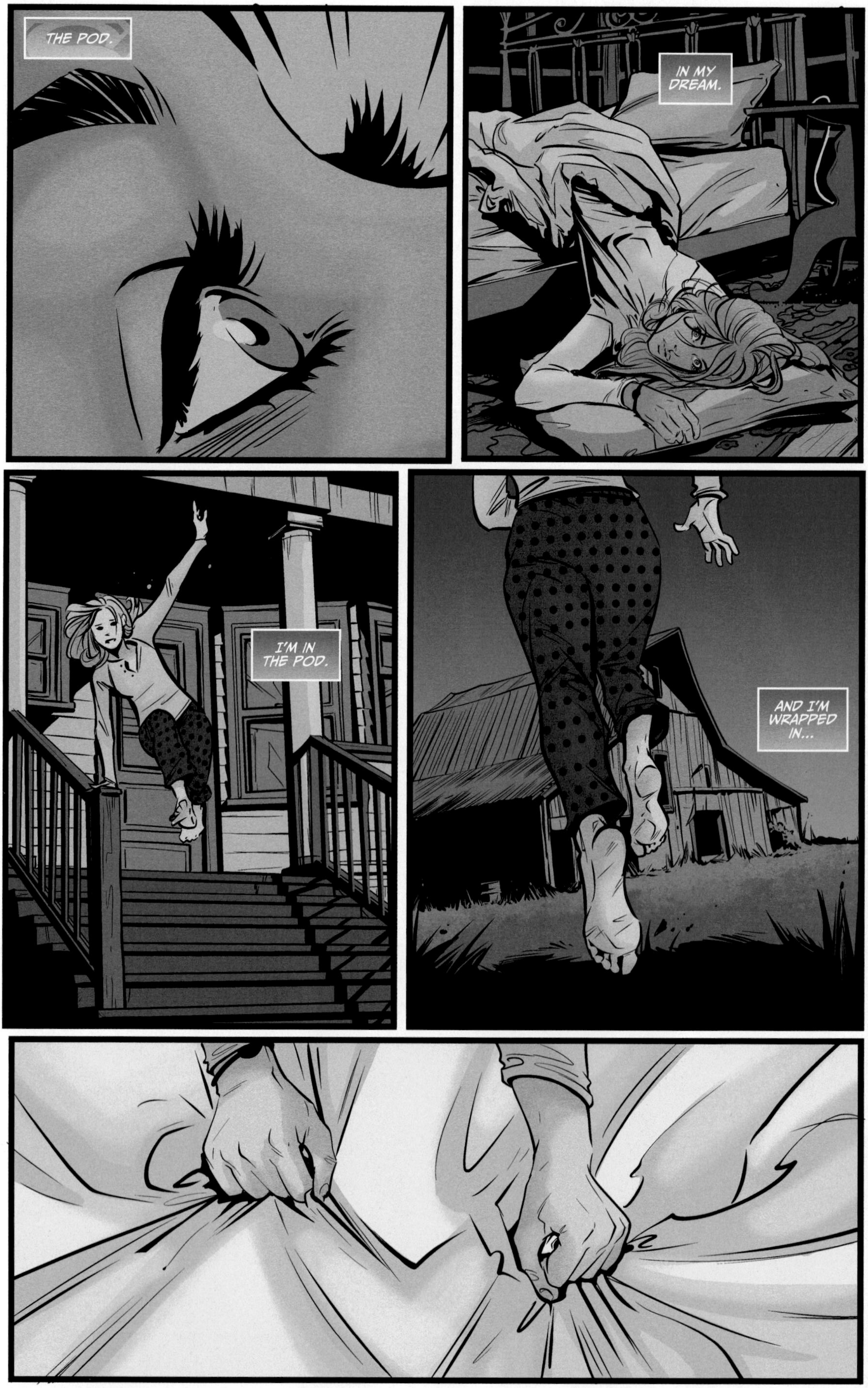
THE POD.
IN MY DREAM.
I'M IN THE POD.
AND I'M WRAPPED IN...

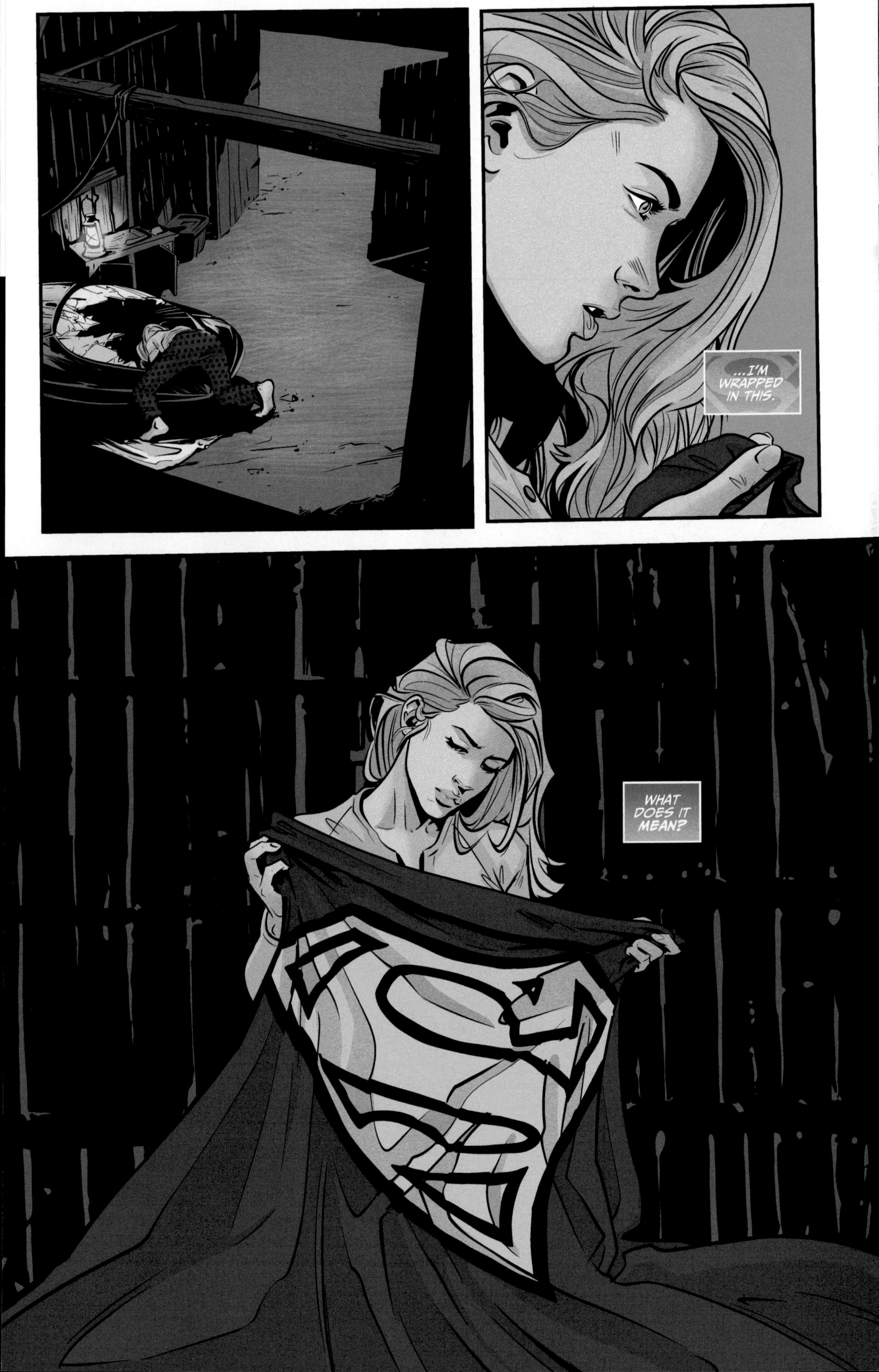
...I'M WRAPPED IN THIS.
WHAT DOES IT MEAN?

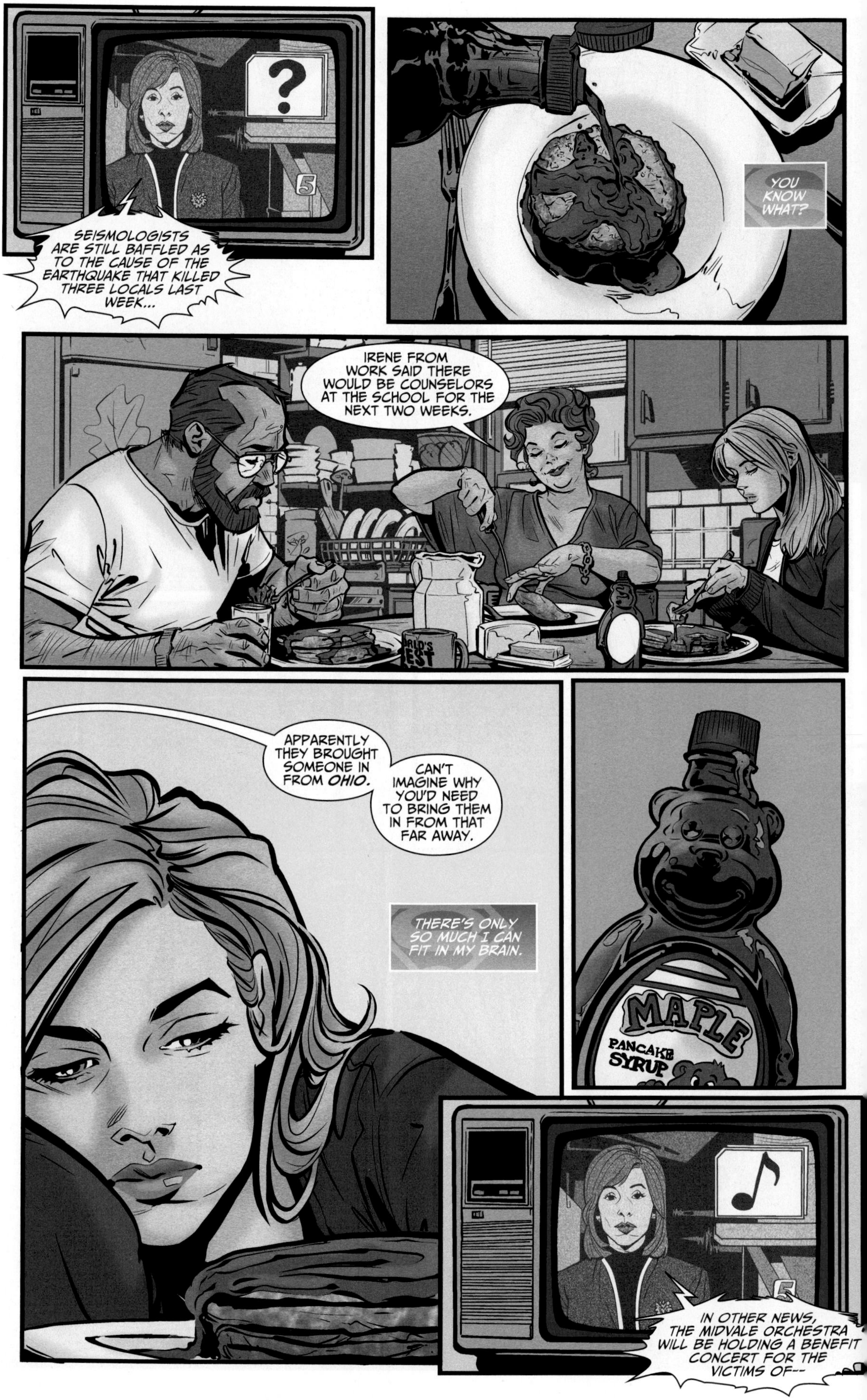
SEISMOLOGISTS ARE STILL BAFFLED AS TO THE CAUSE OF THE EARTHQUAKE THAT KILLED THREE LOCALS LAST WEEK...
YOU KNOW WHAT?
IRENE FROM WORK SAID THERE WOULD BE COUNSELORS AT THE SCHOOL FOR THE NEXT TWO WEEKS.
APPARENTLY THEY BROUGHT SOMEONE IN FROM *OHIO*.
CAN'T IMAGINE WHY YOU'D NEED TO BRING THEM IN FROM THAT FAR AWAY.
THERE'S ONLY SO MUCH I CAN FIT IN MY BRAIN.
MAPLE
PANCAKE SYRUP
IN OTHER NEWS, THE MIDVALE ORCHESTRA WILL BE HOLDING A BENEFIT CONCERT FOR THE VICTIMS OF--

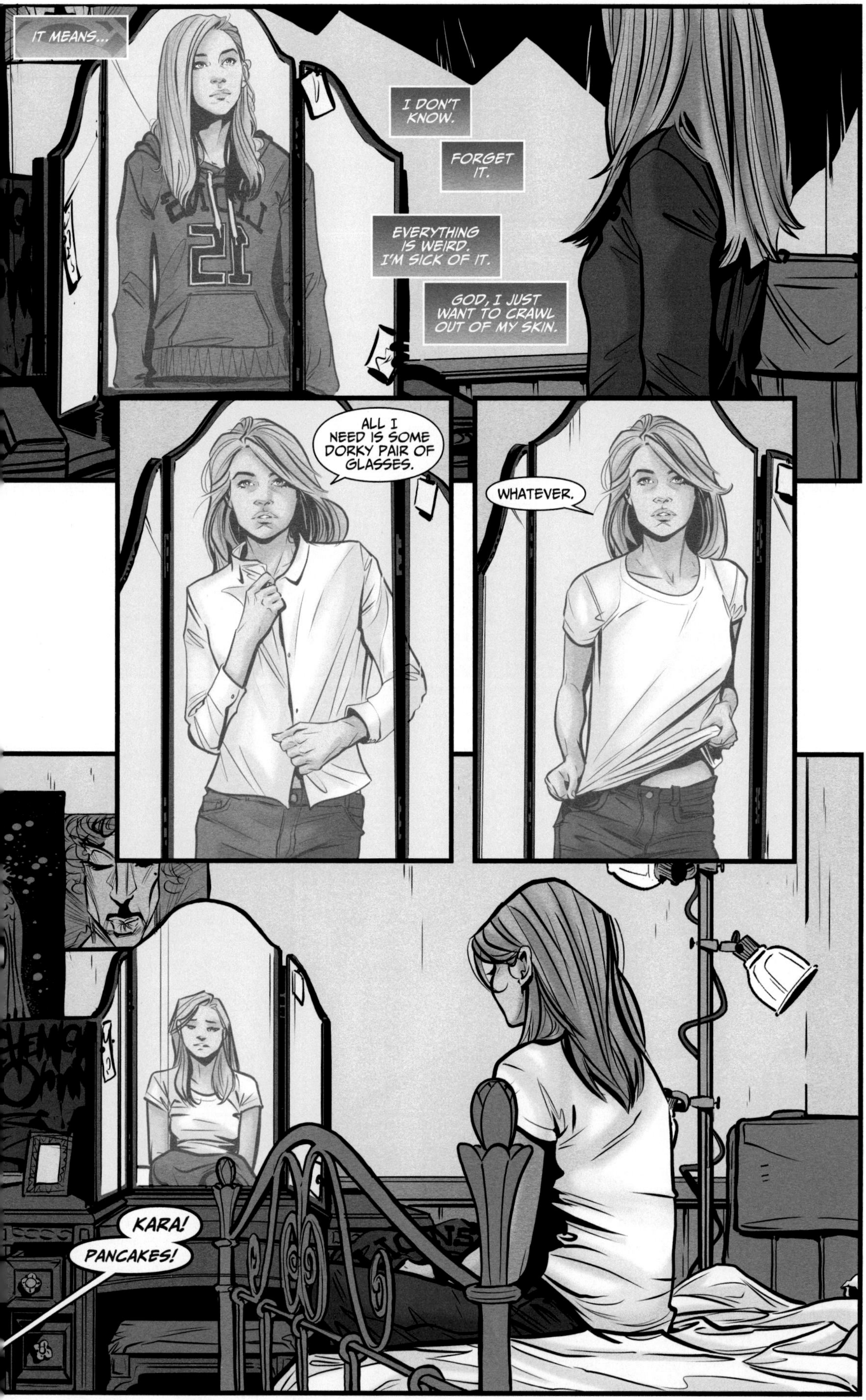
IT MEANS...
I DON'T KNOW.
FORGET IT.
EVERYTHING IS WEIRD. I'M SICK OF IT.
GOD, I JUST WANT TO CRAWL OUT OF MY SKIN.
ALL I NEED IS SOME DORKY PAIR OF GLASSES.
WHATEVER.
KARA!
PANCAKES!

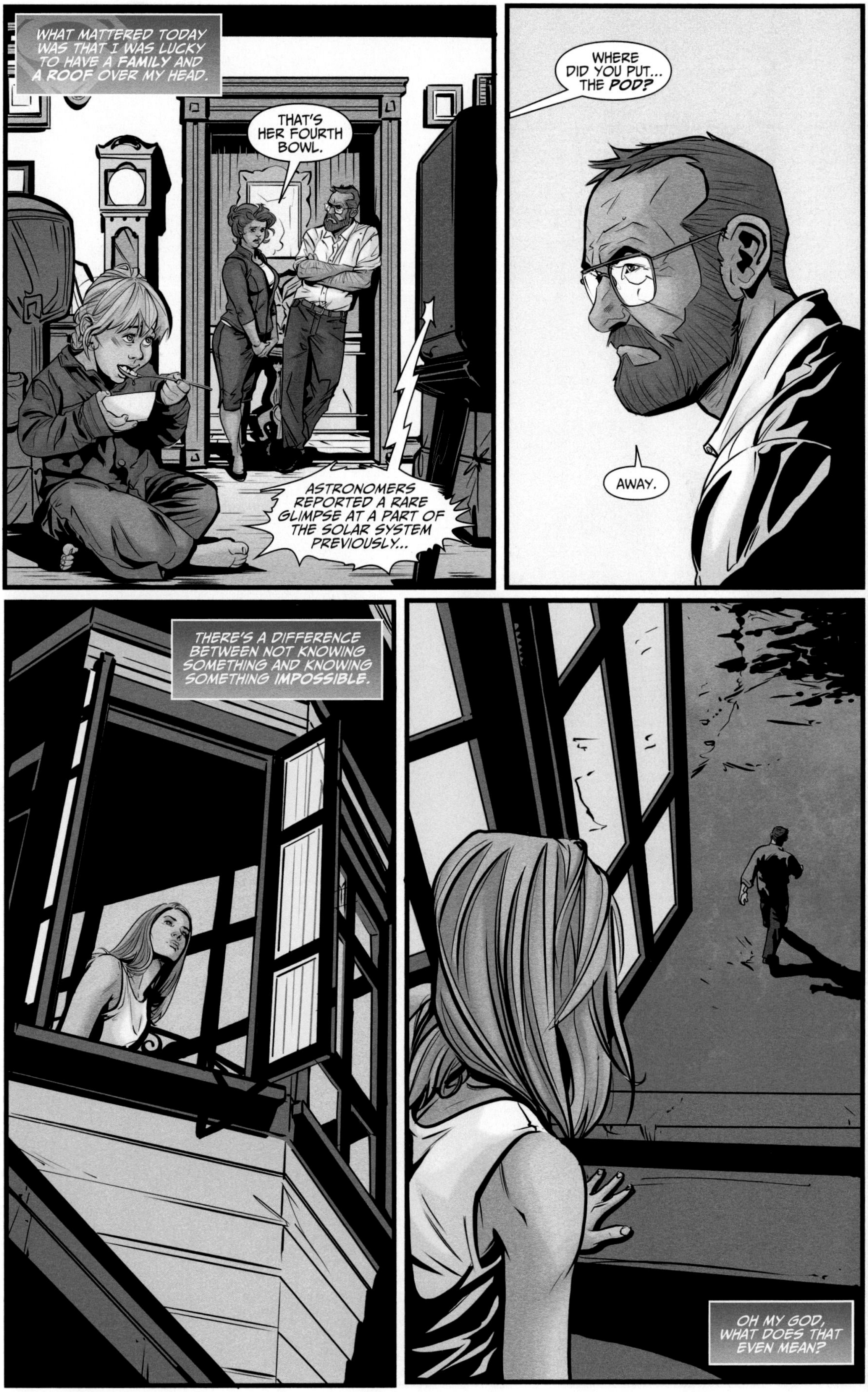
WHAT MATTERED TODAY WAS THAT I WAS LUCKY TO HAVE A FAMILY AND A ROOF OVER MY HEAD.
THAT'S HER FOURTH BOWL.
ASTRONOMERS REPORTED A RARE GLIMPSE AT A PART OF THE SOLAR SYSTEM PREVIOUSLY...
WHERE DID YOU PUT... THE POD?
AWAY.
THERE'S A DIFFERENCE BETWEEN NOT KNOWING SOMETHING AND KNOWING SOMETHING IMPOSSIBLE.
OH MY GOD, WHAT DOES THAT EVEN MEAN?

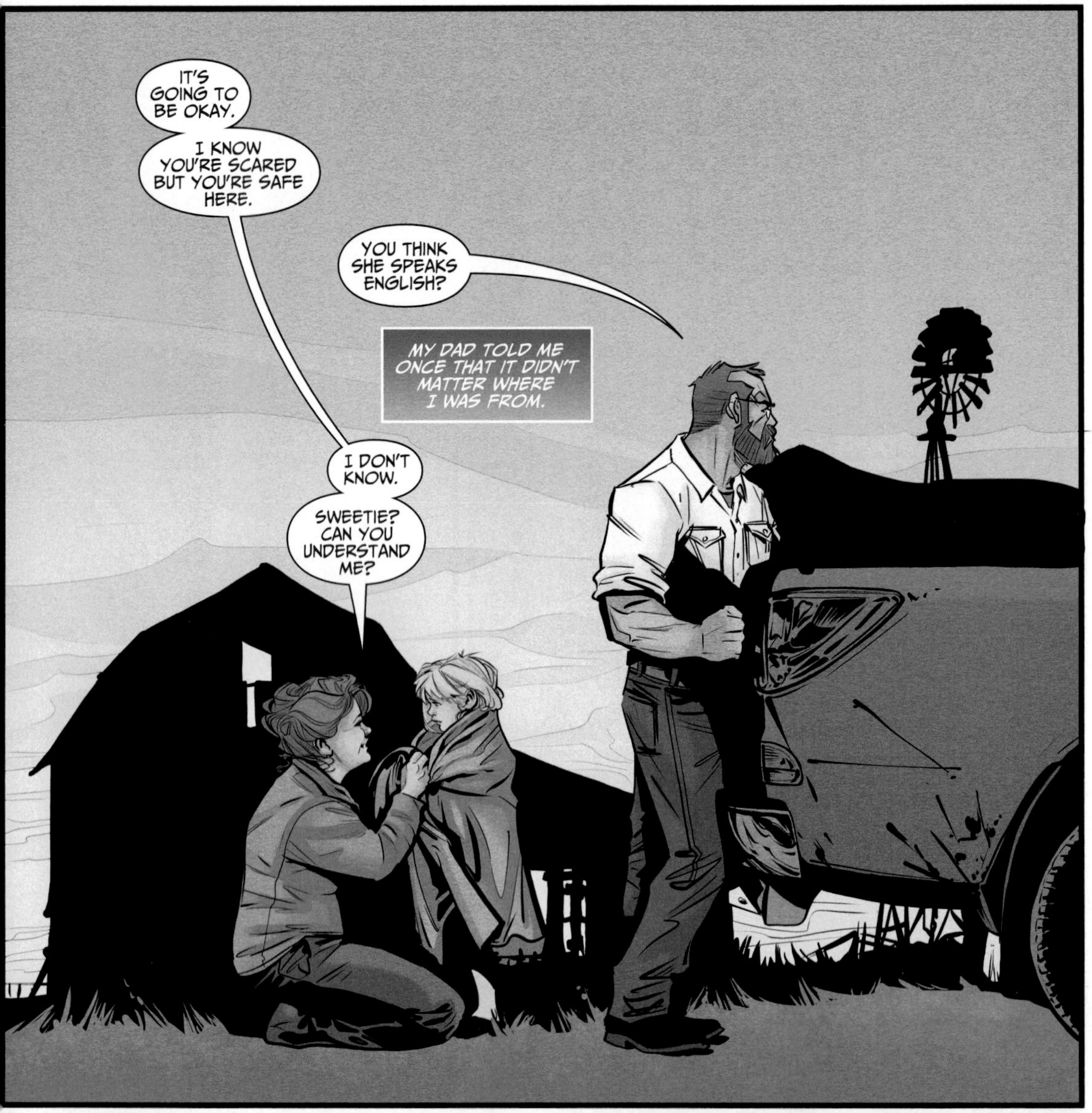
IT'S GOING TO BE OKAY.
I KNOW YOU'RE SCARED BUT YOU'RE SAFE HERE.
YOU THINK SHE SPEAKS ENGLISH?
MY DAD TOLD ME ONCE THAT IT DIDN'T MATTER WHERE I WAS FROM.
I DON'T KNOW.
SWEETIE? CAN YOU UNDERSTAND ME?

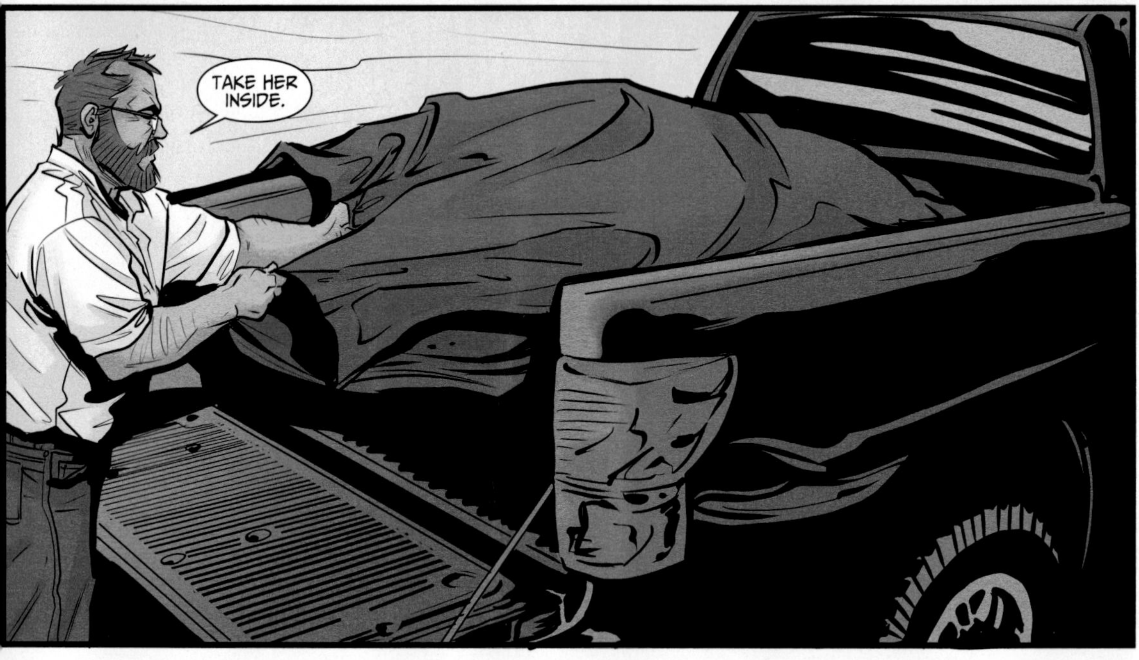
TAKE HER INSIDE.

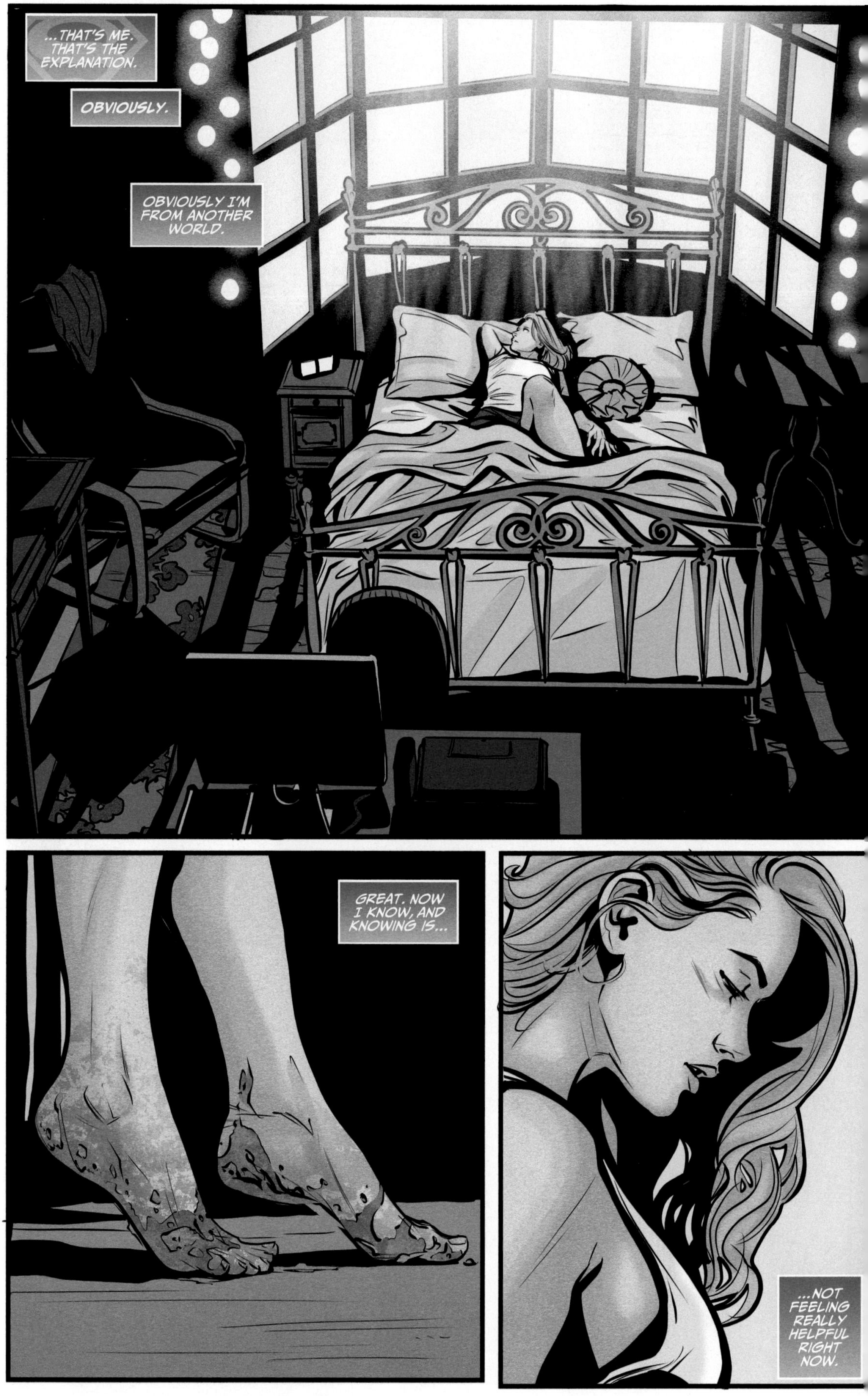
...THAT'S ME. THAT'S THE EXPLANATION.
OBVIOUSLY.
OBVIOUSLY I'M FROM ANOTHER WORLD.
GREAT. NOW I KNOW, AND KNOWING IS...
...NOT FEELING REALLY HELPFUL RIGHT NOW.

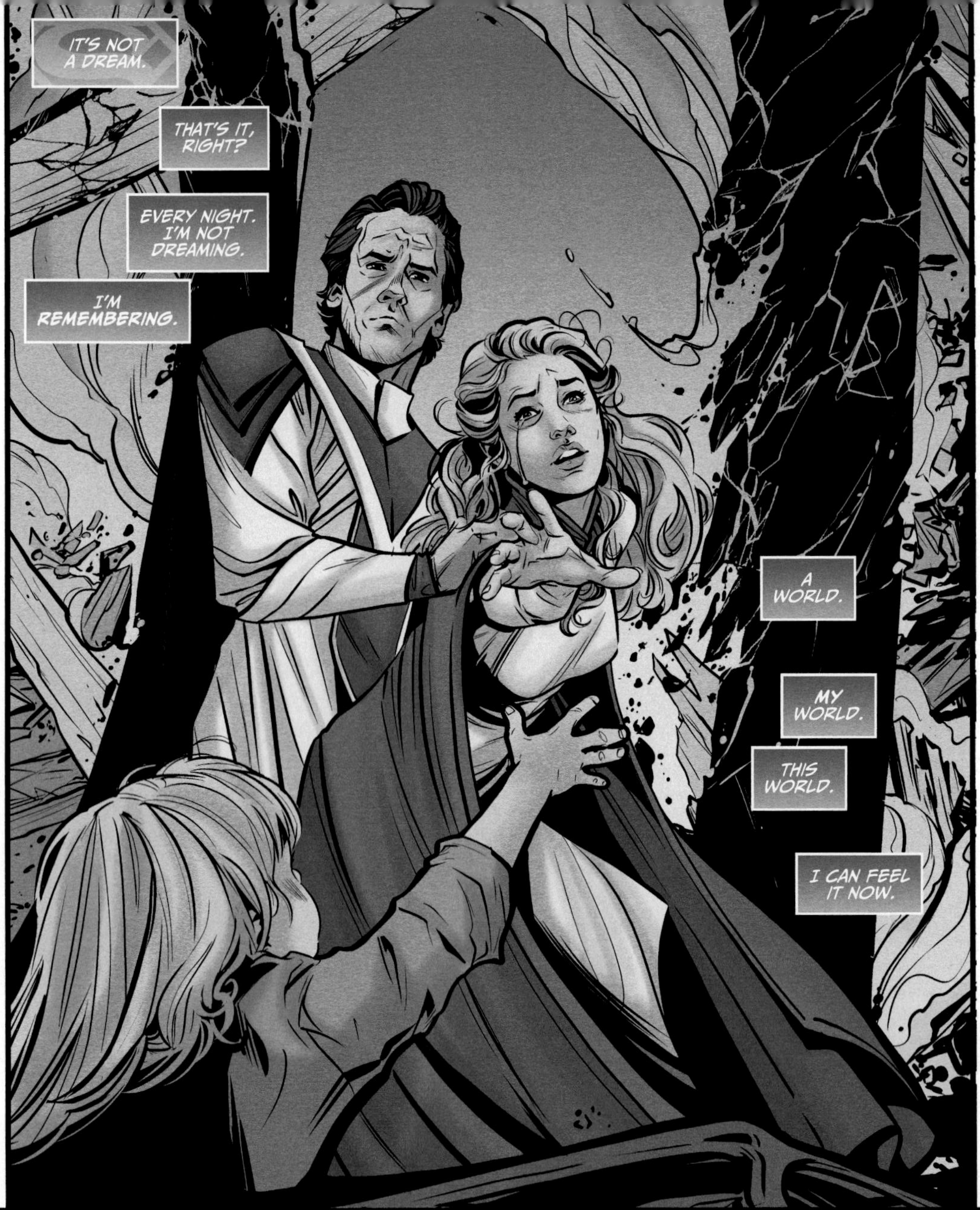
IT'S NOT A DREAM.
THAT'S IT, RIGHT?
EVERY NIGHT. I'M NOT DREAMING.
I'M REMEMBERING.
A WORLD.
MY WORLD.
THIS WORLD.
I CAN FEEL IT NOW.

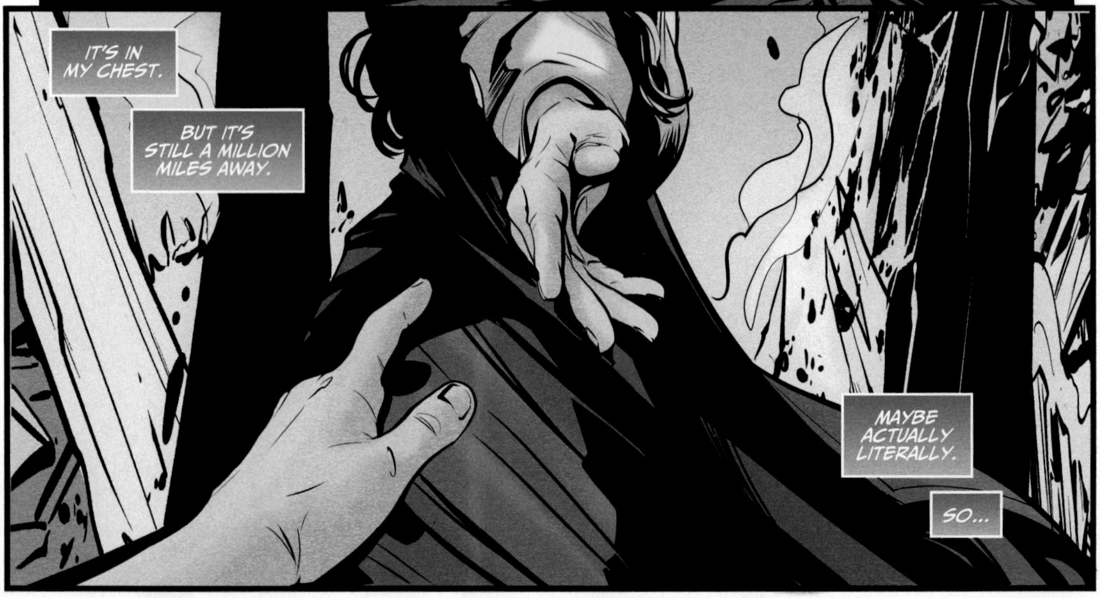
IT'S IN MY CHEST.
BUT IT'S STILL A MILLION MILES AWAY.
MAYBE ACTUALLY LITERALLY.
SO...

SUPERGIRL: BEING SUPER

CHAPTER THREE: WHO ARE YOU?

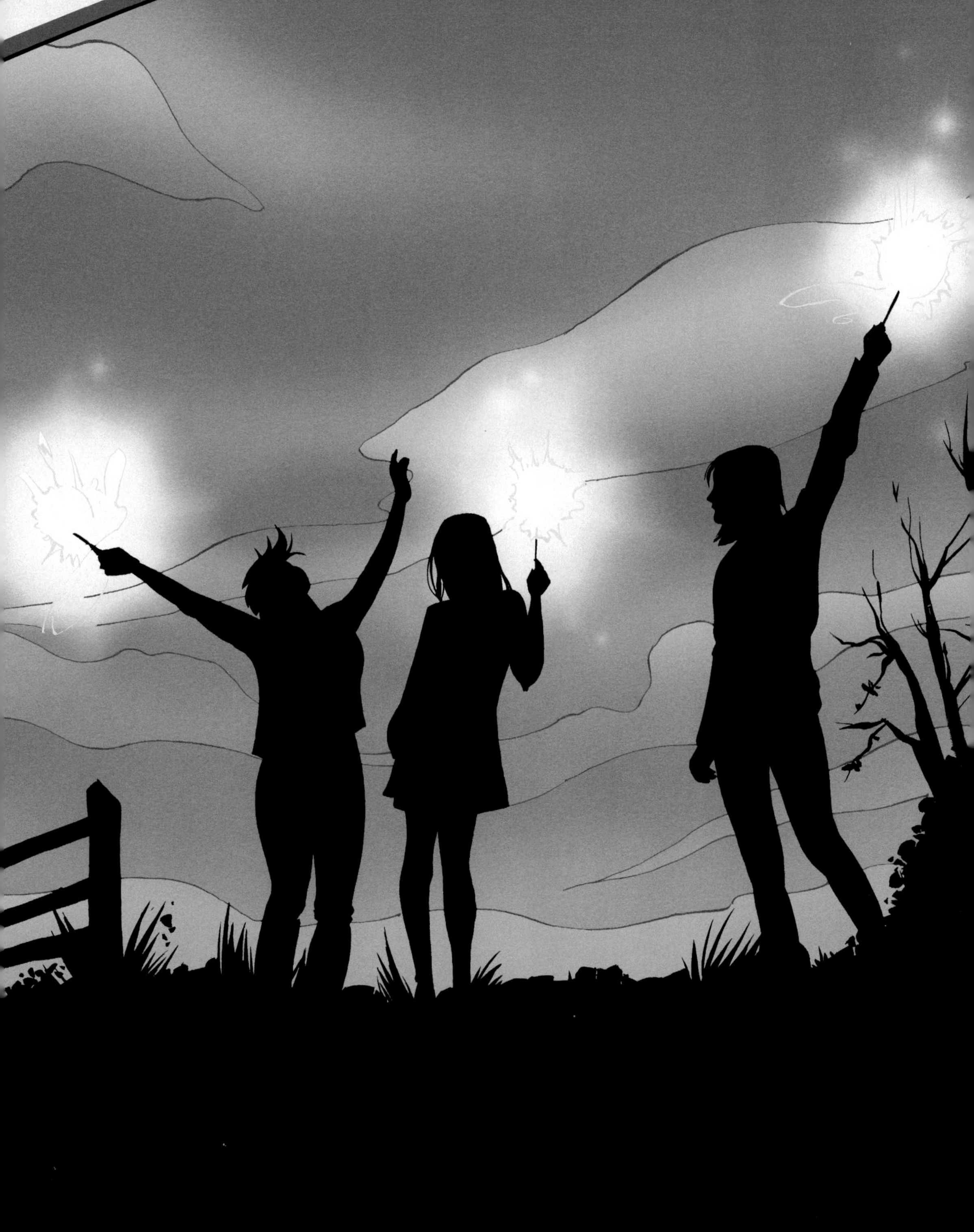

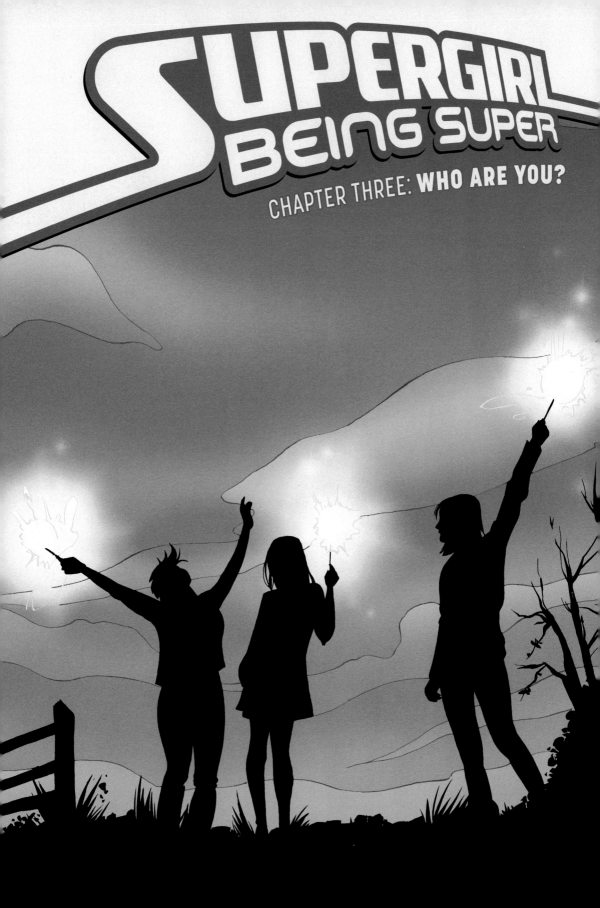

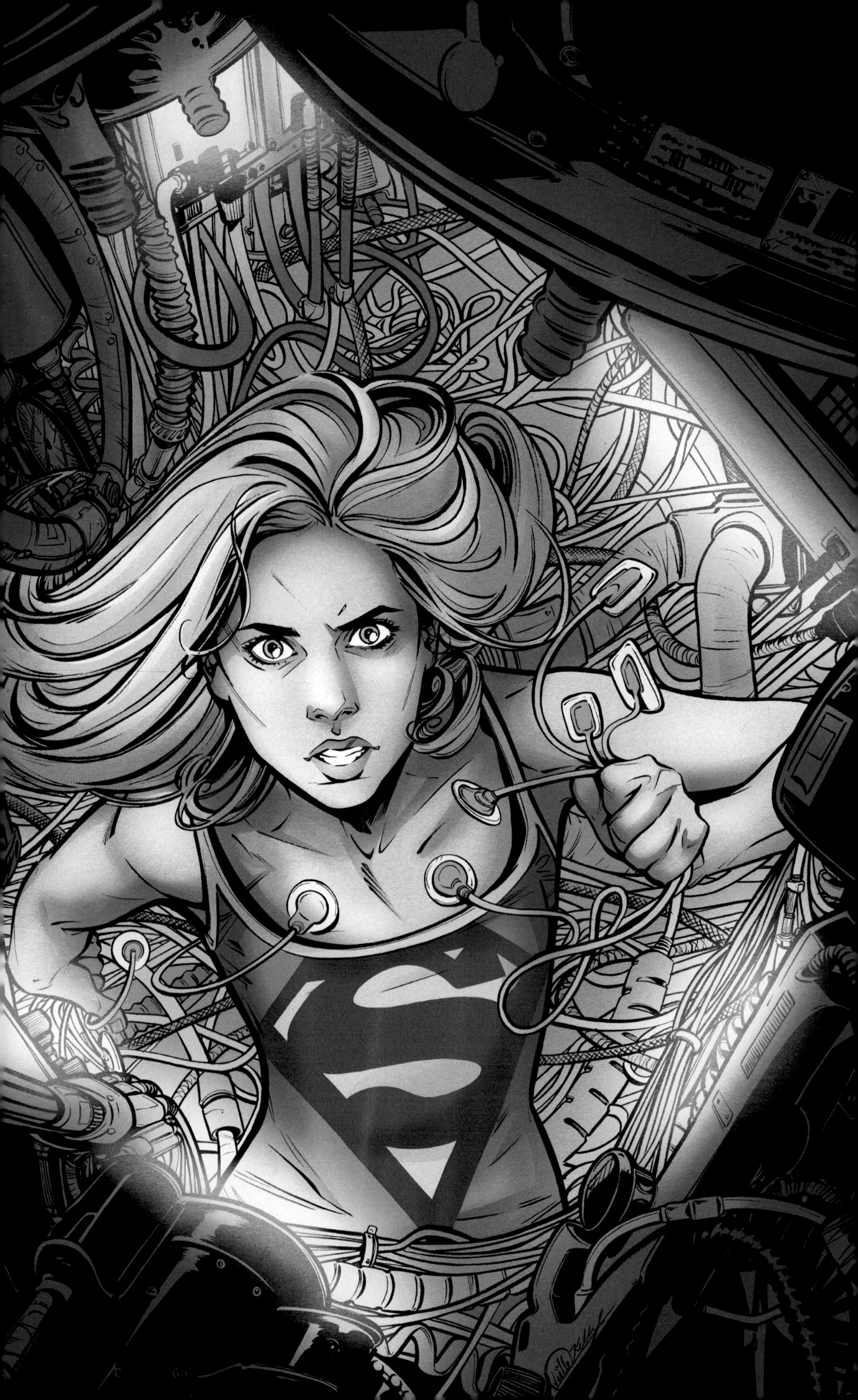

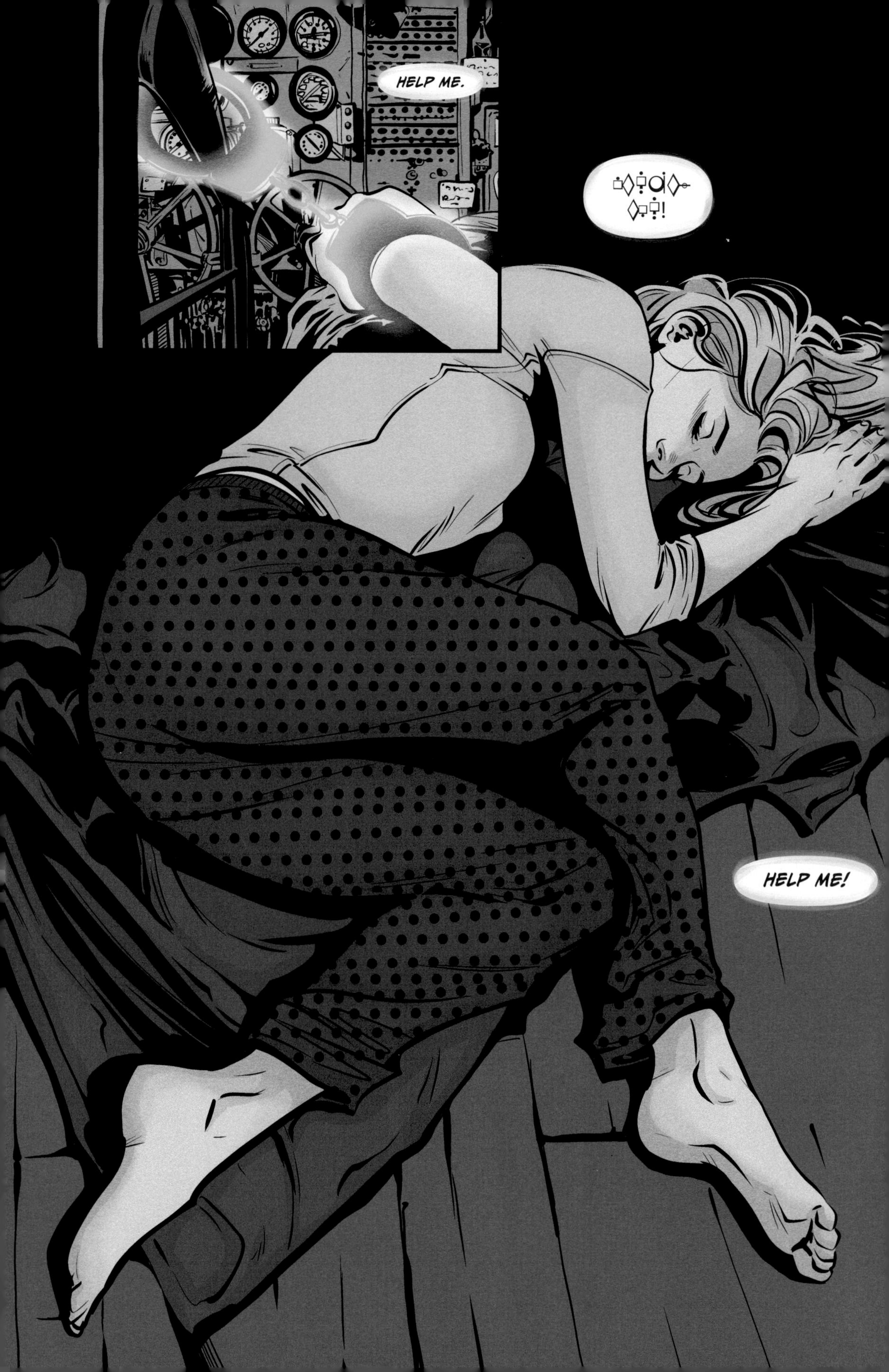
HELP ME.
HELP ME!

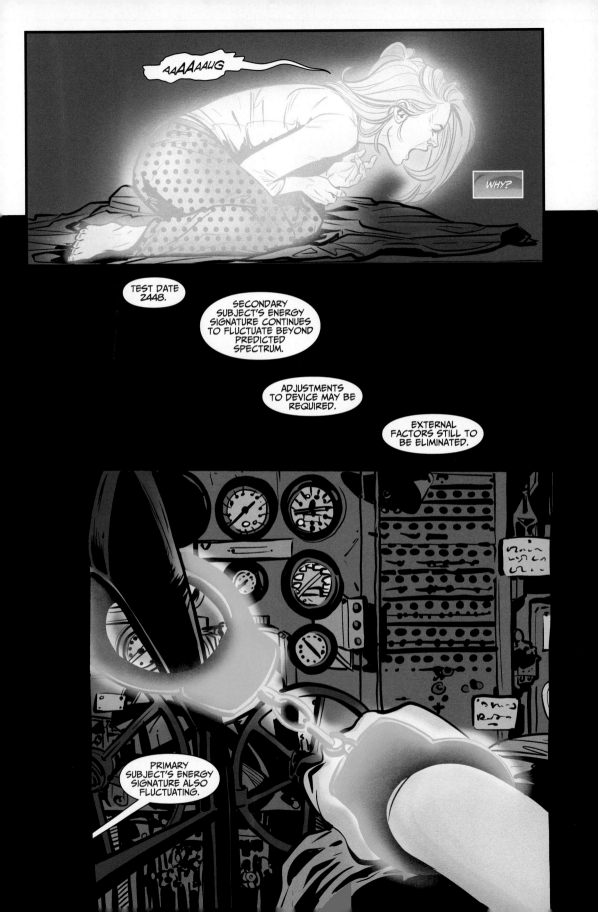

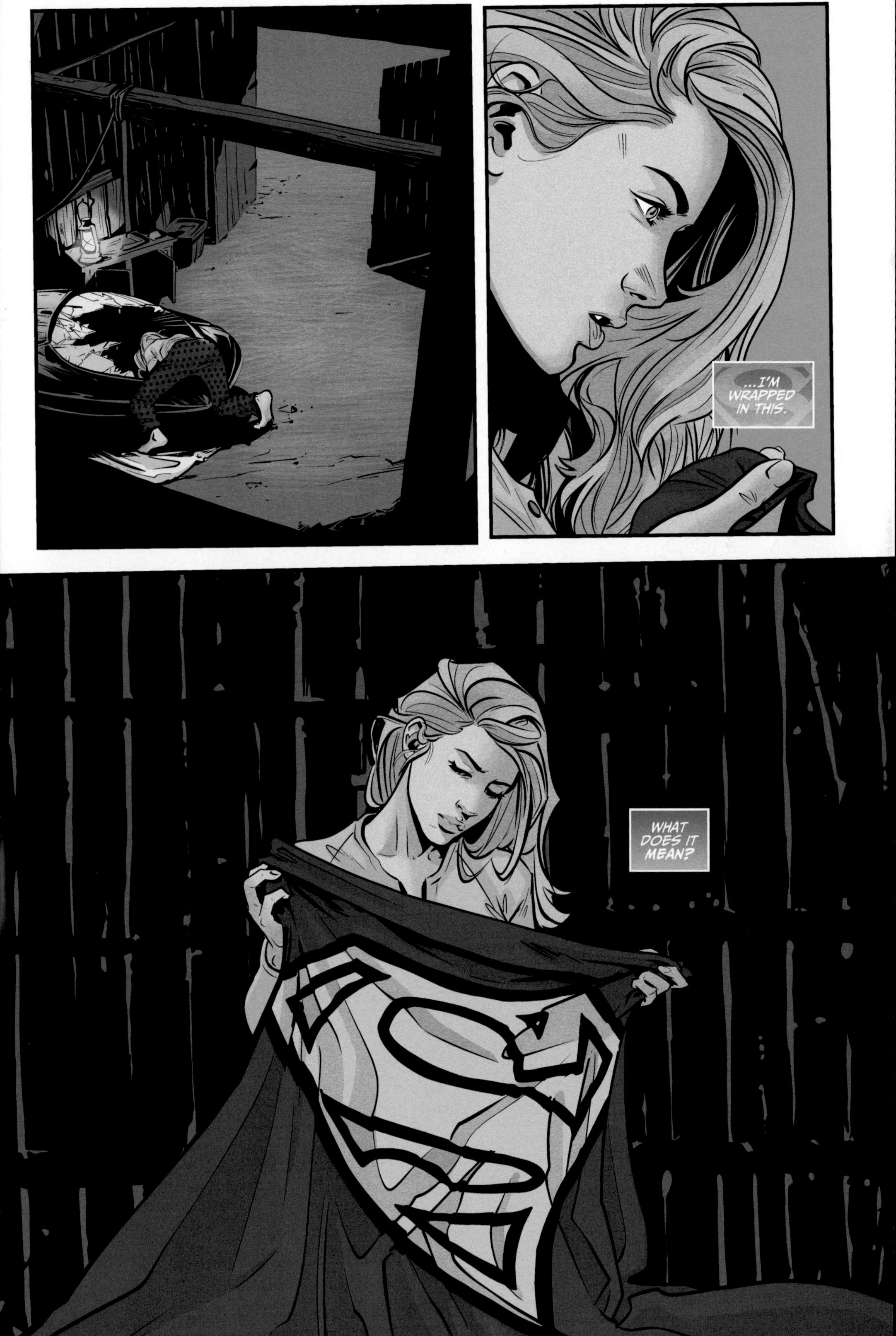
...I'M WRAPPED IN THIS.
WHAT DOES IT MEAN?

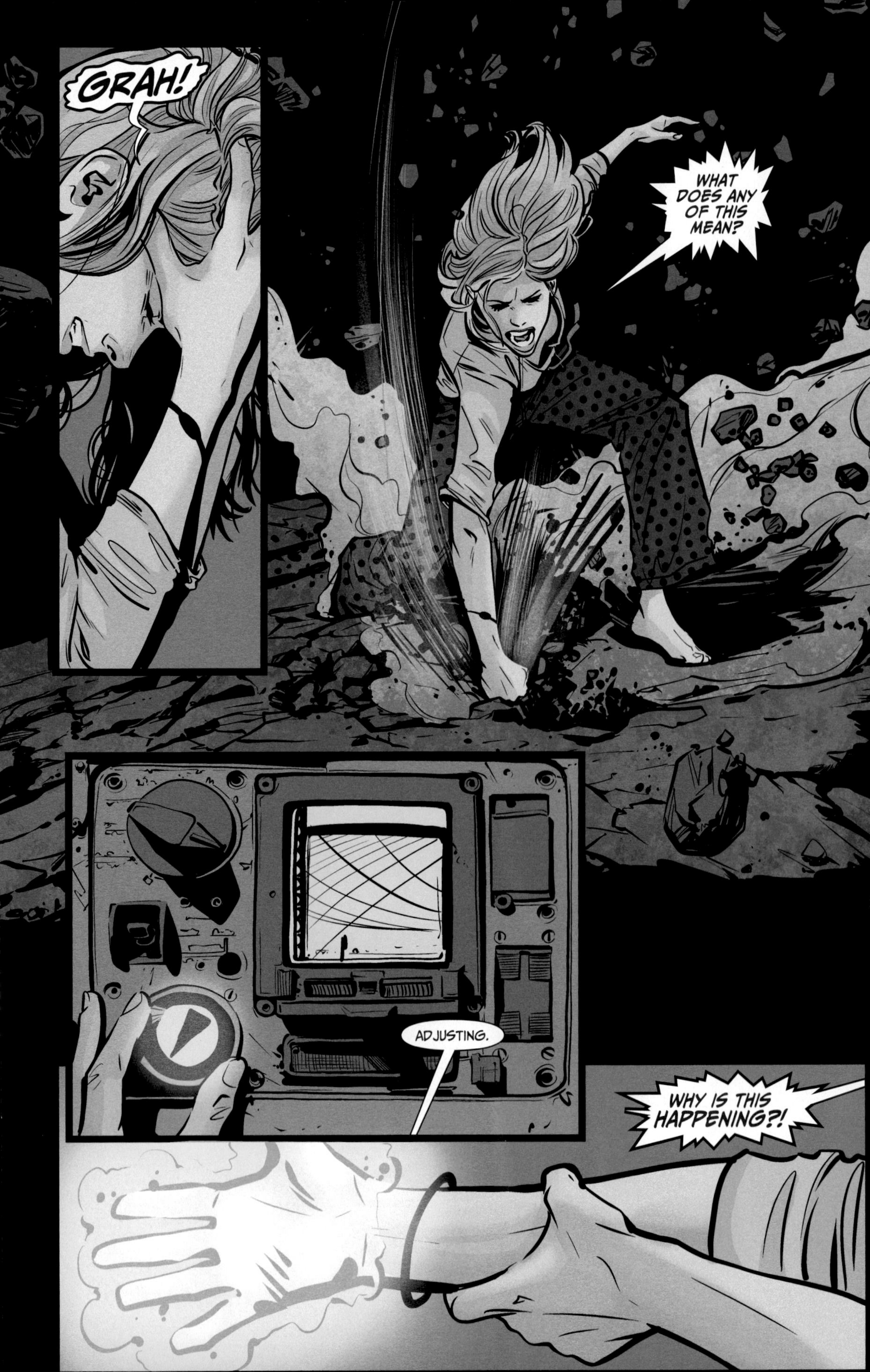
GRAH!
WHAT DOES ANY OF THIS MEAN?
ADJUSTING.
WHY IS THIS HAPPENING?!

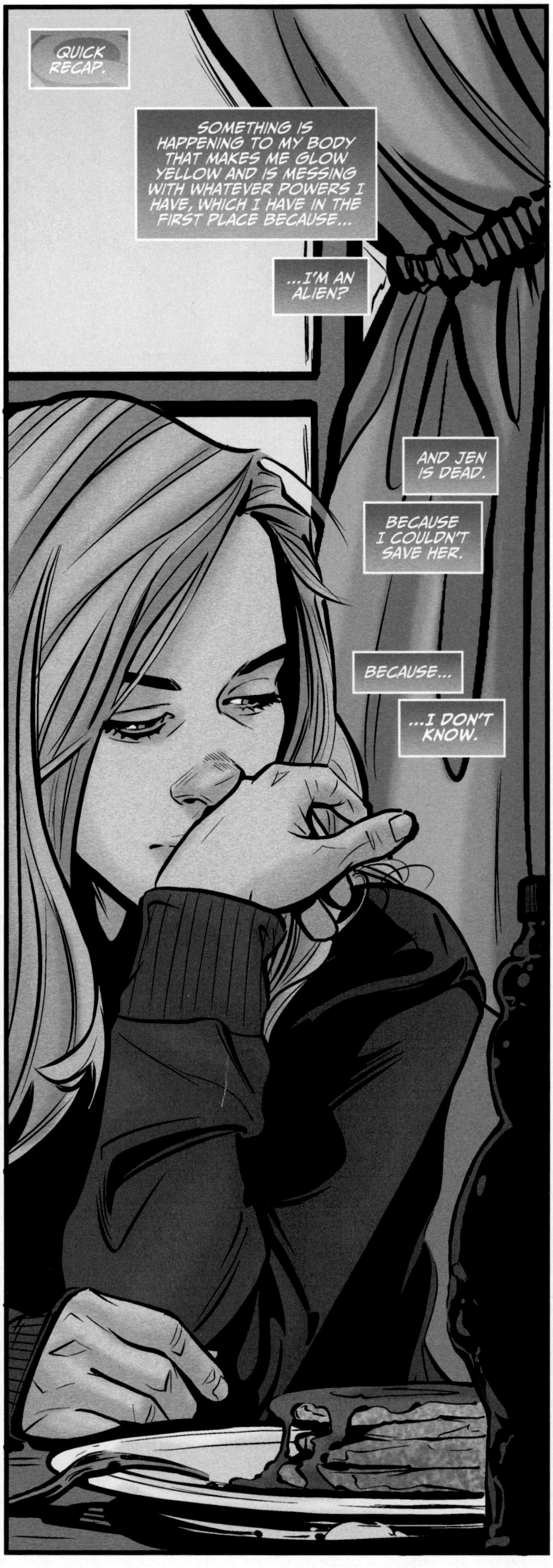
QUICK RECAP.
SOMETHING IS HAPPENING TO MY BODY THAT MAKES ME GLOW YELLOW AND IS MESSING WITH WHATEVER POWERS I HAVE, WHICH I HAVE IN THE FIRST PLACE BECAUSE...
...I'M AN ALIEN?
AND JEN IS DEAD.
BECAUSE I COULDN'T SAVE HER.
BECAUSE...
...I DON'T KNOW.

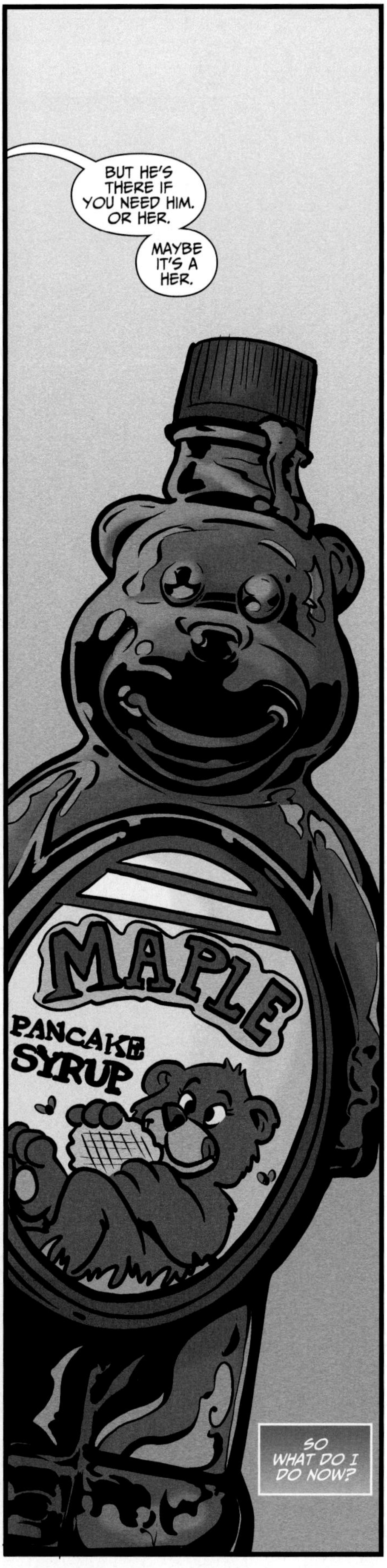
BUT HE'S THERE IF YOU NEED HIM. OR HER.
MAYBE IT'S A HER.
MAPLE
PANCAKE
SYRUP
SO WHAT DO I DO NOW?

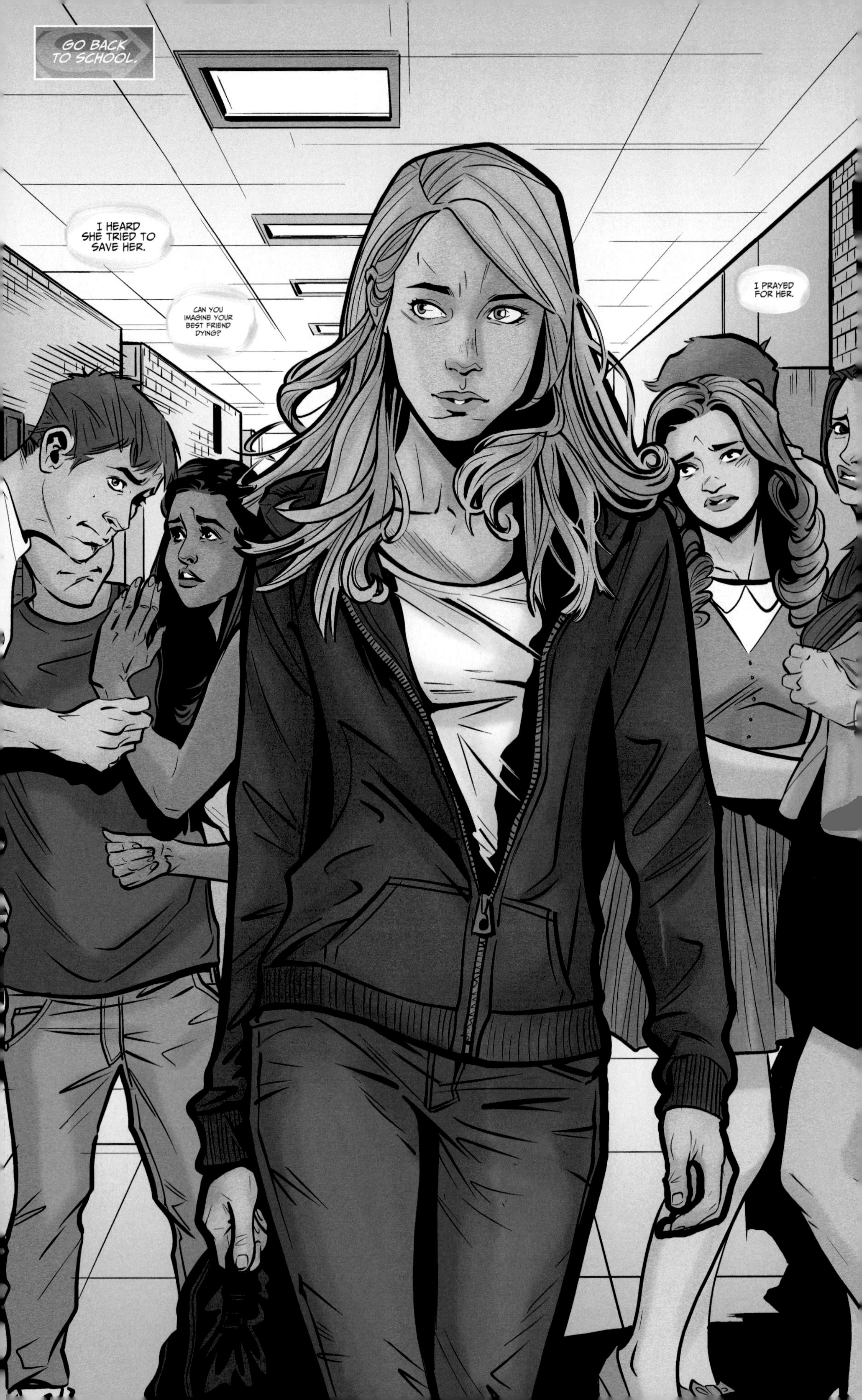
GO BACK TO SCHOOL.
I HEARD SHE TRIED TO SAVE HER.
CAN YOU IMAGINE YOUR BEST FRIEND DYING?
I PRAYED FOR HER.

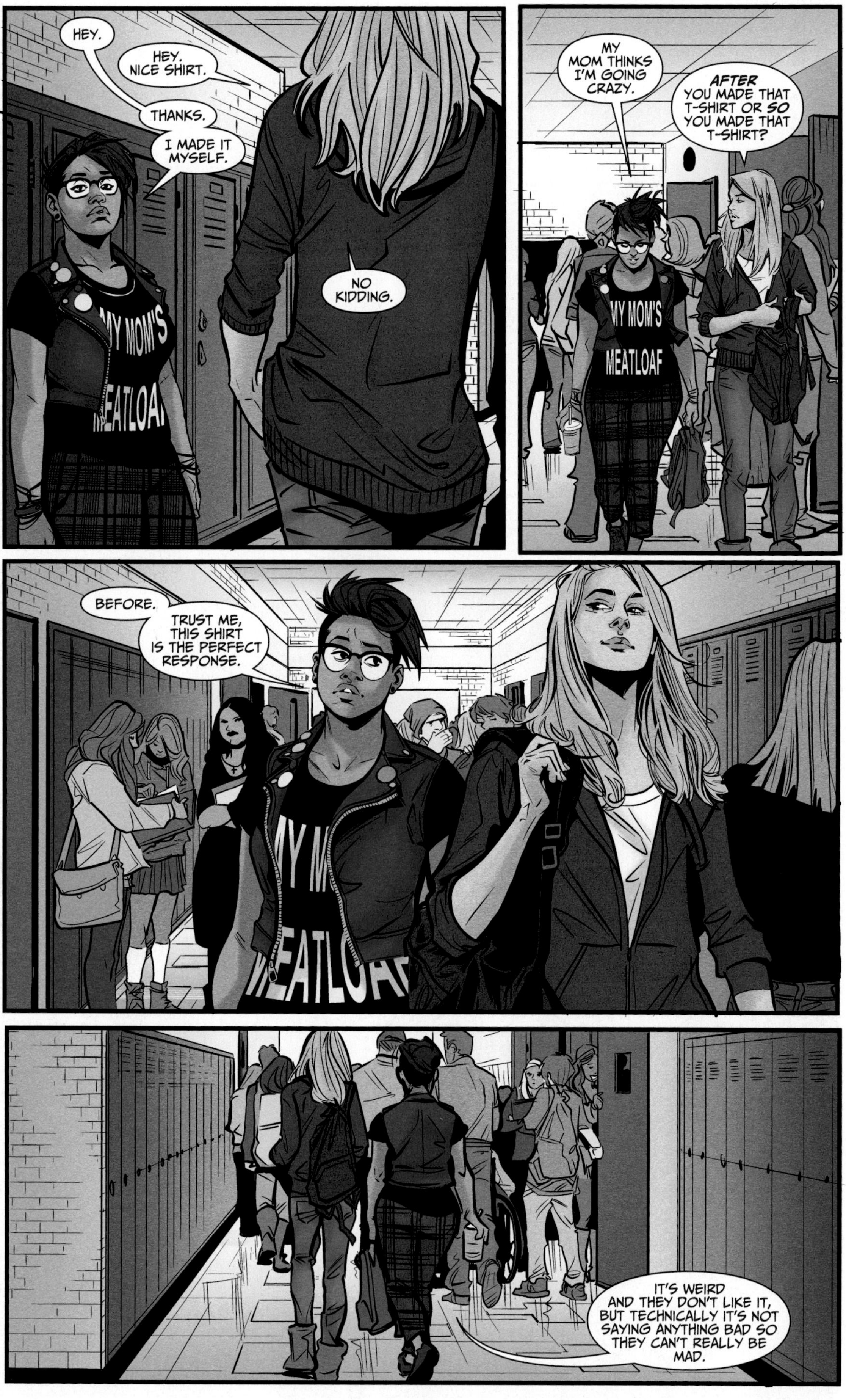
HEY.
HEY. NICE SHIRT.
THANKS.
I MADE IT MYSELF.
NO KIDDING.
MY MOM'S MEATLOAF
MY MOM THINKS I'M GOING CRAZY.
AFTER YOU MADE THAT T-SHIRT OR SO YOU MADE THAT T-SHIRT?
MY MOM'S MEATLOAF
BEFORE.
TRUST ME, THIS SHIRT IS THE PERFECT RESPONSE.
IT'S WEIRD AND THEY DON'T LIKE IT, BUT TECHNICALLY IT'S NOT SAYING ANYTHING BAD SO THEY CAN'T REALLY BE MAD.

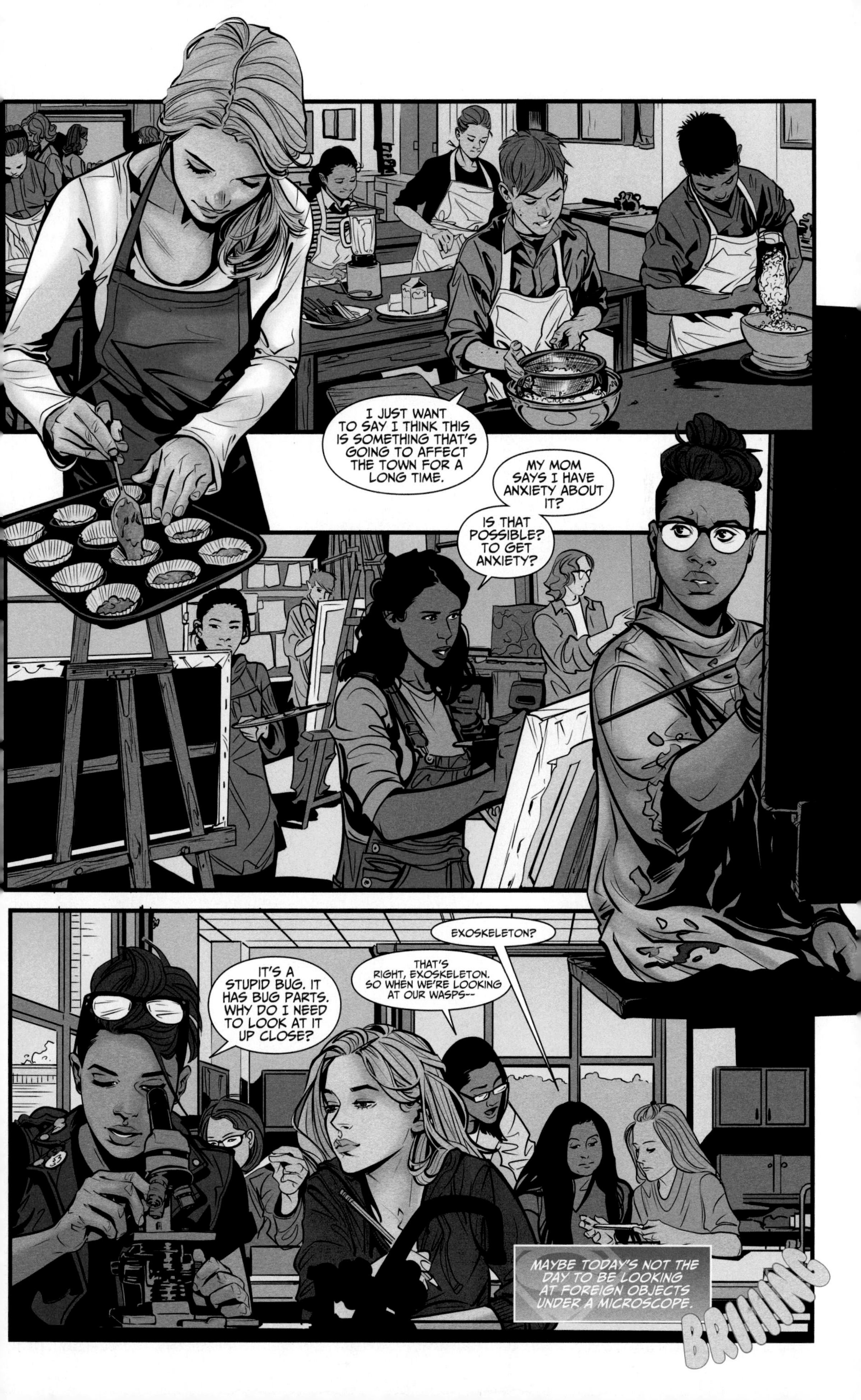
I JUST WANT TO SAY I THINK THIS IS SOMETHING THAT'S GOING TO AFFECT THE TOWN FOR A LONG TIME.
MY MOM SAYS I HAVE ANXIETY ABOUT IT?
IS THAT POSSIBLE? TO GET ANXIETY?
EXOSKELETON?
IT'S A STUPID BUG. IT HAS BUG PARTS. WHY DO I NEED TO LOOK AT IT UP CLOSE?
THAT'S RIGHT, EXOSKELETON. SO WHEN WE'RE LOOKING AT OUR WASPS--
MAYBE TODAY'S NOT THE DAY TO BE LOOKING AT FOREIGN OBJECTS UNDER A MICROSCOPE.
BRIIING

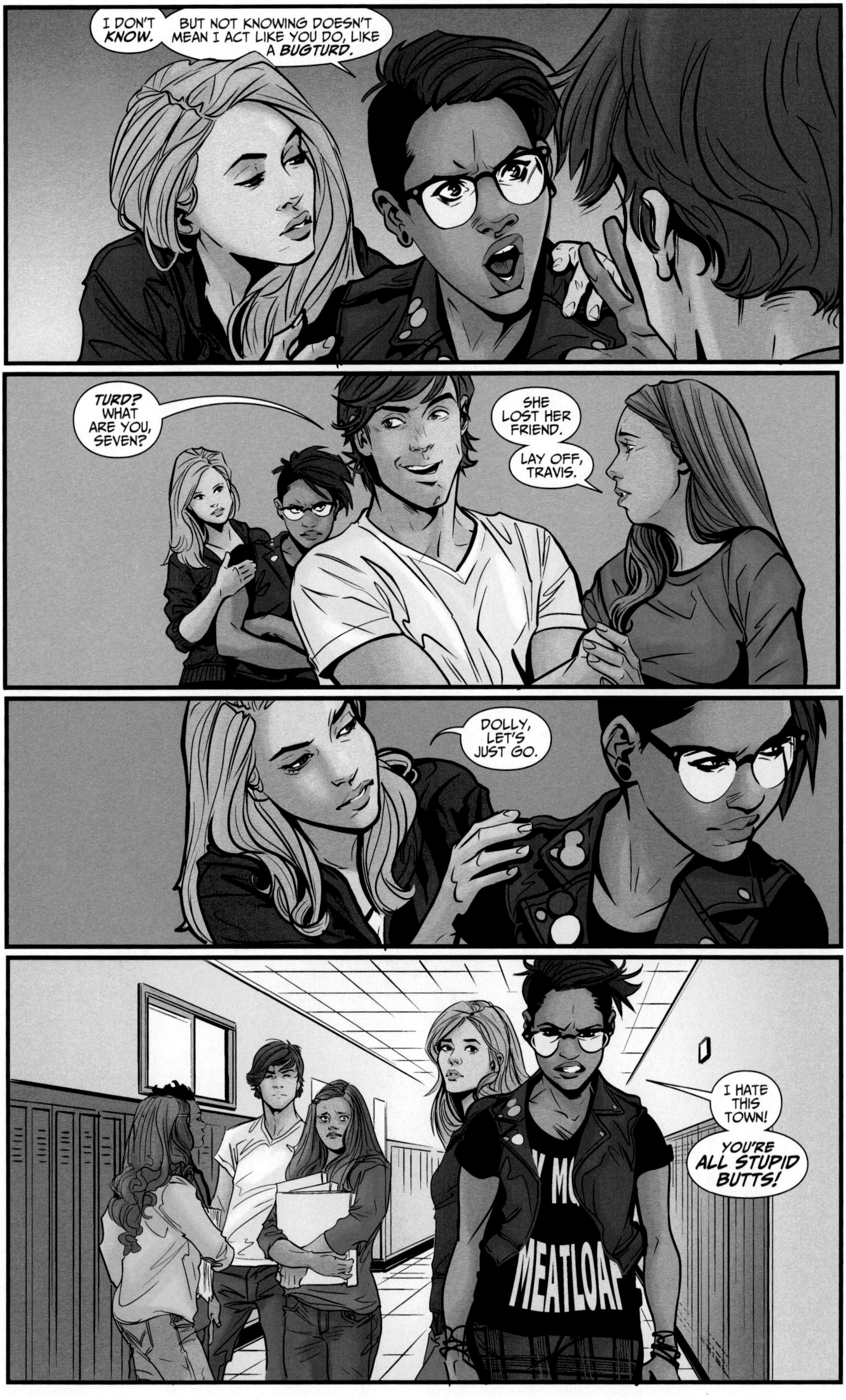
I DON'T KNOW.
BUT NOT KNOWING DOESN'T MEAN I ACT LIKE YOU DO, LIKE A BUGTURD.
TURD? WHAT ARE YOU, SEVEN?
SHE LOST HER FRIEND.
LAY OFF, TRAVIS.
DOLLY, LET'S JUST GO.
MEATLOAF
I HATE THIS TOWN!
YOU'RE ALL STUPID BUTTS!

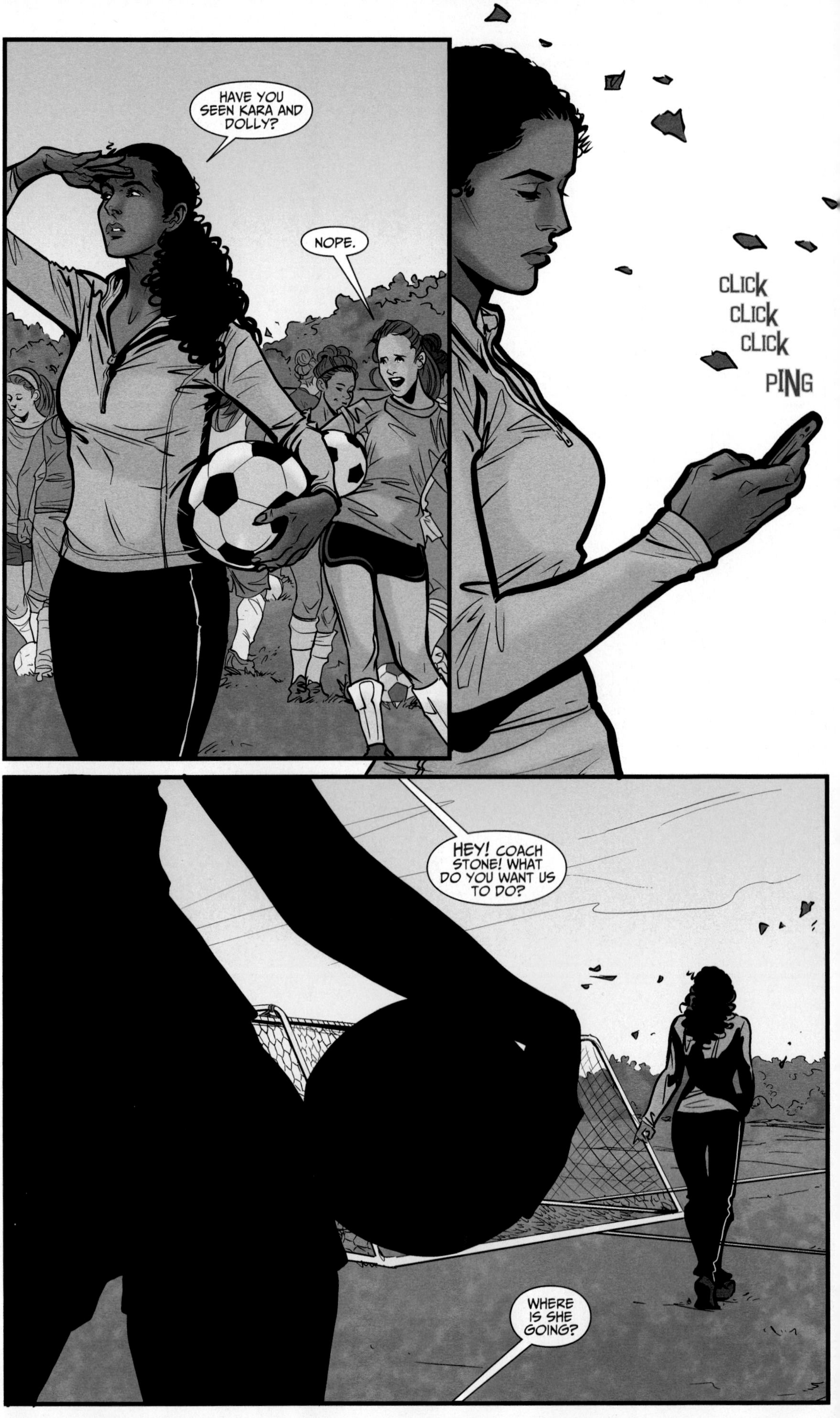
HAVE YOU SEEN KARA AND DOLLY?
NOPE.
CLICK
CLICK
CLICK
PING
HEY! COACH STONE! WHAT DO YOU WANT US TO DO?
WHERE IS SHE GOING?

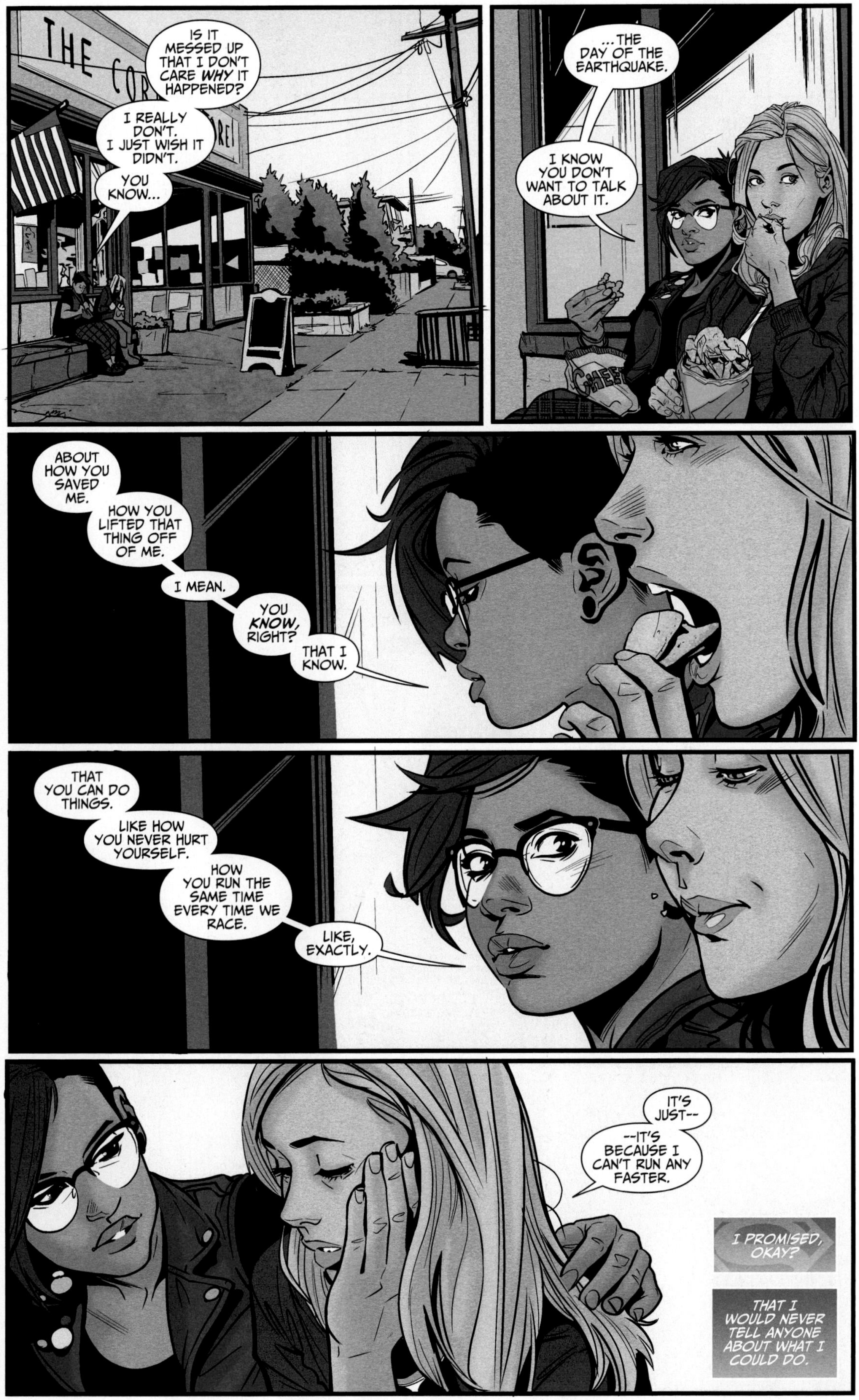
THE COR STORE
IS IT MESSED UP THAT I DON'T CARE *WHY* IT HAPPENED?
I REALLY DON'T. I JUST WISH IT DIDN'T.
YOU KNOW...
...THE DAY OF THE EARTHQUAKE.
I KNOW YOU DON'T WANT TO TALK ABOUT IT.
ABOUT HOW YOU SAVED ME.
HOW YOU LIFTED THAT THING OFF OF ME.
I MEAN.
YOU *KNOW,* RIGHT?
THAT I KNOW.
THAT YOU CAN DO THINGS.
LIKE HOW YOU NEVER HURT YOURSELF.
HOW YOU RUN THE SAME TIME EVERY TIME WE RACE.
LIKE, EXACTLY.
IT'S JUST--
--IT'S BECAUSE I CAN'T RUN ANY FASTER.
I PROMISED, OKAY?
THAT I WOULD NEVER TELL ANYONE ABOUT WHAT I COULD DO.

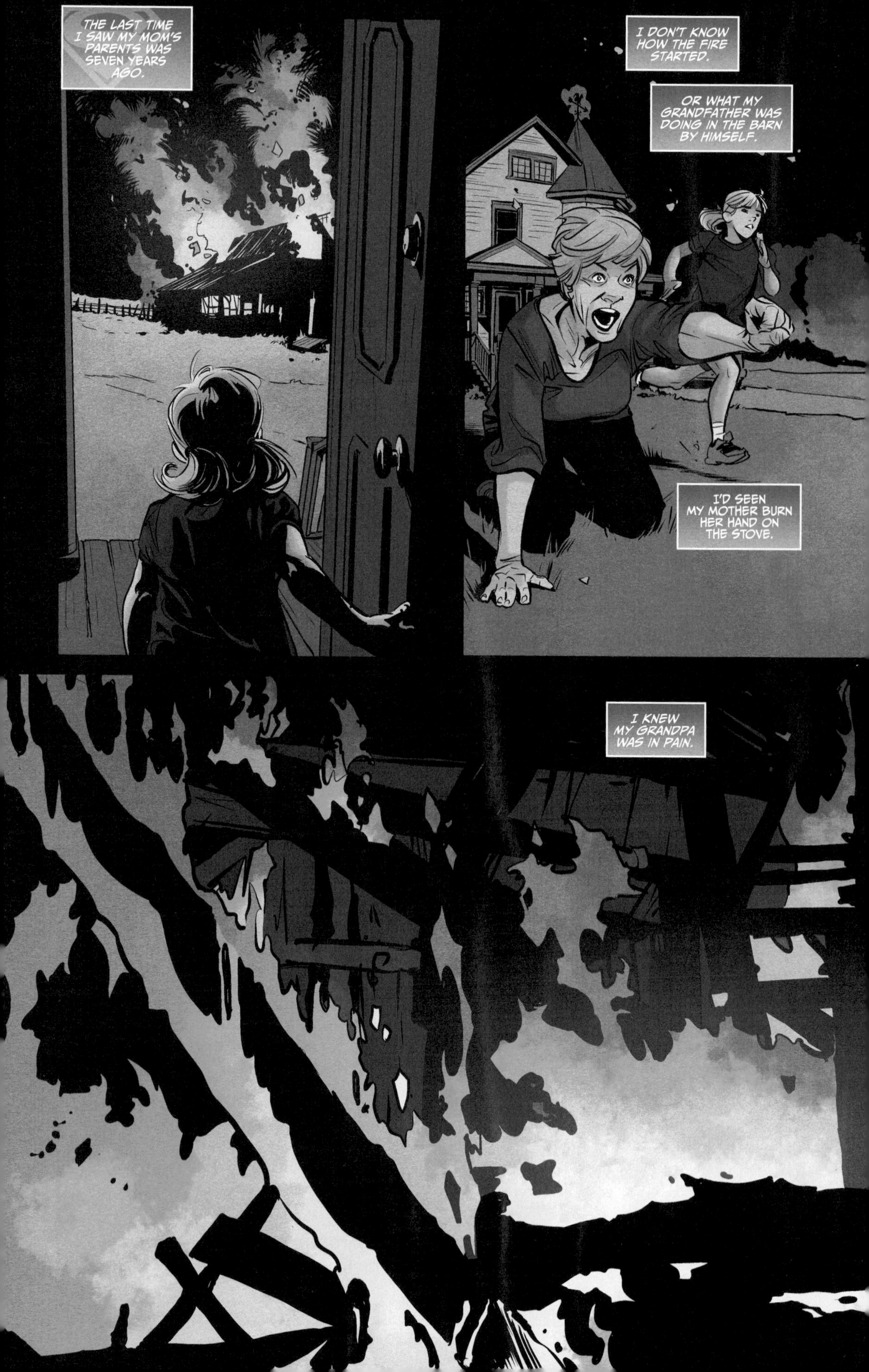
THE LAST TIME I SAW MY MOM'S PARENTS WAS SEVEN YEARS AGO.
I DON'T KNOW HOW THE FIRE STARTED.
OR WHAT MY GRANDFATHER WAS DOING IN THE BARN BY HIMSELF.
I'D SEEN MY MOTHER BURN HER HAND ON THE STOVE.
I KNEW MY GRANDPA WAS IN PAIN.

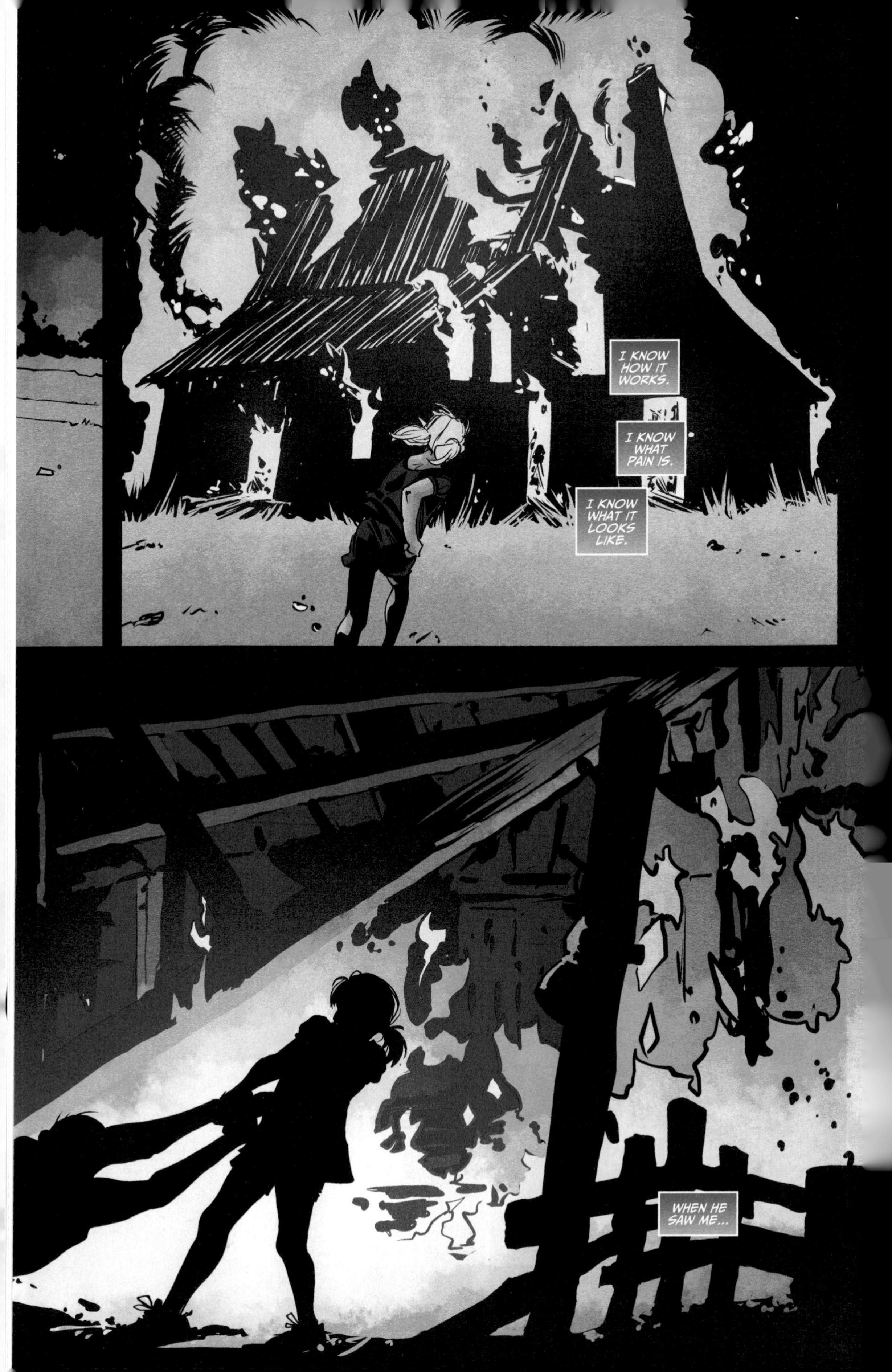
I KNOW HOW IT WORKS.
I KNOW WHAT PAIN IS.
I KNOW WHAT IT LOOKS LIKE.
WHEN HE SAW ME...

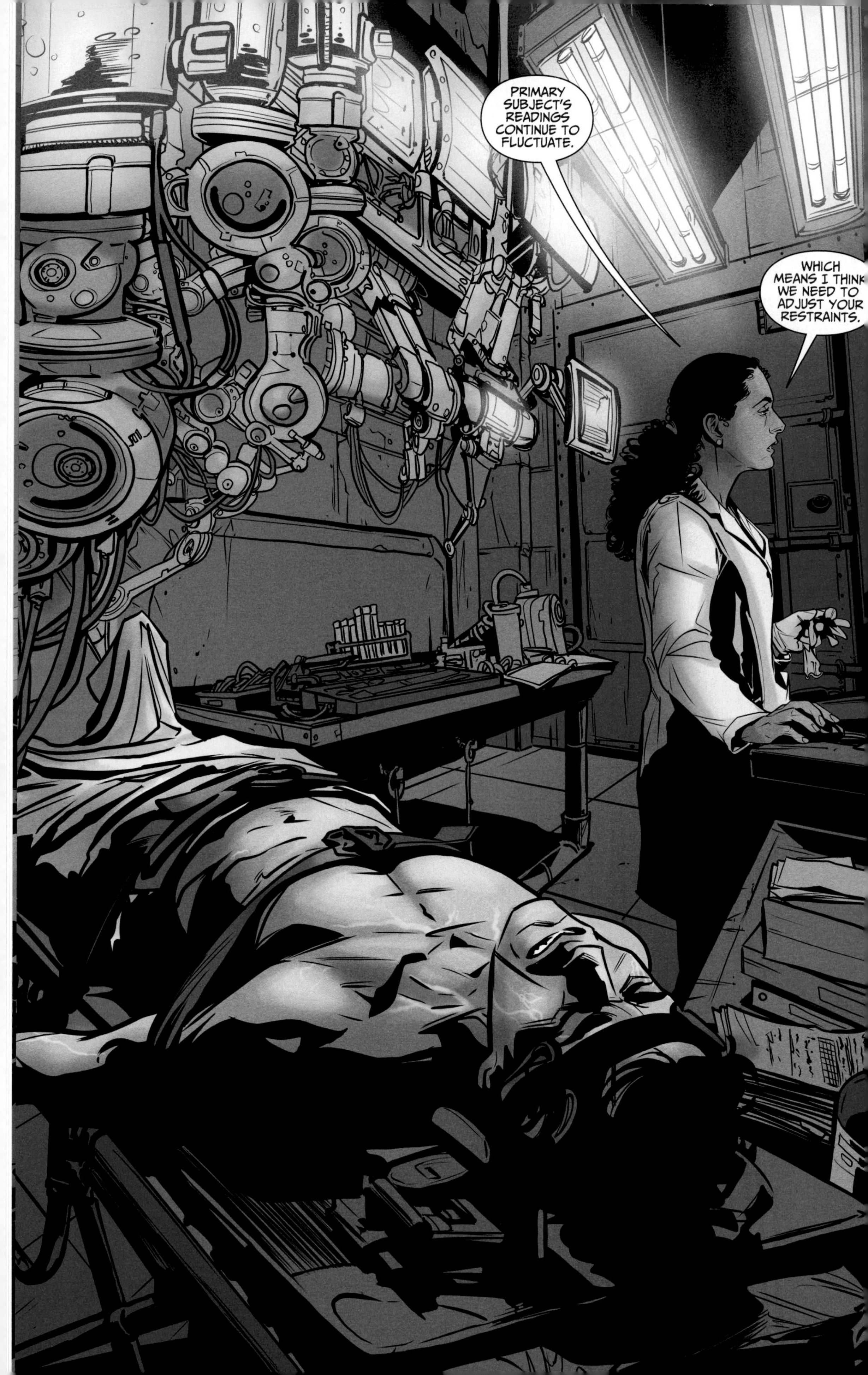
PRIMARY SUBJECT'S READINGS CONTINUE TO FLUCTUATE.
WHICH MEANS I THINK WE NEED TO ADJUST YOUR RESTRAINTS.

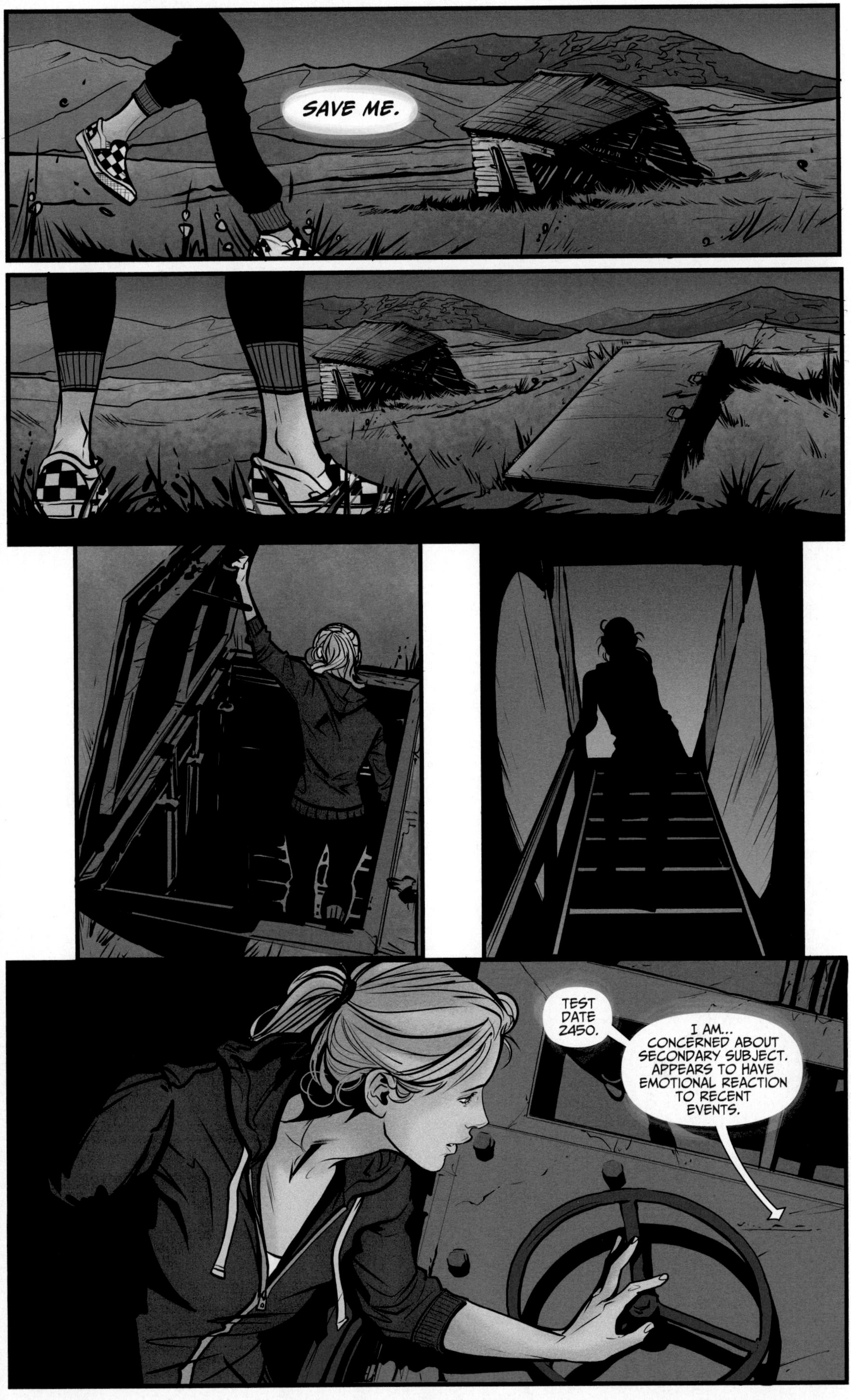
SAVE ME.
TEST DATE 2450.
I AM... CONCERNED ABOUT SECONDARY SUBJECT. APPEARS TO HAVE EMOTIONAL REACTION TO RECENT EVENTS.

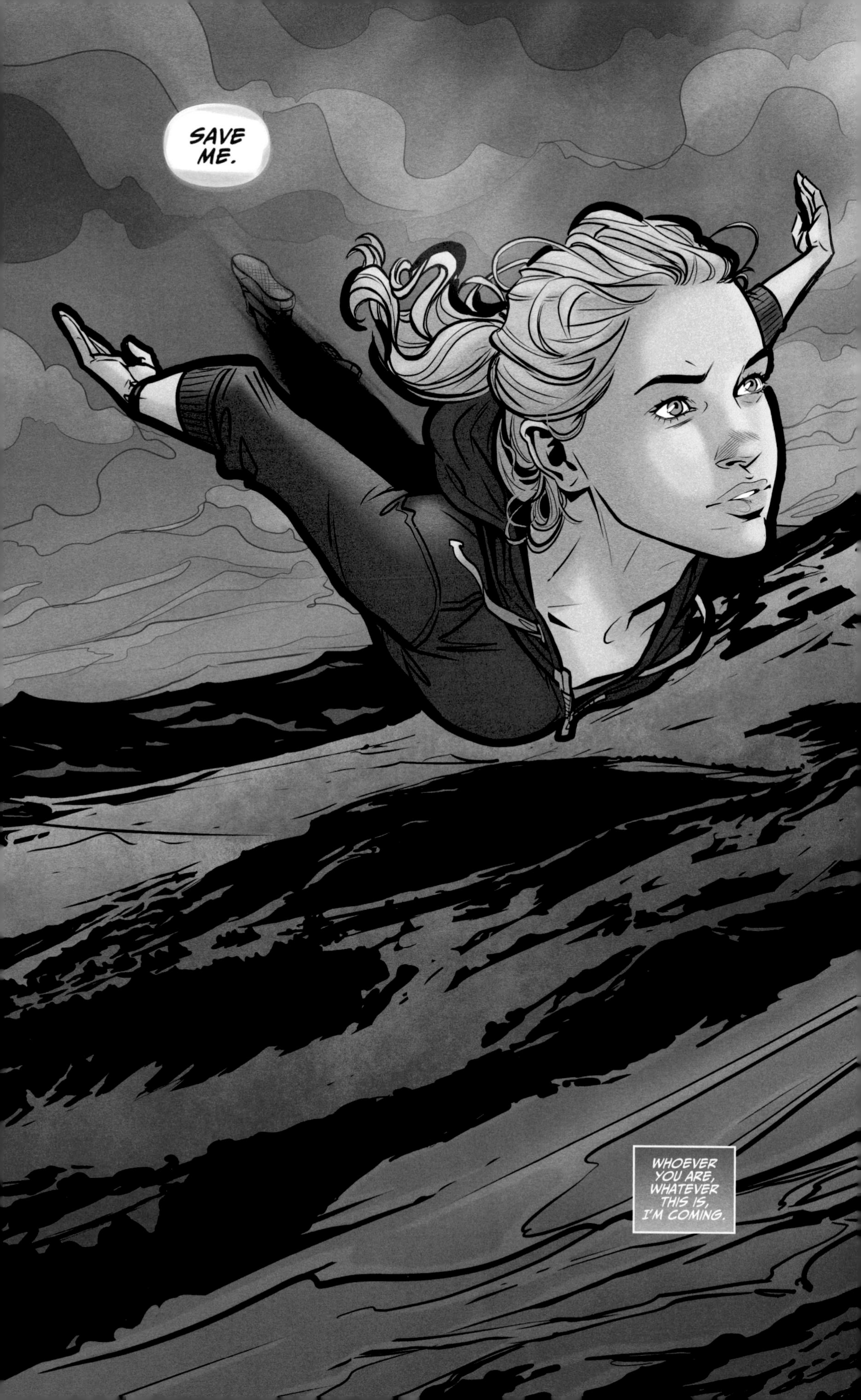
SAVE ME.
WHOEVER YOU ARE, WHATEVER THIS IS, I'M COMING.

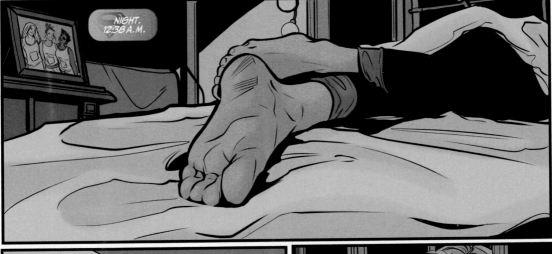

NIGHT. 12:38 A.M.

SAVE ME.

JEN?

SAVE ME.

HOPEFULLY I DON'T FALL OUT OF THE SKY AND BREAK MY NECK.

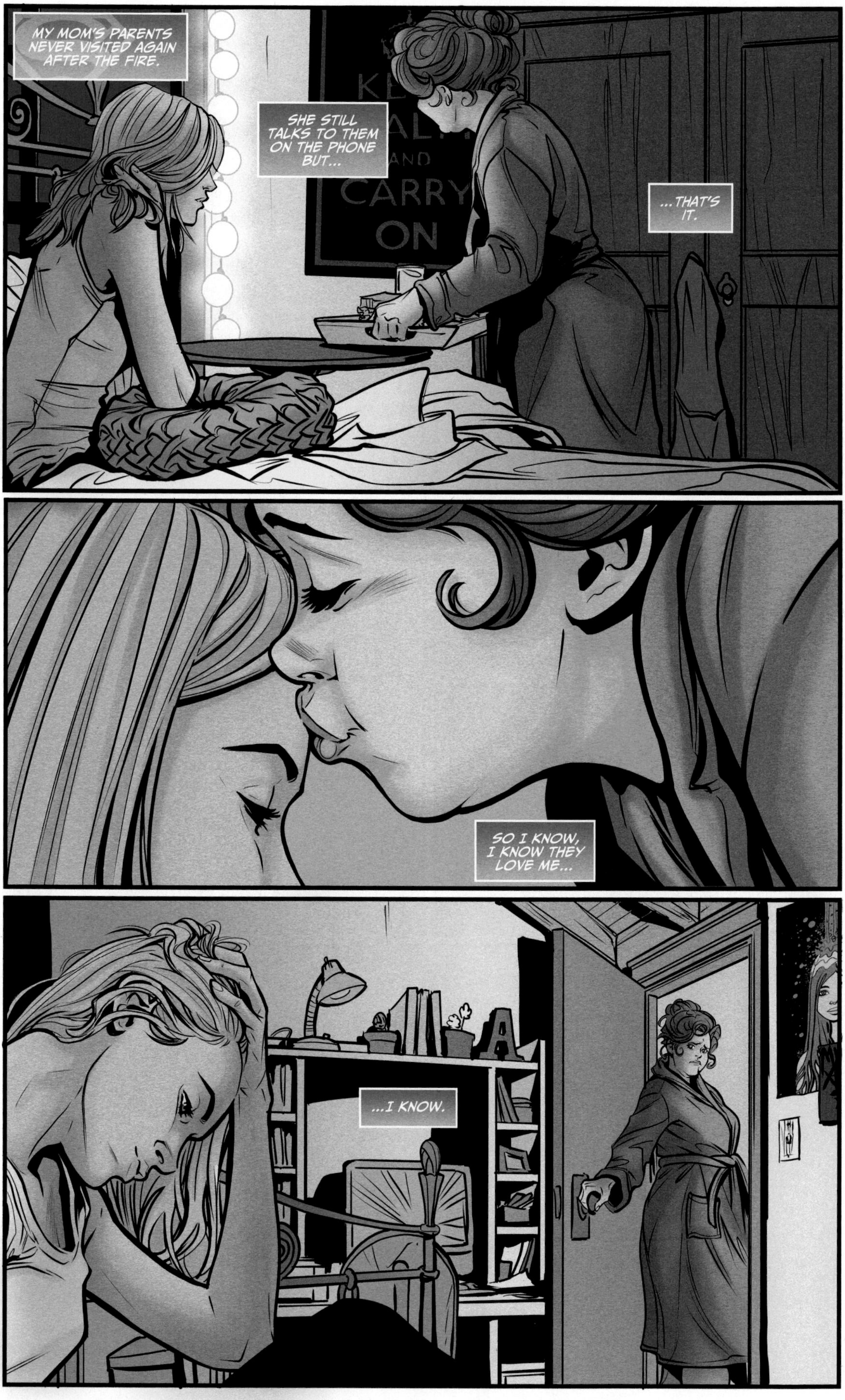
MY MOM'S PARENTS NEVER VISITED AGAIN AFTER THE FIRE.
SHE STILL TALKS TO THEM ON THE PHONE BUT...
...THAT'S IT.
SO I KNOW, I KNOW THEY LOVE ME...
...I KNOW.

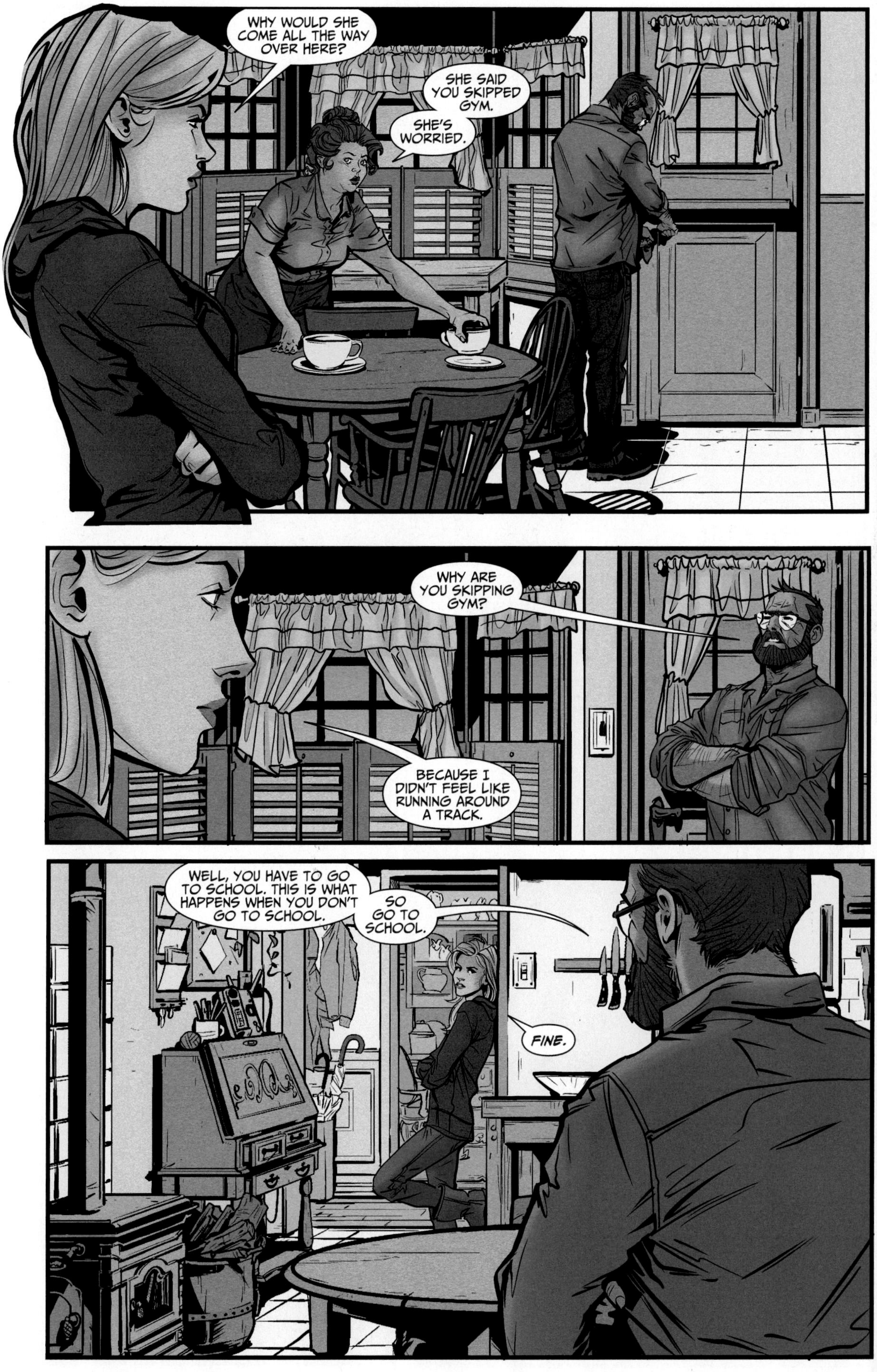
WHY WOULD SHE COME ALL THE WAY OVER HERE?
SHE SAID YOU SKIPPED GYM.
SHE'S WORRIED.
WHY ARE YOU SKIPPING GYM?
BECAUSE I DIDN'T FEEL LIKE RUNNING AROUND A TRACK.
WELL, YOU HAVE TO GO TO SCHOOL. THIS IS WHAT HAPPENS WHEN YOU DON'T GO TO SCHOOL.
SO GO TO SCHOOL.
FINE.

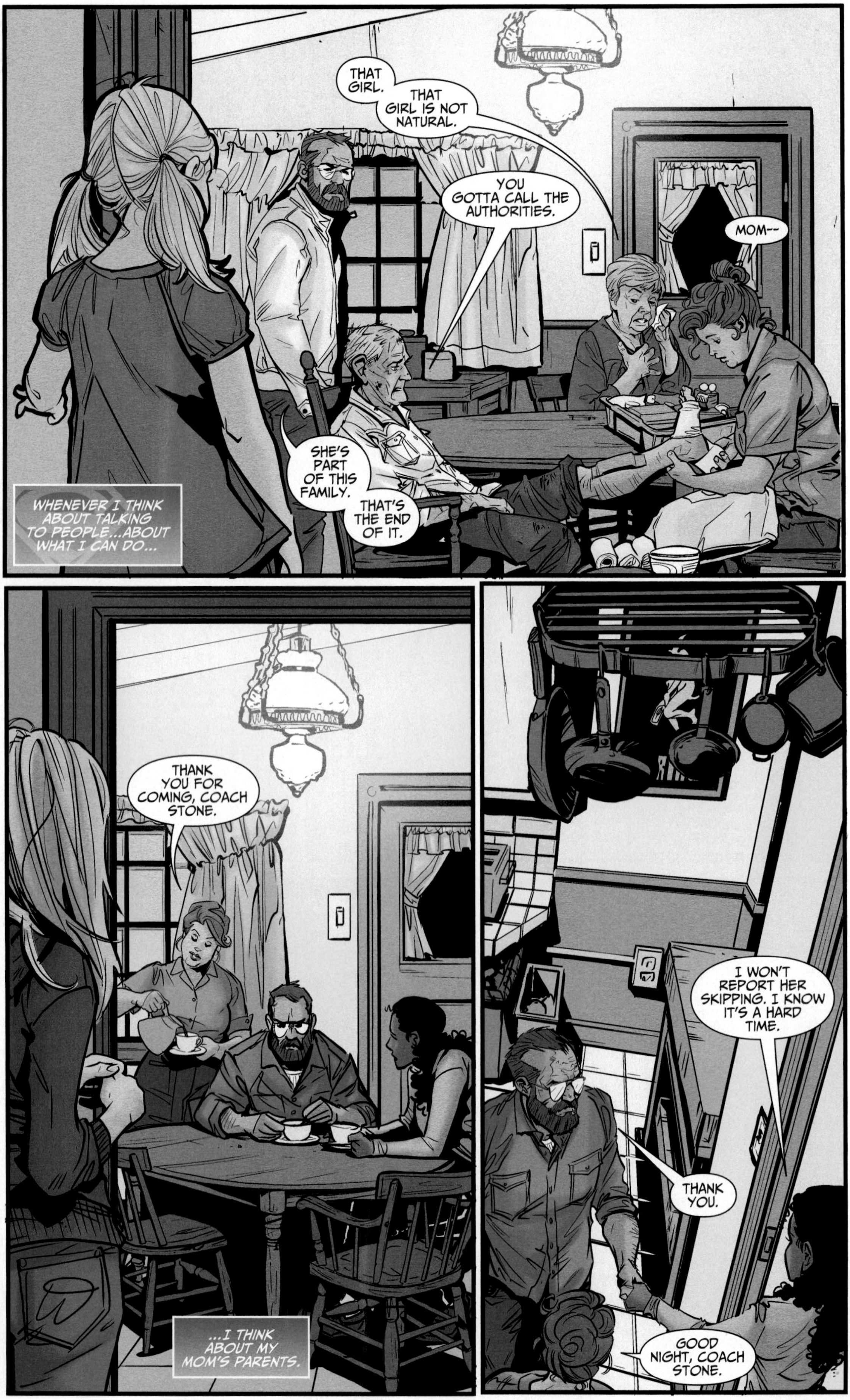
WHENEVER I THINK ABOUT TALKING TO PEOPLE...ABOUT WHAT I CAN DO...
THAT GIRL.
THAT GIRL IS NOT NATURAL.
YOU GOTTA CALL THE AUTHORITIES.
MOM--
SHE'S PART OF THIS FAMILY.
THAT'S THE END OF IT.
THANK YOU FOR COMING, COACH STONE.
...I THINK ABOUT MY MOM'S PARENTS.
I WON'T REPORT HER SKIPPING. I KNOW IT'S A HARD TIME.
THANK YOU.
GOOD NIGHT, COACH STONE.

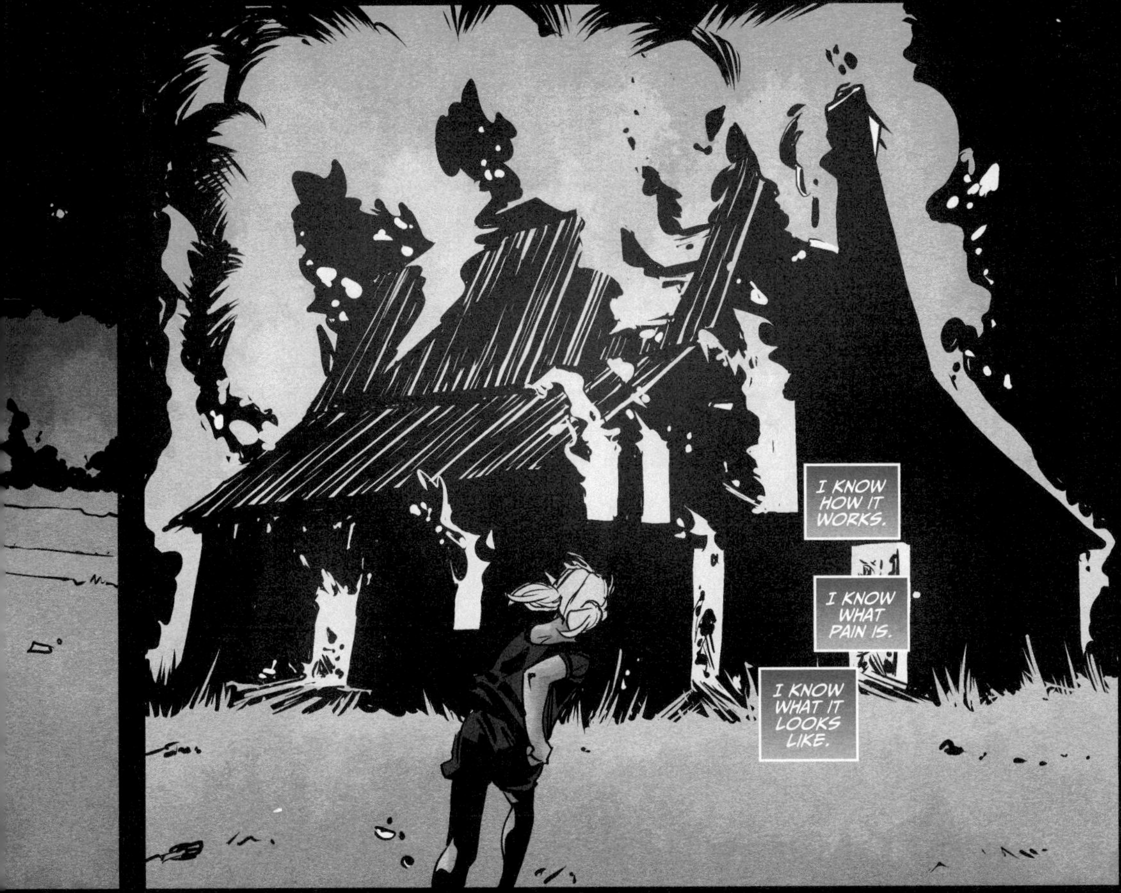
I KNOW HOW IT WORKS.
I KNOW WHAT PAIN IS.
I KNOW WHAT IT LOOKS LIKE.

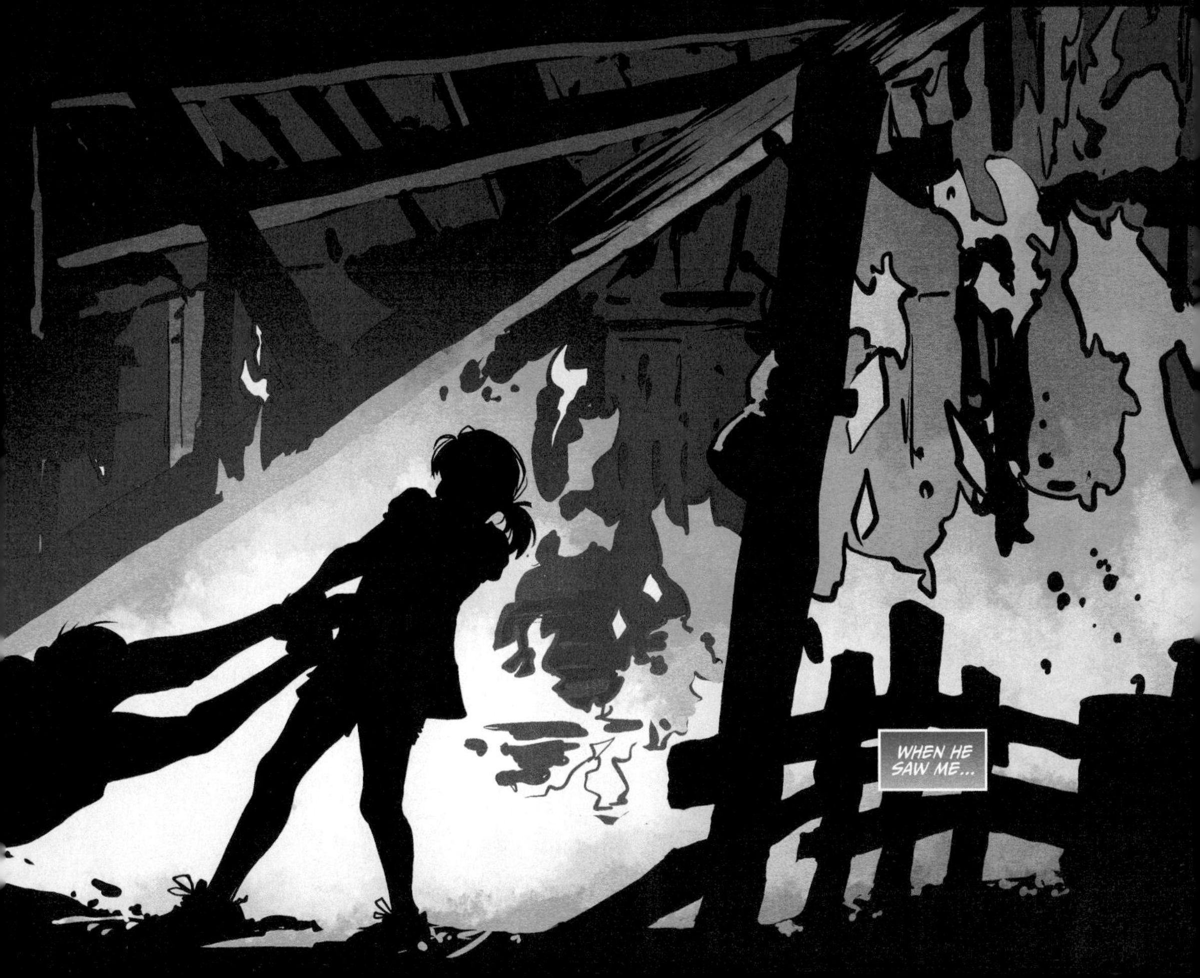
WHEN HE SAW ME...

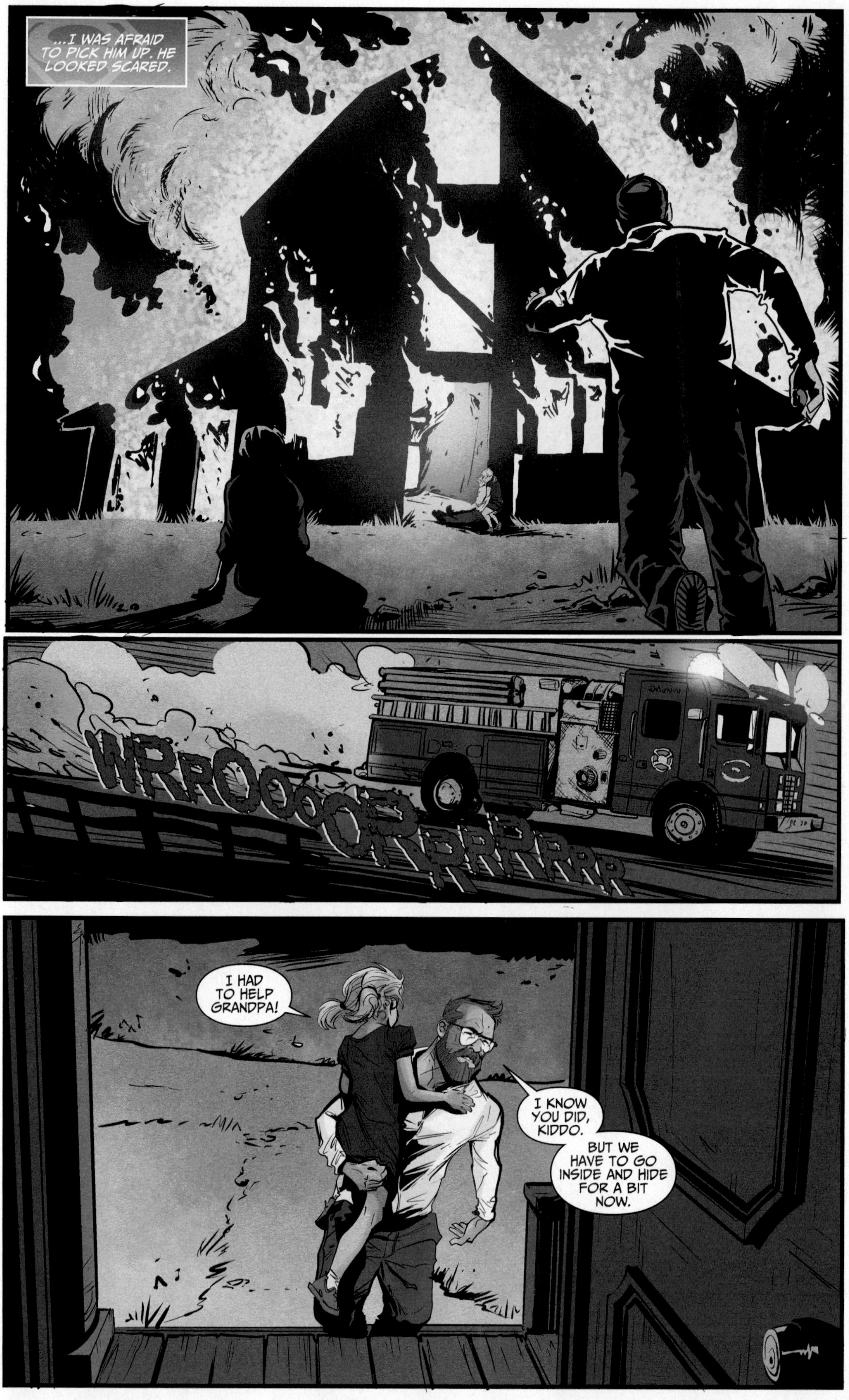
...I WAS AFRAID TO PICK HIM UP. HE LOOKED SCARED.
WRROOOOORRRRRRRR
I HAD TO HELP GRANDPA!
I KNOW YOU DID, KIDDO.
BUT WE HAVE TO GO INSIDE AND HIDE FOR A BIT NOW.

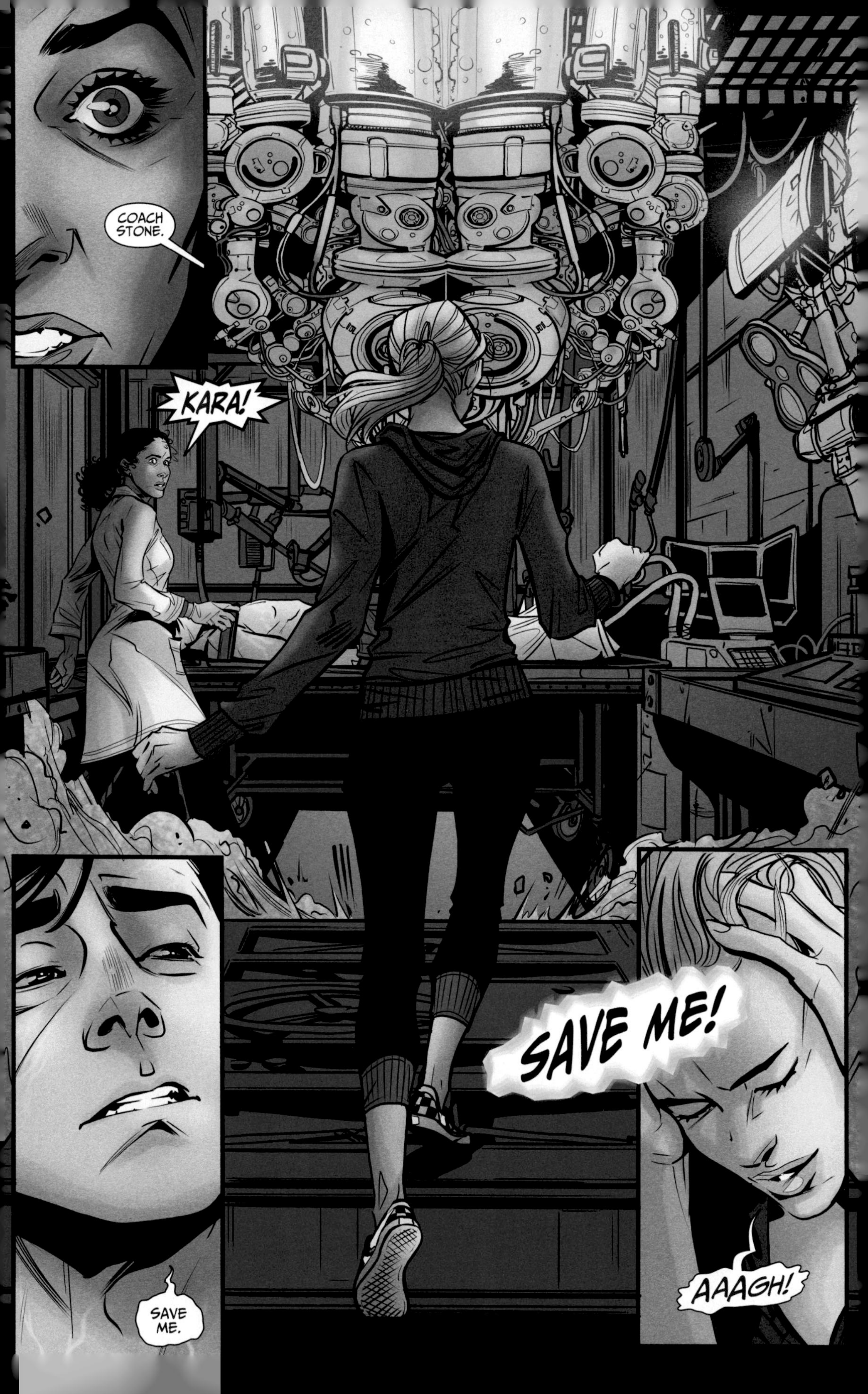
COACH STONE.
KARA!
SAVE ME.
SAVE ME!
AAAGH!

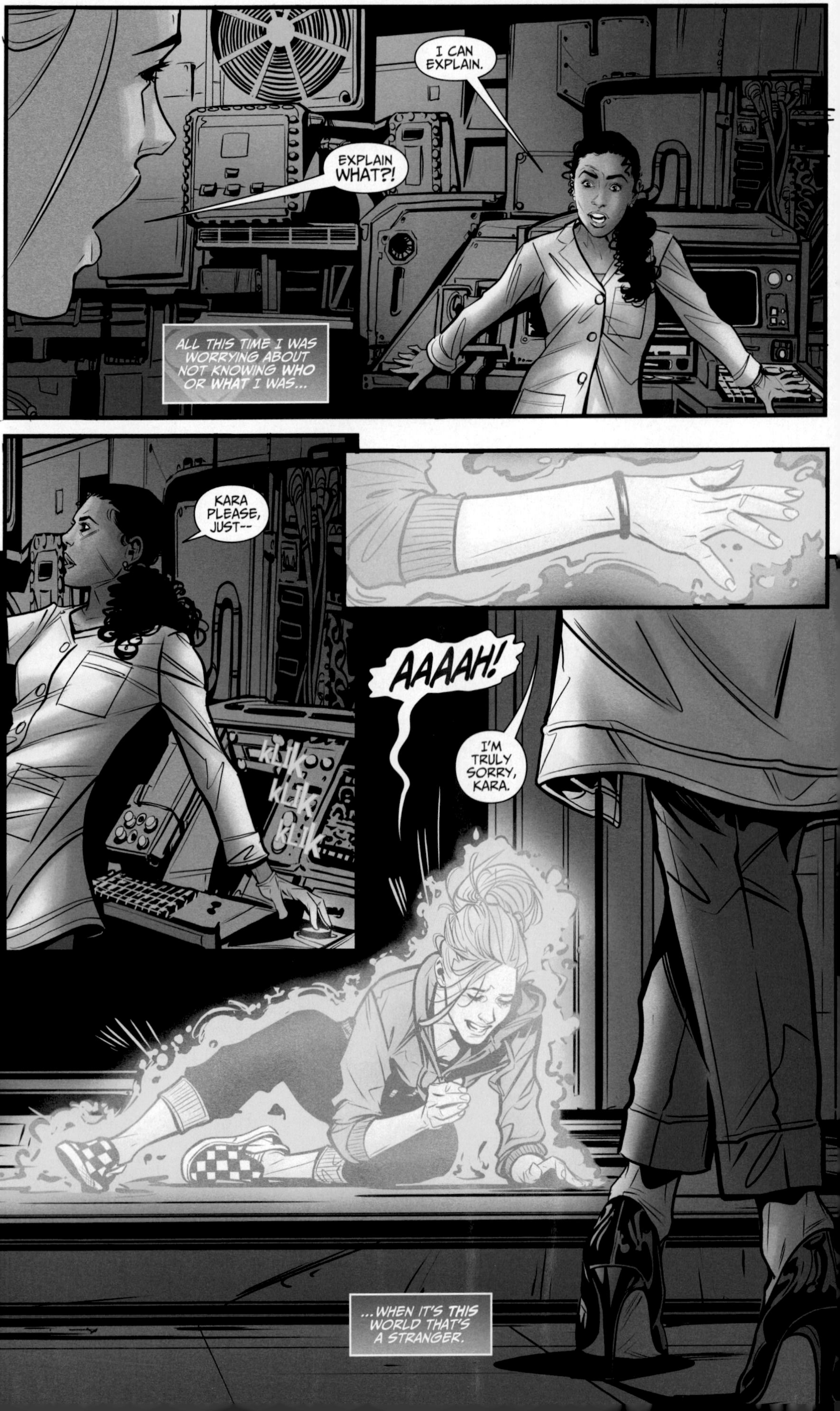
I CAN EXPLAIN.
EXPLAIN WHAT?!
ALL THIS TIME I WAS WORRYING ABOUT NOT KNOWING WHO OR WHAT I WAS...
KARA PLEASE, JUST--
KLIK KLIK KLIK
AAAAH!
I'M TRULY SORRY, KARA.
...WHEN IT'S THIS WORLD THAT'S A STRANGER.

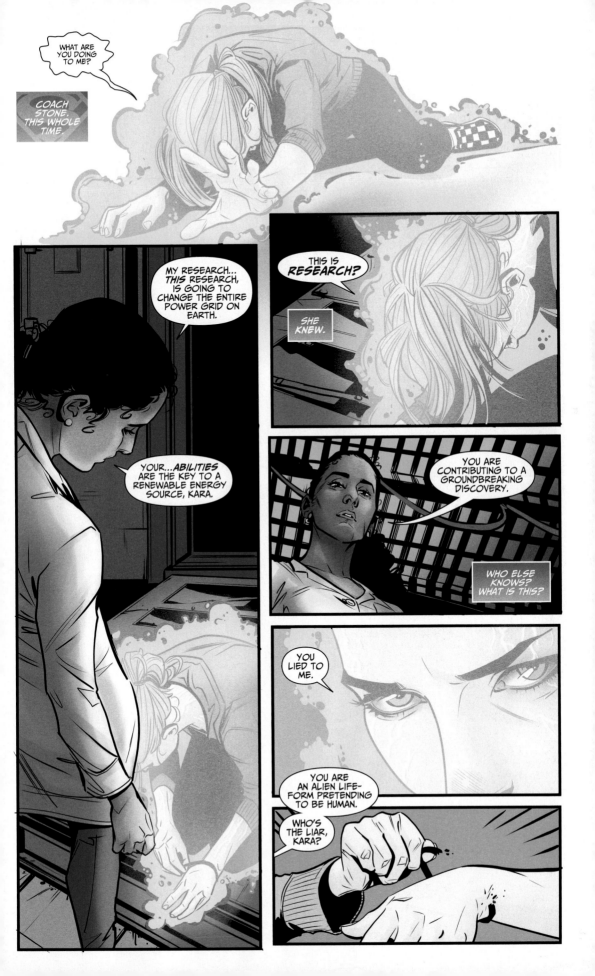

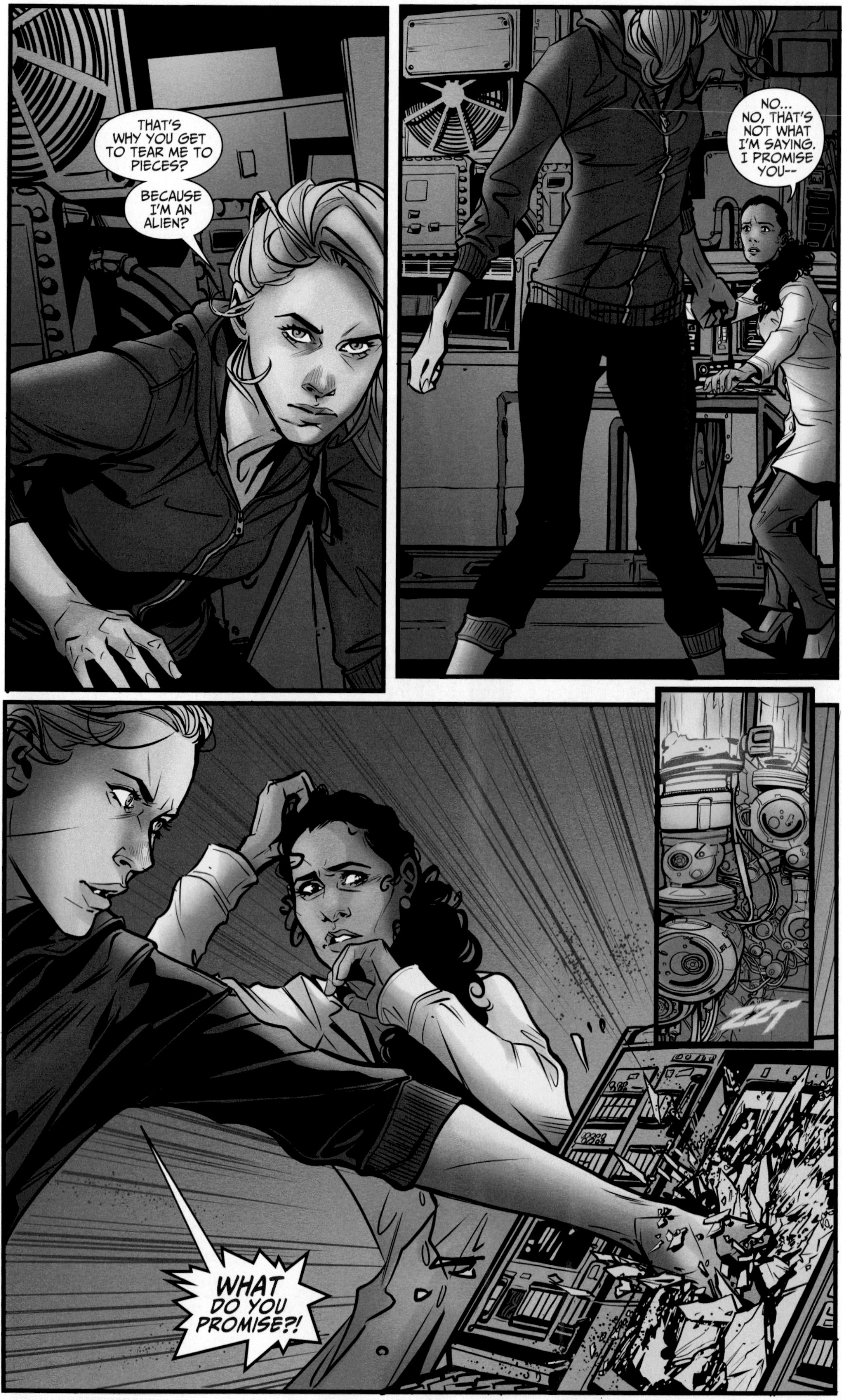
THAT'S WHY YOU GET TO TEAR ME TO PIECES?
BECAUSE I'M AN ALIEN?
NO... NO, THAT'S NOT WHAT I'M SAYING. I PROMISE YOU--
ZZT
WHAT DO YOU PROMISE?!

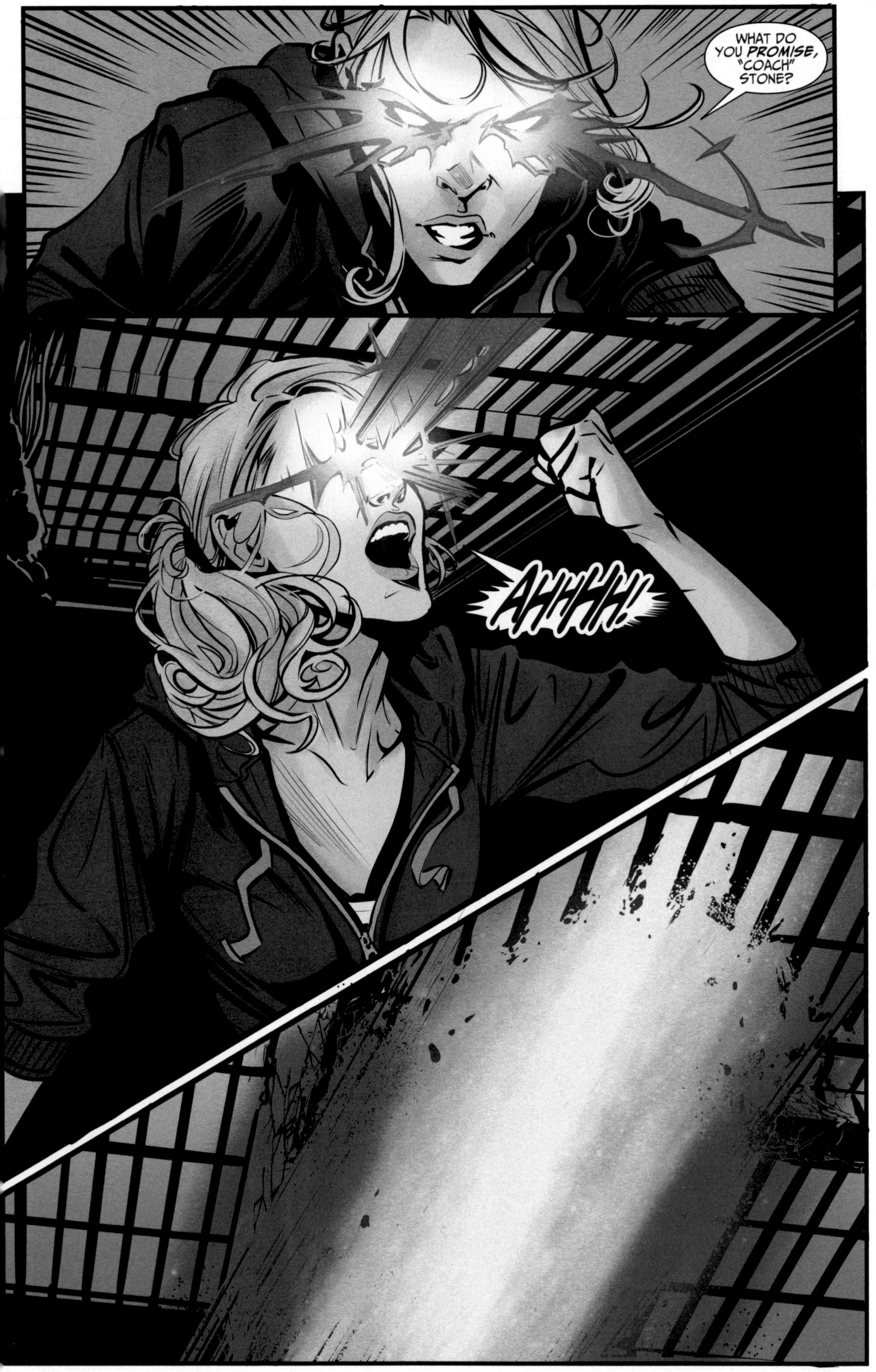
WHAT DO YOU PROMISE, "COACH" STONE?
AHHHH!

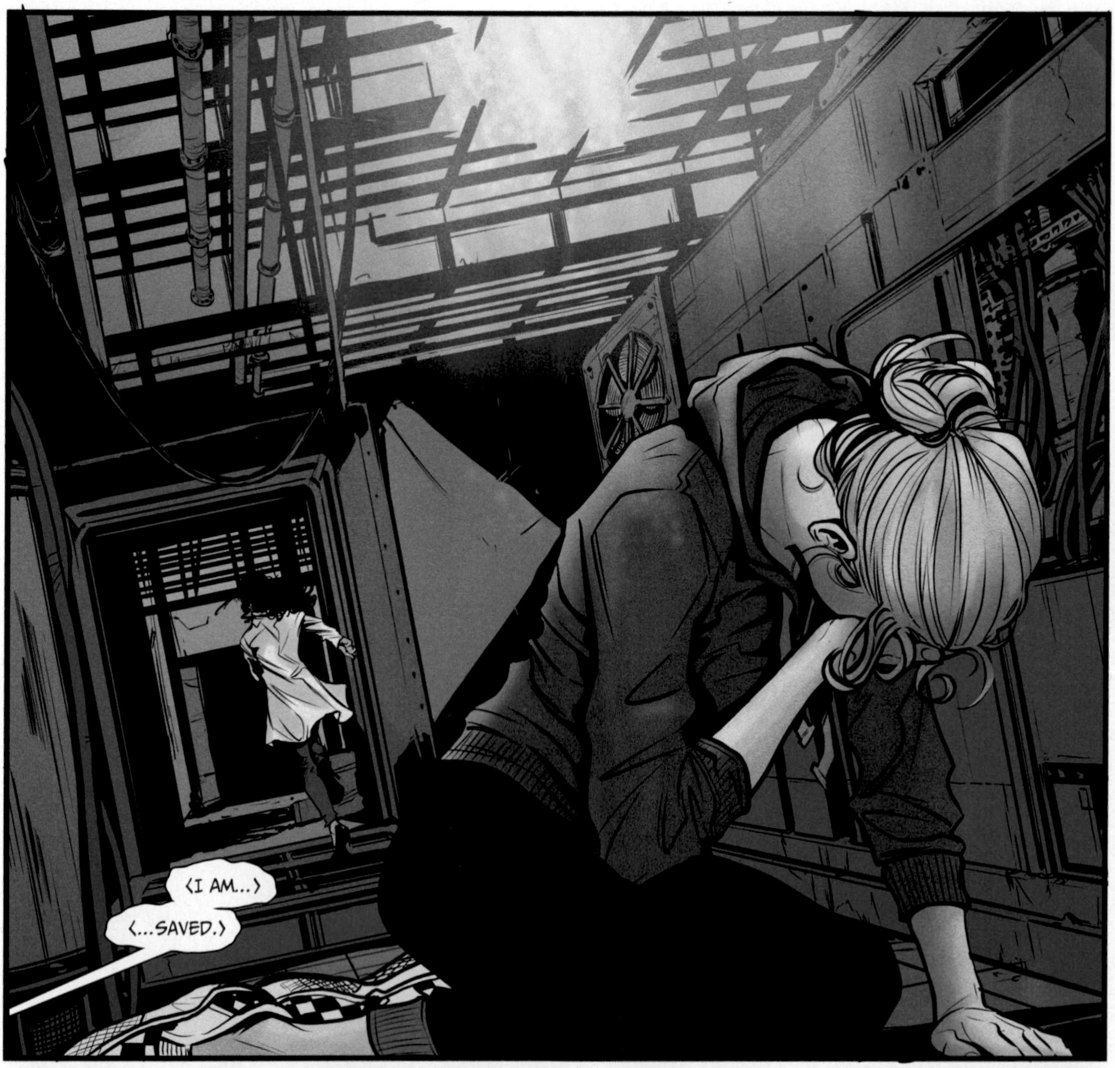
⟨I AM...⟩
⟨...SAVED.⟩

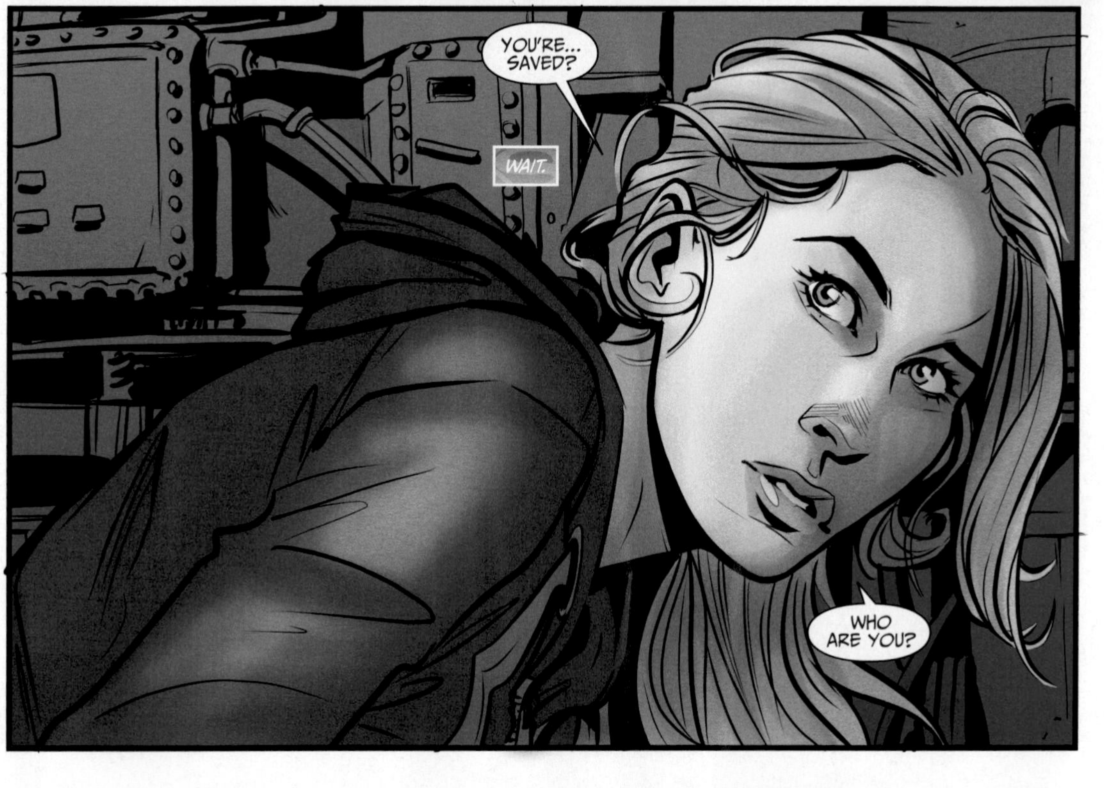
YOU'RE... SAVED?
WAIT.
WHO ARE YOU?

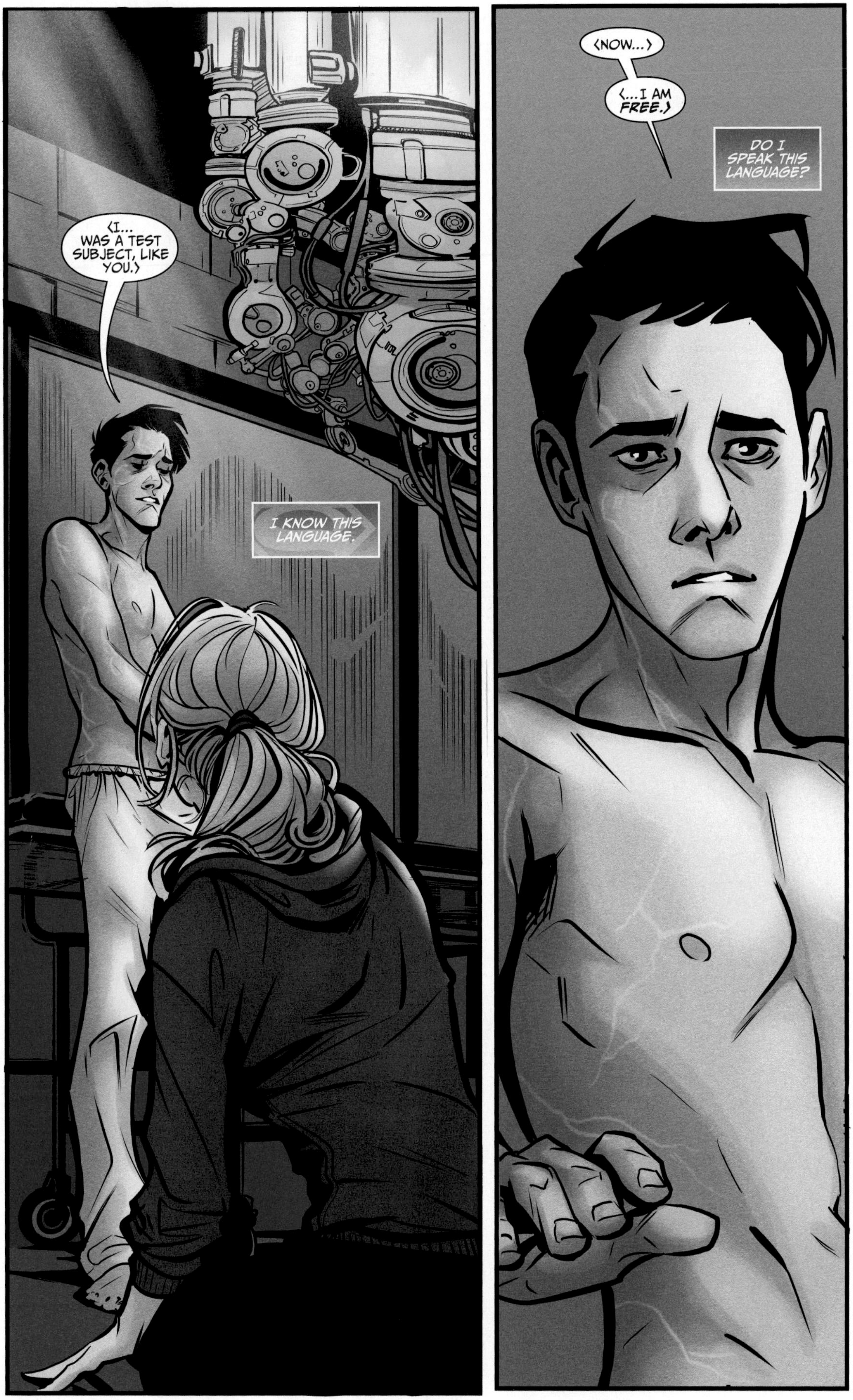
‹I... WAS A TEST SUBJECT, LIKE YOU.›
I KNOW THIS LANGUAGE.
‹NOW...›
‹...I AM FREE.›
DO I SPEAK THIS LANGUAGE?

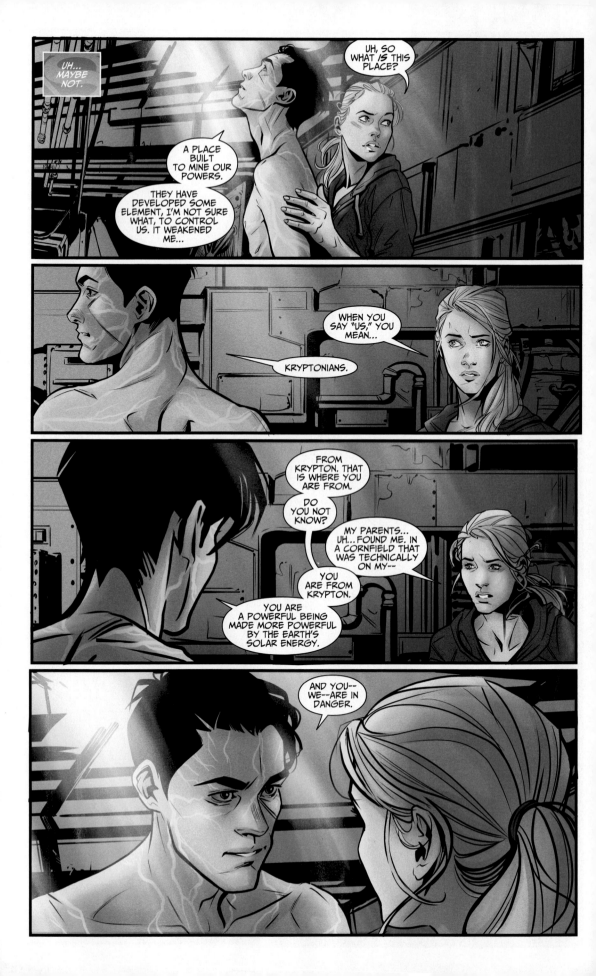

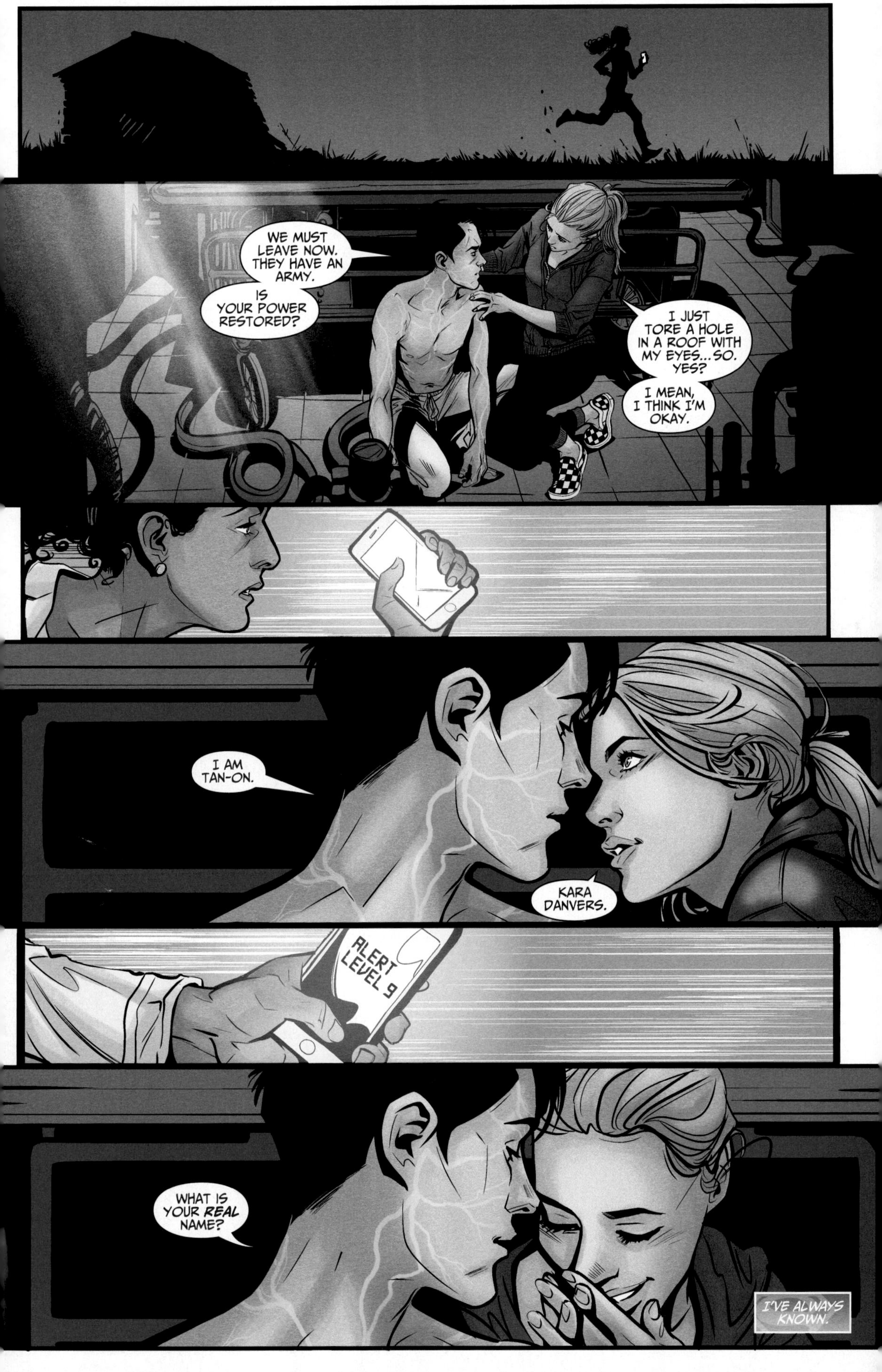
WE MUST LEAVE NOW. THEY HAVE AN ARMY.
IS YOUR POWER RESTORED?
I JUST TORE A HOLE IN A ROOF WITH MY EYES... SO. YES?
I MEAN, I THINK I'M OKAY.
I AM TAN-ON.
KARA DANVERS.
ALERT LEVEL 9
WHAT IS YOUR *REAL* NAME?
I'VE ALWAYS KNOWN.

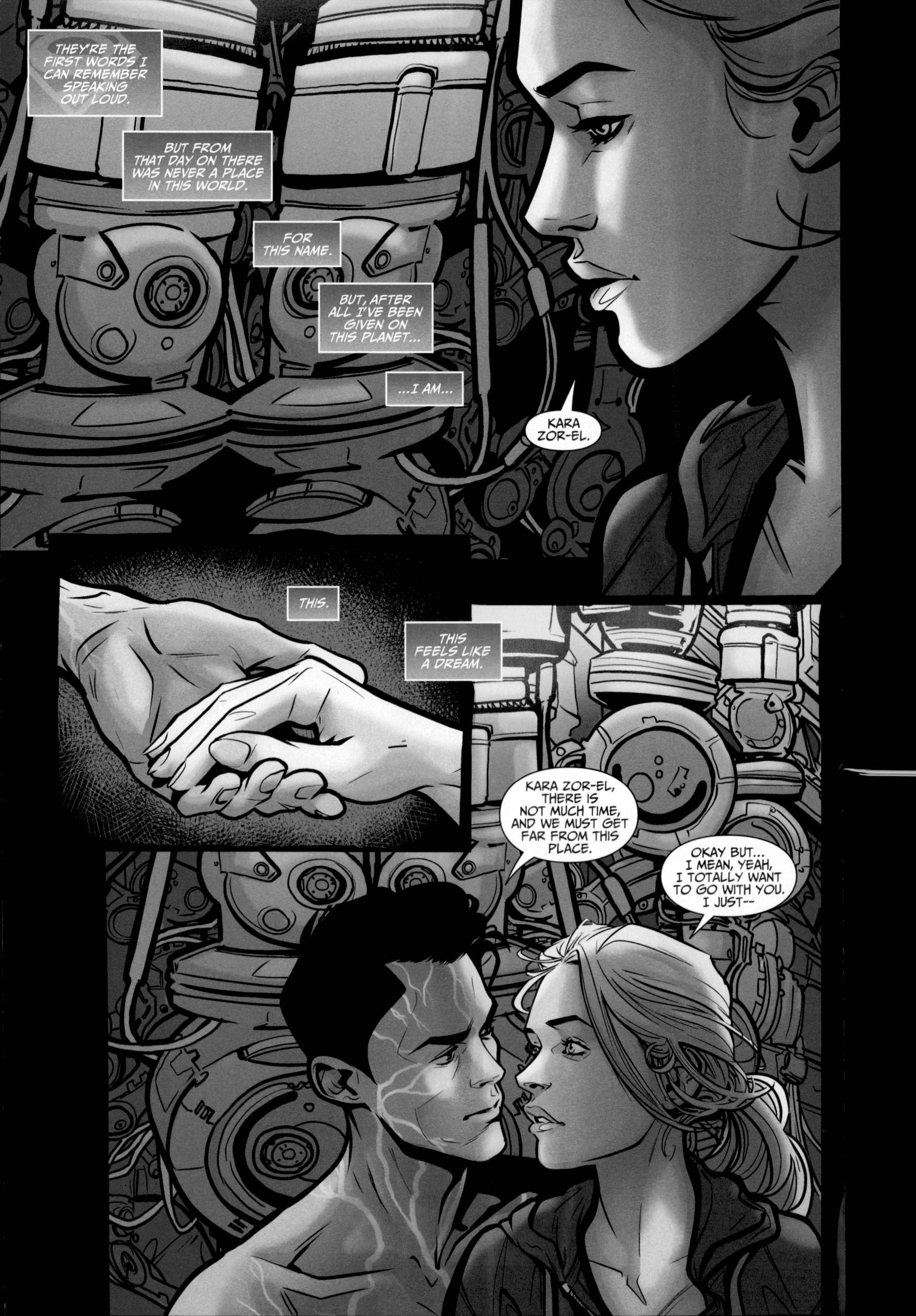
THEY'RE THE FIRST WORDS I CAN REMEMBER SPEAKING OUT LOUD.
BUT FROM THAT DAY ON THERE WAS NEVER A PLACE IN THIS WORLD.
FOR THIS NAME.
BUT, AFTER ALL I'VE BEEN GIVEN ON THIS PLANET...
...I AM...
KARA ZOR-EL.
THIS.
THIS FEELS LIKE A DREAM.
KARA ZOR-EL, THERE IS NOT MUCH TIME, AND WE MUST GET FAR FROM THIS PLACE.
OKAY BUT... I MEAN, YEAH, I TOTALLY WANT TO GO WITH YOU. I JUST--

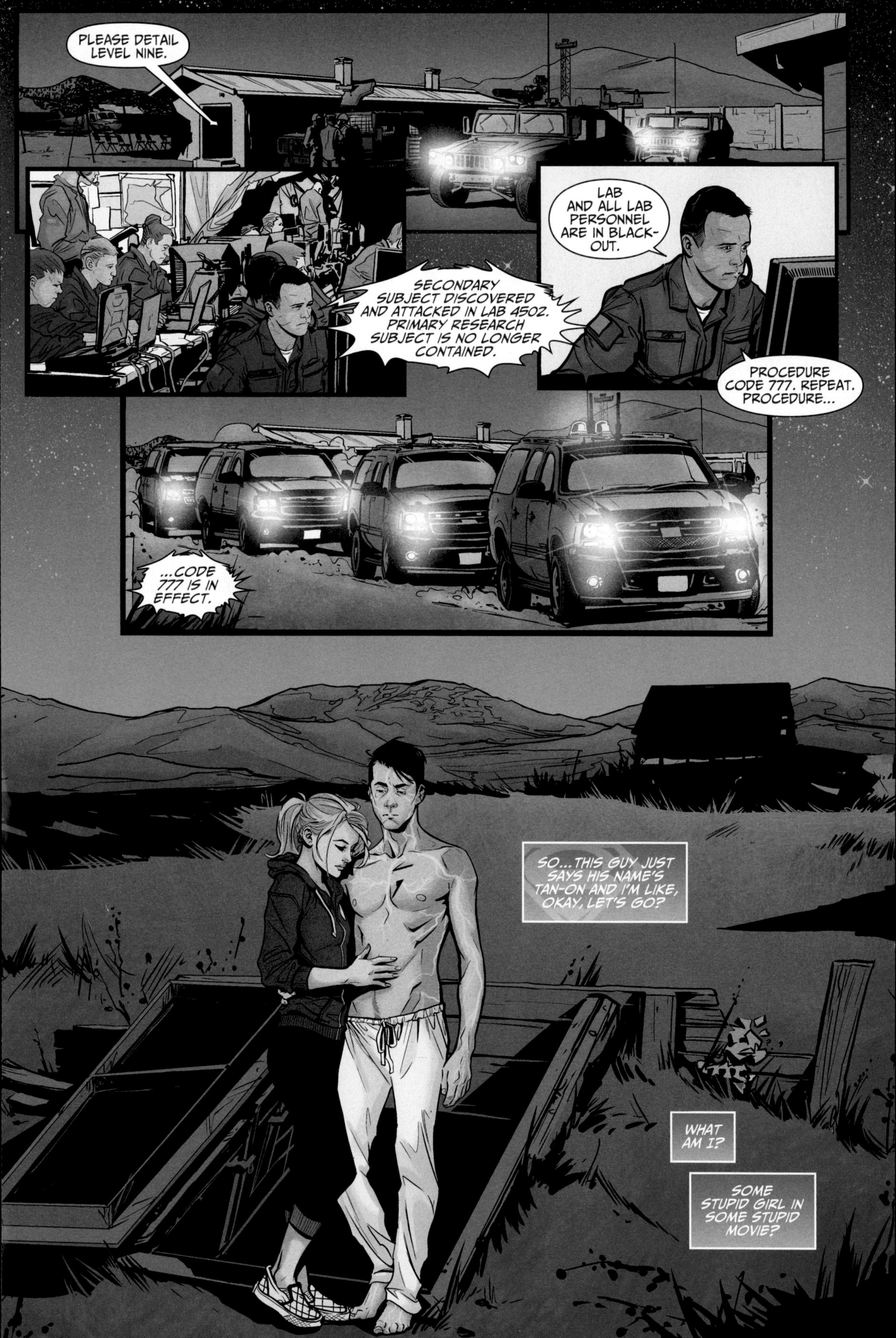
PLEASE DETAIL LEVEL NINE.
SECONDARY SUBJECT DISCOVERED AND ATTACKED IN LAB 4502. PRIMARY RESEARCH SUBJECT IS NO LONGER CONTAINED.
LAB AND ALL LAB PERSONNEL ARE IN BLACK-OUT.
PROCEDURE CODE 777. REPEAT. PROCEDURE...
...CODE 777 IS IN EFFECT.
SO...THIS GUY JUST SAYS HIS NAME'S TAN-ON AND I'M LIKE, OKAY, LET'S GO?
WHAT AM I?
SOME STUPID GIRL IN SOME STUPID MOVIE?

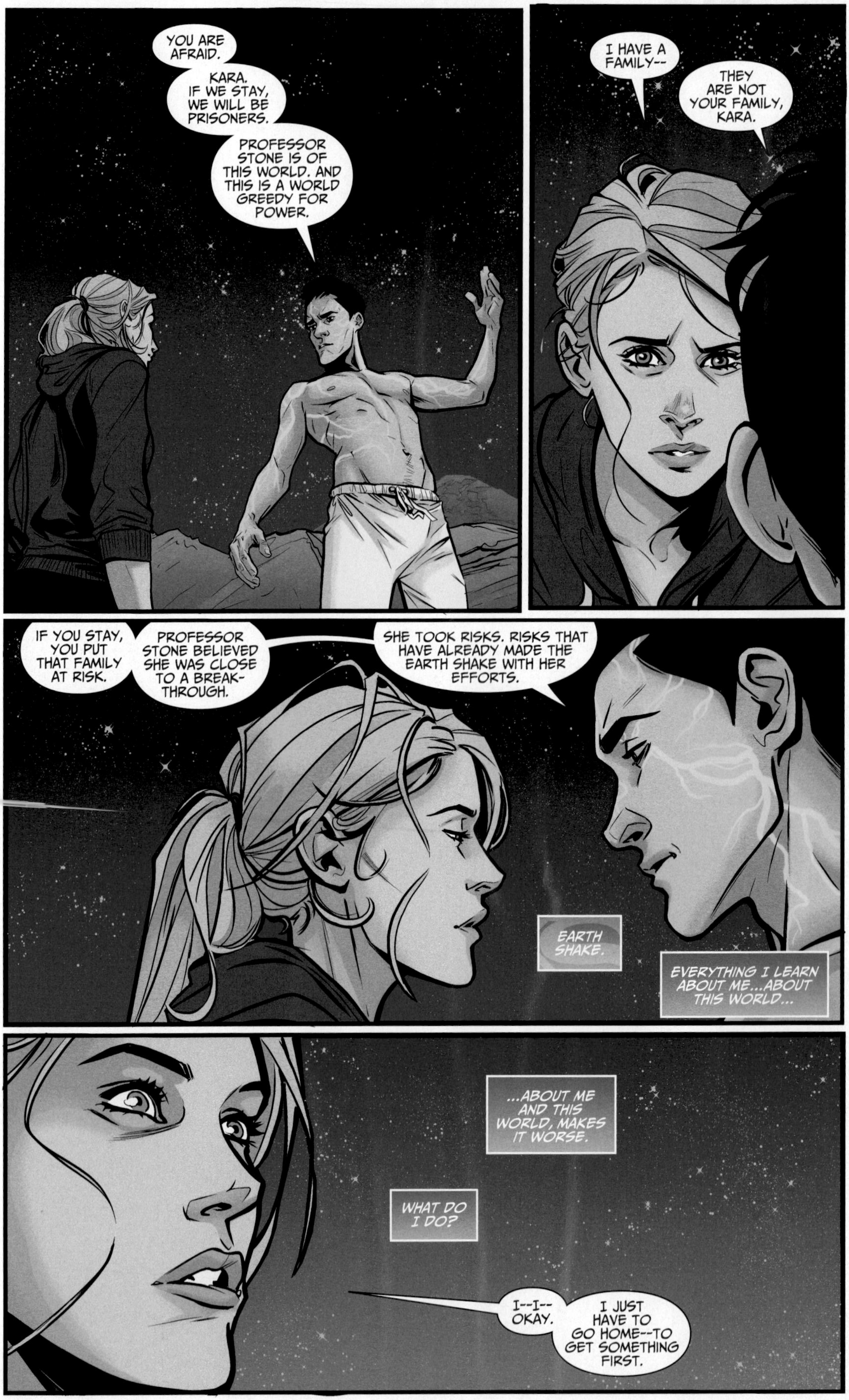
YOU ARE AFRAID.
KARA. IF WE STAY, WE WILL BE PRISONERS.
PROFESSOR STONE IS OF THIS WORLD. AND THIS IS A WORLD GREEDY FOR POWER.
I HAVE A FAMILY--
THEY ARE NOT YOUR FAMILY, KARA.
IF YOU STAY, YOU PUT THAT FAMILY AT RISK.
PROFESSOR STONE BELIEVED SHE WAS CLOSE TO A BREAK-THROUGH.
SHE TOOK RISKS. RISKS THAT HAVE ALREADY MADE THE EARTH SHAKE WITH HER EFFORTS.
EARTH SHAKE.
EVERYTHING I LEARN ABOUT ME...ABOUT THIS WORLD...
...ABOUT ME AND THIS WORLD, MAKES IT WORSE.
WHAT DO I DO?
I--I-- OKAY.
I JUST HAVE TO GO HOME--TO GET SOMETHING FIRST.

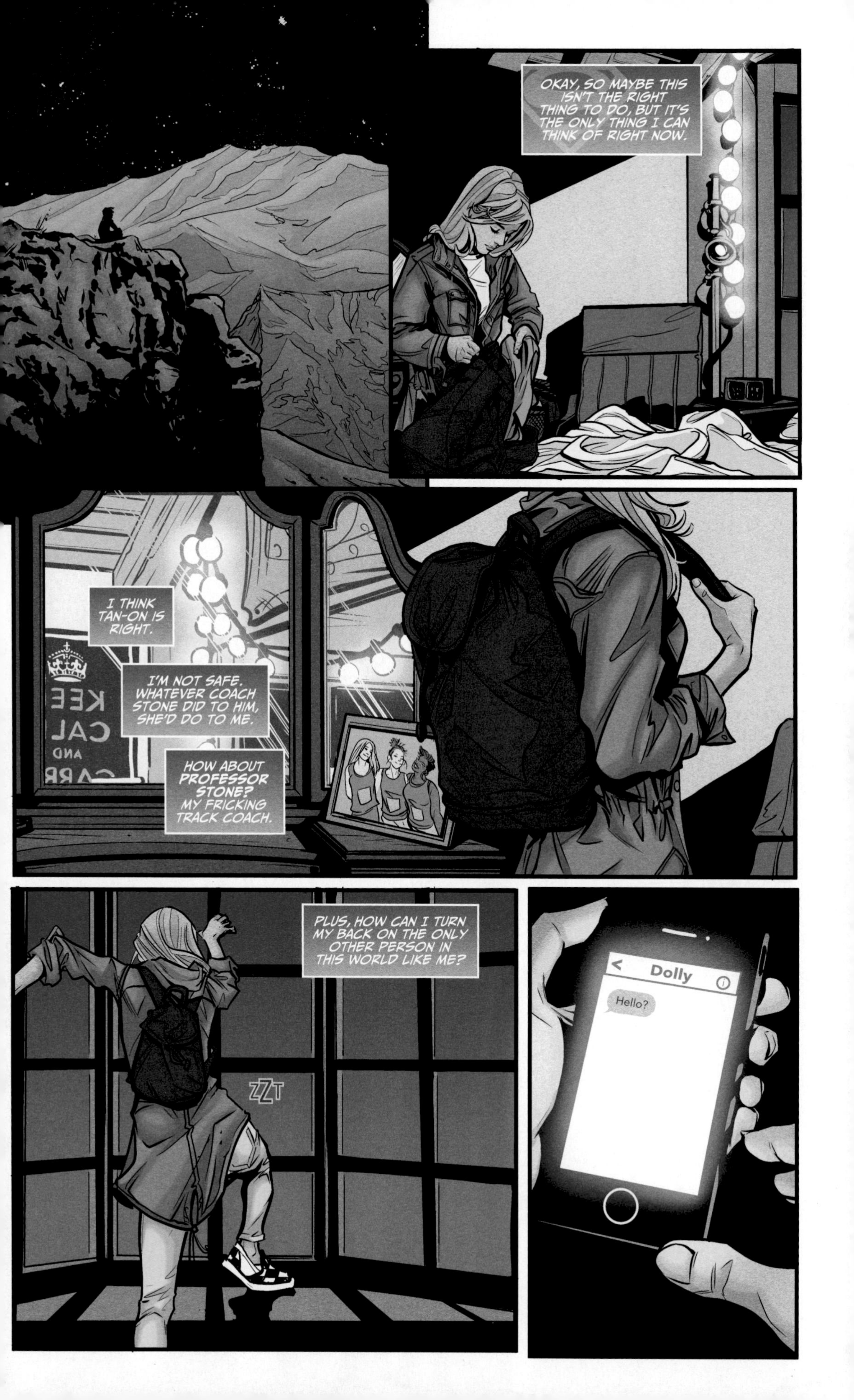
OKAY, SO MAYBE THIS ISN'T THE RIGHT THING TO DO, BUT IT'S THE ONLY THING I CAN THINK OF RIGHT NOW.
I THINK TAN-ON IS RIGHT.
I'M NOT SAFE. WHATEVER COACH STONE DID TO HIM, SHE'D DO TO ME.
HOW ABOUT PROFESSOR STONE? MY FRICKING TRACK COACH.
PLUS, HOW CAN I TURN MY BACK ON THE ONLY OTHER PERSON IN THIS WORLD LIKE ME?
ZZT
Dolly
Hello?

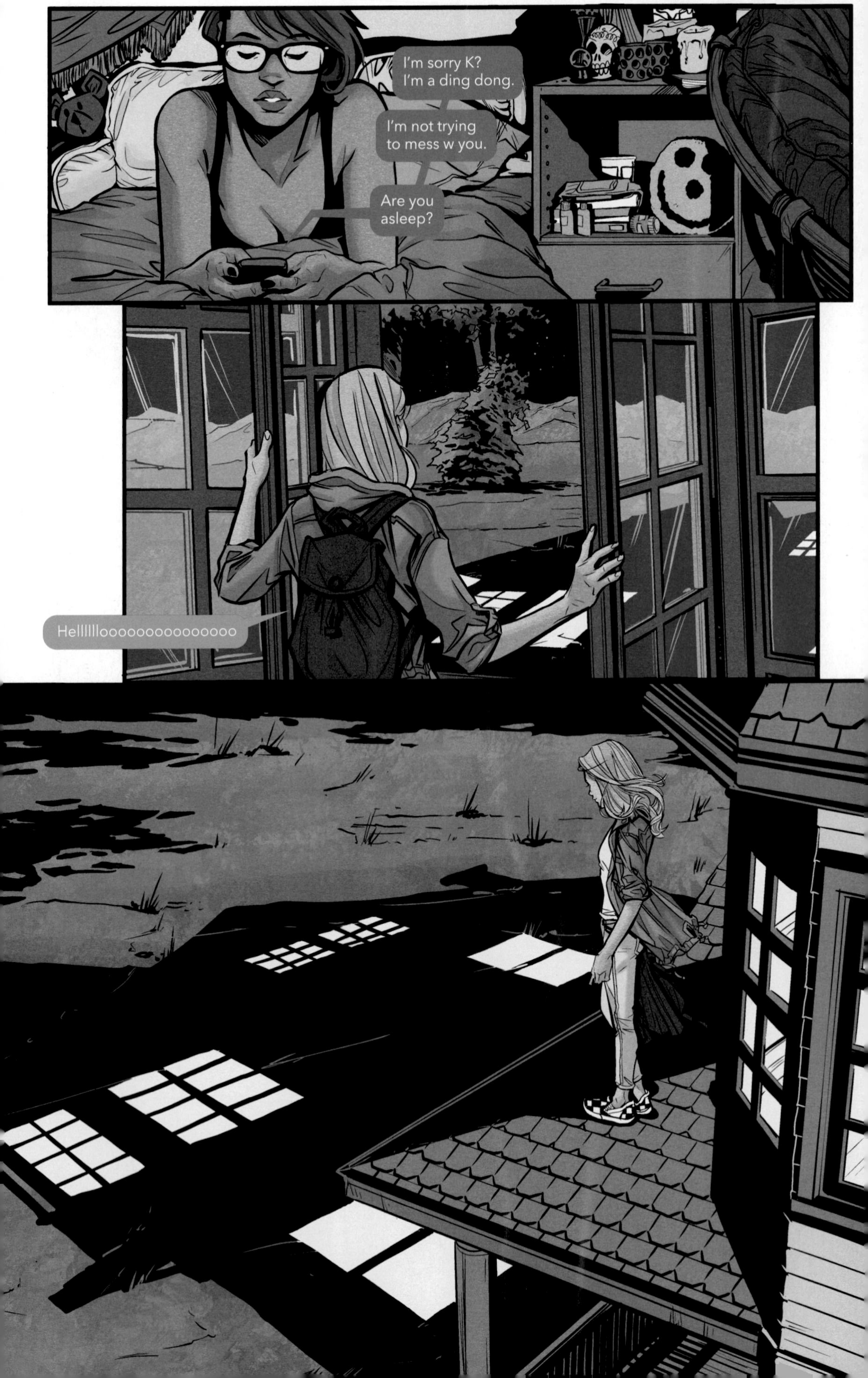
I'm sorry K?
I'm a ding dong.
I'm not trying
to mess w you.
Are you
asleep?
Hellllllooooooooooooooo

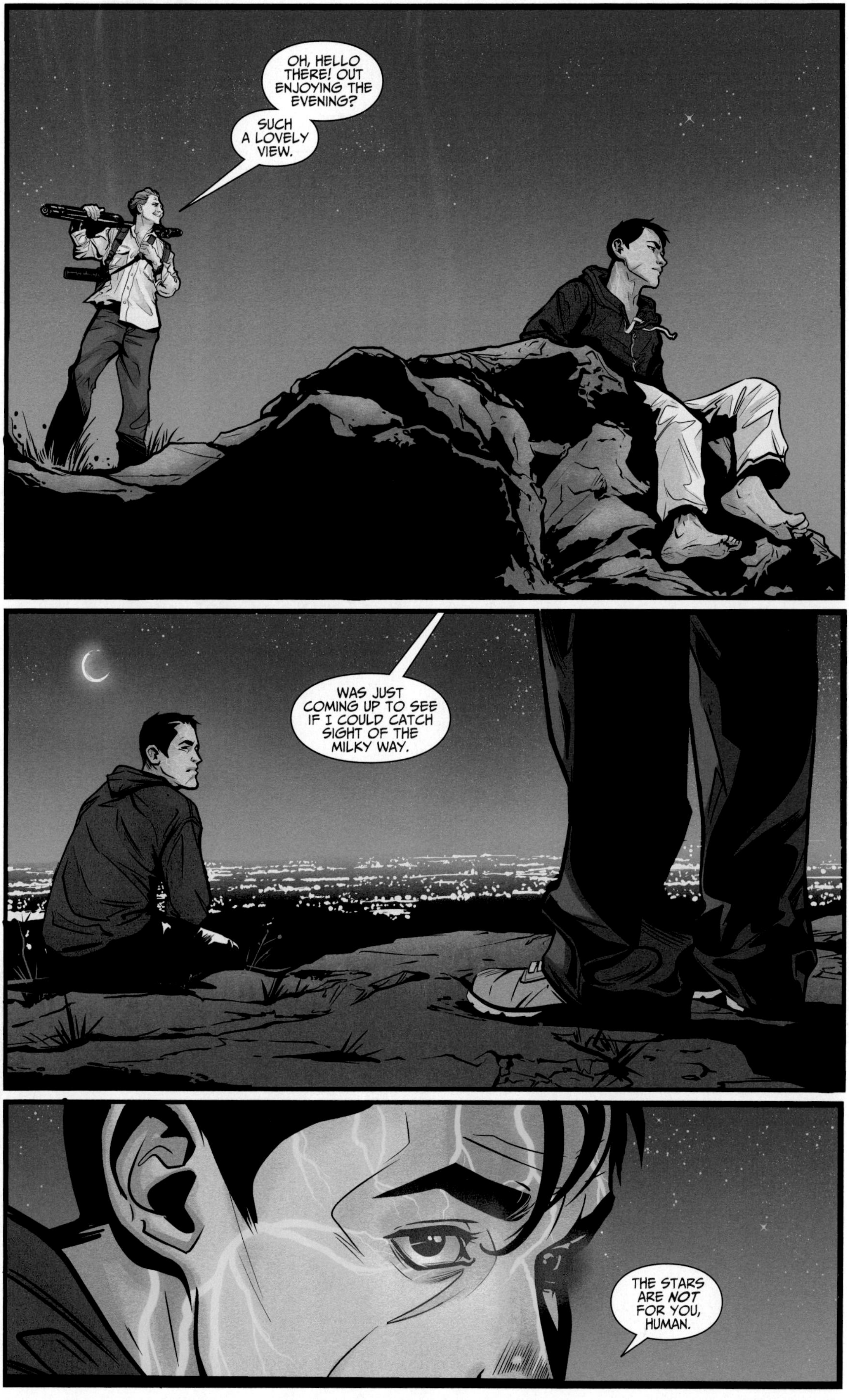
OH, HELLO THERE! OUT ENJOYING THE EVENING?
SUCH A LOVELY VIEW.
WAS JUST COMING UP TO SEE IF I COULD CATCH SIGHT OF THE MILKY WAY.
THE STARS ARE *NOT* FOR YOU, HUMAN.

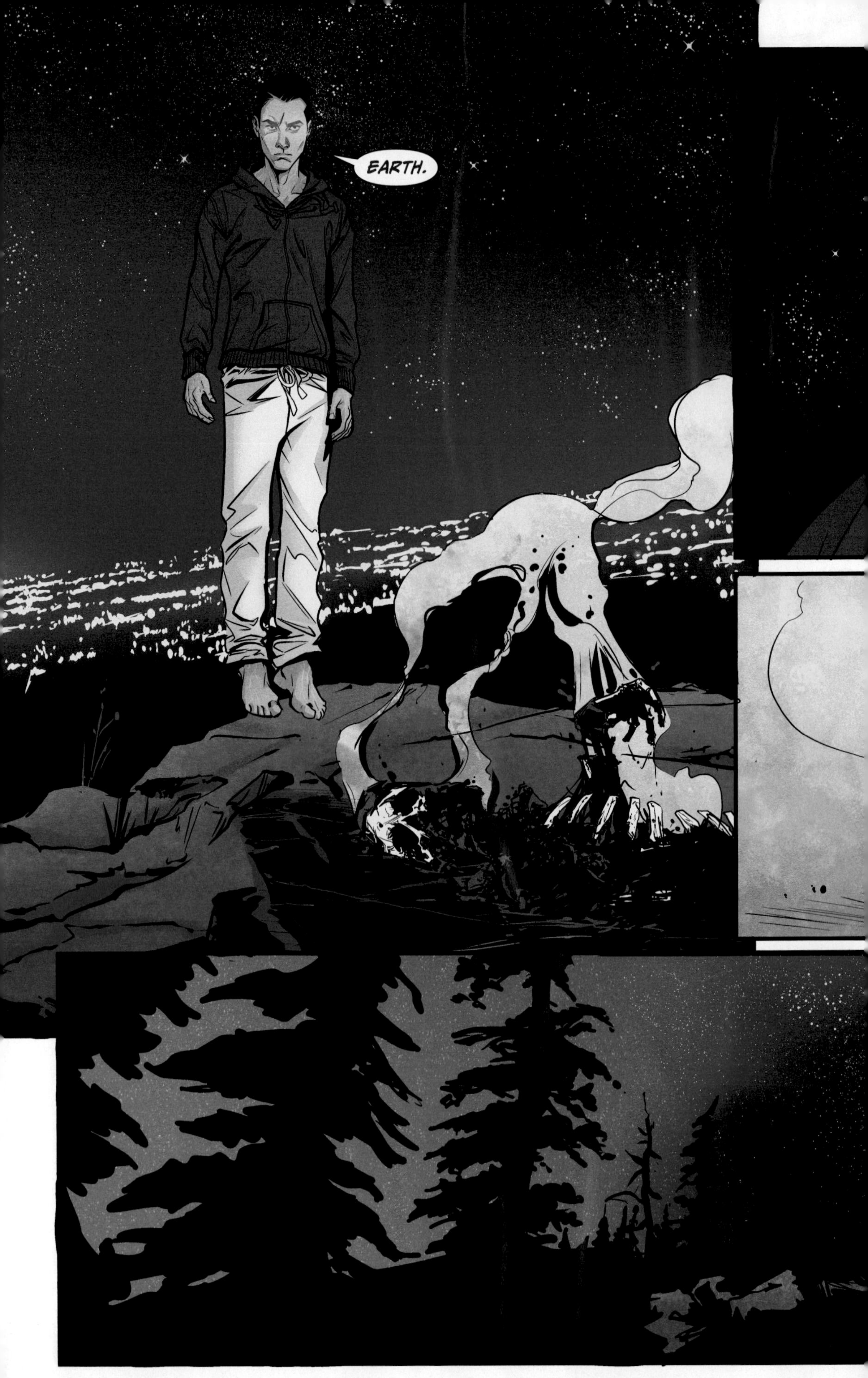
EARTH.

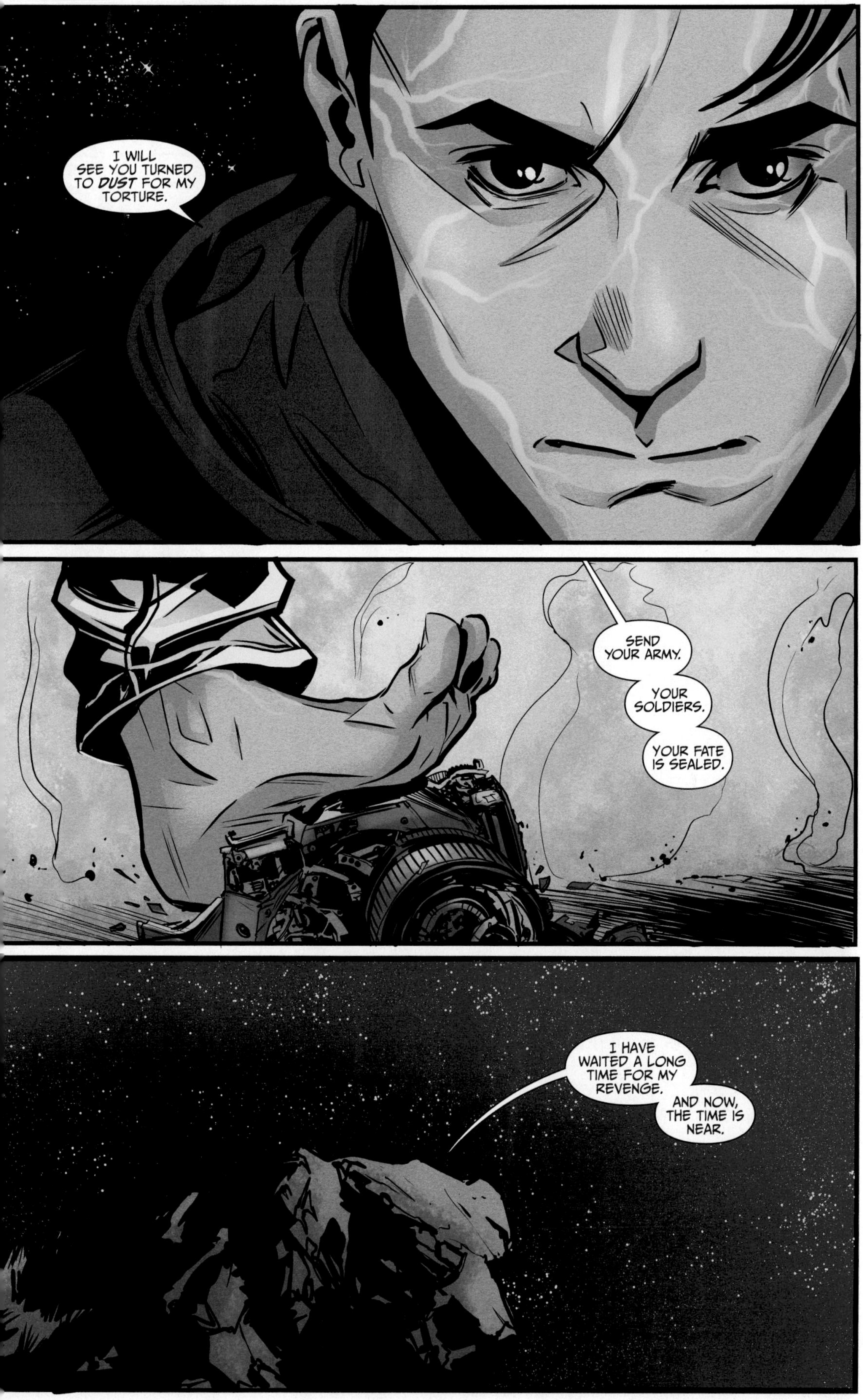
I WILL SEE YOU TURNED TO *DUST* FOR MY TORTURE.
SEND YOUR ARMY.
YOUR SOLDIERS.
YOUR FATE IS SEALED.
I HAVE WAITED A LONG TIME FOR MY REVENGE.
AND NOW, THE TIME IS NEAR.

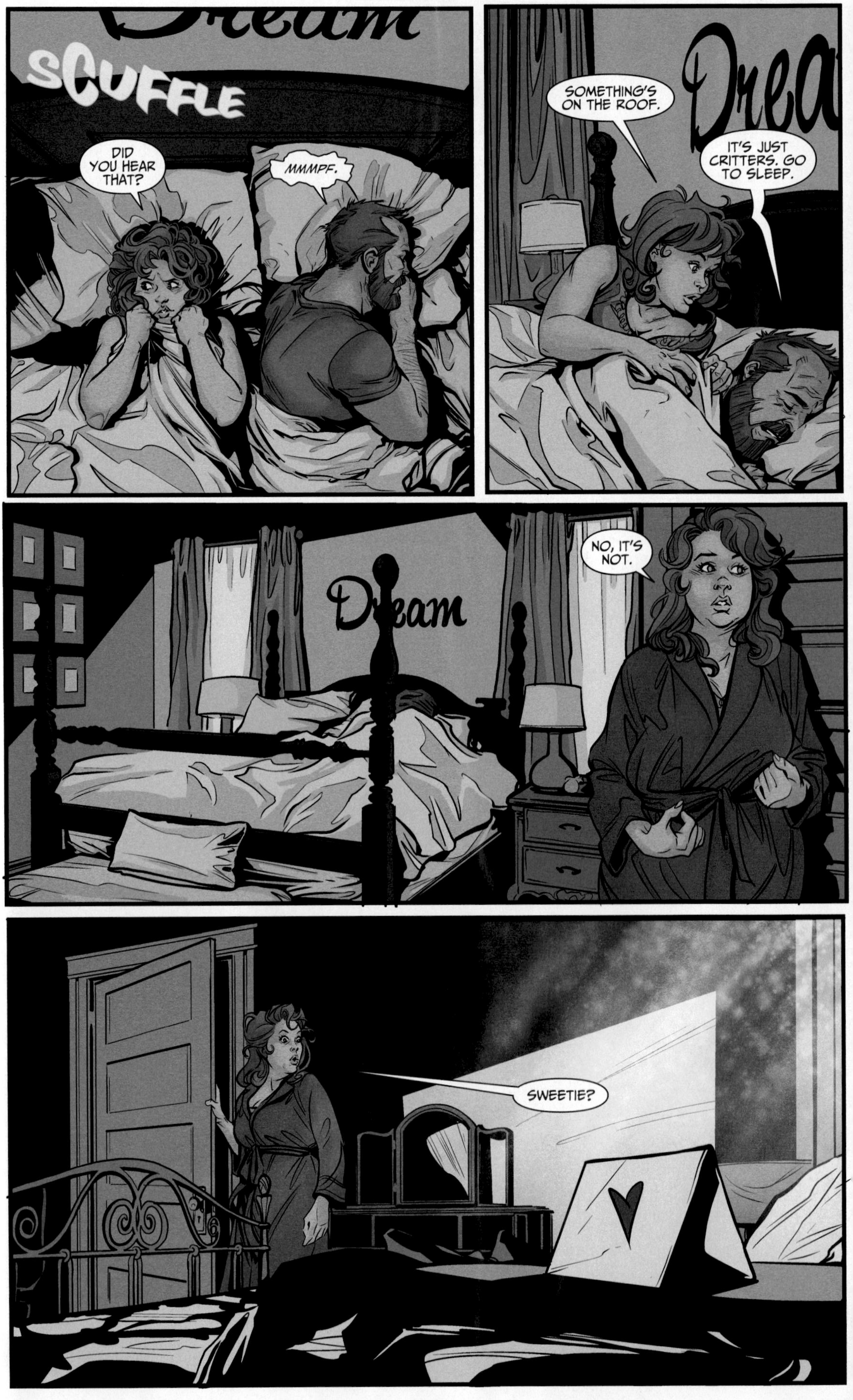
SCUFFLE
DID YOU HEAR THAT?
MMMPF.
SOMETHING'S ON THE ROOF.
IT'S JUST CRITTERS. GO TO SLEEP.
Dream
NO, IT'S NOT.
SWEETIE?

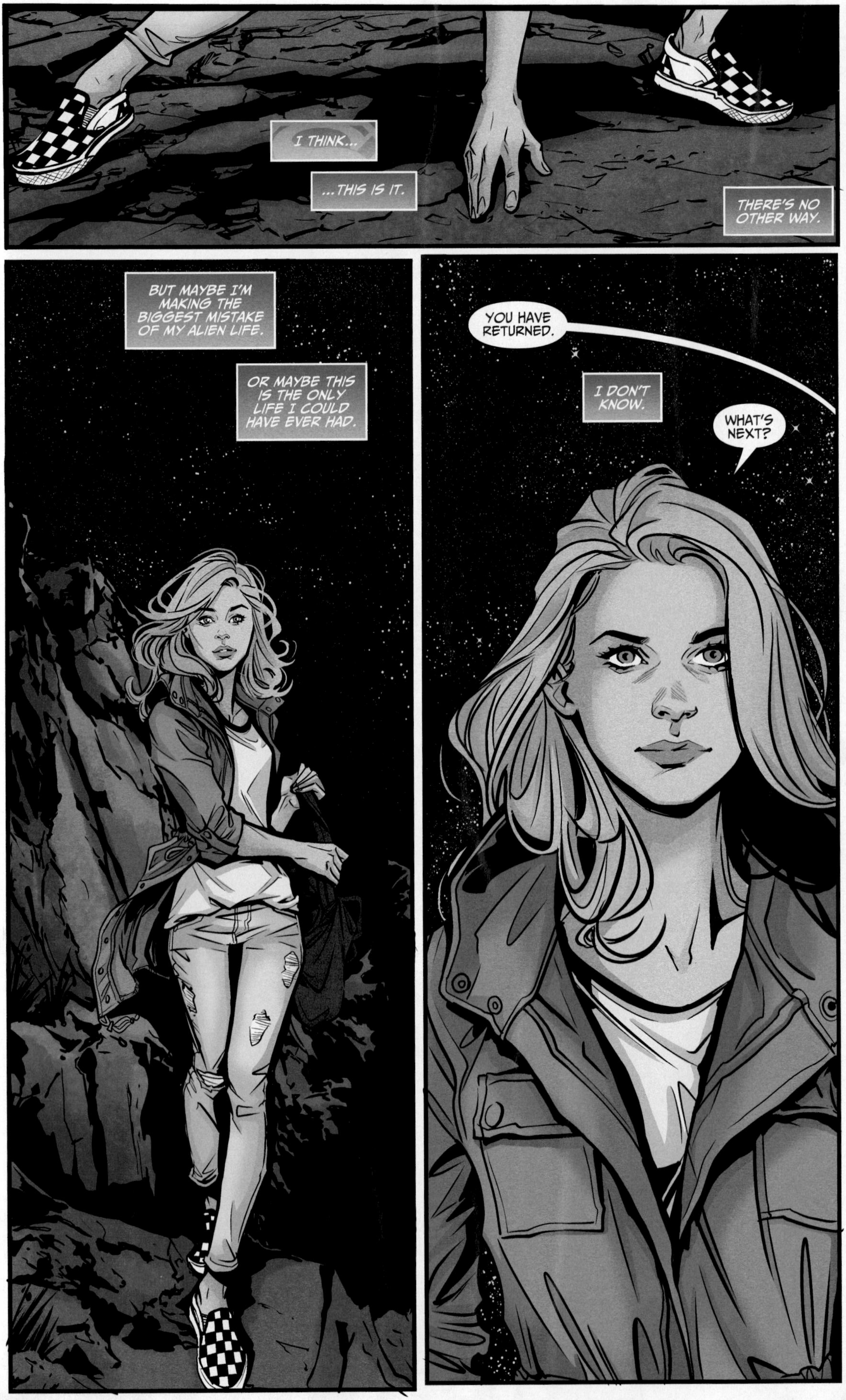
I THINK...
...THIS IS IT.
THERE'S NO OTHER WAY.
BUT MAYBE I'M MAKING THE BIGGEST MISTAKE OF MY ALIEN LIFE.
OR MAYBE THIS IS THE ONLY LIFE I COULD HAVE EVER HAD.
YOU HAVE RETURNED.
I DON'T KNOW.
WHAT'S NEXT?

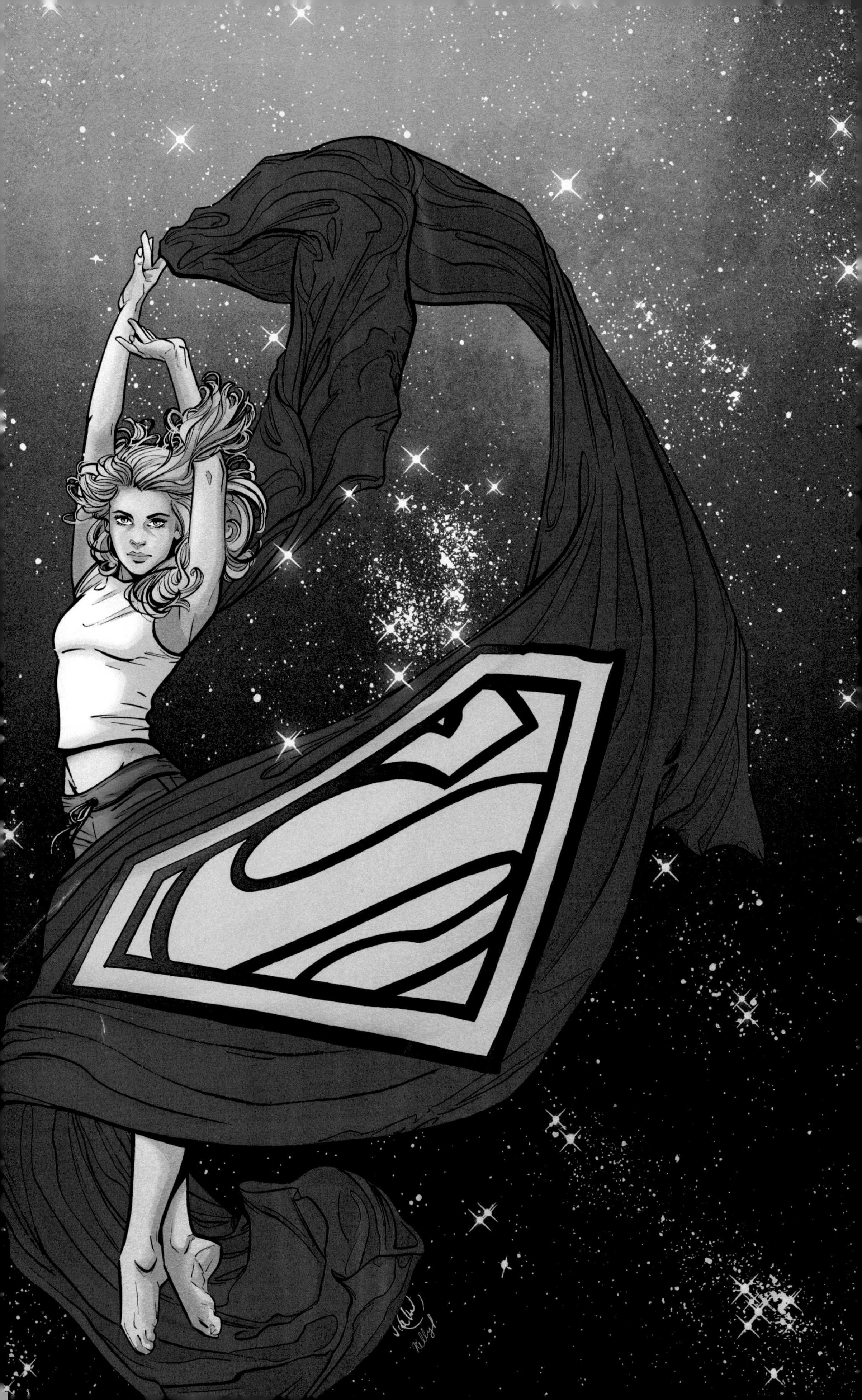

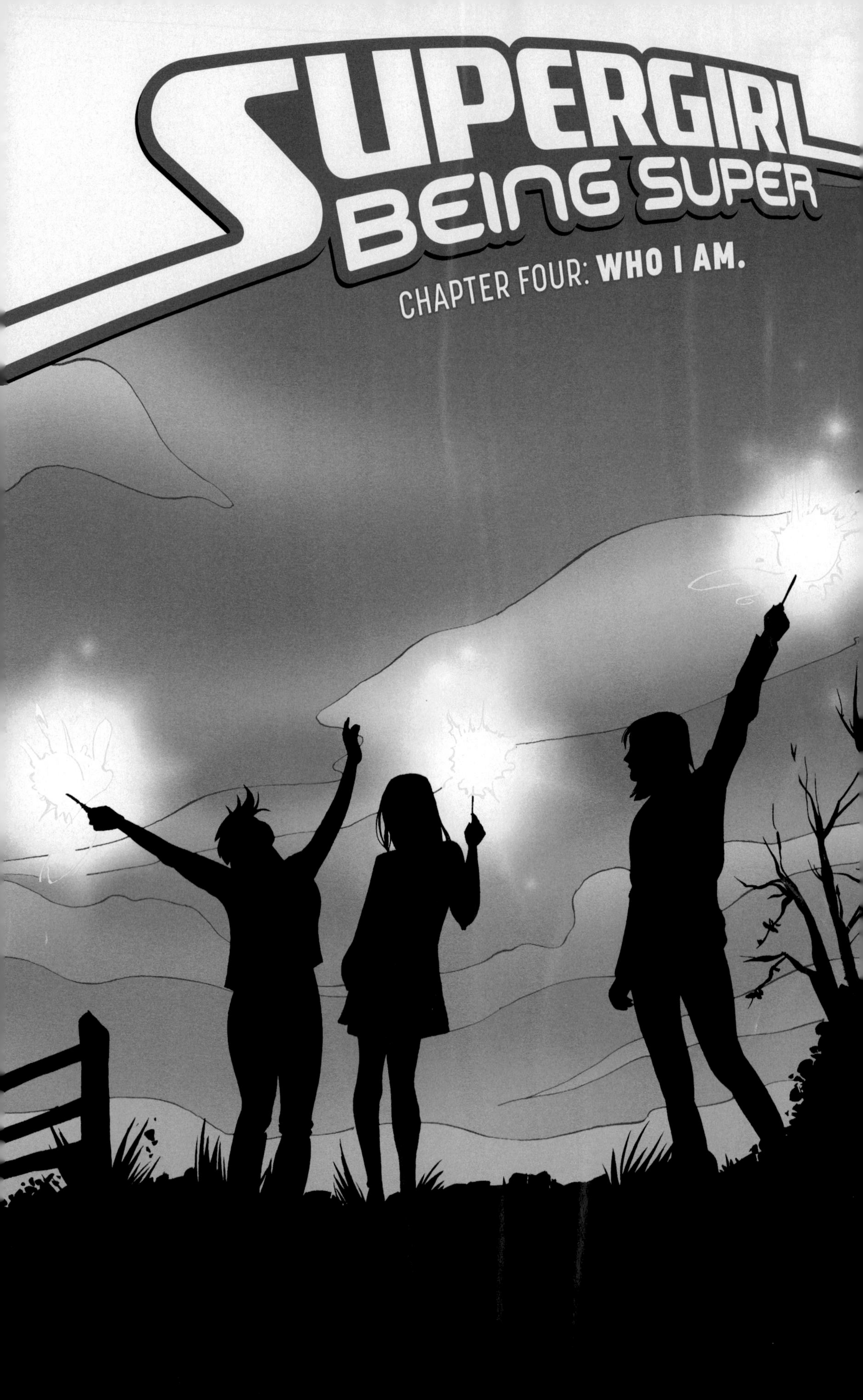
SUPERGIRL
BEING SUPER
CHAPTER FOUR: WHO I AM.

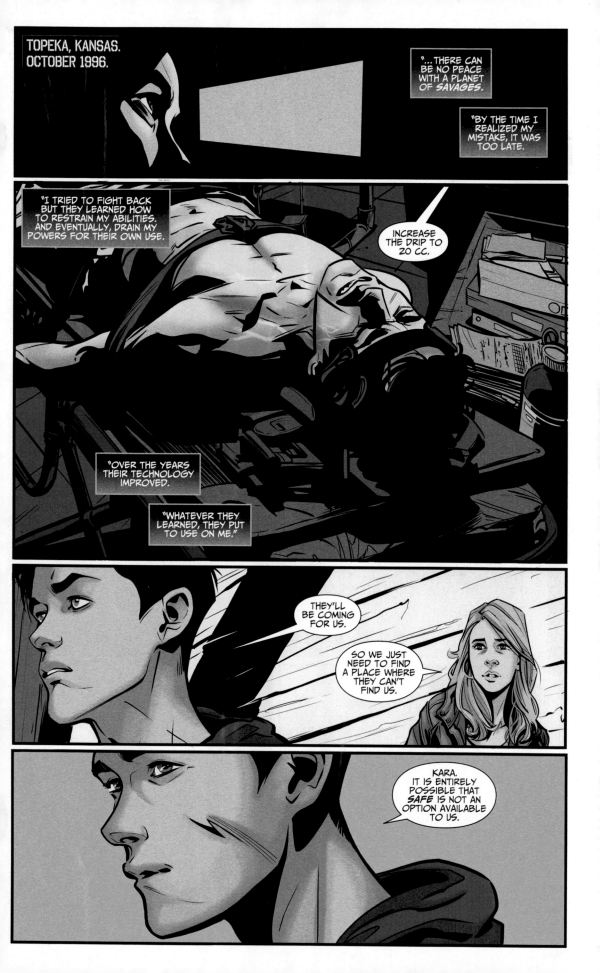

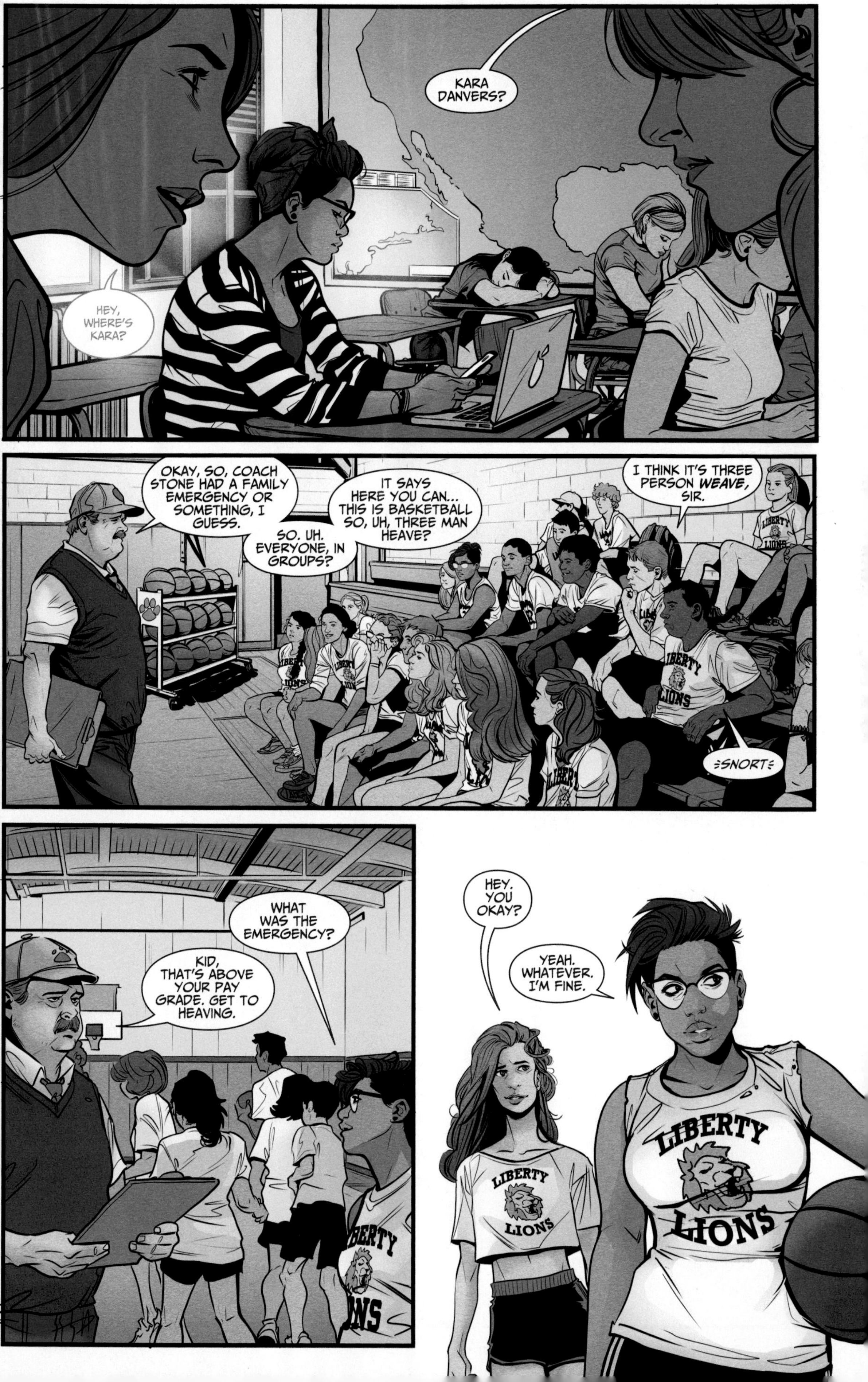
KARA DANVERS?
HEY, WHERE'S KARA?
OKAY, SO, COACH STONE HAD A FAMILY EMERGENCY OR SOMETHING, I GUESS.
SO. UH. EVERYONE, IN GROUPS?
IT SAYS HERE YOU CAN... THIS IS BASKETBALL SO, UH, THREE MAN HEAVE?
I THINK IT'S THREE PERSON WEAVE, SIR.
SNORT
LIBERTY LIONS
WHAT WAS THE EMERGENCY?
KID, THAT'S ABOVE YOUR PAY GRADE. GET TO HEAVING.
HEY. YOU OKAY?
YEAH. WHATEVER. I'M FINE.
LIBERTY LIONS
LIBERTY LIONS

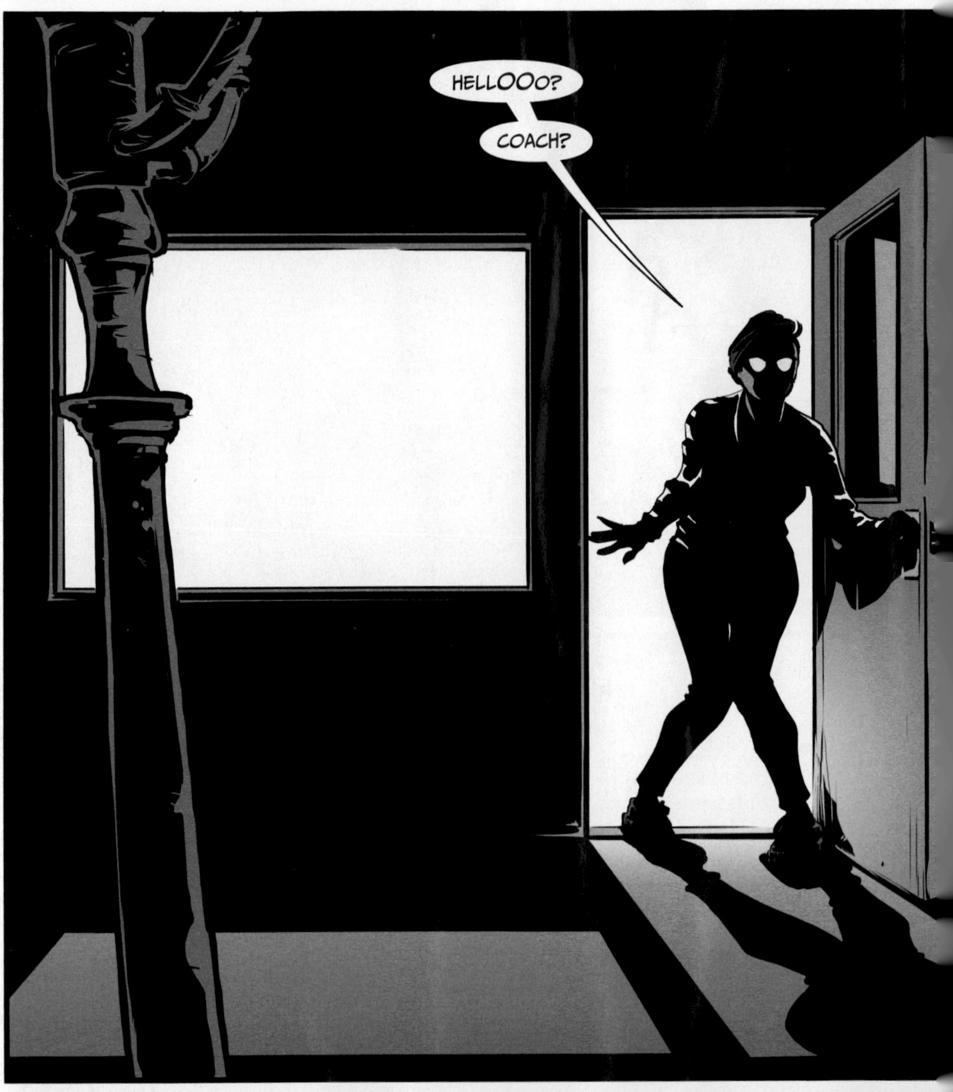
HELLOOOo?
COACH?

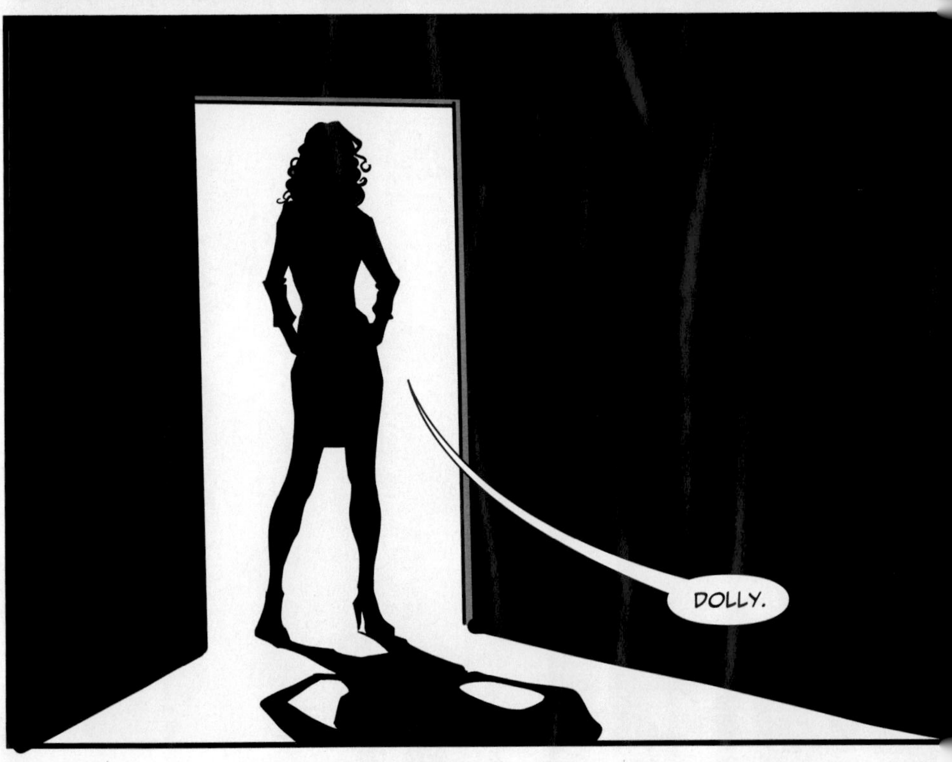
DOLLY.

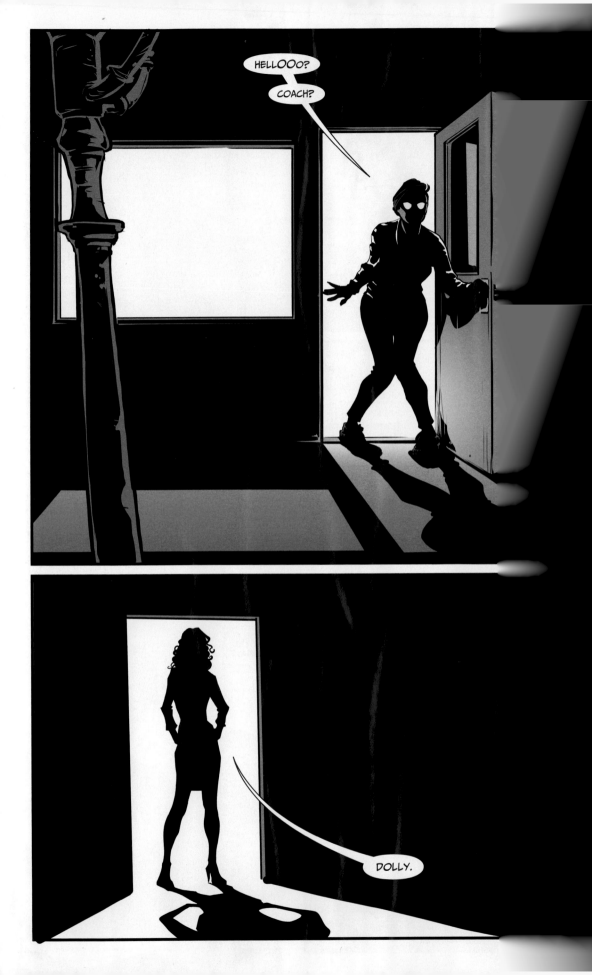

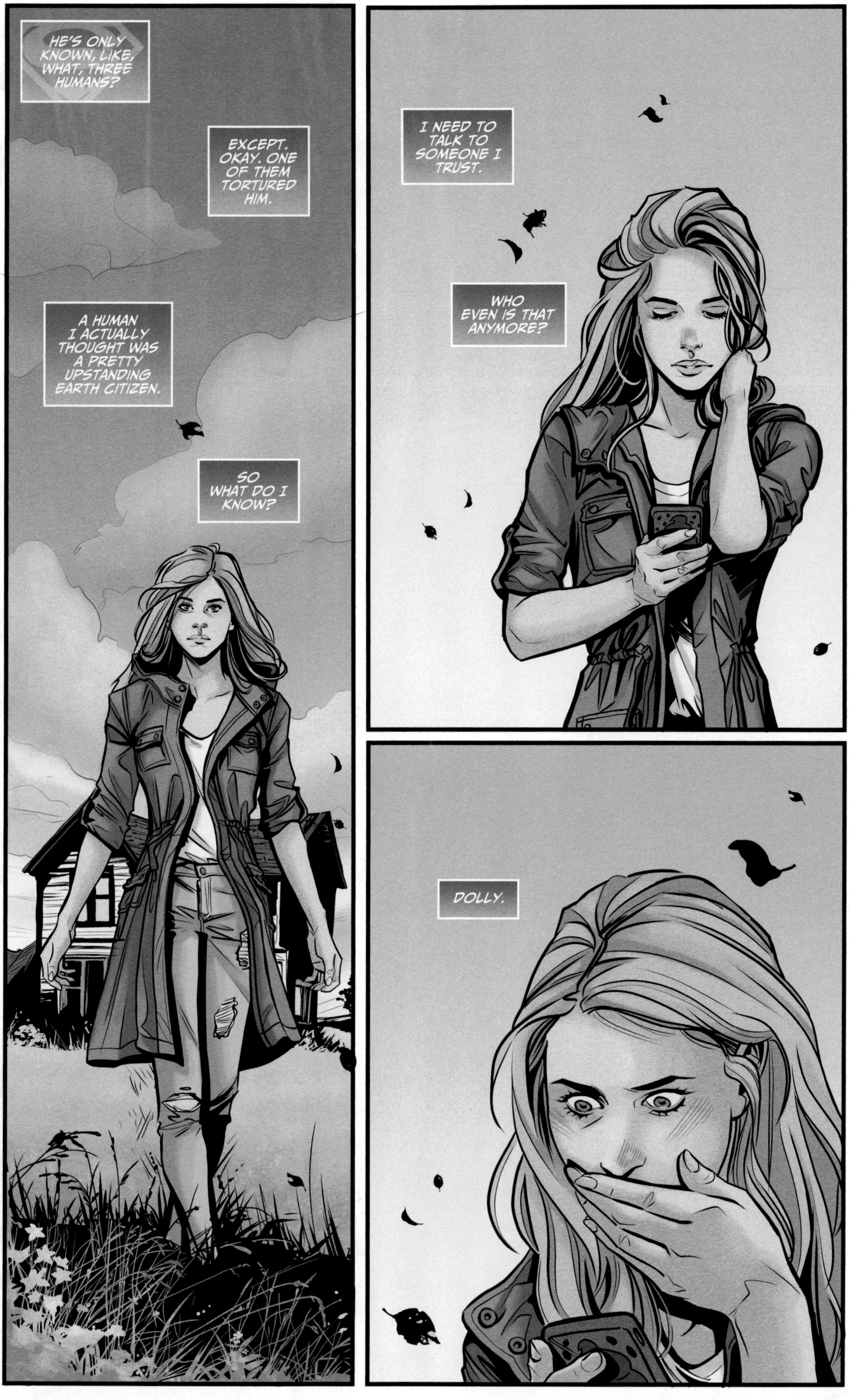
HE'S ONLY KNOWN, LIKE, WHAT, THREE HUMANS?
EXCEPT. OKAY. ONE OF THEM TORTURED HIM.
A HUMAN I ACTUALLY THOUGHT WAS A PRETTY UPSTANDING EARTH CITIZEN.
SO WHAT DO I KNOW?
I NEED TO TALK TO SOMEONE I TRUST.
WHO EVEN IS THAT ANYMORE?
DOLLY.

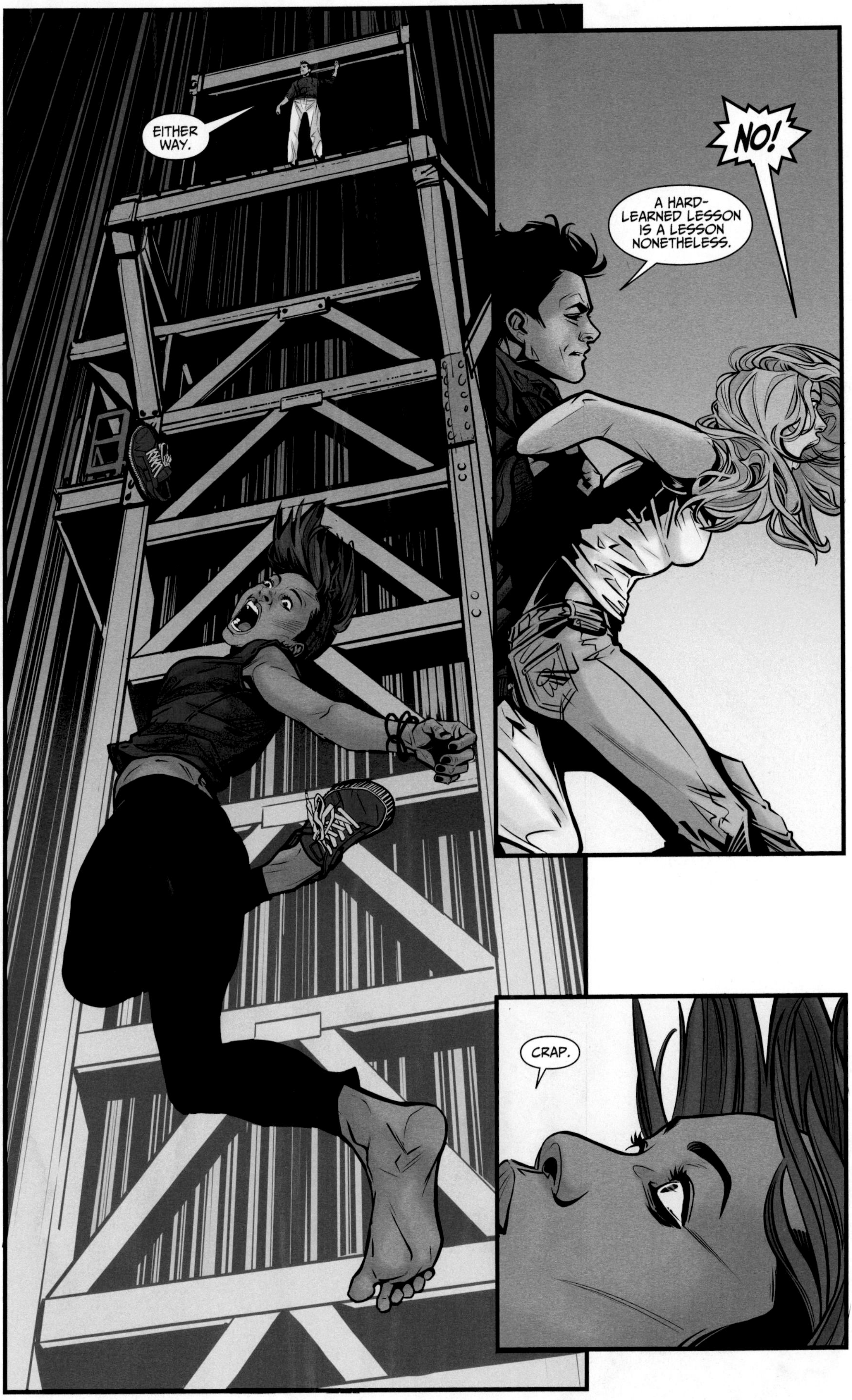
EITHER WAY.
NO!
A HARD-LEARNED LESSON IS A LESSON NONETHELESS.
CRAP.

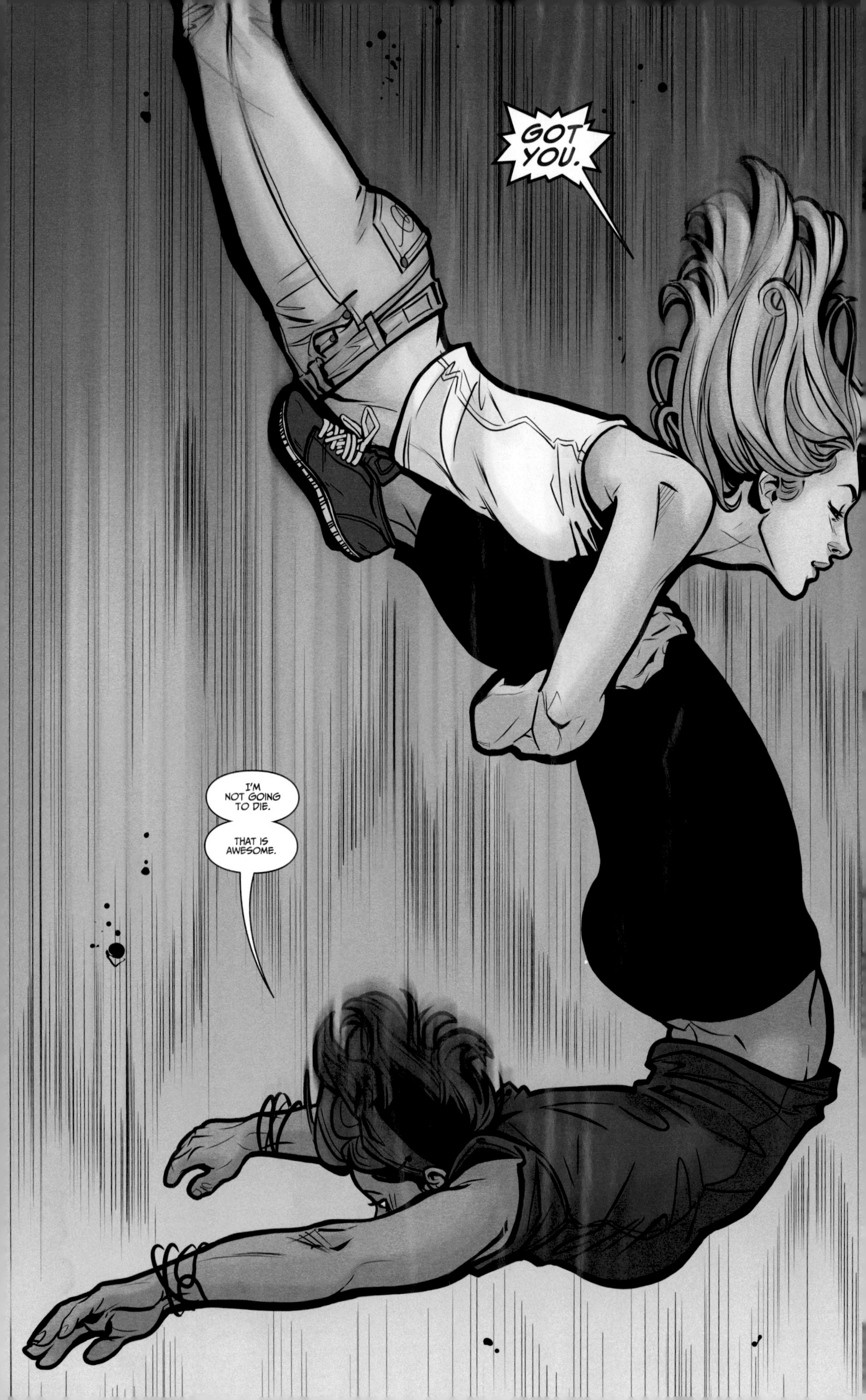
GOT YOU.
I'M NOT GOING TO DIE.
THAT IS AWESOME.

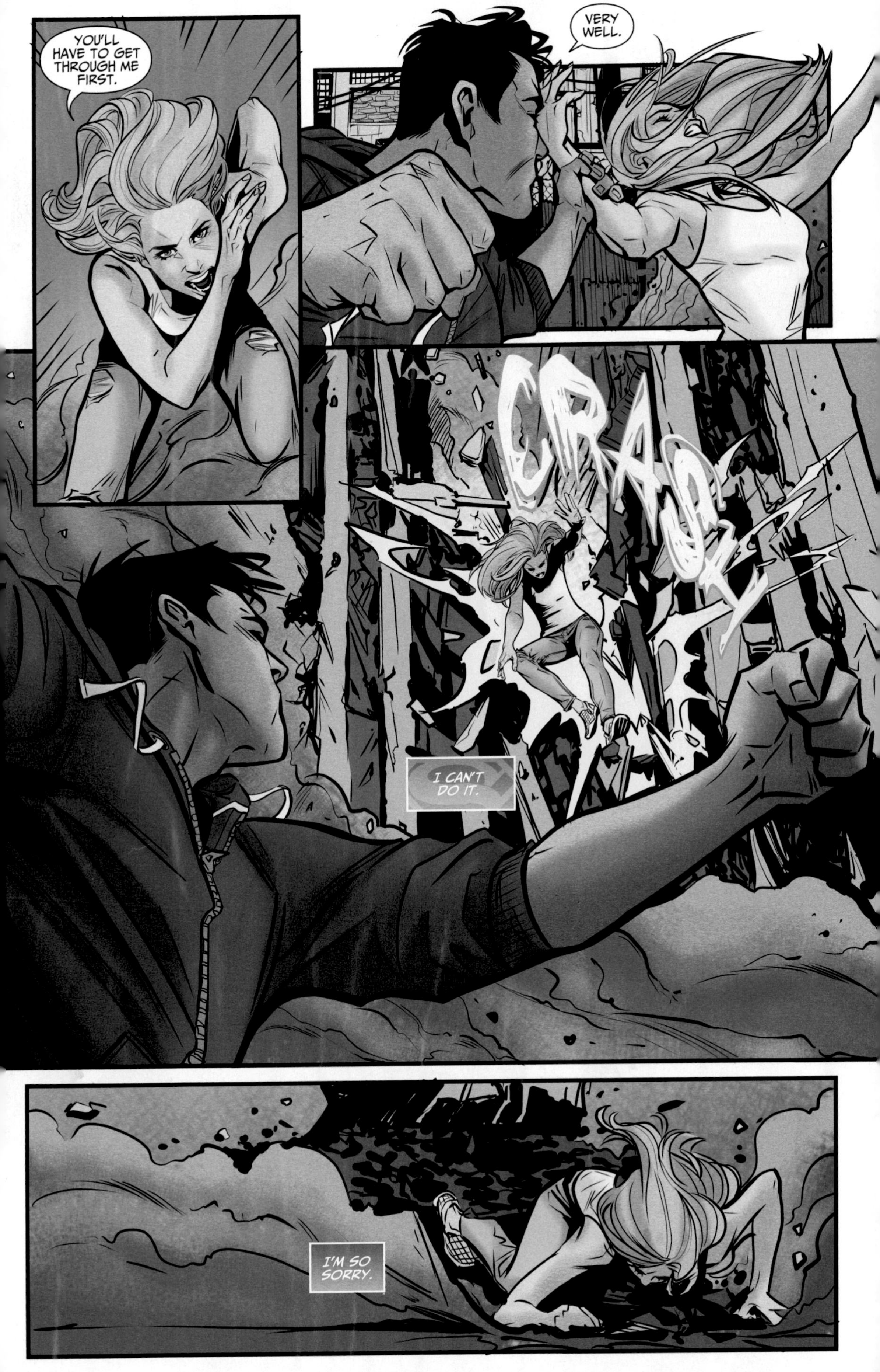
YOU'LL HAVE TO GET THROUGH ME FIRST.
VERY WELL.
CRASH
I CAN'T DO IT.
I'M SO SORRY.

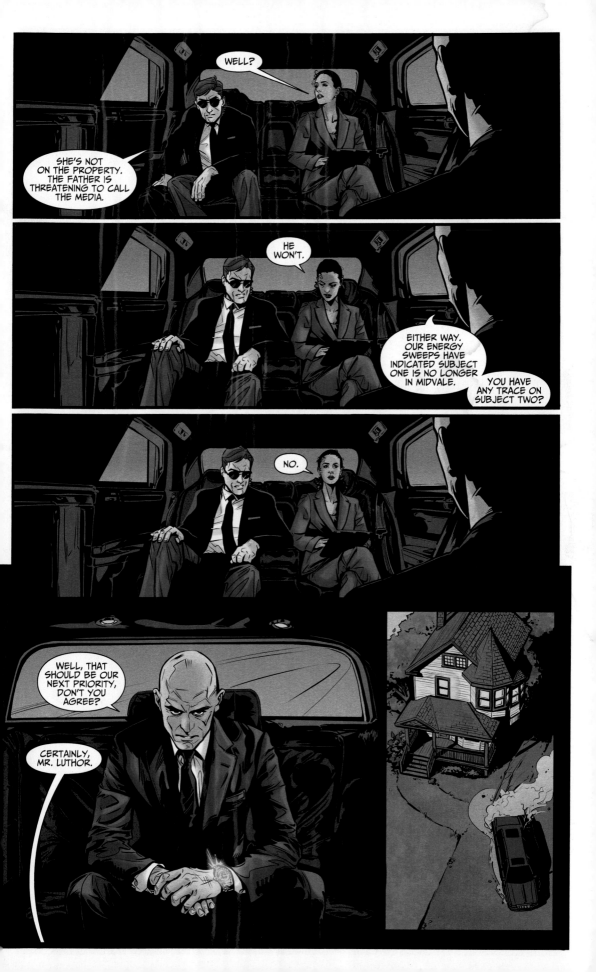

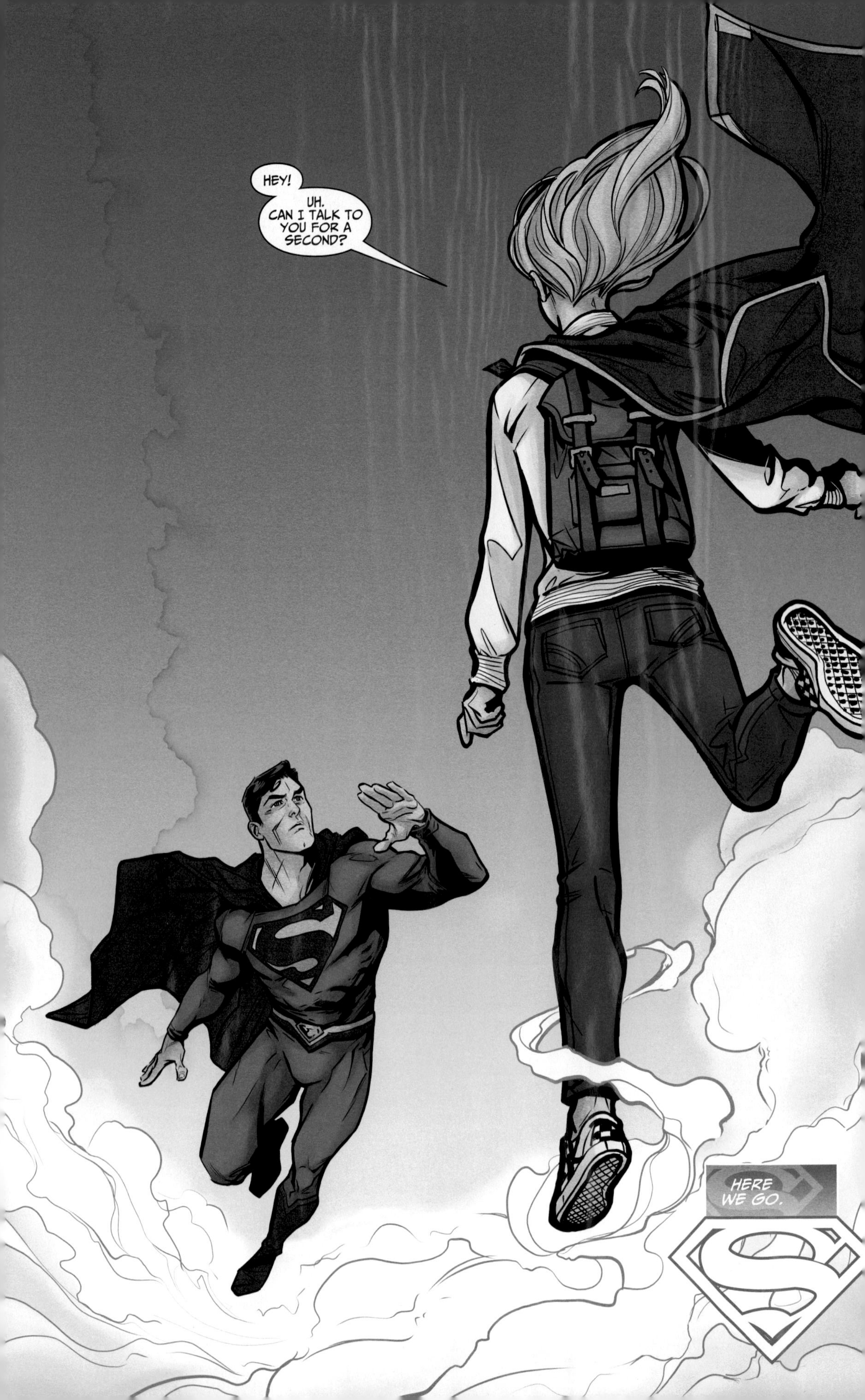
HEY!
UH. CAN I TALK TO YOU FOR A SECOND?
HERE WE GO.

Character sketches by Joëlle Jones

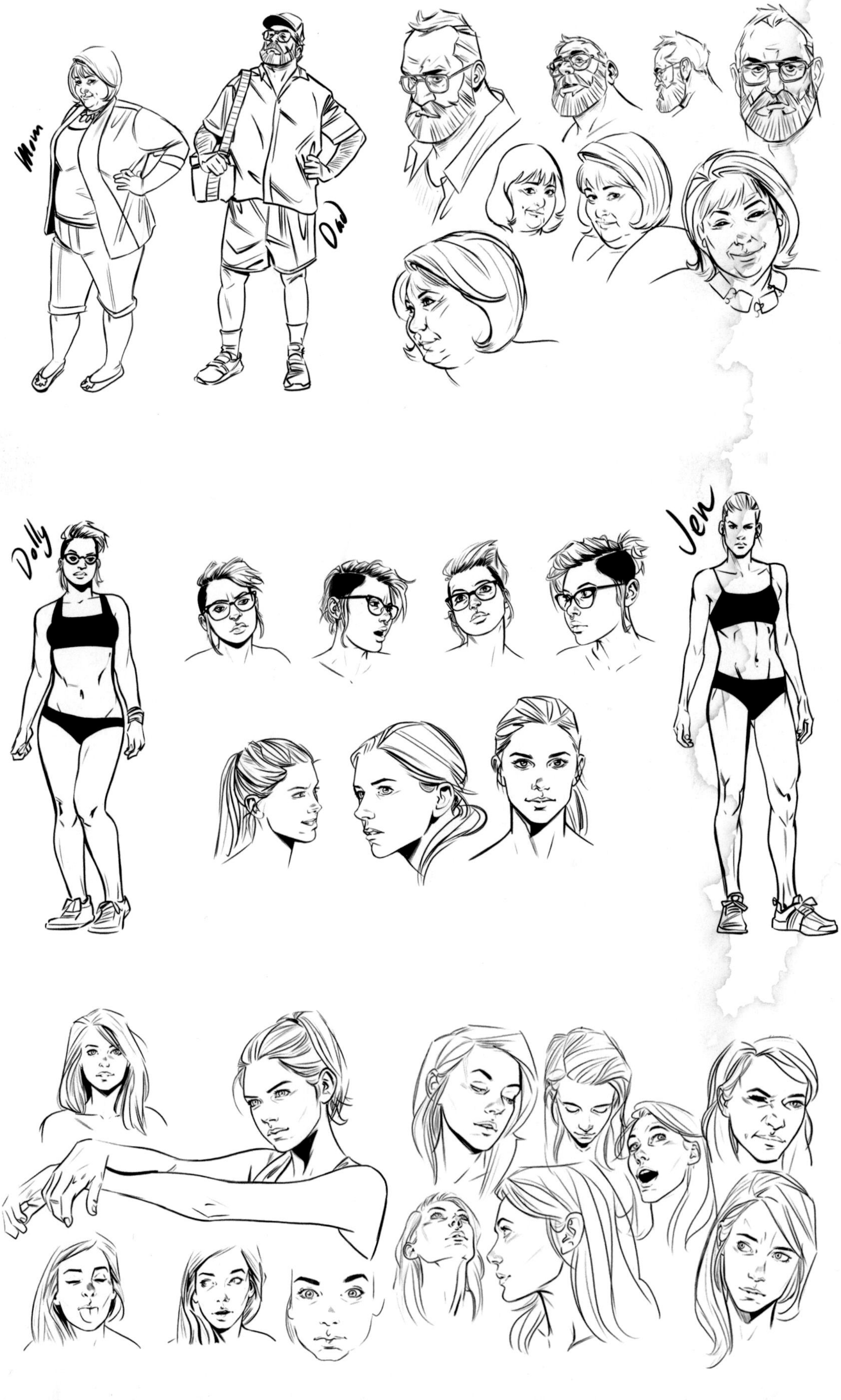
Mom
Dad
Dolly
Jen

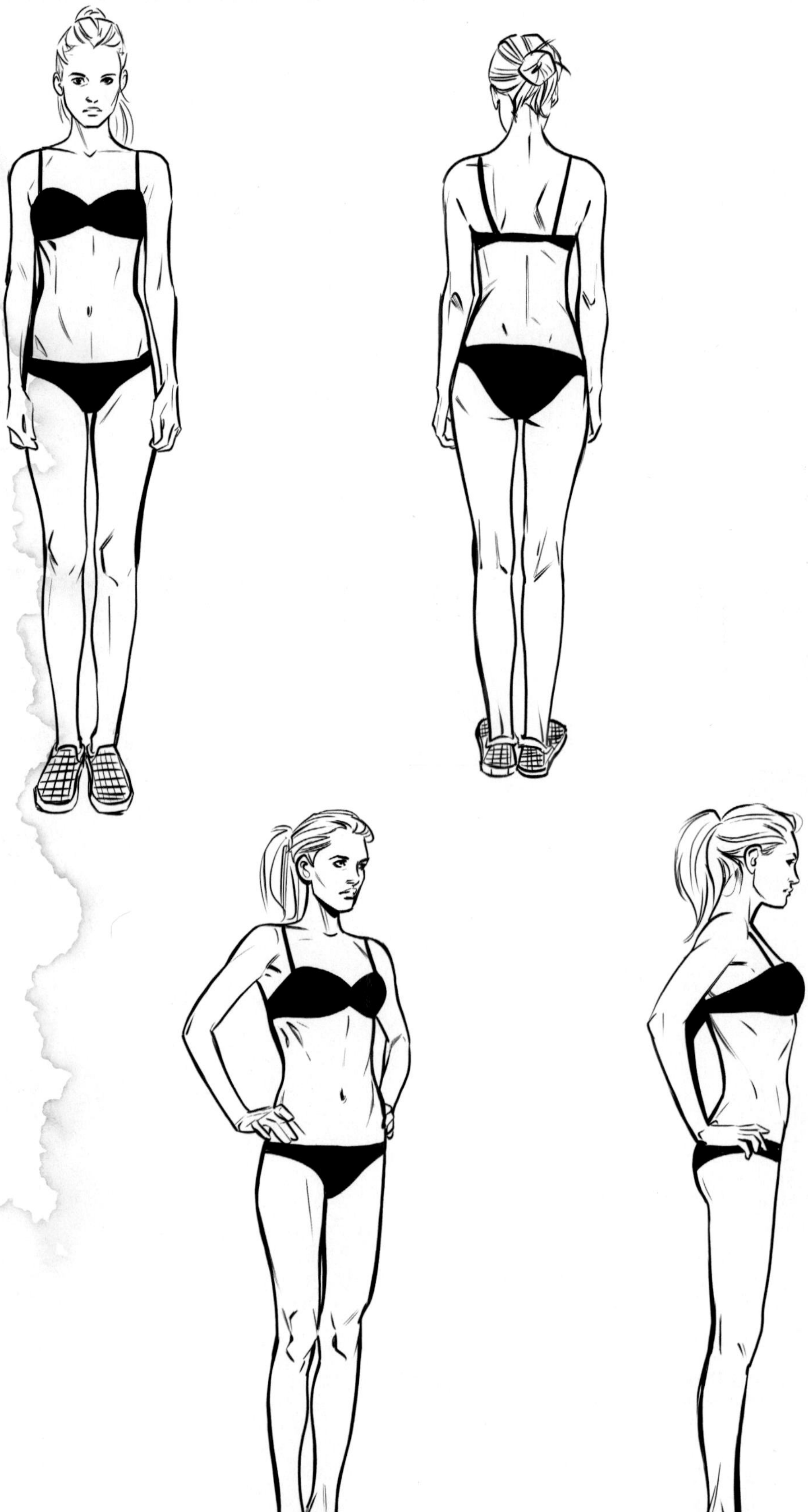

Unpublished character sketches by Kevin Wada

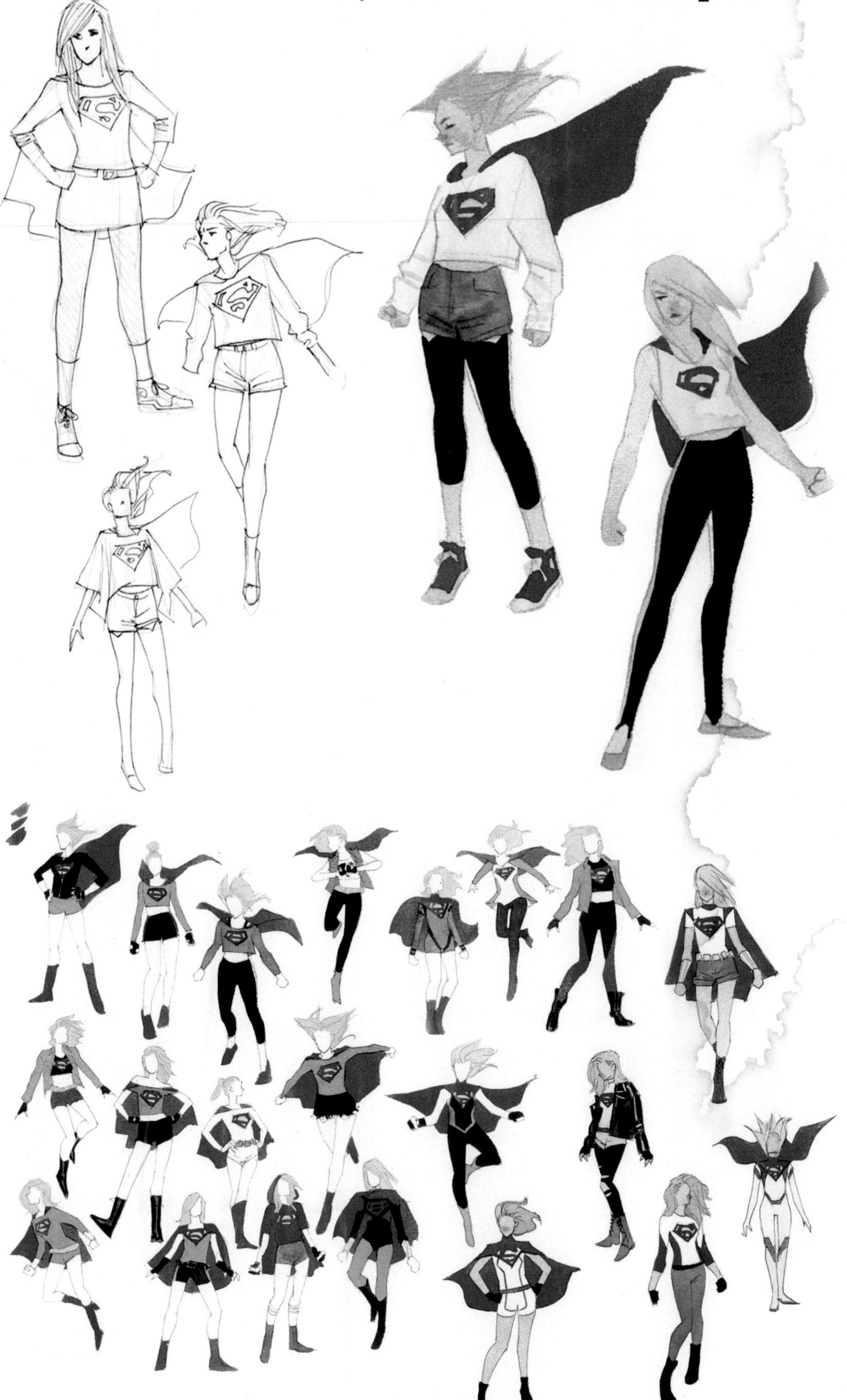

Unpublished cover by Tula Lotay

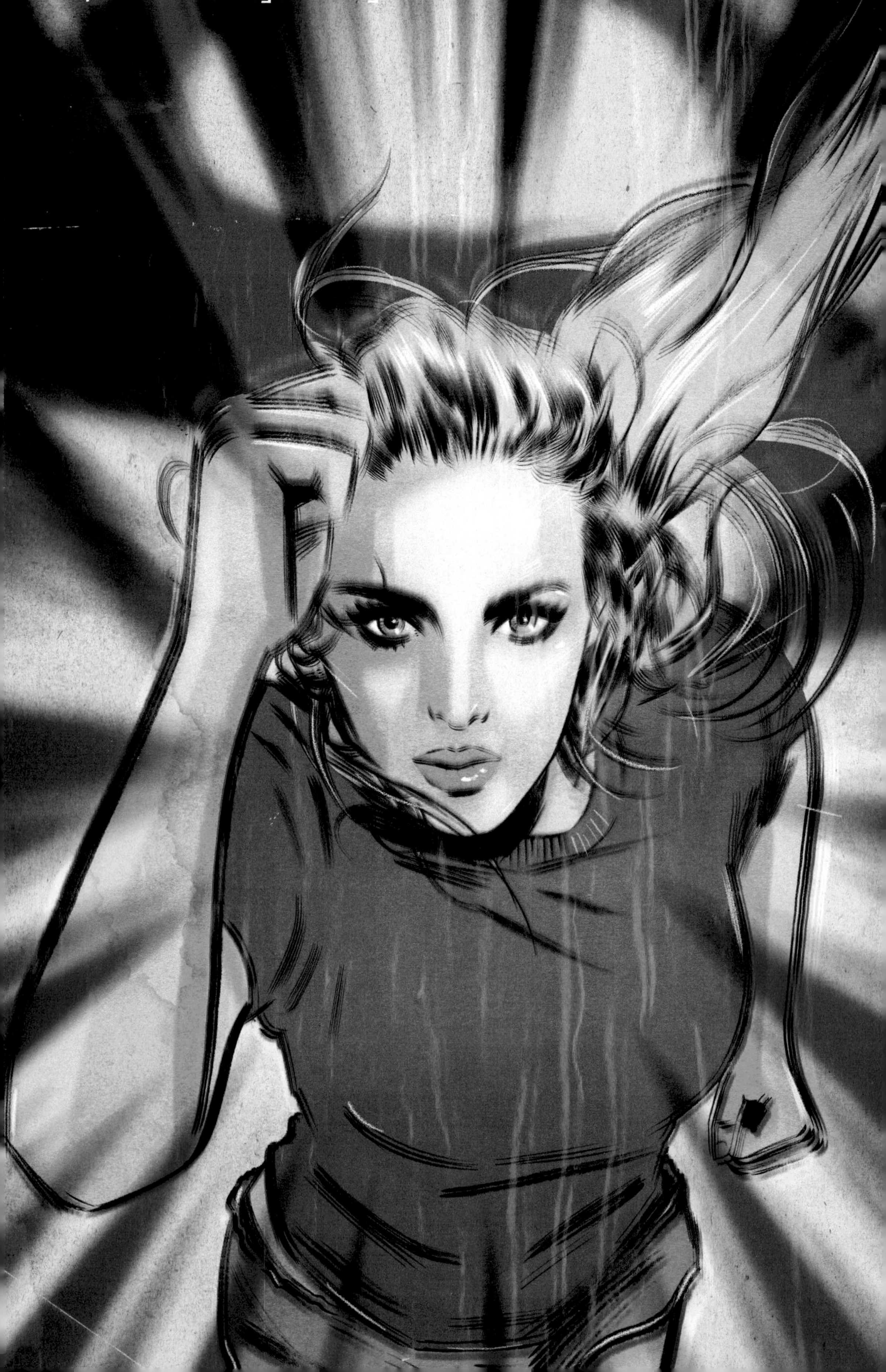